"He doesn't bring people

Shaking her head, she

leather sofas in the front ro

cushion and slinging it over her shoulder. "I've said too much. Goodbye, dear. Do me a favor and keep this visit between us, hmm? He'll be angry if he knows I disturbed his guest."

And with that, she throws open the door, leaving me alone. It slams shut behind her, the sound rattling off the windows on the upper level of the foyer, and I just stand there for a second, wondering what the hell just happened.

Laurel and I blink at each other, and then I shrug. "I don't know, bud. This island is fucking weird."

He snorts, presumably in agreement.

We head down the hall together, passing a chef's kitchen and another sitting room, which widens, morphing into an octagonal-shaped library with built-in shelves and probably thousands of dusty books.

The far wall boasts an array of different hunting rifles and bows, strung up on display like trophies. But there aren't any of the traditional animal carcasses hanging, which intrigues me.

Perhaps Alistair's trophies aren't the kind you can hang up in your home.

Laurel and I stop inside of it, and I tilt my head toward the domed ceiling. There's a mural painted on the plaster; the Greek gods convening on their mountain, looking down at the mortals they rule. Marble sculptures of each Olympian are mounted above each bookcase, making the library look as though it belongs in a museum.

I'm suddenly too scared to touch anything.

Rolling my eyes at the pretentiousness of it all, I can't

help wondering why I'm surprised in the first place. The man based his entire political persona around the arts, so some snobbishness is bound to be built into his character, right?

Frankly, I'd probably have been more shocked if there wasn't a single mythological reference to be found on the premises.

Leaving the room, I go down the hall and through the sliding glass door in the back. It lets out onto a gray stone patio with a firepit with ornately trimmed hedges lining the yard and walkways that seem to lead to country club–esque amenities, like a tennis court and some sort of driving range.

A mechanical digger sits beyond the hedge line, working at the dirt in one section of the yard. Laurel barks at the machine as it beeps, clawing away at the earth. Some men in bright neon vests stand around, chatting as they look over a blueprint on the side of a white pickup truck.

One notices me and breaks off from his group, walking over. "Shit, we didn't disturb you, did we? Mr. Wolfe told us to be out by noon, but we wanted to get this part done, so we could pour concrete first thing in the morning."

I glance out past him at the massive hole in the yard. "What are you building?"

"A pool." Removing his ball cap, he scratches at his receding hairline, shrugging. "I've never known the mayor to step foot in the water, but I guess there's a first time for everything, eh?"

Dread fills my stomach as I stand there, watching them work for a few more minutes. What kind of psychopath doesn't swim or at least lounge in a pool? *Ever*?

The same kind, I guess, who might build a permanent pool for a girl who can only be temporary in his life.

DAUGHTER OF TRUTH

A VERITAS AND MORI NOVEL

BY: S. FRASHER

First published 2022

Book cover design by Hannah Ridge (creativebyher)
Some images were designed using Freepik.com

ISBN: 9798821949844 (paperback)
ISBN: 9798821991645 (special edition)

Self-published via Kindle Direct Publishing

Trigger warning(s):
Mental health struggles, trauma, emotional abuse, gaslighting, prejudice, imprisonment, scars, nightmares, PTSD, panic attacks, death, murder, torture, mutilation, decapitation, gore, slut shaming, hostage situation, female oppression, kidnapping, sexual harassment, sexual assault, general suggestive/sexual themes, politics, war, blood, and violence.

Feel free to message me @frasherwritesandreads on Instagram for any details or questions on these warnings.

The heart is deceitful and desperately sick.
Who can understand it?
Jeremiah 17:9

Preface

I haven't truly lived yet, the devastating thought crossed Thea's mind and added emotional pain to her physical suffering. Thea had never felt so much pain. A pampered life of ballroom dancing and tart tasting had not prepared her for hours of torture and interrogation. Her cheek was raw and swollen from all the hits it had taken. Her delicate arm was hanging at a sickening angle, dislocated. The once beautiful lingerie she wore was now covered in mud and blood. Its once ornate neckline was ripped, and the matching hem lay against her bruised ribs, now wholly tattered. Thea winced when she licked her dry lips, discovering yet another bleeding wound. But, to her horror, she was so dehydrated that she welcomed the blood, for at least it was something wetting her dry tongue.

Time was incalculable without sunlight to mark the days, but Thea figured her captors had detained her for no more than two days. However, she had passed out from pain so frequently that any amount of time could have passed. They were currently holding her in what looked like a grand, yet small, dining hall. Two men had chained her to the leg of a table. Not that it was necessary. With the combination of injuries and general weakness, she doubted she had the strength to stand, let alone escape or fight back against them. She cursed her family for never exposing her to any kind of combat training. Maybe if she had that, she wouldn't feel so helpless or hopeless. Perhaps if she had training, she could at least pretend she stood a shot of surviving this. At that moment, she didn't even know if she would survive the night, not if the gusto with which they had tortured her most of the day continued much longer. In stark comparison to the hell she was experiencing, revelry took place all around her as her tormentors took a break from tormenting her. The king had gone to bed – and left his men to their own devices. After taking turns spitting and pissing on her, the tormentors had taken to drinking ale and dancing around the room. About a dozen men and women drank and laughed around her, acting as if there wasn't the crumpled mass of Thea's body lying on the floor beneath their feasting table. They callously sang victory songs as she lay broken, covered in her own blood and their bodily fluids.

Thea's fevered and exhausted mind drifted to Kol, of his smile and how he would often brush his soft lips against her knuckles. If she closed her eyes, she could almost feel his fingers rubbing lazy circles on her bare legs. In stark comparison, she also remembered how he had looked when he had stabbed a knife into the hand of a man who had disrespected her. Fierce and unforgiving. He had promised to always protect her, and he had meant it, of that she was certain. She knew that the promises he made her came from a place of unwavering devotion, maybe even love.

In her heart, Thea knew Kol would be willing and capable of saving her – if he knew where she was and if she realized she was missing in time. But panic and sorrow gripped her again, as the fear in her mind told her that neither of those things were possible. She had to force herself to hold on to hope, for without hope, she knew she would surely die.

After hours of revelry, someone had remembered her presence there. The sound of heavy boots ambling toward her pulled her from her thoughts of Kol. Her swollen eyes peeled open, and her head lulled painfully toward the direction of the shuffling feet. A large ruddy hand placed a cup on the floor near her.

"Thirsty?" He offered, gesturing toward the cup. Despite herself, she lunged toward it, primal thirst taking the reins from her resentment for the people around her. The chains around her ankles pulled, clinking loudly as she fell flat on the ground. She groaned in pain – but continued crawling forward and braced her weight on her good shoulder as she stretched toward the cup. It was just inches out of her reach.

"Please." She begged, voice raspy and barely above a whisper. Her sandpaper tongue rubbed roughly on the roof of her mouth.

"Let me help you." The man offered, before he callously kicked the cup over and spilled its contents all over the floor. He cackled maliciously as she wailed in disappointment.

Thea used all the will left in her, actively fighting the urge to give up and collapse to the ground, to look up at him with death in her eyes. "You will regret that." She swore with all the energy left inside of her.

The man laughed again, looking around at his comrades as he did so. "Little lady, no one is coming to save you, so you can keep your threats to yourself." Lie. Hope filled her chest as she detected his lie, and then the door to the room was kicked open. Splinters shot out as the wooden mass burst open and then hung to the side, tittering off its hinges.

"Where is she?" Thea shivered, even knowing his anger would never be directed at her; at that moment, his very voice

9

incited fear. She looked up at him from under the table, he had yet to see her, but she could see him. Blood dripped from both swords he held, and his dark, curly hair was dripping with sweat. Rage-filled eyes scoured the room, and his chest heaved with substantial breaths as he searched desperately for her. "I will not ask again!" He shouted.

The women screamed and fled the room knocking over chairs and dropping their glass cups as they ran. Metal chinked as the five remaining men in the room pulled their swords and began to walk toward Kol. He ignored them – as if driven by a single desire that turned off even his self-preservation skills. Kol had to know she was alive.

His eyes finally found her, and then he allowed himself to draw in the first steady breath he had inhaled since he discovered her missing. A strange combination of relief and horror flashed through him. He was relieved to find her – but also horrified and filled with shame that any of his past actions had led his enemies to do this to her. Horror reigned supreme in his mind to see the state she was in. Though he never raised his own hand against her, he felt as if every bruise on her body was directly his fault. It took all his willpower not to run to her immediately. He vowed to take care of her, but first, he had a job to finish.

"They did this to you?" He asked her calmly, strangely calm given the circumstances. She nodded slowly, unable to speak. "All of them?" She confirmed with another weak head nod. He dipped his head grimly, before raising his gaze back to the men around him. He smiled sharply, showing nearly all his teeth in a wicked smile. "I want you all to know – I'm going to enjoy this immensely."

Chapter 1

History of All

Not much is known of the world, but luckily only two lands are important to this tale, specifically, two continental lands – one large and one small. Those who live on the larger call their homeland The Continent, and the other they call The Lesser Continent. For those who live on the smaller one, the names of the lands are as different as the people who live on them, but that's a story for another time.

Long before the beginning of recorded history, when God created man, and the first civilizations had only just begun, Blessings were bestowed upon those who were most righteous. The Blessings were miraculous gifts, far above what any person could simply be born with or obtain from skillful practice. These gifts became known as Controls, and like anything, man found a way to corrupt them after only a short time. Those who had Control lorded over those who didn't, dividing the lands of the continents between those with Controls to do with as they pleased. But over time, lording over the powerless bored them, so those with Control began to war between themselves as well. Children were born, and Controls were passed down through generations, as was the power over the people of their respective realms. Though God, called the Blessed long before those with Control used that word to describe themselves, intended for these gifts to be used to better the world – they became weapons they waged war with. Over time some Controls died out, leaving only those most powerful, cunning, or lucky to survive the test of time. God stopped being worshipped, his temples went into ruin, and the Blest became the new gods.

Althea Torianna of Pache

They say names have meaning, an ability to shape one's destiny. Althea's name was carefully chosen, six long months after she was born, as a means of strategy on her parent's part. Not to manifest intelligence or adventure in her life, only to make her more appealing in marriage to a powerful family.

Before she was born, her father, of noble blood and powerful in his own right, had no children to leave his small seaside kingdom to. Like all powerful families of nobility, they had a Control. Their family had the Control of Veritas, truth in all ways. But as helpful as this power could be, it was nothing compared to the sheer power that others were gifted with. This led their family to survive off the marriages and political ties they created – rather than physically battling for power or supremacy. For many generations, the war had not touched their land, and peace had existed in their realm. But her father feared this would not last should he leave no children to inherit his noble status. He feared that his realm would be vulnerable due to his advancing age and lack of heirs.

They prayed for many moons for a child – but continued to have none. Finally, a Healer Blessed by God himself came to them. The Healer used her gifts to reach out to Althea's mother's womb. They were told that her healing would be enough to bring one healthy child into this world. Though they prayed day and night for a son, not even the most powerful could change fate.

After months of worrying and countless pleas to God, it was discovered that the child was a girl. Rather than raise his daughter to be the ruler of his realm, he sought a powerful marriage for her instead. He didn't believe a daughter would ever be strong enough to rule independently, especially a daughter of mere Veritas. He hoped that if he gave up the rights to his ancestral lands, they would avoid war, and his daughter and future generations would be taken care of.

When her father would tell this story years later, he would say, "Luck was on my side when I sought a marriage for Althea, as the High King and Queen themselves were seeking both things I had to offer: a girl of noble blood for their son to wed and land with access to the coast to be added to their Empire."

A treaty was drawn up, the marriage terms agreed upon, and once the dowry was settled, she was finally named – Althea Torianna. Althea translated to mean: wholesome, truthful, alluring, and a loyal mate. Torianna meant conqueror. Althea had been chosen by her parents, and Torianna by his. And before the age of one, she was betrothed to Kol Arius of Cativo.

While many arranged marriages were completed after both reached puberty and finished their educations, Kol's parents deemed his education in kingly ways too precious to pause at a young age for something as frivolous as marriage. They instead decided the appropriate age of marriage to be twenty-three. Then they were to ascend to the throne after paternal death. Like everything in their world, twenty-three was a carefully chosen symbolic number. "A number of importance to God." As his mother would say in her letters to Althea's parents, outlining their decision of when to wed. She wrote:

"The angel number 23 is a blend of the energies of the numbers 2 and 3. The number 2 symbolizes teamwork, spirituality, and stability. The number 3 symbolizes development and hope. This is what we want for the future of the Kingdom and their union."

And that was the final word to be said on the matter. Althea would travel to Cativo after her twenty-third birthday, only a few months after Kol's twenty-third birthday. They would live in the Palace together for one moon phase, learning about one another and their roles to come, and as long as Kol found her pleasing – they would be wed after that. Althea's opinion – was not to be considered.

One may wonder if Althea resented this marriage agreement, being forced into a marriage without her consent, but such was the way for every high-ranking lady in her time, and it is all she had ever known. Her parents spent much of her life romanticizing her future marriage and spouse. They told her of the grandeur of his Palace and the beauty of the countryside in which it was located. Once, when she was small, she sat at her mother's feet and asked again what her future home would look like. Her mother put her needlepoint to the side and began the same story Althea had heard many times before.

"The Palace, it is a beautiful place, little Thea. One day you will take a grand carriage up the stone laid path to the outer entrance of the Palace. A gate will close, keeping you in, nice and safe. You will look up and see ahead a beautiful castle, bigger than any you've ever seen before, covered in gold detailing and standing several floors high with windows all around. As you ride up all around, you will see lush gardens, with flowers, fountains, and statues. And lucky for us, it is

located a mere one-day journey away from home, so Mama will
always be close by.''

When she was young, this story often placated her when
she felt scared about leaving home, as did the stories of her brave
and handsome future husband, who would make her Queen. But
as she got older, stories of his father's brutality frightened her.
His Control, one that he unleashed with little restraint, devastated
the lives of many who would not give in to his demands. And by
the time she had reached adolescence, stories of Kol's brutality
were added into courtly gossip as well, and they called him the
Prince of Death. Her mother assured her that they would never
allow her to be taken away if it were unsafe, she allowed this to
comfort her, but deep down, she knew they had as little choice as
she did. The High King could do whatever he wanted.

While both of noble blood, Kol and Althea did not reside
in the same realm, and therefore their courts did not ever overlap,
meaning that it was not likely they would cross paths until they
were to be wed. On occasion, her parents would be invited to
grand events at the Palace, but even they had not met the young
Prince. Kol and Althea were not to meet until they were both
trained, educated, and ready – to avoid a potential social faux pas
that might leave either with a poor impression of the other. But
that did not stop her from being curious.

Being a daughter of nobility entitled her to an education,
but as the future wife of a Mori King, this education was
carefully chosen by her future husband's family, of course. Her
lessons included: reading, writing, equestrian, music, art, and
culture, amongst other similar things. She even was to take
classes on the art of sexual arousal and pleasure. The letter sent
with this instruction came well into her adolescence from Kol's

mother, reading: *"She is to be able to enchant the mind and the body."*

But she was never taught philosophy or state affairs. They said it would bore her, but she began to suspect it was to keep her ignorant and unproblematic. But she did not want to challenge her lot in life, she was fortunate, and she did not want to hurt her family or future by appearing ungrateful.

As she grew in grace, she also grew in beauty. She was everything her parents hoped her to be: generous in spirit, benevolent, kind, and talented in all her studies. But two things they did not like were her rebellious spirit and that many young boys at court desired her. Out of fear, and the urging of her parents, she became skilled at fending the attentions of males off, else the Prince of Death incur his wrath upon them. To fend the boys off, she was often sharp-tongued with them, giving her the ability to engage in battles of wit from adolescence – a powerful tool in court. And despite her beauty, she learned to move through social gatherings unseen, preferring her own company to that of a group and putting up a wall of practiced indifference around others. All her parents hoped was that if she were uncomplicated and pleasant, she would never anger her future husband, and both she and their realm would be protected.

Kol Arius of Cativo

Kol Arius of Cativo. His name meant both death and immortality. Although his name is a contradiction at first glance, it was given deliberately as a message to those who may challenge him. Kol to remind them of his Control, death, and Arius as a hope he would never die. While the latter is a fruitless wish for us all, and his mother feared it would taunt God, his father would not budge on it. It was symbolic of the longevity of their Empire more than their actual son. Kol Arius became the next tyrant born into a line of powerful rulers.

Kol's family was one whose Control often dominated over others. Their Control was called Mori. While translated to mean death, in actuality, it was a complete dominance of essence. They could bend the will of others, even unto death. As with any Control, some individuals who wielded Mori were more potent than others. Kol had a cousin that could barely force a servant to dance on command, while stories say his great-grandfather could kill an entire enemy army with only his mind. Since a war like that had not happened in generations, the Mori line had not been able to showcase their powers at large; therefore, many in the kingdom did not know that Kol had power much closer to the latter than the former. This being the case, much of the Continent was under the rule of Mori. Some realms were taken by force or manipulation, and others were taken over by marriage.

Marriage is an inevitability to a future king, so like Althea, he was raised knowing he was to be wed. His father raised him to be ruthless and spoiled. He was to think he was more powerful and more deserving than every other living being on this planet. But his mother took special care that he did not think this way of his future wife, for she had been wed for negotiation and power, not love. She was afraid of her husband and had often felt like a symbol and nothing more. She did not want that life for another unsuspecting girl. She would use her Control, Sway, on Kol often, "You bow to no one, other than your Queen. To the world, you may be harsh and unrelenting, but for her, you are to be soft and gentle. She is to be your equal. To all but Althea, no mercy." She also taught him how to do many things in secret, such as dancing and reading poetry. She even would sneak him into the kitchens late at night and show him how to prepare sweets. As Kol got older, he learned other things from the boys at court, such as how to flirt and seduce women. But he never forgot what his mother forced into his head, as was her Control. She was born with the power of Sway, the closest Control known to Mori. His father had married her with the hope that his children would have his Control – but felt Sway was the next best thing if they were to inherit their maternal Control. She could not Control the mind like a Mori, but she could highly suggest to it. So, everything she spoke to Kol about his future bride, especially in his vulnerable youth years, would stick as truth.

During his 'kingly lessons,' his father would encourage him to push his powers as far as they could go. It started when Kol was young, and his father would instruct him to make his servants walk in circles around him. Kol would practice his Control on his own as well, forcing maids to bring desserts to his room after dinner or willing his peers to do his bidding. But as he aged and grew stronger, his father would even encourage him to do more sinister things, and Kol found he could do them with ease. At age sixteen, he went to a battle camp and made as many as a dozen soldiers, at the same time, march through freezing waters against their will and stand there for hours, resulting in lost toes for all and death for an unfortunate few. But despite all this, he did not yet know the extent of his Control.

Like his father, once he began engaging in courtly duties at eighteen, he would use his Control to bend the will of those around him so they may not betray him. He simply spoke in a deep and commanding voice, "You will get no lofty thoughts of overthrowing my will." And so, they did not, even if they wanted to – and many did.

Growing up this way, he did not have many friends. He had peers who tolerated his presence and, as he aged, courtiers began to hang around him more, hoping to elevate their status within the court by befriending him – but they feared him. He always felt it was better to be feared than loved, but his 'relationships' occasionally left him wanting more. But of those he trusted, he had his pets, a dog and a horse, and his mother, and that was it. But he would dream of the day he would have a companion, an equal he could share meals and laughs with. As a young boy, he would beg his mother to tell him of his future bride so often that she eventually had yearly portraits commissioned of her for him to have so he would stop asking what she looked like. And as he grew older, he kept his ear out in court for any gossip that may come of her. While persuaded to be soft for Althea and trained to be diplomatic and charming in court, he could never have been accused of having a soft heart, and that became even more true after his mother died. She was kind where his father was harsh, and thankfully she lived into Kol's adult years to help Sway him toward even a hint of kindness, and luckily, for Althea, the effects of most Controls last even past death.

The years following her death were hard. Kol was left with only his father, who grew increasingly angry and volatile without the Queen to ebb his rage, but Kol held onto hope for his twenty-third year, the year in which he would finally meet his Althea. He considered her the only light in the darkness. He did enjoy his courtly duties, which mainly consisted of attending meetings with nobility and interrogating prisoners for his father's gratification. Still, they were mundane and merely a distraction until he could have the thing he had wanted most since he was a young boy – connection and love with another.

Chapter 2

Birthdays had always excited Thea. Every year on her birthday, she would be awoken to the smell of warmed chocolate and pastries and was allowed the whole day to do whatever she pleased, no lessons or rules, and then the night would be filled with a lavish party. While some things were the same, in reality, this year was completely different – because her whole life was about to change. This year would be her twenty-third birthday party, and the day after, she would leave for Cativo to be married.

Over the years, her feelings toward this marriage had ebbed and flowed. As a child, she was only excited. Her mother would tell her stories of the grand Palace, her handsome Prince, and the beautiful dresses she would get to wear. As an adolescent, she had her qualms, especially when stories of the Prince of Death began to circulate. Then, her qualms grew even more when her lessons began to include information on how to please a man sexually. As an adult, she would tell herself that courtly gossip should not dictate her opinions of her future husband, and convinced herself that nothing could be a more comfortable life than being Queen. However, leaving all she had ever known to be married to a stranger still gave her pause at times. She occasionally felt it a curse, but more often considered herself lucky. She had many friends who were taken as young as fifteen to marry men twice their age. At least her husband was to be High King, and at least he was her age. And many women in court reported him to be very pleasing to the eye and charming, though victims of his Control would disagree.

Thea woke up that morning, no different than any other birthday. Her parents came in, a servant following them, carrying a tray of warmed chocolate drinks and citrus pastries. She opened her arms to them as they wrapped her in a practiced embrace. Despite their rather frigid hug, Thea fought back tears, knowing this would be the last time she ever got to experience this tradition.

As Thea sat there, wrapped in a forced hug, she eyed the servants who carried in her breakfast. One of them sat the tray down and rolled her eyes, no doubt jealous of Thea's lot in life and annoyed with how spoiled she seemed from the outside looking in. But Thea felt that in reality, she was hardly different from this servant, for they both were at the mercy of others. Thea had always been told when to speak, what to wear, and how to act. She was to serve a future king, giving him heirs when he demanded and doing as she's told. *Not unlike a servant at all,* she thought.

Her parents released her from the hug, and for a brief moment, Thea thought they looked quite sad. She often wondered why they had always kept her at a distance, emotionally speaking. She had always assumed it was because they knew they'd have to give her up one day, and the less close to her they were, then the less it would hurt to do so, but that assumption hadn't made the loneliness Thea dealt with her whole life easier to bear. Despite her nervousness and apprehension, she prayed this marriage would mean no longer feeling alone.

"What would you like to do today, little Thea? Attend the festival in town? Picnic in the citrus grove with your friends? Watch a play at the local theater? Anything you want." Her mother listed activities she has liked to do on previous birthdays, but today she had something else in mind.

"Can we all spend the day together? We can do any of those things, but I'd like to do them with you both."

Her mother's eyes welled with tears. "I don't know that we have time for that today, Thea. Someone has to see to your party plans." Her mother responded, looking toward her husband for validation. Her father nodded in agreement. Thea had not expected anything less, but it did not cushion the blow of sadness she felt at thinking of spending another day alone. "Enjoy your treats and get dressed. Perhaps a stroll through town would be something you'd enjoy?" She looked to Thea's father again, who had yet to say anything. Thea often wondered if he ever regretted her marriage agreement, if he saw the impact of being promised to the Future High King had on Thea. But if he did, he never said so, and it really wouldn't matter because no one could back out of a contract with the High King.

"I think that sounds wonderful." He cleared his throat, kissed Thea's temple, and left without another word.

"Is father okay?" Thea asked.

"Of course." Her mother replied dismissively over her shoulder – before exiting the room herself.

Thea took a few deep breaths trying to calm her nervous energy. At that moment, she decided that even exciting change was hard. She wondered if having known about her marriage contract her whole life made this change easier or harder to deal with. While she didn't like surprises, she also had a lifetime of expectations and fears to build around this marriage. *Introduction before marriage*, she had to remind herself as he could dismiss her and call off the marriage contract if he so chose, and that thought sent a shiver of fear through her. The lack of say she had in the matter was glaring in that regard. She took another breath and considered what would happen if he sent her away. If he decided he didn't want her, she could stay in her family realm forever, marry one of the nice men from her own court, and have a predictable life. A small smile spread across her lips at this thought, but she quickly dismissed it, for losing this marriage contract would disgrace her family, and it would mean she would not be queen – the only thing she had prepared her whole life to do. She didn't know who she was outside of the bride of the future High King. No one had ever let her try to figure it out.

Her legs dangled over the edge of her lush bed, and she curled her fingers into the duvet as she rolled her shoulders out. A golden pastry from the tray called to her, she inhaled deeply, and the aroma immediately calmed her down. The tart and sweet dough felt like comfort and tasted like home as it rolled around her mouth. Amongst the things she was bringing with her to her new home was a large catch of citrus fruits, the pride of her home realm, that she would be giving as a gift to her new family – in addition to her dowry. Like much she was forced to do, it was symbolic of her generous spirit and desire to share her past with her future.

After enjoying her treat, she drank half a cup of chocolate in one gulp and then hopped up to get dressed and start her day. At her party that night, she would be wearing a new gown, one custom made for the occasion in her signature color, a deep plum, and the final touch would be her new necklace, a gift this year from her future husband.

Every year he sent her a gift for her birthday, as she did for him, and this year had been no different. A beautifully wrapped box had been hand-delivered to her estate the day before her twenty-third birthday, with a note instructing her to open it at her pleasure. Of course, she opened it immediately, not even considering for a moment waiting for her actual birthday. She would take any chance to choose for herself, even if it was the most mundane choice. Inside, the box was satin lined and perfumed to smell like lavender, a scent he had no doubt been told was one of her favorites. The gifts he had sent in the years prior had been lovely, but the scent detail alone made this one seem much more personal. Thea grabbed the satin between her thumb and index finger, pulling it to the side to reveal a sparkling gemstone. It was teardrop-shaped and nearly the size of a walnut. The stone was attached at the tip to a small ornately carved mounting, that fused it to a dainty silver chain. A gasp left her lips – as she knew the cost of such a gift. She smiled, heart filling with hope as she thought, *the Prince is already spoiling me*. She carefully picked it up by the chain and held it to her chest, and then began to daydream while looking at it, imagining the life she could live surrounded by so many beautiful things and a husband who spoils her.

She was pulled from her daydream by her mother asking if she would like the staff to put the gift somewhere safe for her. "I can't imagine a safer place for it than right beside my heart, Mother." She said with sass and then turned, looking toward the man who had delivered her gift. "Thank Prince Kol for my gift and let him know I am eager to meet him." He nodded and left without another word. A lady's maid had helped her put it on. One side was flat, allowing the gem to lay flush against her skin, and the color was almost clear though faintly blue. She had found herself staring at the necklace periodically throughout the day; that gaze was always followed by a jolt of excitement – then a tidal wave of nerves at the thought of meeting the Prince. Marriage is all she had prepared for, all she had waited her whole life for, and she was growing afraid that she may somehow mess it all up. At the end of that day, she had taken the necklace off and placed it on the vanity in her room, and there it remained as she got ready on the day of her birthday.

With the assistance of a lady's maid, she picked out a more casual outfit for the day of her birthday, a light blue cotton dress, corseted with a tan band around her abdomen, and a white overskirt. As a woman of her standing, she was expected to wear outfits like this every day, but she had been known to rebel and even wore pants at times. In fact, she planned to wear pants on her journey to her new home the next day, partly for comfort and partly as a statement. Her mother would not be thrilled, and Thea giggled at the thought of one more mundane argument with her mother before she left home for good.

Thea wondered if her new home would allow her the frivolous joys of picking out her own attire – or would her new husband be strict. She hated that it was something she had to consider, but she knew she did. One of her friends had married a man who had slapped her across the face, busting her lip and bruising her cheek for wearing pants around their manor – she cringed, remembering how afraid her friend had been of her husband. Thea considered the less than loving moniker the public had bestowed upon her future husband, the Prince of Death didn't sound like the type of man who let anyone around him do very much choosing – least of all a woman who was to represent him to the public. A sigh left her lips, and her head was spinning from the whirlwind of thoughts running around her mind. *If I can only have one, I'd give up my power to choose for true love,* she told herself while praying to God the Prince could be like the princes in the stories she read as a girl. Chivalrous, handsome, and charming. She continued to imagine what he might be like, twiddling with her hair as she left her room and walked to the front entrance of the house, where a carriage sat waiting for her.

During the ride into town, Thea had nothing but time to consider what the next few days of her life may look like. The girlish, I part of her mind romanticized all of it. Her imagination took control, and she could see herself rolling up to the Prince's Palace in a gilded carriage and being met immediately by her roguishly handsome fiancé. He would run to her, place his hands gently on her waist, and then twirl her around. Once her feet hit the ground, he would look deeply into her eyes and then place a delicate kiss on her lips. A heavy sigh escaped her slightly agape lips as she imagined this. A bump in the road temporarily sent the carriage wobbling – and caused Thea to tip over in her seat, sending her daydream to a screeching halt. Once she righted herself and smoothed her clothes with a few quick wipes, she released a melancholy sigh. Though she was quite I, she was not without logic. She knew of the Prince's reputation, and she knew their meeting was likely to be curt and awkward more than romantic.

Once in town, she mindlessly milled about, spending money here or there on tchotchkes or food from vendor carts and considering her day of solitude. Solitude was always a mixed experience for Thea, because she often felt this earth-shattering loneliness deep in her bones –and hated it. But on the other hand, when she was alone, she didn't have to hide any facet of her true self, and it was freeing. One of the reasons Thea loved her birthday so much was because she was permitted to do anything

26

she wanted. Even as a young child she was allowed to do anything on her birthday. For example, on her seventh birthday, she had eaten cake for dinner and brought her pony inside the house to ride in the ballroom, and no one had even dared question her. But every other day of the year belonged to someone else. Most days, she was in lessons learning how to be the perfect wife, a poised dancer, and a skillful conversationalist, all while they attempted to strip her of her individualism and rebellious spirit. As she got older, she preferred to spend her birthdays alone, away from the watchful eye of her instructors and parents, though she was certain her parents always had a guard stalking somewhere close by her. After all, she was their only child and had also become their salvation from war with the Mori's, and that was something they could not afford to risk. They had been made abundantly clear.

This birthday was different for many reasons, and one of them was that Thea felt not even this day belonged to her, as she had to spend it getting ready for her life to change. Thea had made a list of what she wanted to buy while out that day, and while some were items for her, most of the things she hoped to purchase were to give to her husband-to-be upon their first meeting. Desperation to make a suitable first impression and get into his good graces as soon as possible was the main motive behind the gifts.

Thea remembered from his list of likes and hobbies that he enjoyed archery and exotic spices, so she wandered around the town to find such items for him. About halfway through her day, she walked into a carving shop, hoping to find arrows for the Prince, but instead of simply being able to shop, she was confronted with a sad example of what happens to many women of her time.

"Haven't sold anything all day?" A rotund, middle-aged man yelled at the teen girl before him.

"We haven't had many people in today, but-" The girl began – but was cut off when his large ruddy hand collided with her face. Thea winced more than the girl did, sorrow settling deep in her core as she watched.

"No excuses! When I bought you, your father promised you'd be useful!" He grunted and walked toward the back door of the shop. "If you don't start selling my wares, I'll send you out and make you use the only thing God gave you to make me my money back." With that, he slammed the door. Thea watched, tears brimming in her own eyes as the girl put her face in her hands, still unaware anyone had witnessed her being reprimanded.

Thea cleared her throat. "Excuse me."

The girl jumped, nearly falling off her stool, and aggressively wiped her cheeks with the sleeve of her shirt. "May I help you, my lady?"

"Are you okay?" Thea asked quietly. "I saw what happened."

The girl forced a smile. "I am great. What brings you in today?"

Despite her desire to help, Thea let it go and settled for saying a silent prayer of safety for the girl instead of intervening. Thea told the girl of her desire to buy arrows as a gift and was guided to a set of ornamentally carved archery arrows. Looking at their beauty made Thea wonder how something so grand could be created by a man so terrible. The girl offered to wrap them, and Thea paid extra to have them secured by an emerald green ribbon – the Prince's favorite color. After she paid, Thea placed an extra gold coin into the girl's hand and eyed the girl knowingly before leaving. *I cannot complain,* Thea thought, *at least I'm not her.*

As she left the carving shop, a myriad of smells immediately wafted into Thea's nose, and she found herself being drawn into the town's herbal shop. Walking into that shop filled her with a sense of nostalgia and sadness, knowing this was likely another last for her that day. When she was a girl, one of her instructors had educated her in the power of herbs, both for medicinal purposes and cooking, and together they spent many afternoons in that shop studying. Thea walked carefully past the 'Table of Danger' as her instructor had called it. She gave it that name as it was covered with powerful herbs – some of which could cause a rash while others could kill you from even a single touch. Thea remembered one day in particular when she had carelessly plucked a stem from that table, thinking herself so daring, but ended up with two large welts on her hand. One from the poison of the herb and the other from the smack on the hand her instructor had given her. The instructor had yelled, "If you had picked up that stem beside it, you'd be dead!" Thea knew now that the most dangerous herbs on that table were encased in glass jars, but she had been scared senseless at the time. She had cried all night, apologizing to her mother for putting her own life in danger – and therefore endangering her whole realm at the same time.

The middle-aged woman behind the counter smiled at Thea, eyes crinkling at the corners as she did so. Thea told her of her day's mission and was assisted in creating a boxed set of exotic spices: cinnamon, cardamom, nutmeg, vanilla beans, and ginger. The smells reminded Thea of cakes, and she again allowed herself to imagine a pleasant scene. The smells aided her in imagining the Prince and herself sitting together at a large table, surrounded by hundreds of pastries and cakes, laughing, and enjoying one another's company as they ate the confectionery. *I wonder if that is wishful thinking,* Thea wondered. The shopkeeper walked Thea out and placed a kiss on her cheek, the smell of patchouli lingering in the air around them, and then sent her off with well-wishes on her life's journey.

After several hours in town, she successfully completed shopping and deemed it time to head home. Exhausted, physically and emotionally, she climbed back into the carriage and set off toward home to prepare for the party. Once she arrived, Thea lingered in a corridor, sorting through things she had purchased that day, when she heard a hushed conversation and sniffling. Around the corner, she could see her mother and father talking, and her mother was furiously wiping tears from her cheeks.

"It's normal to be upset when your only child is marrying and moving away." Her father tried to comfort his wife.

"I am not just upset. I am scared. We were sending our only child into a warzone." Thea's heartbeat increased at this. *Warzone?*

"The Palace is not a warzone." Her father reassured her.

"Well, figuratively, I would disagree. And physically, it is very close to one. You know better than I, that the Mori's have amassed quite a few enemies, and our daughter is going to inherit all of them." She barked out in a harsh whisper.

"We have to believe they will keep her safe."

"So you aren't worried?" She countered.

"No, I am." He admitted, defeat clear in his voice. "There's just nothing to be done about it. This is a signed treaty and contract with the High King – one we have benefitted from for over two decades. There's no way out of it. Besides, this is all she has ever known or prepared for. What would she even do if she wasn't his wife?" He almost sounded like he was scolding her.

"We could figure it out." His wife pleaded.

"It is done. As is this conversation." And with that, he stomped away, leaving his wife to her silent sobs and his daughter to fearful pondering. *Am I in danger?* Thea wondered, but that thought was quickly replaced by seething anger. She was hurt that not even her parents believed she could be more than someone's wife, not even in some hypothetical conversation.

Thea worked to push away the earlier conversation she had eavesdropped on, distracting herself with idle chit-chat as she was aided by lady's maids in bathing and prepping for the night. She sat, humming and playing with the hem of her dressing gown as her hair was braided around her head and decorated with tiny clear gemstones and a few curls left out to frame her delicate face. Deep, deliberate breaths filled her lungs as she was corseted into her dress, and the full skirts fell around her as her body was pulled into a perfect hourglass shape. She fingered the delicate lace that made up her low décolletage and smiled at herself in the mirror when her gift from Kol was placed around her neck. She felt beautiful and confident, ready to enjoy her night with her friends and family. At that moment, she refused to let worries of what was to come to darken her mood. *This is my last hurrah.*

Thea walked with purpose toward the ballroom, pausing only briefly to smooth her dress and stand up straighter before motioning for the servants to open the doors for her. Two grand doors were opened before her, allowing her to step on the platform overlooking her party. She spotted her parents immediately, both beaming up at her with pride. Pride was the

31

most common emotion they felt when looking at her, for her birth had saved them and given them notoriety throughout the Continent. Thea looked around the room, impressed with the turnout, but then again, who wouldn't want to be at the party being thrown in honor of the future High Queen. All eyes gazed up at her as she descended the stairs into the ballroom. She smiled and nodded at her guests as she glided through the room, making her way down the stairs and toward her parents. They greeted her with cold smiles and gestured to the people around them to begin mingling again.

Thea made deliberate attempts to spend as much time as she could that night in the presence of her family, whom she would not get to see again until her wedding. But they often excluded her, making their way to the corners of the room to discuss business out of sight of Thea. A deep sense of loneliness filled Thea's heart, a thing that was not uncommon for her.

Thea thought about her travels to Cativo – and life in general. She had high hopes the loneliness wouldn't continue once she met her future husband. In addition to having a future spouse in Cativo, one of her friends, Lady Dorothy Farler, had agreed to accompany her to Cativo. Dorothy's parents thought she might rise through the courtly ranks and find a suitable marriage match if she were seen in the presence of the future High Queen. Though it was a decision made mainly on strategy, Thea didn't mind; she was just happy to have a familiar face going with her. Thea stood there, laughing with Dorothy near the dance floor – when the music changed, and couples began to line up for her favorite dance.

"I love this dance!" Thea declared, "Go get a partner and join me." She urged her friend – as she looked around the room for a partner of her own. Dancing thrilled her, not only because

she loved the feeling of gliding on air to the rhythm of music –
but also because it was the only socially acceptable time she was
allowed to be touched by anyone. Her eyes scanned the room,
and she watched, disheartened, as all her usual dance partners
were snapped up by others – some even actively avoided eye
contact with her as she searched. The closer she had gotten to her
marriage, the more of a social pariah she had become. Just as she
thought she'd have to sit out on her favorite dance on her
birthday, a man stepped out from behind her and extended his
hand to hers.

"May I have the honor?" He asked, bowing slightly as he
pulled his lips up into a seductive smile. Her stomach clenched,
looking at the tall, beautiful stranger before her. She had never
seen him before, and for some reason, that disappointed her. He
gazed at her intently, blue eyes tracking her every move. She felt
a desire pool in her stomach and, suddenly, didn't feel
comfortable accepting a dance from someone who enticed her so
much – given her engagement status.

"Thank you, but I promised a friend they could have this
dance." She lied smoothly, for she would rather miss her favorite
dance than potentially damage her future marriage by untoward
actions. And his face had her feeling quite untoward.

"I don't see anyone around waiting for you, and I heard
you say this was your favorite dance, did I not?"

"It is, but-" She hesitated, looking at the couples lined up
on the dance floor – she knew the musical cue to begin was only
a few moments away.

"I insist. It's only one dance, please." He continued to
hold his hand out to her, an open invitation. She could see
Dorothy gesturing to her from the dance floor, she regretted not
just asking Dorothy to be her partner, but it was too late for that.

When another look around the room yielded not one familiar face willing to help her, she placed her small hand atop the stranger's large one. His calloused hand was warm in hers.

"Just one." She said excitedly, forgetting her former trepidation. She thought, *what could one dance hurt?* He allowed himself to be pulled around from behind her as she rushed to line up before the dance began. He laughed, deep and breathy, content to allow her to pull him along because he was just as entranced by her as she was by him. Two lines had been made on the dance floor, a partner in each one, facing one another. Thea pushed her partner toward his line and took her place in the other. An urgent thought came to her mind, "Are you even familiar with this dance?"

"I am." He drew his lips up into that same alluring smile, "It's all about the intimacy of the almost touch." He looked her up and down slowly, and she swallowed, unable to break eye contact with him. The men bowed deeply when the music swelled, and the women curtsied down. "Very good." He mouthed, followed by a cheeky wink. And though he didn't speak, she could hear his voice sultry in her mind, and she felt her face heat in response to his praise.

To begin, all the couples took a few steps toward one another and stood a step aside from their partner. One partner raised their right hand, and the other their left. They mirrored one another, hands inches apart as they turned in a circle, holding eye contact. Thea felt his unbroken eye contact a challenge – one she did not want to back down from. They stood back in their original positions, only to step forward again, raising their other hand this time. Thea took uneven breaths as her deep caramel eyes stared into his thoughtful blues. She had never before been quite so taken off guard in this way by anyone, especially a man.

Guilt made her stomach churn; she was beginning to regret the dance – simply because of how alluring she found him. She had been forced her whole life to repress these desires, and she wasn't about to let herself fall short so close to the finish line. Once that turn was complete, the couples rested again, only to step forward, both hands raised, still not touching, and completed a full turn again. Thea could feel the intensity roll off her partner as they danced through the final, slow turn. The longer they stared into one another's eyes, the more self-conscious she became, and she was acutely aware that soon they would be touching. She remembered how carelessly she had dragged him onto the dance floor, how forward he must consider her, and regretted that too. Suddenly, she felt a spark run through the ring finger on her left hand. She gasped audibly, this sensation pulling her from her thoughts. Her partner had ever so lightly placed one of his fingers against hers. He had touched her in an act of defiance, and now he was looking at her with a knowing and mischievous grin. Her brow furrowed, and she gave him a withering stare, which only seemed to fuel his amusement, as evident by the arrogant look in his eyes. They separated once again, only to quickly step toward one another once more, but this time they were supposed to touch. Due to his insolence, she considered walking away, but she told herself that leaving during a dance wouldn't be proper; in reality, despite her annoyance, she couldn't bring herself to walk away from him.

She placed her hand in his, cautiously stepping forward into his embrace. All her life, she had to take the first steps with people; they always treated her like a porcelain doll because she belonged to the future High King. In all honesty, she often treated herself the same way, cautious not to put herself into compromising situations out of fear of response or punishment.

Her gaze turned cautious, but the energy between them stayed palpable. In her mind, she could remember dozens of times she had danced with men, but never before had she felt this drawn to another. This time was different – some part of her desperately wanted to be close to him, even though she considered it dangerous. Her partner placed a hand on the small of her back and gracefully, but forcefully, pulled her close to him. His hand felt hot on her back, and she was very aware of every single place they were touching. Hands, back, arms, and an occasional graze of the hip, all his touches ignited a fire on her skin. Her body was responding to him in ways she had not expected, and she had never considered herself touched starved until that moment. His touch intoxicated her. With one inhale at this proximity, his scent was a shock to her senses as well, cedarwood and lime and undeniably masculine. She placed her other hand on his shoulder, and he began to lead them around the dance floor.

Trying to alleviate some of the tension, knowing they had several more minutes dancing together, she cleared her throat and spoke. "You're a very accomplished dancer, are you classically trained?" She said formally and with little inflection in her voice, putting up her wall of cold indifference.

He laughed again, almost mockingly, and shrugged. "You could say so. Growing up in court, you visit enough parties like this that you learn the basics just to survive."

"Growing up in court? How have I never seen you before?" She wondered aloud.

"I'm here visiting family. I grew up in the north." He replied, and she sensed no lie. She decided to allow herself to relish in engaging in a conversation with someone who wasn't from her court, who didn't know anything about her.

"North? Anywhere near Cativo? I'm moving there…tomorrow actually." She paused. "And then getting married." She reported, sadness unexpectedly seeping into her tone.

"I sense sadness about that." He responded, with gentleness in his voice.

"Yes and no…it is my fate. I have known that my entire life. Plus, I hope adventure lies there." She paused. *Adventure and love*, she hoped wistfully. "I really hope it does." Another pause. "But change can be hard, and this-" she gestured all around. "Is all I've ever known." Some may consider her too frank or open, but she valued honesty and authenticity when possible – such was her Control.

He nodded his head thoughtfully, considering her words. With that small gesture, he made her feel seen, but that moment was fleeting as a wry smile appeared on his face. "So, marriage? And your fiancé doesn't mind us dancing? Or is that why you were so hesitant to be my partner? I know it can't be because of my looks." He quipped confidently. She smirked at his ego.

"Someone thinks highly of himself." She savored the amusement on his face. "But no, he is not here to object. I did, however, still want to be respectful of him."

He nodded his head thoughtfully again, *something he must often do*, she thought. "He must be quite the man for your family to be willing to send such a beautiful asset all the way to Cativo just for a marriage." *Or the trade deal was too good to turn down, and even before the age of one, my parents doubted my ability to figure life out on my own.* She kept this thought to herself.

"Well, I'll have you remember I am a person, not an asset." She replied quickly, in anger, easily triggered after a lifetime of feeling more like the latter than the former. "And it is quite the match, something I'm sure you couldn't understand."

He feigned insult, "You can put the claws away, darling, I'm only joking. I have misspoken, being in the presence of one as gorgeous as yourself tied my tongue. The way you move your body alone has kept me distracted all night." Disgust covered her face, and she listened to him spew flirtatious language in her direction.

"You'll do well to remember yourself." She whispered, as to not draw attention toward them from other guests. "I think you do not realize others do not find you as charming as you find yourself."

He pulled her closer and spoke softly in her ear, breath sending chills down her spine, "But you do find me at least a little charming then."

She quivered; his close physical proximity and her continued tracking of every place he touched on her body acted as a distraction from her better sense. She whispered back, "I suppose." Despite his ego, she could not help herself from finding him alluring, and she made note that he was unlike any man she had ever met before. She felt she could be a little bold in his presence, as she assumed he didn't know who she was – and more importantly, didn't know to be afraid of her future husband.

"I suspected as much." He leaned back, a smirk resting on his lips and a small dimple forming in his left cheek. "And my physical form, it's pleasing to the eye, correct?" She did not answer, instead she looked over his shoulder and released a breath she had been holding for quite some time. "Your silence speaks volumes." He took his hand from hers and placed it gently on her chin, turning it toward him. Her face warmed instantly from being near and under such scrutiny from this man.

Lust filled her chest, but then as if cued by the song's final note, the feeling of panic followed replaced it. *What am I doing?* Thoughts of guilt filled her mind. She placed both her hands on his chest and shoved, garnering gasps from passersby. He looked on in shock. "Are you daft to think a pretty face entitles you to my affections?" She said quietly. "Clearly, you forget the occasion, so I'll remind you. It's my birthday and engagement party. You know I am to be married, as we spoke about it earlier." She laughed, feigning pity. "You don't even know how stupid you are, to be flirting with me." He looked at her with confusion, but never let the smile fade from his lips. "You don't know who my future husband is. Else you would have stayed far away from me." Despite being reprimanded, his grin remained, masochistically enjoying being scolded by her. She continued, trying to keep her voice low. *These people will never see me again, what do I care if I make an ass of myself*, she thought. "I'm to be wed to the future High King of this realm, a man of a reputation that I am sure you know, and if you have an ounce of wisdom inside that head, you'll know not to become his enemy." She looked him up and down, in an attempt to make him feel small – a task not made easy given his tall and muscular frame. "Now, as I said before, if you have any intelligence at all, you will leave me alone while you still can."

He laughed, genuine joy in his eyes. "Is that a threat, little princess?

"It will be a promise if you keep this up, goodbye." She turned away, grabbing the hand of the nearby, mouth-agape Dorothy and marching away. Her parents watched on in abject horror.

The stranger chased after them and whispered in Thea's ear. "The future High King, really? Is he aware of your temperament? Or is that to be a surprise for him on the wedding night? Though in my opinion, I can't say the feistiness will be a deterrent at that moment." He paused, and she froze – embarrassment and anger threatening to bubble over.

She turned back, fire in her eyes, "I will not be spoken to by the likes of you in this manner. I scarcely believe you could have been raised in court and would knowingly speak to me in this fashion." She was aghast. "And I can assure you that my husband shall never incur my wrath in this way. He is an honorable man, whom I will freely give the pleasure of placing his hands on my body, unlike you who attempts to take what is not his without permission." She paused.

In her pause, he responded with a devilish look in his eye, "Will you now? Lucky man indeed." She sensed no lie in this statement.

She bawled her fists, face hot with embarrassment and fury, "Leave at once or be forced off this premise by my guards. You're spoiling my fun and good mood."

"You'd do well to listen to my daughter." Her father added, from behind the man.

He raised both hands in defeat, "As you wish, little princess." And with that, he sauntered off.

"Who the hells was that?" Dorothy asked, face still frozen in shock.

"Who fecking cares, just some nobody who found his way through the gates tonight." She watched him leave, burning holes into his back with her eyes.

"Language, young lady." Her father reprimanded quietly, but unlike most reprimands she had been given in her life, she ignored this one.

"I have never heard you speak that way before," Dorothy whispered as they walked away from the dance floor.

"You likely never will again. Once I am married to the Prince, no man will dare speak to me in that way." Of that, she was sure, no one would speak to the future High Queen like that, and at least not live to talk about it. *No one could speak to a queen that way – except a king,* she thought.

Thea attempted as best she could to shake off her encounter with the alluring and infuriating stranger, but a bit of lingering irritation pulled at her brain for the rest of the night. She ignored it enough to have fun, dancing and eating with her friends and family, but that night when she was alone, she worried about some things that man had said. Was she too brash for her future husband? Would he be displeased with her? She at least took comfort in remembering that she detected truth when he said the Prince was a 'lucky man.' *Maybe he will like me*, she hoped. But she knew, the tricky thing about her Control was that it was often literal. It is a fact that someone considered Kol lucky to have her, but maybe he wouldn't.

Chapter 3

Thea stood in front of her childhood home, tears filling her eyelids as she looked at her around for one final time. Of course, she had been on holidays away from home, and her parents had left for months at a time for court tours, but leaving that day felt different as she didn't know when she would be back, if ever. She wasn't sure what she was feeling more, grief over leaving home, or the fear of what was to come.

Once her luggage was loaded onto the carriage, all that was left to do was say goodbye. Her father stepped forward, "Do not cry, little Thea. This is your big adventure." He embraced her in a hug, "Your whole life has led up to this day. You will make us proud." That felt more like a demand than encouraging words.

She nodded her head. His words rang true; she had been raised for this, and this alone, and it would be an adventure – but she knew from books that adventures were not always easy.

She turned next to her mother, wrapping her arms around her. Her mother pulled her back, looked her in the eyes, and simply said, "You are capable. No reason to worry at all." She nodded again, making this phrase one of her mantras. *I am capable*, she thought to herself.

Thea joined Dorothy in the carriage but looked out the window to wave one final goodbye to her family, and as she did so, the convoy began to pull away. With a deep breath, she turned and looked to her friend, "Onto my new life." She smiled as the part of her excited about what could be started to take control of her mind. Hope filled her thoughts, hopes that she could have a relationship of love and equity. Lately, she had considered this change a loss, a loss of her identity and known life, but suddenly she started to wonder if it could be a rebirth. If she was no longer 'little Thea,' who could she be? While considering this, another part of her mind remembered her husband-to-be. *He will decide who I am to be now.* A shiver ran down her spine as she remembered that many refer to her betrothed as the Prince of Death. *Will I be under his thumb until the day I die?* She wondered: would he dictate whom she spoke with, what she wore, and what she was allowed to do? She looked down at her pants, a visible sign of the rebellious spirit many desired her to repress, and wondered what he would think if he saw her in them.

Dorothy's voice pulled her from her thoughts. "What are those?"

Thea's eyes land on the box of red roses sitting beside her. "The Prince sent them this morning. Well wishes for safe travels, I suppose. My mother insisted I bring them." Her voice remained monotone as she explained, not a hint of inflection rising from her.

"What are you thinking about?" Dorothy asked, sensing unease in her friend.

"I wouldn't even know where to start," Thea responded honestly. "I'm mostly just nervous about what he will be like. You know as well as I do that entitlement can make men unbearable, and he is the most entitled of them all. Not to mention the fearsome reputation he has built for himself." Dorothy nodded, listening thoughtfully. Thea continued to spill her thoughts out, never having spoken them aloud to anyone before. "I want to be free to be myself and pursue my passions. I know my role will come with some required duties but outside of that, what will my life look like? What if he is intolerable and scary? I have no say in any of this." She quickly swept away the single tear that rolled down her cheek. "I just want love, and I don't know what I'll do if he is horrible."

Dorothy looked at her, sincerity in her gaze. "Well, Thea, you will do what women in unhappy marriages have done for centuries."

"Deal with the unpleasantness silently until it drives them mad, and they are sent to a cottage in the Mores while their families are told they have hysteria, and they die alone in a hideous white nightgown?" Thea said quickly, causing Dorothy to laugh and raise her eyebrows in amused horror. "It was in the novel I read last week. She saw apparitions while she was locked away."

"You're ridiculous. No, my sweet, simple girl, you kill him." They looked at each other grimly – before breaking into nearly hysterical laughter.

When the laughter dissipated, Thea continued, "You're not taking me seriously…" She paused, "I am afraid of two things. One, that he won't love me, and two, that I won't love him. I don't know which is more frightening though." She sighed, "If he doesn't love me, he could be cruel. We have known many whom that has happened to." Dorothy nodded in agreement. "And if I don't love him, my life will be long and miserable. However, I would prefer that to him being cruel. And I think I could grow to love a man as long as he was kind to me. But that's the scenario I fear to be less likely, married to the

Prince of Death…." She sighed. "Is it possible he has even one kind bone in his body?"

"I thought you didn't listen to courtly gossip?" Dorothy retorted.

"That was when I had the luxury not to, now that I sit in a carriage on my way to meet him, the court gossip is all I can think about." She sank deeper into her seat, and Dorothy rested a comforting hand on her leg and patted it a few times. The sensation of her hand worked to ground Thea.

"All I know is that we could worry ourselves into madness with what-ifs. I wonder if I will ever marry. Or even create my own life. Will I meet someone at the Palace? The list goes on." Thea nodded at her friend, knowing her worries were just as valid as hers. "Or we could distract ourselves. Tell me more about this horror novel you've been reading instead!" Dorothy smiled mischievously.

At that moment, Thea was more grateful for her friend than she had ever been before. "Okay, so in her case, she isn't even crazy. Her husband wants her out of the picture so that he can wed his mistress…."

They distracted themselves for hours, talking about books they had read and the lives of their friends. Dorothy even mused about the man she may meet in court. She made Thea spit tea all over the carriage when she suggested she could marry a court jester.

"Your mother would kill you. Hells, she'd kill me, if I let you even look at a court jester," Thea choked out between fits of laughter.

"She'd never get the chance. Your husband would protect you, and mine would whisk me away, never to be seen or heard from again." She replied casually.

"What power does a jester have to whisk? He could maybe take you down the path to a local pub and inn," Thea teased.

"A place my mother would never dare look. She always said pubs are full of miscreants and pox." Dorothy said in a mocking tone. "I know you were sad to leave, but I couldn't be more ready."

"Why?" Thea questioned. "You had a nice life."

"I did. But the older I got, the less subtle my mother became about her disdain for my lack of marriageable matches. Forget the tongue lashing I received when she caught me in the stables making out with Petry." She sat up straighter, "*'Dorothy, with the help?'*" She spoke, mocking her mother's shrill voice.

Thea chuckled but grew serious again. "And how was that?

Dorothy looked surprised, "The sex? It was fine, but I was picking straw out of my arse for days." She said with a laugh. "Why do you ask?"

"Just another thing I worry about, you know, with him."

"You've never?" Dorothy asked, surprised.

"No, everyone has always known I was to be married, to a man of reputation no less, so everyone stayed away. And I've always felt waiting would be special, and honoring to God," Thea paused for a moment. "I mean, I've had my education on the matter, and they were thorough, believe me. I just still wonder."

Dorothy interrupted her. "We aren't doing any wondering on this trip. I'll tell you a story this time. Have I ever told you about the time I went with my parents to visit Lords in the West, and I knocked over a sacred artifact and nearly started a war between our families?" Thea looked at her friend in shock. "They leave all these important items out on pedestals in a hallway, then serve wine throughout the night and expect people not to stumble through the hallways on their way to bed. It was the first time I ever drank and-" Dorothy continued, distracting her friend as best she could as the journey crawled on. Fortunately, the trip was not a full day and night, else they would have to stop somewhere to spend the night. Halfway to the Cativo, they made a stop, allowing everyone a chance to stretch their legs, relieve themselves, and eat in the town tavern.

Thea had not been to many places. She had traveled some, but only to equally wealthy lands to her own. Neighboring realms, manors, and seaside beaches. Nothing like the dusty forgotten town she found herself in that day. The town's structure reminded her vaguely of the one near her family home. It had a tavern and inn, a church, and a few people selling wares from carts. But that's where the similarities stopped. The tavern sign was hanging off on one side, the vendor carts looked dilapidated and broken, and everywhere she looked, she could see beggars and children running around without shoes on.

"Sir?" She called for the attention of the head guard of her convoy.

"Yes, my lady?" He answered. She paused for a moment, stunned by looking at him. He was the tallest man she had ever seen, and his broad shoulders easily blocked the sun as he stood before her.

"Are all towns on this side of the realm so…" She looked around and lowered her voice. "Destitute?" Dorothy nodded in agreement while looking around, concerned and clutching her satchel closer to her.

The guard sheepishly rubbed his neck. "I believe this is an anomaly." She sensed a lie.

"Do you forget with whom you're speaking with? Do not lie." She commanded sternly.

His face reddened. "Apologies, I just – the High King doesn't want you to think poorly of his realm. There are areas of lesser renown than others." Truth.

Considering this, she asked a follow-up question. "Were we supposed to stop here?"

He rubbed the back of his neck sheepishly. "No, ma'am. We were not."

"Thank you." She looked around again and looped her arm with Dorothy's.

"Despite the poverty, I hope there isn't crime we need to be worried about?" Dorothy asked.

"No, you are safe, my lady." Lie.

"What did I say about lying?" Thea spoke, irritation growing in her voice.

"Apologies, I don't want you to worry. We will be keeping watch over both you and lady Dorothy. No harm will befall you." Truth. "Just stay with one another and make your stay in town brief. One of my men will follow closely behind you." He gestured to a rider to follow them. "Don't speak to anyone about our purpose here." He added quickly.

She and Dorothy went to the tavern, hoping to find water and a bathroom. The inside of the building exceeded the expectations Thea had from seeing the outside. While outside, the building was dusty and falling apart, the inside was colorful and full of life. Women danced in the center of the room, and men laughed as they played cards at various tables. A barmaid walked up to them as they stood mesmerized and watched the merriment.

"Anything from the kitchen?" She said with a plucky accent.

"What's fresh today…?" Dorothy asked, leaving a pause and hoping the woman filled in her name.

"My name is Elaine, and the porridge is fresh." She responded quickly.

"Two servings of that would be fine," Dorothy said, and then ended the transaction by handing her a few coins.

Several minutes later, Elaine returned with bowls of food and two cups of water. "Water is fresh too, from the well," Thea and Dorothy nodded and thanked her. "So what brings you to town? We don't get many passersby that aren't on the road to the Capital."

"We are on our way to the Capital," Dorothy said with confusion.

"Oh pardon, the men you are with said this was a family trip," Elaine responded.

Thea thought that an odd way to describe their purpose, but she supposed it technically was. "I mean, I suppose that isn't wrong. We're traveling for my wedding." Thea felt that was vague enough.

Elaine smiled, and Thea noted that several of her teeth were missing. "Well, congratulations! Is it a local family? I know most everyone within a hundred miles or so."

"Yes, sort of." Thea considered the guard's words; his warning not to say why they were in town rang in her ears.

A guard, sporting the Mori crest upon his chest, walked up behind them and bowed as he spoke. "We should be back on the road promptly, my lady."

"Thank you," Thea replied dismissively, eyes staying on the now suspicious Elaine.

"Well, as I said, congrats. Anything else you two need?" She asked quickly.

"Are there bathrooms here?" Dorothy asked.

"In the back there, to the left," Elaine curtsied and walked away briskly.

"That ended weirdly," Thea said first.

"So weird," Dorothy agreed. They watched as Elaine went behind the bar and whispered to the bartender, his head whipped around to stare at them. "And getting weirder," Dorothy turned back to face Thea.

They finished their food quickly and used the bathrooms in the tavern before heading back outside. While they waited for all the members of their party to get sorted, they walked down the dirt road, talking and peering into the various shops along it.

A young mother with several children trailing behind her walked alongside them, prompting Dorothy to ask, "What do you know of the Prince's family?"

"Probably as much as you. His mother passed a few years ago, his father is a rake that has a less than favorable reputation, and his sisters all live abroad – married to powerful rulers themselves."

"That's it?" Dorothy asked.

"Yes, that's it." Thea walked towards a flower cart, not wanting to dwell on the fact that she knew very little about her husband-to-be.

Thea walked up to the woman standing by the cart and smiled. She was a pretty girl, barely out of adolescence, and her abdomen was already swollen with child. The smock she wore over her dress was worn and tattered, making Thea think she was of little means. The girl greeted them warmly and asked how their travels had been. As they engaged in polite small talk, and

50

as they did, Thea felt more and more guilt on her shoulder. She had never seen a whole town so impoverished before, and she wished she could help. She did not need flowers, but asked the girl nonetheless.

"Can you show me a flower special to your realm?" She thought fondly of the lilies that were favored in her own realm. The girl smiled and pulled a bundle of lavender. "This is the flower of your realm? This is my favorite herbal scent." She pulled the bundle to her face and inhaled deeply. For a moment, she felt as if she could feel at home in this realm. However, that moment was fleeting, as homesickness already tugged at her heart. She suddenly remembered the gifts she had purchased for her husband-to-be and felt this lavender would be a good addition. Citrus in honor of her realm, lavender in honor of his, and spices and arrows to make him feel endeared to her. To make him feel like she already knew him and was serving him. Thea requested an additional bundle from the girl and paid her ten times what they were worth.

Tears sprung in her eyes, "Lady, I couldn't accept this." This made Thea feel worse. She looked at her abdomen, so swollen with child.

"May I?" She gestured to her stomach.

"Of course." She pulled Thea's hand to her abdomen. Thea could feel her child moving beneath the surface. She had always been fond of children, as they were so wholesome and uncontaminated. It was one of the perks of her future marriage she looked forward to, having a child. She smiled kindly at the women.

"Please, consider it a gift for the baby."

The woman looked at her knowingly and nodded. "Thank you." She said quietly. "Times have been hard, with the men off battling for the High King and the taxes continuing to rise." She said 'High King' as if it were a curse. Clearly, no love was lost in this part of the realm for royalty, and Thea began to feel the distinct need to get back to the safety of her carriage and leave this town as soon as possible.

Thea pulled both bundles of lavender into her arms, almost as a shield, and began her walk back toward the caravan. "Blessing to you." She yelled over her shoulder.

Dorothy spoke, having been quiet throughout the entire exchange. "Seems she hates the High King."

"Yes, seems that way," Thea replied absent-mindedly.

"Can you imagine being born into this mess?" Dorothy asked and gestured to the town, decrepit and destitute.

"No-" She paused thoughtfully. "I cannot," Thea said guiltily.

They took the items they had bought in town and stowed them away before getting back into the carriage. But as they were settling into their seats, all of a sudden, a commotion drew both of their attention's outside. The carriage pulled to an aggressive halt, throwing both girls from their seats.

"What is that noise?" Thea asked.

"I think it's people yelling," Dorothy replied. They both cautiously peered over the edge of the window. Outside half a dozen men, dressed head to toe in black, stood in front of the caravan – blocking the road. They wore black stockings over their faces, concealing their identities. Some stood still, fists raised in the air, while others threw things at the guards. But all were shouting.

"What are they saying?" Dorothy asked.

"Shh!" Thea shushed her as she cracked the window open and pressed her ear toward the opening.

"Oppressors! Down with the oppressors!" The men repeatedly shouted in unison.

"Are they talking about us?" Thea asked. Dorothy only shrugged in response. "What are we going to do?" Her words were laced with fear.

Before Dorothy could answer, Thea watched as the large guard, who had spoken to them earlier, jumped down from his horse and walked toward the men in black. He raised his sword and swiftly swung it, seamlessly chopping the head clear from one of the men's bodies. Blood spurted from the headless neck, and Thea watched in horror as his head slowly rolled away from his lifeless body. Once his body hit the ground, she finally turned away in disgust. A scream sounded from the tavern, and Thea turned her head in time to see Elaine collapsing to the ground, clutching her chest.

"Now leave before the rest of you face the same fate!" The guard yelled. The men hesitated before slowly backing away from the road.

"Thank God the guards are here," Dorothy said as she settled back into her seat.

"Yeah..." Thea sat back and tried to forget the image of the man's head rolling off his shoulders. She reasoned that those men shouldn't have been threatening them, that if they had minded their business, no one would have gotten hurt. But she also felt that had they just continued their journey and not stopped in town as planned, none of the violence would have happened. *This is partially my fault.*

Thea watched through the carriage window as dilapidated towns turned to rural country and then into forest. She considered how much of the realm must be living in this way, impoverished and isolated. She didn't know much about war or politics. The tutors sent by the High King made sure of that, but she had heard talk at parties that the constant battles the High King waged were leaving many dead and even more poor. Her family had been exempted from tax increases, as a part of her marriage contract, but many had not. Even Dorothy's family, once the richest in her realm, had lost several assets and even sold one of their holiday estates to cover the excessive taxing.

"Dorothy?"

"Yes?"

"What do you know of the war?" Thea asked.

"Not a lot, likely more than you considering the Mori's seemed pretty determined to shield you from it, but still not much. Why are you thinking about the war?" Dorothy asked curiously.

"Yesterday, before my party, I overheard my parents talking." She took a deep breath before continuing. "My mother was sobbing, actually scared for me to leave because she considered the Palace and the capital not safe – because of the war," Thea admitted, fear in her voice. "Or perhaps she's worried because she knows about whatever the hells those protesters we saw in the town were going on about," Thea cringed.

Dorothy nodded, understanding Thea wasn't ready to speak about it, while trying to figure out how to reply in a way that wouldn't scare her friend. "Well, I have heard my father talk about it, and he has always said that the capital is a very safe place to live. Less poverty, more soldiers and guards to protect. Plus, we'll be living in the Palace, arguably the most secure building in the Empire ."

"But?"

"But capitals are often targets for enemies, and the royal family can be targeted as well."

"Why?" Thea asked, trying not to cry.

"Probably to send a message, hit them where it hurts. I don't really know."

"Are you afraid?" Thea asked.

"I am…aware of those realities. But I don't think we need to be afraid, none of the actual fighting is being done close to the capital, and I'm sure they will keep you very safe. You are the future princess, after all."

They both settled into silence for a few moments, but Thea's mind was still buzzing with consideration. "I wonder if my fiancé will allow me to engage in royal duties at all?" Thea pondered aloud.

"Why would you want to?" Dorothy snorted, peering over the edge of the book she had started to read.

"I think men often get caught up in their plans, like with war, and are more concerned about winning."

"Okay?" Dorothy mused.

"And they forget what damage the path to victory may be leaving in its wake. They are all hard and powerful, but being soft is important too."

"I thought we weren't going to worry about His Highness's hardness anymore on this journey?" Dorothy raised her eyebrows suggestively.

"Stop!" Thea laughed and swatted playfully at her friend. "I'm serious. I think they forget about the casualties of war, about what happens to the widows and children of soldiers, or about the towns too overtaxed to survive. Maybe I can help there." Thea rested her dainty chin in her palm and looked out the window again.

"I think that's a noble idea…." Much was being said in the pregnant pause.

"But?" Thea provided.

She closed her book and sighed, placing it in her lap with umph. "They purposefully left all things political out of your lessons your whole life. You don't know the first thing about money or the war or the poor." She paused, letting those words sink in. "And the previous High Queen did nothing of that sort. She planned parties, raised her child, and looked pretty. Quiet and pretty on the lap of the High King while he ordered beheadings and taxation. I don't know that the Prince will feel much different." Thea deflated at these words, feeling small. No one, not even Dorothy, believed she could do anything besides the frivolous. Tears welled in her eyes. Dorothy noticed her shift in mood and added, "I have been wrong before, but I just don't want you to get your hopes up. This is a political marriage, not a love match. And you are to be Queen, not King, and that is a big difference."

"Is it too much to hope for equality and love?" Thea begged aloud, contempt in her heart. Dorothy ignored her question, going back to reading her book rather than continuing the conversation. As Thea pondered this question the rest of their ride, her thoughts drifted to the rumors she'd heard of the Prince of Death – would a man like that even be capable of love. Would a man like the High King, a man obsessed with conquering at all costs, have been capable of teaching his son to have any goodness in him? She heard stories of what happened when the High Queen died. The High King brought in consorts from all over his realm within a month. Rumors went as far as to say he didn't even cry at his wife's funeral. Was this to be her fate? A life of frivolous parties and childbearing, only to be forgotten the moment she's dead, overshadowed, and mocked by her powerful husband even in death. She shed a single shimmering tear, and it warmed her cheek as it went down, keeping her grounded in the present moment. She repeated the words her mother had said to her before she left over and over in her head, *I am capable of handling this*, while praying to God the Prince would have even a shred of goodness in him.

Chapter 4

The sky glowed vibrantly with colors as dusk began to settle over Cativo. Blue, pink, and orange swirled in intricate patterns through the clouds and around the falling sun. Thea's muscles ached, stiff from sitting in a carriage all day, and her stomach was churning from nervousness. With each turn off the carriage wheels, she grew more nervous. The growing proximity to her new life weighed upon her. She was only moments away from pulling up to the Palace. The carriage bumped and crawled at a painstakingly slow pace, and the noises of the town around her grew irritating in combination with the frantic thoughts swirling in her mind. She tried to focus on her senses: the smell of bread baking somewhere in the distance, the whinnying of her carriage horses, and the supple cushions beneath her – but nothing could help calm her at that moment. Not when she was about to begin the rest of her life – or potentially a worse fate awaited her, to be sent away for not pleasing the Prince, bringing shame to her family.

She shook her head – as if she could physically shake away her anxiety. "Everything will be okay." She mouthed to herself as she forced her wringing hands to pause.

Dorothy noticed her friend's growing anxiety and spoke up, "Everything is going to be great, Thea, and just imagine the feast they'll have planned for us tonight." Dorothy gave her friend a kind smile. "Have you looked out the window at all? There are so many people gathered around to watch your arrival. Children are even throwing flowers on the ground before the carriage." Dorothy scrunched up her face in stunned adoration of the children's actions. "They adore you already." A hint of jealousy could have been detected in her town had Thea been paying attention.

Thea pulled open the curtain from her window, giving passersby as much a view of her as she had of them. People cheered, clapping and waving as she passed. As Dorothy had said, children were throwing flowers down before the horses. One girl tossed a crown of wildflowers toward the caravan and then smiled up at Thea, and beside her, a much younger child hid behind their mother's leg. Thea waved, causing both children to squeal in delight.

Men whistled and women gazed in jealousy while watching her carriage roll by. The people's reactions utterly amazed Thea. When she was growing up, everyone around her had always known she was to be a queen one day, and she was sure they treated her differently – but never with utter exaltation like the people had that day. Pride filled her chest as she looked at the happy people around her. *My people,* she thought. Unexpectedly, her attention was caught by a single person in the crowd: dressed in all black, stocking covering their features, with a single fist raised in the air.

"Dorothy! Look!" She pointed toward where the man had been, but he was nowhere to be found.

"I know this is so exciting!" Dorothy said with a smile.

"No! I saw a man in all black with a mask on, like in that town!" Her breath was coming in short rapid puffs.

"Thea, I don't see anyone. Take a deep breath. We're fine." Truth. "It is just your imagination." False. Thea pulled her attention away from the mystery man and tried to distract herself by taking the sights the carriage moved past.

Thea considered Cativo a proper city rather than a simple town, which she was more accustomed to. Well-constructed shops lined the streets, as well as taverns and what looked to be a well-staffed brothel. She noted a bakery and several restaurants, which looked much more opulent than the shops she had in her hometown. Every building around them was made from white brick and black mortar, each door its own muted color, and the streets had even lines through the cobbling. Manicured bushes and flowers had been planted in front of many shops, and decorative signs hung outside of each establishment. Ahead of them lay a large bridge. Thea heard the river before she saw it and was delighted once she could see through the black iron fencing of the bridge a deep blue river running through the middle of the city. Several small boats bobbed on the water, and some sat on the edge, tied up on conveniently placed posts. As they went across the bridge, a small child ran toward the water and threw a large rock in, her mother scolded them, but Thea couldn't help but join in the child's laughter as she watched the splash and rippling water.

Soon enough, they were pulling through the gated arch that served as the entrance to the stone wall that blocked access on all sides to the Palace. Thea's mouth hung open. Neither her mother's stories nor her imagination could have done the Palace justice. Her mother had been right with the vague details, but the grandeur of this place could not be described, and she wondered if anyone could have even painted it to justice. Her eyes traced every gilded inch of the Palace. The structure stood several

60

stories high, each floor boasting windows that were at least ten feet tall and delicately outlined in gold. She imagined herself basking in the afternoon sun by one of those windows, carelessly draped over a chaise lounge. She pulled her attention down to the ground level, and she was met with the eyes of several dozen staff that stood lining the stairs to the Palace's grand entrance. At the top of the stairs sat a set of golden doors well over double the size of any she had seen before. *Surely no one person could even open those alone*, she thought to herself.

"They're all here to meet you!" Dorothy shrieked with glee. Thea suppressed a smile, remembering her lessons in decorum. Ladies are never to be overly delighted by anything, and that is even more true of a Queen.

The carriage pulled to a slow stop, right in front of the awaiting Palace staff. Trumpets sounded, and with a flourish, the large, gilded doors opened. The High King stepped out, dressed in a regal jacket with gold buttons and a train that flapped behind him as he walked. He stopped at the top of the stairs and motioned for the carriage door to be opened. Thea swallowed the lump that had formed in her throat and wiped her glistening palms on her pants. She had momentary regrets over her choice of travel outfits, she would never have assumed the High King would come out to greet her immediately upon arrival.

The High King stood proudly, his young wife a few steps behind him, head bowed submissively. This wife would never be queen, she had to know her place or risk someone else taking it. No doubt the High King wanted her to stay quiet, gorgeous, and agreeable.

Many centuries ago, there was a Mori King with a wandering eye and loose pant strings. He had taken many people to his bed: his wife, consorts, sex workers, Palace staff, and lovers. One said lover had this King's favor. The King would send gifts to them and openly parade around parties with them on his arm. But one day, this lover got greedy, and with an Icarus-level ego, thought they were more important to the King than they were. They killed the Queen, hoping to take their place in the royal family beside the King in place of her. They later grew to regret this, a beheading later and a new law in place: a King could only ever have one Queen. They hoped this would take a target off the Queen's back, at least from jealous lovers.

Thea felt a twinge of sympathy for the woman, barely older than she was and married to a man twice her age. She wondered, had she been given a choice in her marriage? *Do any of us get one?* Thea thought ruefully. She looked at the High King again, given name Kairo, and noted the differences in the man she saw standing before her compared to the portraits she had seen of him. The man she had seen in the portraits was no older than forty, had thick black hair, a chin cleft, and well-chiseled muscles. The man she saw now was well into his sixties, hair more gray than black and more missing than thick, with a gut protruding over his black pants. Chin cleft the same. She smirked at the vanity of powerful men. A small voice in her head whispered, *vanity can be manipulated.* This thought was fleeting, she knew not from where it came and let it go just as fast as it came. *Ideas like that do not often serve women well.*

She looked past the High King – to his wife. From her lessons on the Mori court, she knew that this woman's name was Dove. She was a niece of the late High Queen and was given as a "grief gift" to the High King by her father, who was likely desperate to remain in the good graces of the High King after his sister's passing. *Scum,* Thea thought to herself. She often felt relieved that at least her father had arranged her marriage to

62

someone of her age. From her lessons on the court, she knew that Dove had not been born with her paternal gifts, but with her maternal ones. Her mother's family was Flora, and they had the ability to grow or tend to any plant in existence. Naturally, Floras mostly worked on the agricultural lands in the realm, but her mother had married above her station, and her daughter had followed in her footsteps in that way. Though it was an advantageous match, maybe not a wise one if the rumors of the High King's cruelty were true. *She and I may soon have much in common,* Thea worried, *married to Mori men.* She shook her head again, willing away her worry thoughts and focusing her attention on Dove once again. She was wearing a muted gown, likely to coordinate but not outshine her husband, and had her waist corseted to please the male gaze. She had flowing golden hair that came down nearly to her waist, and her skin was sun-kissed, which was not uncommon for those with the Control of Flora – as they often preferred being outside to in. Thea hoped they could be friends, and she knew she'd have to create many alliances to survive in the Palace. Both for political reasons and her general sanity.

Two men, dressed in black and white uniforms, opened the doors to the carriage, and one presented Thea with his hand. She took it, gingerly, and attempted to steady her breaths as she exited the carriage. She remembered her training: *chin high, chest out, walk with purpose, address the staff with a faint nod, do not smile, curtsy to the High King, refer to him as Your Majesty, and do not make eye contact until he addresses you!* These commands raced furiously around in her head, she used them as a mantra, and if she were being honest, she felt better to be distracted with decorum and rules than to think about the reality of her future playing out in front of her. *Is the Prince here?* She wondered. She didn't dare glance around, not that it would help anyway, given she didn't know what he looked like. But she couldn't deny that she was desperate to know if the Prince was in attendance. She hoped he wasn't somewhere nearby watching, but she knew that she would be if the roles were reversed. This thought made her knees wobble and saliva thicken. Her new mantra became – *one step at a time.* She knew she could handle each moment as it came, but she couldn't handle thoughts of her whole future all at once.

When she was finally at the top of the stairs, she dropped her gaze to rest on the High King's feet, forcing herself to blink in regular intervals because it suddenly felt like a foreign action. She placed her feet in position, one she had practiced for years, and lowered herself into a low curtsy. After many moments, she heard him grunt in approval.

"Rise." He spoke with authority – as if she had no other option than to obey him. But upon consideration, she realized that because he was a Mori, that was true. She didn't have a choice. Bile began rising in her throat as she felt her body responding without her consent, and fear coursed through her veins at the thought of being subjected to this level of subservience for the rest of the High King's life. *Maybe for the rest of mine too, if the Prince is like his father.* Once she stood before him, he quickly looked her up and down and clucked in distaste. "You couldn't find more suitable clothing to meet your High King in?"

"Apologies, Your Majesty, I thought I would be given a moment to change before introductions were made." She felt that she shouldn't have to explain herself, and her sorrow for Dove was increasing by the moment. Dove looked up at Thea and gave her a small smile – as if apologizing, or at least acknowledging, that her husband's actions were rude. Despite how well planned many aspects of this marriage treaty were, the small details like when she would meet the High King were not given to her, and at that moment, Thea found this incredibly annoying.

He dismissed Thea with the wave of his regal hand and motioned an older woman forward. "See that she knows the grounds." He looked at her like dust beneath his shoes. "And the rules." With that, he was off, strutting back into his Palace with his properly dressed, quiet wife behind him.

Thea looked to the older woman, hoping to assess her character in a glance. After that exchange with the High King, Thea was already desperate for allies. The woman bowed to Thea, an act that made her uncomfortable but one she knew she'd have to get used to. When the woman stood up, Thea noted she had kind eyes and smile lines.

"Welcome, Althea, I am your head of household." She spoke with a gentle voice. Thea nodded and looked her up and down. Thea felt it imperative to know whom she could trust in this house, but even asking certain questions could be dangerous, as everyone knew what her Control was. She and Dorothy had discussed in length how to ascertain allies in this court, even going as far as to practice how to ask the questions that would give Thea the answers she wanted. Thea had always been careful with how much of herself she shared with others. In reality, she could force the truth out of anyone at court and easily know who was to be trusted. Years of practice has taken her from simply being about to detect truth from people, to being able to demand it, but very few people knew this, and she wanted to keep it that way.

"And why are you in charge of my tour?"

"The High King trusts me with this task." Truth. The woman looked at Thea knowingly. "I am one of his most loyal servants." Lie. Thea looked to Dorothy, who nodded, encouraging her to question the woman before them.

"Are you to be my ally?" Thea asked quietly.

"I will be whatever you need." True, but vague.

"Can I trust you?" She countered.

"Of course." Truth.

"Will you keep secrets for me?"

"If you ask me to." Truth.

Thea smiled, unsure what she had done to earn this woman's favor but pleased all the same. "If we are to be friends, may I know your name?"

"It is not customary to call staff by their given name." She smirked slightly – as if appreciating Thea's small act of defiance.

"Let it be the first secret I ask you to keep then. And I grant you the same. You may call me Thea."

"Ruth."

"Ruth, would you mind showing me to my apartments then?" Ruth nodded, still smiling, and led Thea, Dorothy, and the staff carrying their vast belongings into the Palace. She then began what was likely a rehearsed speech while walking them toward their accommodations.

They approached the golden doors. "As I'm sure you know, this Palace was constructed many centuries ago, by another Mori King. Since the Great War, the Mori line has been in power in this realm and will be until the end of time."

"Until the end of time." The servants around her repeated in reply, in unison no less. Dorothy gave Thea a confused look, but Thea knew from her years of court education what that phrase meant.

She leaned in close to Dorothy and whispered, "It's like their version of 'Long live the King,' it shows loyalty to the throne."

Dorothy nodded in acknowledgment of this and then turned her attention back to Ruth's speech. "These statues were given as a gift to High King Kairo after his most recent battle conquest. Hw is *quite* proud of them." The girls giggled at the inflection in Ruth's voice as she gestured to the statues flanking the doors. They were a loose rendering of His Majesty's likeness, but like his portraits, not a true resemblance could be seen other than the deep cleft of his chin.

Thea looked around in awe again, feeling she would never get over the beauty of this place. She stepped into the first room, out from under the arched structure that served as the doorway, and was speechless. This room, much like the outside of the Palace, was lined in gold at every turn. Large crystal chandeliers hung down from the three-story cathedral ceilings. In every direction, arched doorways led down as many as eight hallways away from the entry room they stood in now. Deeper into the entry room, twin staircases bent around the sides of the east and west walls and led up to a second floor held aloft by large marble pillars. Ruth's high-heeled boots clicked on the white and gold marble flooring beneath them as she led them toward the stairs.

"All hallways to the east lead to rooms you will rarely have to be in. Meeting rooms, the war room, the ballroom, and the High King's study. All hallways to the west lead to daily use rooms, the library, ladies' waiting room, the dining hall, entrances to the gardens and stables, and so on. To the south and subfloors are for the kitchens, service staff housing, and the dungeon – which you will never need to see. The only exception is in the event of danger, you will be taken to a sub-room that is a safe room, but we haven't had to use them in a great while." She paused for a moment, remembering that last time they had gathered in the safe rooms, the night the High Queen had died. Dorothy and Thea exchanged a look, Thea shrugged in reply, not knowing what horrors were haunting Ruth's memory at that moment.

"Continuing on," Ruth started up the stairs. "The second floor is where your apartments will be, on the west side. These are not the only stairs up – in fact, there are stairs on the other side of your apartments that lead you down to all the aforementioned dayrooms."

"And on the east side of the second floor?" Thea asked as they walked westward.

"The Prince's wing is that way." A chill ran through her, she had yet to see her future husband, and the anticipation was starting to get unbearable. "And the High King is on the third floor with various other rooms you will not need to use." Thea wondered what would happen if she found herself in one of the rooms she was not encouraged to be in her new home. *Probably nothing good,* she thought glumly. "The south of the second floor is combat rooms and education centers. You will likely never find yourself there either." They continued down a hallway. Hard marble had given way to a plush carpet as they left the landing and began to pass door after door. At the end of the hallway, Ruth produced a key and unlocked a set of double doors, she pushed them open, and Thea found herself amazed once again.

The room was bright and airy, decorated not unlike her old bedroom at her parent's home, but this room was larger and much finer. The wall across from the entrance was covered in several floor-to-ceiling windows, set deep with cushioned benches inside them. Large glass doors in the middle of the wall led to a balcony that overlooked a sprawling garden. Thea covered her mouth and turned around. The walls beside the doors were set with many shelves – some containing books but others containing art and beautiful pottery. The room was well furnished with plush couches, a piano, and enough seating to host at least a dozen people. Each end table was decorated with a bouquet of lilies, and one table even held a crystal bowl of jeweled citrus fruit. Thea knew someone had gone to great lengths to make this room remind her of home.

Thea looked to the right to see yet another set of doors. Ruth followed her gaze and led her toward this door. She opened them, and Thea stepped into a bedroom that did not remind her at all of the rest of the Palace. More rustic and homey than glamorous and regal. Unlike all the arched windows all over the rest of the Palace, this room had one rectangular floor-to-ceiling window, draped in thick dark purple curtains. The curtains had been pulled open for her arrival, allowing natural light to pour in through the window. A large four-poster bed sat in the middle of the back wall, canopied with smokey, silky fabric. The duvet atop the bed was light purple, much like hers had been at home. A small black leather settee was in front of the bed, draped in a gray fur blanket. The floors were large planks of darkly colored wood, and several plush rugs lay around the room. On the south wall, a sizable was a dark brick fireplace, contrasting the stone-colored walls. Two oversized chairs sat in front of the fireplace, atop what once was the skin of a small black bear. On the black mantle was a portrait of her and her parents beside a vase of flowers that contained both lilies and lavender sprigs. Tears welled in her eyes as she noticed the great care someone had taken into designing this space for her. Hope filled her chest, *surely a place this beautiful could not be so bad.*

Ruth cleared her throat behind her, "Lady Thea, I just have two more things to show you, and then I will let you settle into your accommodations." She motioned to two doors opposite the windowed wall. "The left is your dressing room and the right your bathing room. I'm sure you can find your way around those just fine." Thea nodded and gave Ruth a small smile.

"Thank you for the hospitality, and for the future friendship, we are to have," Thea said genuinely.

"It is my pleasure." She nodded in return. "I would love for you to get settled into your new home. Tonight, we thought to have dinner brought up to your apartments, for you and Lady Dorothy to enjoy alone. I'm sure your travels were exhausting." She paused, allowing Thea to process that information. Thea was slowly growing tired from overstimulation, and Ruth could tell. "Perhaps a nap before that would be wise. I can have a lavender and honey tea sent up for you." Thea smiled in gratitude and walked to sit on the settee. "Tomorrow, as I'm sure you remember, is a ball that Lady Dove planned to welcome you to your new home." Home. Ruth kept calling this home. Thea wondered when it would feel like it. "The dress your mother had designed was sent along and will be unpacked with your things. Lady Dove gifted you a mask to wear with your gown, it is in a box in your dressing room."

"A mask?" Thea questioned, tiredly, a yawn escaping her full lips.

"She planned a masquerade. Slightly ill-advised, in my opinion, as you have yet to meet anyone and now will be meeting them with their faces covered and therefore will likely have to be reintroduced to them again later...." She blew out a breath and laughed, "But she is Lady of this Palace for now and I am but a humble servant." Thea laughed, happy to have Ruth here, easing her into her new life. "If you don't need anything else, I will show Dorothy her room and be on my way. It is just outside your doors – the first room on the right."

"Ruth, I have one question," Thea asked suddenly.

"Yes?"

"When..." She paused, taking a deep breath, as she wrung her hands together. "When am I to meet the Prince?"

Ruth gave a sympathetic smile, "He has been away on travels lately and will meet you at the ball tomorrow, as agreed upon by your families."

Thea unclenched her jaw, something she hadn't realized she was doing until that moment. She pulled the gemstone from beneath her shirt and looked at it longingly, willing herself to be excited to meet the one who had gifted it to her.

Hours later, after a nap and luxurious bath in a rather large tub, Thea relaxed and read on the couch in her drawing-room, waiting for dinner to be brought up. Dorothy had gone to her room shortly before, wanting to clean herself up.

A knock came from the door. "Lady Althea?" A deep voice inquired from the other side of the door. She put a page holder into her book and closed it, placing it on the couch cushion beside her. Her feet found their way into her fuzzy slippers, and she slowly padded her way to the door. She paused before it and tied her silk night robe around her, securing it with the belt. The door opened, and the servant before her bowed, his mop of dark, slightly curled hair falling askew as he did so.

"That's nice, but unnecessary. You may call me Thea. Please come in." She gestured into the room and looked at the cart he began to push in. It carried several covered dishes. Her stomach growled rebelliously.

"As you wish, little princess." She turned, confused by that title, then her stomach clenched upon seeing him.

"What are you doing here?" Her mouth was agape with shock, while his bent up with an arrogant smile, just as it did the last time she saw him – the handsome stranger from her birthday party.

"I work here." Truth. He pushed further into her room.

"I would like to request a different servant bring my meals up, given your lewd behavior last time I saw you." She retorted scornfully, her body betraying her as a blush rose to her cheeks when she remembered their dance.

He feigned hurt and placed a hand to his chest, "You scorn me, Thea – we both know you rather enjoyed yourself that night. And you don't have to worry. I do not typically deliver food anyway. I just couldn't resist seeing for myself once I heard who exactly was being brought to the Palace today." He looked around the room. "You know if you're lonely, I could stay for dinner." He paused a devilish grin pulling his lips up at the corners. "Or other things." He raised a suggestive eyebrow. Her mind betrayed her as well, imagining his large, muscled body lying in her new bed, fire crackling in the background.

He looked at her, "I like this outfit. It gives me insight into your nocturnal habits." He reached toward her, but she slapped his hand away. "Feisty." He smirked again. "Though I don't like it as much as your traveling outfit from today. Please tell me you have more tight pants in that closet of yours."

72

She ignored him, as much as part of her didn't want to. "At first, I wondered, but now I know you must be stupid…or reckless or both. Flirting with the future High Queen is treason."

"That's what makes it fun, Thea." He winked as he plucked a strawberry off her plate, biting and sucking on it seductively. As arrogant and annoying as he was, Thea considered those annoying qualities were equally matched by his beauty and boldness, which she appreciated.

"Do not call me that." She demanded slowly.

"You told me to." He said obviously.

"That was before I knew it was you."

"And now that you do, would you like me to call you something more special instead? Would you prefer darling? Or love?" He teased her, enjoying every minute of making her uncomfortable. "And I am hurt that you have never asked me my name."

"Because I don't care." Lie. "Please leave." She placed a hand on his shoulder and shoved hard, catching him off guard. He swayed, thrown off balance, and used this as an opportunity to pull her against him. His smell, as strong as she remembered, wafted into her nose. Strong arms wrapped around her as the world tilted, threatening to pull them both to the ground. He quickly righted them, his muscles more than just for show.

"Thea, if you wanted to get horizontal with me, all you had to do was ask." She looked at him, incredulous.

She lingered in his arms, again relishing the feeling of being touched, but then quickly pushed away from him. "You may call me Lady Althea. And next time we see each other – you may remember your place – beneath me." She spoke with conviction, aiming to sound intimidating.

73

He smiled again, perfectly straight teeth showing. "I will lay in bed tonight dreaming of being beneath you, *Lady Althea*." He grabbed her hand and placed a kiss on it. She observed it happening in slow motion, his full lips spreading over her delicate hand, and she swallowed gently as she watched. "Until next time." He looked back at Thea, who was still standing there stunned, and laughed wickedly as he walked away.

Thea stood there in stunned silence until a question pulled her from her thoughts. "Are you okay?" Dorothy asked as she approached, picking up a strawberry from the charcuterie plate. Thea suddenly remembered what he had done with his strawberry. Dorothy looked up at Thea, who had yet to answer. "Hello? Thea? What is wrong?" Thea dove into the story without hesitation, all of it spilling out of her mouth quickly. She started from the beginning, telling Dorothy every single detail of her encounters with this gorgeous, infuriating man. No touch was left undetailed, but she did spare some of the details of her conflicting inner dialogue.

"So the very man from your birthday is here? At the Palace?" Dorothy was smiling devilishly and fanning herself.

Thea nodded. "Well?" She asked after several moments of Dorothy's processing. "What do you think of it?"

"I think that things will be quite interesting around here. Sounds like he would make a fun plaything," Dorothy giggled.

Thea shoved her friend, repressing a laugh. "Stop!" She lowered her voice. "Be careful what you say. You know that infidelity, even joking about it, in my position is not a laughing matter. The Prince could have me killed if he even suspected it." Thea looked around nervously, hoping no nosey staff had heard their conversation.

Dorothy ignored her. "That face and attitude to match – honestly isn't fair." She looked around. "Tell me again." Thea exhaled a breath, and the girls giggled together, and she told the story again – indulging herself as she merely glazed over his annoyances and lavished them in the salacious details. *His hands and the scorching trail they left in their wake.* Despite elements of the encounter being annoying, Thea found herself less anxious to be in the Palace now. He had allowed her and her friend a moment of normalcy – gossiping and enjoying laughs together. And if nothing else, she was grateful to him for that.

Chapter 5

Thea awoke the next morning, stomach fluttering with nervous excitement about the day to come. The day she was to meet the Prince. She wished she could meet him alone – to have a private moment with him instead of being watched by dozens of people as they meet. But this, like much of her life, was not up for debate. Thea had learned that morning that the High King, or maybe his late wife, had planned the meeting years ago. They would meet in front of the Lords of the realm, not in private, and would be expected to immediately share a dance. The reasons why were unknown to Thea, but she was sure someone had figured out an arcane symbolic reason to make those specific choices.

Thea felt as if the day was going by in a blur, she willed it to slow down so that she could savor moments before her life changed again. But she has always found time to be a fickle master during the biggest days of her life. Instead of being present, she perseverated over the knowledge that he could send her away for any reason, end their engagement, and dishonor her in the eyes of both the realm and her parents. As much as she longed for a say in what happened in her life, being dismissed by the Prince was not how she wanted to receive it. Plus, him dismissing her wouldn't grant her freedom anyway, it would just cause her father to make a far less opulent match for her.

Thea spent much of the morning in bed, eyes closed, as she tried to will herself back to sleep. Half-woke dreams of a romantic prince and a grand love story danced in her head, only interrupted by fleeting fears and nightmares. Breakfast was a blur, as was lunch, and Thea found that when her hands weren't busy – she took to pacing. When the ladies arrived to help Thea get ready for the ball, they had to all but force her to stop moving about and sit in a chair long enough for them to paint her face and style her hair. She felt nauseated as she sat in silence, chewing nervously on peppermints, as several well-meaning made her presentable.

The only event that broke the day up was when a delivery came to her door mid-day. A lady's maid with bouncing blonde curls and a large smile brought a velvet box to her. "From the Prince." She said with a bow and ridiculous giggle. Everyone made a show of gathering around to watch her open the box, and some of the ladies even had jealous glints in their eyes. Thea couldn't bring herself to swoon, as she was still actively grappling with the anxiety growing in her stomach. The box snapped open, audibly cracking, and all the ladies in the room gasped at the sight of the sparkling earrings shining up at them. Thea forced herself to smile, and demurely plucked them up and handed them to one of the ladies to place on her earlobes. She tried to ignore her feelings and play into the role she had been groomed her whole life for.

Beneath the facade, no one knew the fears that swirled in her head, the battle that was waging behind her face. She spoke in small pieces about these fears to Dorothy, but never all the details. She had never told anyone of her secret desire to run away and leave this all behind. To make one choice for herself. But she knew she couldn't, she had been raised for this reason and this reason only – to be the wife of a powerful man. She couldn't even begin to think how she would survive alone. Her thoughts drifted back to that poor pregnant girl in the town she met on her journey to Cativo. She shivered at the thought of her life being like that. All things being considered, she knew that being pampered as Princess and Queen was better than being destitute or alone. All these thoughts were manifested out of fear of a miserable life. So instead of dwelling on them, she turned her worries to prayers – prayers that the Prince could be a man in which she could find even one thing to love.

She paced outside the doors to the ballroom, heels clicking on the marble flooring as she did so. Opposing thoughts warred in her mind, one side wished to get this over with and the other wished for the ability to freeze time and stop this moment from coming at all. Her gown ruffled around her as she turned to continue her pacing loop around the hallway. She adjusted her mask again, feeling frustrated with the ball's theme. With everyone in disguise, it felt like she was being introduced to many cast members in a play rather than important people she needed to remember.

"Stop messing with your mask, you look great," Dorothy chastised her. Thea looked at her friend, appreciation for her filling her chest.

"I'm so glad you're here with me, I would be going absolutely mad if I was alone," Thea confessed.

"Would be? So, this isn't you going mad?" She teased. Thea laughed lightly, her smile not reaching her eyes. Again, she tried to focus her attention on tangible reality rather than her fears. She watched Dorothy sitting gracefully in the chair, red gown flowing around her. Thea noted that red always looked good on Dorothy, a compliment to her dark skin and hair. She looked down at her own dress, which had been carefully planned and constructed over the course of the last year with her mother's help. The gown complimented her figure, with an accentuated waistline and a high slit that put her legs on display. She had always favored muted tones, given her olive complexion, and had picked a deep green for the fabric of her gown. This color also happened to be the Prince's favorite. Unlike the flowing and chiffon elements of Dorothy's gown, Thea's was silken and banded at the waist to flow around her. The bodice was tight and corseted, as many of her gowns were, and dipped low enough that the gemstone gifted to her by the Prince was visible. Even though she was in turmoil on the inside, she felt beautiful on the outside – and she was determined to derive her confidence from that alone, if necessary. She breathed in deeply, gathering all her confidence and positive thoughts. She would deal with bad things if they came, and not a moment sooner.

"Ladies, you look lovely!" Thea turned to see Ruth scurrying down the hall toward them. "Now the High King will be escorting you into the event and the Prince will arrive shortly after." She looked at Thea's now calm demeanor and smiled. "Everything will be okay, you will see." She said as she patted her hand.

The doors at the end of the hallway opened with authority, drawing all their attention toward the High King as he strode down the hall. He was dressed very similarly as the day before, but this time he wore his obsidian crown upon his head. His mouth was set in a hard line, and Thea noted that not one smile line could not be found upon his face. She hoped desperately he wasn't a glimpse into her future. And at that exact moment, she considered another bad side to finally meeting the

Prince. All her life she could pretend he was perfect for her, but once she meets him that will be impossible – as reality will replace fantasy and she will have to face the truth.

"Are you ready? I have been informed that they are all ready for your entrance and I'd like to get on with my night." He spoke tersely.

"Yes, Your Majesty." She dipped her head as she spoke.

"Let's get on with it then. You, show her little friend to the guest entrance." He waved them away.

Thea repressed the urge to roll her eyes. She looked to Dorothy, who did it for her, and then smiled and gave Thea a thumbs up. "See you in there." Dorothy mouthed silently before being ushered away.

"Thank you," Thea said to Ruth as she walked away with Dorothy.

"Thank you?" Kairo scoffed. "Who are you thanking?"

"Ruth?" Thea answered slowly.

Kairo laughed, mirthlessly. "We don't thank the staff. You naive, insolent idiot." Thea flinched, his words hitting her like slaps to the face. Her mouth hung open, in shock. "Close your mouth, you look like a fish." She snapped her teeth together so fast it hurt.

He wordlessly held his arm out for Thea to grab. She followed the silent order and they both stepped toward the doors. "Open and announce us!" He barked at the guards by the door. He turned to Thea, "I do hope you know how to behave yourself tonight. I need no more scandal in my Kingdom." Thea nodded – but wondered to what 'scandal' he was referring to. "And you'll do well to remember that you represent the Mori empire now. If you appear weak, I appear weak, and I will not stand for that. We do not show weakness, ever. And we do not show kindness, because it is a form of weakness." He placed a vice grip on her arm. "Do you understand?" She silently nodded, fighting back tears. "And you will not cry, else you'll regret it." The tears that had been threatening to betray her immediately dried up under Kairo's command.

The doors opened, "High King Kairo of Cativo escorting Lady Althea Torianna of Pache, promised in marriage to Prince Kol Arius of Cativo." Her mouth dried. She reminded herself to take steady breaths and solid steps, as well as to smile at the people around her as she glided through the room. They clapped and awed at her, ladies whispering and men leering. She felt as if she were floating, the grand room around her a dreamscape. She looked around the grand but dimly lit room, wondering again why anyone thought a dark room of masked people was the best way for her to meet anyone. As impractical as it was, she faintly considered it a blessing. The mask and lack of light were, in a way, shielding her from all the unknowns around her.

They reached the middle of the room and Lady Dove walked forward to meet her husband, and without any other words, the High King released Thea's arm and left her standing on the edge of the dance floor alone. *Rude,* she thought to herself. Thea looked around the room, desperate for a familiar face – or even just a friendly face. Everyone around her stared at her with grave interest but refused to approach her. Yet again she felt alone in a crowd of people. She restrained her hands to her sides, forcing herself not to nervously ring them in an unladylike fashion.

Dorothy quickly found Thea, praised her entrance, and commented on the state of the room. They mingled around, eating and drinking what they could snatch from passing serving trays. As Thea was accustomed to, no one came up to introduce themselves to her, likely out of trepidation. She had spent her whole life being both the center of attention and an outsider at the same time – and it seemed that wasn't ending any time soon. *It may even get worse.*

One man, however, did introduce himself to Dorothy, and asked her to dance. She accepted immediately, turning to Thea as they walked away to jokingly fan herself behind his back. Thea smiled, though she struggled to maintain it. She was as happy for her friend to be meeting new people at court as she was nervous for herself. The High King stopped by periodically, introducing her to members of his council and other prominent Lords and Ladies, but mostly she stood on the edge of the party, alone. Every time the doors opened, Thea would whip her head toward them, wondering if it was the Prince. She grew more anxious and frustrated with every new arrival that wasn't him.

Eventually, her attention was drawn toward the main doors as a man declared, "Prince Kol Arius of Cativo." She felt the world around her shift into slow motion. Her stomach dropped and the applause around her seemed to fade away as her vision zeroed in on the tall, masked man approaching her. His body was wrapped in a black suit and his obsidian hair was perfectly coiffed, yet somehow also looked as if it had just been carelessly pushed to the side. A few errant curls dangled over his black mask. His hair made her believe he had either spent much time or zero time on his appearance that night. She really couldn't tell which. He, like his father, walked into the room with unquestioning authority. All eyes were on him as he strode toward her, but his eyes were locked onto her alone. *This is it,* she thought to herself. As much trepidation as she had, she still wanted to remember every piece of this moment. She drank in his strut, the way the candlelight danced off his dark hair, the pull of his jacket over his arms as he moved, his pleased closed-lip smile, and the not-so-subtle way his eyes traced up and down her body. She felt her whole body blush under his imposing stare. And before she knew it, he was in front of her, and he was speaking.

"Althea." He bowed and held out a hand. "May I have the honor?" She, thrown off by the break-in protocol, hesitated to answer. He wasn't supposed to bow to her; she was supposed to bow to him. She looked at his father, noting the anger on his face.

"Of course, Your Highness." She curtsied and hurriedly placed her hand in his. He led her, without show, to the dance floor, and pulled her in as the music around them turned to a classical slow song. Thankfully, other couples began to swirl around them as well, giving her the reprieve of continuing to be the only entertainment and center of attention.

Thea felt senseless, all but her eyes failing her at that moment. She stared into his eyes, and he stared back, his gaze was warm and kind – much unlike his fathers. Tension released from her shoulders at that detail alone and a genuine smile found its way onto her face. Slowly, her senses began to return to her. She could feel the warm skin of his hands on her lower back, hear the beat of her own heart pounding in her ears, and smell masculine wafts of citrus rolling from the Prince. The moment felt utterly surreal to her.

All too quickly, without much interaction aside from piercing eye contact, the song ended, and he gently pulled her to a private alcove in the corner of the room. People around them tried to watch – but quickly lost interest when the couple stepped out of view. Her head was spinning as they walked. *What is about to happen?* Fear gripped her again, crashing down around the pleasantness she felt from the dance they had shared. He cleared his throat and somberness settled on his face.

"Where are we going?" She asked as they skidded to a halt.

"I didn't want to share our first official conversation with others, even we deserve something that is just our own."

She smiled, stunned at the thoughtfulness. "Thank you, I agree." She felt utterly exposed under his gaze, as he caressed her body with his eyes again. She cleared her throat and continued. "I'm so happy this moment is here, I've been waiting for this moment..." She paused, searching for the right words, "Well, my whole life actually."

"As have I." He looked to his side, looking for any eavesdroppers that may be lingering close by. "But we can talk more about that later." He gestured, letting her know they were being listened to, and then changed the subject, "Were your travels safe?" She nodded, remembering she wanted to mention the poor towns they had passed on their way, but assumed later would be a better time to do so. "And have you found your accommodations acceptable?"

"Yes, and your city... it is unlike anything I've ever seen before. And have you been to my apartments? They're beautiful."

"Only once since they were renovated for your arrival. But I know they boast a rather nice view of the estate."

As they spoke, she found herself at ease around him, and oddly enough that caused her heart to race – her mind daring to imagine a life in which they could actually liked one another. She smiled up at him as he spoke about the long journey he was on last month, her eyes glowing from the nearby candelabra. He noticed the look of admiration on her face, and his chest too squeezed with hope, and he took the momentary break in conversation as an opportunity to turn the conversation.

"You are quite pleasant my darling, I had heard talk throughout the court of your ill-temper, I'm pleased to see that's not the case." Thea was speechless and confused. In her court, she had always been known for her pleasant nature and never getting into trouble. She felt disappointment coursing through her veins, afraid something had already ruined their shot at happiness. She looked desperately into his eyes, fearful of meeting disapproval in them, but instead, he wore a mischievous smile. She began to ask what he meant and then he moved his hands toward his face.

He removed his mask and Thea gasped. In her nervousness, she had failed to notice the familiarity of the man in front of her, his eyes, his hair, the gruff sensual tone of his voice. "Your Highness, I am so sorry." Two emotions warred for supremacy inside her again, anger and fear. Anger for being tricked and fear because she had not once, but twice been brash with the future High King, she had even once laid hands on him in anger.

Before her stood the man who had crashed her birthday party and with whom she had yelled at just the night before for being too forward with her. Embarrassment added itself into the mix, for she had let herself be attracted to him in those fleeting moments. Despite her anger, she defaulted to meekness to save herself. "Forgive me and my previous attitude, I didn't know it was you, I was just-" She continued muttering, eloquence leaving her and she tried to find the right words.

He interrupted her. "You were just defending your honor and the vow of your future marriage. I respect you for it." He grabbed both her hands, voice becoming gentle as he rubbed a small circle on the top of her hand with his thumb. "Besides, I enjoy a lady with a little bite." Truth. He carefully pulled her hands to his mouth as he had the night before, but this time instead of kissing them, he nipped playfully at the knuckle of her ring finger. "Perhaps you'll do me that honor one day." She stood stunned, but before she could ask him any questions his father approached, pulling the Prince away to speak with the Lords. He bowed to her again and his father groaned in disapproval, igniting his mischievous smile again. "I will find you later." He promised, releasing her hand and walking away without another word.

Thea stood there stunned, and Dorothy appeared quickly, as if an apparition, beside her.

"Is that-?" She began.

"Yes."

"The same one who was in your room last-"

"Yes." Thea answered, interrupting Dorothy again.

"He was at your party!"

"Mhmm," Thea swallowed.

"Is he angry?" Dorothy asked.

"No," Thea said surprised. She did not know any man, other than a servant, that would take to being spoken to as she had spoken to him not once, but twice.

"As I said before, quite interesting," Dorothy said with resignation.

The rest of the night passed in the same fashion as her day had, a blur. Though this one she was grateful for, she waited all night on the edge of her metaphorical seat for the Prince to return – but the ball ended and he had not been seen again. She worried it was because he was displeased, that he was speaking

86

to his father about ending their engagement. Once again, Thea found herself pacing – this time in her apartments after the ball. Her gown had been traded for leggings and a sweater, allowing full range of motion for her panicked pacing. When a knock on her door came, she ran toward it – expecting Dorothy.

"Thank God, I cannot stand to be alone with my thoughts right now." She admitted desperately.

"Well hello to you too." He grinned wickedly. "Happy to see me?"

Heat crept into her face, she ducked her head to hide it. "Your Highness, I wasn't expecting you."

"I told you I would find you later, who else would you be so eager to greet?"

"I was expecting Dorothy, my friend who traveled here with me." She swallowed nervously, hoping not to insight the irritation of the Prince.

He nodded and looked around her room. "May I come in?" He asked. Shocked, she looked at his face, sincerity covered it as he waited patiently for her to answer. She wouldn't think a Prince would ever ask permission when he could do anything he wished. *To anyone he wished,* she cringed at that thought. He had to know she was in no position to deny him, her fate was entirely in his hands.

"Of course, Your Highness." She hated the formality she was showing the man who was to be her husband – and she did hope that he was still to be her husband. As much as she wished for free will and as angry as she was for having been tricked, she knew that being the disgraced former bride of the Prince was not the life she wanted.

He visibly flinched at her use of his royal title, and without thinking grabbed both her hands in his. "You may call me whatever you wish." He paused. "And I do mean whatever you wish." He grinned wickedly again. "But if I may ask a favor of you?"

She grew goose flesh on her arms at his insinuation, and replied in a breathy tone, "Of course."

"Call me Kol, and I hope to still be granted permission to call you Thea." She continued to be shocked by his submissiveness. The future High King was bowing to her and asking her permission to call her by her familiar name. She hoped again this was a sign of things to come. Of forgiveness, of kindness, and of love. Or perhaps that was her naiveté showing.

She smiled shyly, heat again warming her cheeks. "I'd like that, *Kol.*" He shuddered after she spoke his name.

"Thank you." He exhaled sharply and gone was the man with the ego she had interacted with thrice before. "No one ever has given me the kindness of just treating me like… everyone else." Truth. Her mouth fell open, feeling as if he read a verse from her own mind. She saw in him at that moment, someone like her, desperate for connection.

She reacted without thought and stepped toward him. Her face rested gently against his chest as her arms wrapped securely around him. She later would feel embarrassed about this, even fearful of what his potential reaction could have been, but at that moment she didn't care. His body, one to scarcely know human touch, just like hers, softened under her embrace, his arms effortlessly engulfed her, and their bodies melded together. He placed his chin atop her head, and she felt more secure than she ever had before. She listened as his heartbeat increased to a rapid pace and didn't release him until it had steadied again. When she pulled away, he raised a hand to her cheek and wiped away the tear that had fallen from her left eye. Concern flashes in his eyes, "Are you okay?"

She laughed easily, "Yes, I'm just feeling a lot of feelings."

"Such as?" He asked as he placed his hands on the back of her arms, holding her to him.

"I feel sorrow for you – because I have felt the same my whole life. A little alone. Not always but... often enough." She steadied her breath, afraid to admit the next part aloud, but boldness filled her, and she continued. "And I'm relieved to find that you aren't a monster. At least it doesn't seem like you are."

He let out a sad, breathy laugh. One of irony. "Well, the latter I can't agree with. Many have called me that in my lifetime." Truth. Thea flinched, unsure of the direction this conversation may take. He responded to her movement, concern again flooding in his eyes. "You never have a reason to fear me. I will not act like a monster toward you. This I vow." Truth. He looked into her eyes, hoping to convey his sincerity. At that moment, he hated his reputation – as fair as it may be. And he knew that any trust, or love, she would feel for him would have to be earned and may take time. "I came to speak with you, to clear the air from our previous interactions."

Dread filled Thea's chest, feeling as if discipline was to come. Men of power did not let women speak to them the way she had spoken to him. She nodded her head and followed him to the couch, sitting several feet away from him. He noted the distance and palpated it with his eyes. The expressiveness of his eyes continued to amaze Thea, even as fear seized her. He scooted closer to her, allowing his knee to brush hers. A desire to reach out his hand toward her leg filled him, but he decided against it. *Earn her trust,* he thought, *she is your only chance at happiness.*

"I came here to apologize." He spoke, but despite his confidence, he seemed unsure of how exactly to move the conversation forward. Apologizing was not something he did often. He placed his hand on the back of his neck and rubbed slowly. Thea's eyes darted down at this movement, and she couldn't help but notice how the edge of his shirt pulled up as he moved, revealing taut skin beneath. She gazed so hard at the patch of skin above his pant hem that it took her several moments before the shock of his apology hit her. She agreed that she deserved an apology for being tricked, but she never thought she would receive one.

Boldness again taking the forefront she decided to encourage him. "Go on."

His lips lifted on the left side, dimple pooling in his cheek. "I should not have deceived you, I just wanted…" She raised her eyebrows, awaiting his response. He exhaled, "I don't know what I wanted." He shrugged before continuing. "To meet you without pretense, I guess."

"To test me to see if I was worthy?" She added, filling in the blanks with her fears.

"No!" He spoke forcefully. "Please don't think that! I just-" He grunted in frustration. "I don't want you to think of me that way, I wasn't setting you up or playing a game." Lie, but not an intentional one,

"That isn't entirely true though." She offered,

He grimaced, "Maybe I was playing a game, but it wasn't against you. When I heard you were having a party that night and I was going to be near your town, it felt like fate. I had wanted to meet you my whole life." He sighed. "And I'm not daft, I know

90

my reputation precedes me, and it's earned, but I wanted a chance to meet you without that in the way." Truth. She warred against herself, charmed by his words but sobered by the truth that he felt his Prince of Death reputation was earned. He made eye contact with her after what felt like an eternity. She calmed under his cerulean gaze. "I was pretending I was someone else that night, anyone else, and it got the better of me." Truth. "I found your presence so…thrilling. I was drunk on it, and I let my confidence and attraction to you get out of hand. Putting you in a precarious position and I am sorry for that too." Her face heated again, and she wondered if she would ever manage to stay cool for even one minute in his presence. "I wanted to know you before you put on a mask to meet me, just like everyone else does." Vulnerability rolled off him in waves, and she felt humbled to be in the presence of what she knew must be a rarity. Though she wondered what she could have done to earn his openness. *Why am I so trusted by him?* She wondered. *Why does he care enough to explain himself to me?*

"And last night?" She added.

"You're not letting me off easy, are you?" He jested, dimple showing again.

She shrugged in response. "If you're willing to open up I'm not going to pretend I don't have questions."

"Fair enough. Last night…" He sighed. "I, again, just couldn't help myself. I wasn't home in time to greet you upon arrival, I'm sorry about that too because I'm sure my father was less than welcoming." Despite herself and the seriousness of the moment, she giggled at that. His gaze softened. "I like your laugh." She shifted, again feeling utterly exposed under his gaze. "But anyway, I wasn't permitted to see you, so I found a way to do it, unauthorized. I wanted to tell you about who I was and apologize then and get to know you one-on-one before that stupid charade we had to put on for the nobility tonight. But you were so feisty and authentic, so I gifted myself one more night of pretending. And I know that it was at your expense. and for that I am sorry. I won't lie and say I am not an impulsive man." Truth. "Can you forgive me and allow yourself to trust me despite it?" His eyes quivered, shifting back and forth between hers, waiting for an answer, but in her pause, his eyes landed on her earlobes. "I see you got my gift." A sad smile played on his lips.

"I did."

"Do you like them?"

"They are very beautiful." She responded graciously.

"But that's not what I asked."

"Why did you send them?" Thea asked, but given his apology speech, she felt she already knew the answer.

"As an apology, of sorts, I suppose." He replied quietly.

She didn't have to look that deeply within herself to find the ability to forgive him. Not only because of the hope she had for their future, but also because of the truthful and authentic apology he had prostrated himself through. She knew he didn't have to do that.

"I will forgive you." He shifted forward – as if hundreds of pounds had just been released from his shoulders. "And I hope we can be this open with one another throughout our whole relationship." She shifted in her seat, subtly moving closer to him, her shoulder finding its way in front of the arm he was resting on the back of the couch. She tucked her legs underneath her as he pulled her into him. "Since you were so honest with me, I would like to do the same with you." She couldn't bring herself to look him in the eyes, nor could she allow herself to focus on his arm, which was now grazing her shoulders. She braced herself for the vulnerability she was about to offer him. "I want nothing more than closeness with you, and I hope to have a relationship filled with genuine love one day. I too have spent many of my days feeling lonely and dreading the potential of a loveless life, or worse. But your honesty today makes me hope for better things." She spoke softly, shocking even herself that she was being this open with him.

"I hope for those things as well." Several moments passed in comfortable silence before he spoke again. "Would you like to know what first impression you made?"

"Would you?" She retorted, looking at him with a smile in her eyes – almost like a challenge.

He laughed, the lines around his eyes crinkling as he did. "You made your impression of me very clear that night. I believe the words 'daft, stupid, and not very charming' were batted around." She covered her face, laughing into her hands. "But you did find me quite attractive." He added – the cockiness she had seen in him before reappearing. She snapped her head up.

"I never said that!" She swatted at him playfully.

"Princess, you hurt me. Are you saying it isn't true?" *Princess*, she shivered at the implication. To be a princess, she first had to be his wife – which meant he planned on keeping her around.

She looked deep into his eyes, faces now only inches apart. "No, I'm not saying that either." She continued to shock herself with boldness. She dared a glance down at his full lips before glancing back up at his eyes from under her thick lashes. She spoke gently. "You're also making up for your first impression now."

He matched her tone. "I truly hope so."

93

"I hope I am too." She nervously twisted her hair, causing wayward strands to fall into her face.

"You didn't need to. I was met the night of your birthday with a force of a woman. She was passionate, fun, easy to talk to, and beautiful." He paused, letting those compliments sink in. Thea could feel her heart in her chest, but she wouldn't allow herself to focus on anything but his mouth and the words coming out of it. "And then someone crossed her, and she turned fierce – and I liked that side of her even more." He drew his hand up slowly, pushing the loose strands of her hair behind her ear. His skin felt molten against her face, she again was tracking every single place he touched her. "She was the woman I waited my whole life for. The same one I'm going to attempt to prove worthy of." He looked down – as if embarrassed by his openness.

Thea mustered all the boldness left in her to place two fingers under his chin and lift his eyes to hers. "You're off to a great start." She said delicately. The left side of his mouth tugged up in an exquisite, closed-lip smile. "Well, a good second start." They both chuckled at that statement.

"I know we are strangers, but I feel as if I've always known you, at least the idea of you." She nodded in silent agreement. "The beautiful girl from Pache who was to be my wife. She loves lavender and citrus tarts and dancing. I memorized every detail I could about you. I asked about you so often my mother got sick of me." He chuckled, remembering fond memories of his mother. "Around age eight, she started gifting me a portrait of you every year for my birthday, so I would stop asking what you looked like." He paused again, being sucked into his reverie. "Remember the dance we engaged in on your birthday?"

"You insult my memory, *Your Highness?*" She teased.

He batted her nose playfully. "Try again."

"You insult my memory of our meeting and first grand dance together, *Kol?*"

"Good girl." He smiled friskily. "I learned that dance because my mother told me you loved it." Her heart swelled at all the effort he had been putting into their relationship his whole life – before he even knew her. She again wondered why but thought perhaps being the Prince had made him even lonelier than she had thought. So lonely that he spent his entire childhood waiting for her.

"I-I don't know what to say." His eyebrows pulled up sarcastically. "I can practically hear your thoughts, and to answer – no I am not often speechless." She paused. "You aren't what I expected." His face twisted subtly, "In the best way possible." His face softened. "And I can't wait to get to know you more. Thank you for tonight, it means more than you can know."

They sat in silence for a moment, both considering one another and everything they had just shared. To Thea's surprise, he kept looking at her with adoring reverence. As she sat there, she remembered two of the times she used her Control on him, before she knew his identity.

"Can I ask you a question?" She asked.

"Always." He replied easily.

"At my party, you said that you were in Pache to visit family, and then when you came to my room the night I arrived here and you said you worked in the Palace."

"Those are statements, not questions." He teased.

She shot him a look of annoyance, eliciting a laugh from him, before continuing. "The question is why did I detect those to be truths with my Control – when they were lies?"

"They weren't lies." He stated obviously.

"You're a servant at the Palace then?"

"I never said I was a servant, I said I worked here –
which I do. A Prince, just like a King, must work often to keep
the realm they rule in order. I even have an office here." He
added the last bit with a snarky smile. She thought carefully
about his explanation, either he was very clever, or he was
already trying to manipulate her Control. Her Control that was so
often literal.

"And do you have family in Pache?" She continued her
interrogation.

"You." Truth. He uttered this as if it were the most
obvious thing in the world. All suspicion of him melted away as
he looked at her with care, having just admitted he already
considered her his family. *This will work out*, she thought.

Their eyes met again and for the first time, she thought
they may kiss, and no part of her wanted to stop it. His gaze
slipped to her mouth and up again, as he moved closer to her.
Her hands found their way to his legs, as he snaked his around
her neck. Seconds passed slowly, but neither of them cared –
they soaked in these moments in one another's company. Mask-
free, both literally and figuratively, and truly alone. She could
smell the peppermint on his breath, and she silently thanked God
she had brushed her teeth right before he had arrived. She rose
out of her seat, suddenly desperate to be closer to him, he shifted
beneath her allowing both her legs to settle on either side of him.

"May I ask you a question now?" He asked as he rubbed
a small circle with his thumb over her hip. She nodded, unsure of
her ability to speak. He leaned in closer and asked, barely above
a whisper, "Will you still freely give me the pleasure of placing
my hands on your body?" His eyes twinkled with mischief, and
she shivered in response. She found herself unable to be

embarrassed about the words she had spoken to him in anger the night of her birthday.

"Yes." She replied simply. Their eyes began to close, both in silent consent of what was about to happen. His breath tickled her lips and she inhaled deeply.

The door to her room burst open. "Thea, what are the chances the kitchen can make snacks at this hour? The small fancy food served at parties is never enough for me."

Thea attempted to push herself off his lap but his hands, which had inexplicably found their way to her hips, would not allow it.

Dorothy paused, mouth-agape, when she spotted Thea and Kol on the couch together, intimately close. "I am so sorry, I can deal with my hunger on my own, please continue." She backed toward the door. "As you were." The door clicked softly closed.

Thea hid her face in her hands, nervous laughter escaping her mouth as her face heated to a previously unreached temperature. "I can't believe that just happened."

"The interruption or before?" He teased, using both of his hands to push loose hairs out of her face.

She slowly pulled her hands down to reveal her eyes. "Both." She mumbled into her palms. "The before wasn't..." She searched for the right words.

"Wasn't what?" He asked.

"Proper. I've been told my whole life to do the exact opposite of that."

"Opposite of what?" He asked, confusion in his tone.

"This! Being alone with and touching a man." Her face grew hot in embarrassment.

"You have nothing to be upset about." He rubbed her arm affectionately. "Your body belongs to you, and there's no shame in anything you decide to do with it. I will always honor your decisions, but do know…" He placed his forehead gently on hers. "I can't wait for this to happen again."

"The interruption or before?" She mocked him, pulling her hands off her face before placing them carefully in her own lap, very cautious as to not touch anything else. She was acutely aware of how much of their bodies were already touching.

"The before, because God save anyone who tries to interrupt us again." Defiance filled his features as he spoke with unwavering authority. "I will let you tend to your hungry friend." He carefully pulled their bodies away from one another and placed her on the couch. "May I find you at some point tomorrow?" She nodded, meeting his intense gaze with one of her own. He bent down, placing his soft lips on her cheek, dangerously close to the corner of her mouth. Half of her desired to turn her head, catching his lips with her own, but the other half was too dumbfounded to move. "Have a pleasant evening, Thea."

He turned to leave, but she caught his hand. "Thank you for tonight, for everything." He paused, gaze lingering. "*Kol.*" At the utterance of his name, his fingers tightened around her own and he released a soft breath.

"The pleasure was mine, believe me." He squeezed her hand once more before wordlessly exiting the room. When he opened the door, a surprised squeak sounded. Thea turned her head in confusion, shocked that a noise like that could have come from Kol. But it didn't. "Goodnight, Dorothy," Kol spoke with mirth in his voice.

"Goodnight, Your Highness." She replied, and Thea could hear the shame in her friend's voice, having been caught spying. She entered the room, closing the door behind her.

"Hey, so do you think we can get snacks or not?

Thea looked incredulously at her friend – before throwing a pillow at her. "Were you listening at the door?"

"Are you joking? Of course, I was. And I couldn't hear anything, so I need all the details."

Thea laughed, shaking her head at her friend. "I think I would like to process it all myself before I talk to you about it." She said dismissively.

"Oh, I forgot, someone is shy." Dorothy teased as she poked Thea's sides. Thea swatted her hands away as she attempted to scramble to the other end of the couch. "Fine, be that way, think about it all night, dream about it, and tell me tomorrow morning over scones." She hopped up and walked back to the door. "If your thoughts begin to get too dirty remember, Ruth said that Kol's apartments are down that hall the way at the end and-" Thea threw another pillow at her friend, just missing her head as she slammed the door.

Thea leaned back and sighed, a wide smile spreading across her face as she remembered the events of the nights. Not just the physical proximity, but his words. Words that fanned the spark of hope she had in her chest for their future. The marriage still may not be her choice, but at least Kol could be the man she hoped he might be. She walked herself toward the bedroom, faltering as she went, almost dancing – high on the dopamine that the interactions with Kol had given her. And as she laid in bed, she imagined all the ways the night could have played out had they not been interrupted, but she mostly remembered Kol's promise that they would not be interrupted again – both a scary and thrilling promise.

Chapter 6

With only a month until the wedding, time continued to spin away from Thea frantically. Her mornings were spent with Dorothy and Ruth making wedding plans. The royal family had given her little choice in the planning, but what little she was allowed to decide she was taking very seriously. She found herself going days being all-consumed with what hors devourers should be passed around during the reception or what exact shade of green Kol's pocket square should be.

After her morning wedding planning, she was sent to meetings with members of the royal council to learn all about the Mori Empire. The High King expected her to know which territories were under Mori rule, who their enemies were, which realms were considered allies, the lineages of all the Lords and Ladies of Cativo, and more. But these lessons were given carefully. She was still not provided details on topics they considered too political. When she asked why she couldn't have been learning these things her whole life, a council member sneered at her and said, "This information is ever-changing and too vital to leave in the hands of a daft tutor." During these lessons, she quickly drafted notes as the men talked – and then took the notes with her in the afternoons to study independently. In addition to all of that, she also was given thorough lessons on lineage and items of symbolic importance to the Mori family. For example, she learned that the grandfather of High King Kairo added the title 'High' before his name after he had amassed ownership of almost half the land in the realm; and that they believed seeing a stag was considered a good omen.

She was given a map of all known lands, with the Mori ruled areas highlighted, and was expected to memorize it. It consisted of The Continent, several islands off the coast, as well as the Lesser Continent across the Sea. Three little flags were placed on the map, which she learned were the locations of Kol's sisters, one of which lived on the Lesser Continent. Almost all of The Continent was highlighted, minus the islands, a few coastal territories, and the Strong realm directly to the North of Cativo.

Self-proclaimed nobility ruled the Strong realm, a family of Blest with the gift of immense strength. Their Control made them nearly indestructible; Thea assumed that is why battles for their land had yet to result in a victory for the Mori Empire. When she asked about plans regarding the Strongs, a snippy nobleman just said, "Nothing your feeble mind needs to worry about. The men are working on it." When he turned his back to her, she had held up a vulgar gesture toward him and smiled at her small show of defiance. She wondered if he would talk to her like that when she became Queen, and then she wondered what Kol would do if he had heard him disrespect her.

Kol, she sighed happily as she thought about him. Though thinking of him also brought a wave of disappointment, as her time with him was fleeting and sporadic. During the day, he was hard to pin down. He occasionally ate lunch with her or would send flowers to her, but those gestures felt so formal; he was cold in front of his court and walked around them with menacing energy. But nights were different. He found her every night, and they would spend time in her chambers – alone. They would talk, laugh, and share memories. Thea cherished this time more than anything else, and she often found herself wishing days would pass by faster so that she could have her late-night talks with him. She was becoming more and more captivated by him. She was captivated by his looks and charmed by his personality. He would do things like call her beautiful, and in those private moments, she didn't feel she had to pretend or use courtly decorum around him. He was becoming her safe space and though she had little time to form relationships with others at court – with him she didn't feel alone. Despite that, though, she continued to wonder why he cared for her so much – after only knowing her a short time. She trusted that his affections were true – she confirmed this with her Control, but still she wondered what inspired his feelings and loyalty. She knew he wasn't overly trusting or naive, so why did he throw out logic when it came to so easily trusting her. Not only did she contemplate Kol and the emotional side of their relationship, but she also thought about the physical side. Sometimes he would touch her, a hand on her legs or his lips on her cheek. His chaste behaviors always left her skin burning and her body wanting more. She couldn't help but wonder when things would escalate. This thought both thrilled and worried her.

Thea awoke one morning two weeks after her arrival at the Palace, feeling particularly curious about her future husband. She sat through breakfast with Dorothy, mindlessly talking about court gossip, but all the while, she was planning on how she could gather more information on Kol. She compiled a mental list of who she could question, given her newly arrived status at court; the list was not long. There was always Ruth; not only was she trustworthy, but she also had known Kol his whole life. Thea had yet to learn where the loyalties of everyone at court lay. One

103

thing she did know was that most often, loyalties lay with whoever was most powerful, which was not Thea.

Dorothy watched Thea out of the corner of her eye. "What are you thinking about?"

"Kol." She responded simply.

"Oh Kol, he's so dreamy. I wonder whose eyes our children will have." Dorothy mocked with a smile playing on her lips.

Thea picked up a sugar cube and lobbed it at her friend. "Do you ever get tired of being satirical?"

"No. But I will let you know if it ever happens." She picked up the wayward sugar cube and popped it into her mouth.

"I will wait with bated breath." Thea rolled her eyes dramatically.

"But truly, what are you thinking about?" She prompted again.

"Well, to be honest, Kol's devotion to me," Thea admitted quietly, looking to make sure no Palace staff stood nearby.

"You said yourself that you tested it with your Control. He can't lie to you, for you would know," Dorothy stated in a matter-of-fact tone. "Your eyes are golden brown." Truth. "That dress is unflattering on your figure." Lie. "I once picked up a handsome hitchhiking stranger on my way home from holiday and let him fondle my breasts." Truth. "Your Control is infallible. Tell me which was a lie?"

"The second one," Thea stated obviously. "But the third one worries me." Dorothy laughed, amused by her own antics. "What if he had been a murderer or a ghost?"

"Well, I imagine if he had been a ghost, his hand would have just gone straight through my chest cavity." Thea listened to her friend – with an incredulous look on her face. "Okay, you're right. I won't do that again. But I still think you read too much paranormal fiction."

"That may be the case, but in every novel I've read, picking up or going with strangers is always a bad idea. Remember that. Be uninhibited with men you slightly know or at least know someone who knows them. For my sake, please."

"Cross my heart," Dorothy swore with a laugh – before growing somber again. "So, if you aren't worried that he lied about his devotion, then what are you worried about?"

"I don't know if worried is the word, more curious about why he cares so deeply, so quickly. Why am I so special? Surely, he has grown up with droves of beautiful, charming women around him. It's not like he would be so suddenly smitten by me. I'm not magic." Thea pondered aloud, not out of jealousy but genuine curiosity.

"He was never betrothed to those women," Dorothy added.

"That only explains the commitment, not the feeling behind it. He looks at me like he adores me. He has from the day we arrived here."

"So, what do you plan to do about it?" Dorothy asked.

"Why do you think I want to do something about it?" Thea quipped.

"Because I know you." She stated obviously, tossing a loose loc over her shoulder.

Thea whispered, "I was thinking about asking Ruth what she thought. I mean, I know I can trust her, and she has worked at the Palace Kol's whole life."

Dorothy nodded, considering Thea's plan. "I think that's as good an idea as any." She tapped her chin thoughtfully. "You know, some of the ladies who have been at court a few years might know something too. Especially those married to men on the royal council."

"I was thinking the same thing. They may not know his emotional intentions, but they know more about his general behaviors and how he has acted around the court. They might even know of any other relationships he's had in the past. That definitely would have been fodder for court gossip." Dorothy nodded again, this time in agreement.

As if on cue, Ruth's presence was announced as she strode into Thea's apartments. "Good morning ladies, you look beautiful, as always."

"Thank you, Ruth." Both women spoke in near unison; they looked toward one another afterward and giggled.

Ruth eyed them suspiciously. "What are you two up to?"

Dorothy looked at Thea, waiting for her to lead the conversation. "We were wondering if you'd like to join us for tea."

Ruth continued her skeptical staring. "Any special reason?" She asked – knowingly. Sometimes the girls joked Ruth might be psychic.

"Do you care to dismiss the other staff?" Thea asked nervously.

Without hesitation, Ruth spoke loudly and with authority. "That will be all; see to your other chores, the ladies do not require further services this morning."

Ruth took a seat at the small tea table with them, making herself a cup in silence as the staff that had previously been in the room left silently. Once the door had clicked closed, she ceased stirring her tea and looked toward Thea. "What would you like to know?"

"You're quite direct, aren't you?" Dorothy stated.

"Dear, when you get to be my age, you don't have much time for Blessed burned endeavors or bullshit. Pardon my language." Ruth affirmed casually as she tapped her spoon on the edge of her cup.

"No, I prefer it when you speak to me that way." Dorothy teased.

Boldly, Thea began, having been put at ease by the casual start of the conversation. "I was wondering what you could tell me about the Prince."

"You'll have to be more specific than that, dear; I've known the Prince his whole life. I could tell you many things about him." She took a sip of her tea.

"Well, to be frank, I find it odd how…beguiled he is by me so quickly," Thea stated carefully.

"I have heard many complaints from ladies over the years about their fiancés and husbands, but being too adored is not ever one of them." She chuckled. Despite herself, Dorothy joined in on the laughter.

"No, I'm not unhappy with it – it just doesn't make sense to me. He seemed nearly infatuated with me the first day we met. That's not typical, is it?" Thea whispered desperately.
Ruth placed her cup on the saucer in her hand and a look of debate washed across her face. "He has always been quiet…passionate. And he knows what he wants. Not to mention – that he has had a lifetime of excitement around meeting you." She offered as an explanation, holding it would satisfy Thea. Leaving out that when she said 'passionate,' she meant impulsive, and when she said 'he knows what he wants,' she meant he takes what he wants.

Thea leaned into her interrogation. "You know what I'm talking about, don't you?"

Ruth nodded slowly. "Are you familiar with the Prince's mother and her Control?"

"Of course, she had the Control of Sway."

"Are you aware of what that means exactly?" Ruth prodded, encouraging Thea to draw conclusions on her own.

"She was able to persuade people to do what she wanted. Right?"

"Well, yes. But more than that. She could plant ideas into people's heads and influence them to see things her way. That is partly why she was so well-loved in court. Not because she was, but because she convinced everyone that she was. Understand?" Thea nodded. "She often would use her Control to place ideas in Kol's head. Ideas he wouldn't get on his own or from his father."

Thea sat quietly, contemplating the implications of what that meant. "So, you're saying that Kol's mother used her Control on him to persuade him to love me?" Her chest ached, a small fracture beginning in her heart at that realization.

Ruth placed her cup down and grabbed both of Thea's hands fervently. "Don't go getting upset. Listen, she persuaded him to be kind to you and see you as an equal. The High King was not always kind to her, and she didn't want another woman to feel the way she did. And she certainly didn't want her son to act the way his father did when it came to women."

"That makes me feel like none of this is real," Thea replied sadly.

"If a Mori had told him to love you, then I would agree with you. One would have absolutely no say in what a Mori told them to do. But with Sway, it's only a suggestion. She persuaded him to be kind to you and treat you fairly. But he also has spent most of his life lonely and under the thumb of a less than gentle father. He sees you as hope and companionship. He likely started feeling that way because his mother said you were his equal where no one else is, but any love that grows is outside of her influence."

"How do you know?" Thea asked.

"Did you know that sometimes, when a Mori King conquers a realm, they take members of that family on as members of their council or royal staff?" Ruth asked. Thea shook her head yes. "Many generations ago, my family ruled over a piece of this realm – but a Mori king came in and overthrew us. Several members of my family were integrated into court here, my mother was a lady's maid to Kol's grandmother, and I grew up here in the Palace myself."

Dorothy and Thea listened with rapt attention. "I had no idea."

"Of course, you didn't, how would you? But you'll find that remnants of generations-old Controls linger in many staff or members of the court. Maybe not as strong as they would have been had we been trained or allowed to thrive in our ancestral homelands, but they exist nonetheless."

"What is your Control, Ruth?"

Ruth gave a small smile. "Have you ever heard of Insight, my dear?"

Thea scrunched her face in thoughtful concentration, racking her brain to find this information. "Isn't it... Control of intuition?" Ruth nodded. "I thought it was lost to time."

"All but, my dear, very few of us remain, and it will likely die with us. My mother was so gifted – she could predict the future. But as for me, I am just highly perceptive." Thea

109

could sense Ruth's modesty; it tasted like a lie, and that made her and Dorothy's previous conversations about Ruth's insightfulness seem eerie.

"So, when you say that Kol isn't under some Control to love me, it's true?" She asked hopefully.

"Let's use our powers together, my dear. I will say a statement, and you will tell me if it is true." Thea nodded in agreement. "No one is forcing Kol to care for you." Truth. "The persuasions his mother gave him were about how he should treat you, not how he should feel about you." Truth. "The love you will grow for one another will be true." Truth. Thea shivered in realization. That meant not only would he love her, but she would also love him too. The weight on her chest lifted, and she allowed the hope in her heart to come out of hiding. She fought back tears. Thea looked down at her lap, twisting her hands nervously as she did so. "There is something else you'd like to ask," Ruth stated.

"Do you know anything about people who dress in all black and want to hurt us? That would call us oppressors?" As Thea asked this, Ruth sat up straighter in her chair.

"Where did you hear about this?"

"We didn't just hear about it-" Dorothy corrected. "We saw it! They attacked our caravan when we journeyed from home to the Capital."

Ruth's face shifted from shock to somber apology. "They are called themselves Dissenters, and they are a group of non-Blessed people who think the Mori Empire should come to an end."

Now it was Thea's turn to look shocked. "Why?"

"I couldn't say for sure, my dear, but they say they feel oppressed by the power the Mori's have." She paused. "I really can't say more." But her eyes looked like she wanted to.

"Okay," Thea said, choosing not to pry any further. "Thank you, Ruth. You have no idea how helpful this has been."

"Any time, my dear." She patted her hand lovingly. "Now, would you like to taste some dessert samples for the wedding reception?" Thea nodded, still working to maintain composure given all this new information. Kol would love her. She would love him. That was all she had hoped for her whole life, and she could barely contain her joy.

"What kinds of answers are you looking for now? Didn't Ruth give you enough reassurance today?" Dorothy asked as she walked behind her friend.

"Ruth reassured me about his affections, but I still want to know more of who he is when I'm not around. I have hardly seen him interact with anyone; he always finds himself busy during events or shared meals. I want to know what his goings-on are and how the people perceive him." Thea spoke confidently as she marched toward the day room with purpose. Though named the day room, it was used all times of day, and at this moment, the women of the court were occupying its space for cocktails and gossip after dinner. Thea felt it was the best opportunity to find out this information, and she couldn't find the patience within her to wait any longer.

"And what of the potential consequences?" Dorothy warned fervently.

"If the Prince cares for me so much – as Ruth has said, as my Control tells us is true, then I have nothing to fear." Thea grew braver by the day.

"Just be careful and choose your words wisely. We have no idea how fleeting his affections are." Thea knew her friend's words were valid, but she wouldn't let them stop her.

"I will be covert." She promised before opening the door to the day room and was immediately greeted by the friendly glances of almost a dozen ladies. Dipping her head demurely, she greeted them with respect. "Good evening, ladies." Polite greetings met her. "I thought you might like to help me with a little problem I'm having." Several ladies raised their eyebrows, waiting eagerly to hear her request. Whether to be helpful or mock, Thea was unsure. She took a deep breath and continued. "I seem to have found myself with a surplus of baked goods." She gestured to the door as several carts of cake slices were rolled into the room. "I would love input on which flavor you think would be best to serve at our wedding later this month." She hoped to ingratiate them with flattery, acting as if she cared for their opinions, and then later use that new fond comradery to pull secrets out of them. Despite politics being left out of her education, she had learned to be quite strategic when she needed to be. "I also have personally picked wine pairings for each cake." Alcohol couldn't hurt to loosen them up either.

Several hours later, cork stoppers littered the tables, and giggling ladies could be heard throughout the halls. Thea positioned herself in a semi-private corner of the room, waiting for particularly ambitious ladies to approach her. She would allow them to think they were using her to gain affluence, but in reality, she was using them to gain information.

"Lady Althea, Lady Dorothy." Lady Adams curtsied. "May I join you?" She gestured to the empty chair beside them.

Thea worked to hide her smile. "Of course, you may."

"Lady Althea, I have wanted to make your acquaintance for weeks now. You looked beautiful at your welcome ball, by the way." Flattery – a tell-tell sign of an ambitious lady. And this one was a perfect target. She had grown up at court and was married to one of the men on High King Kairo's council, meaning she was privy to much information. "Please, tell me you're here to give your opinions on the cakes. No other lady has been so bold yet."

"I assure you; boldness is something I am not short on." A drunk hiccup escaped her lips.

"Wonderful." Thea smiled wickedly, something she had inadvertently picked up from Kol over the last few weeks.

"I like the spice cake with the cider wine. For a fall wedding, I think it makes perfect sense."

"I couldn't agree more." Thea nodded.

"Will you not want the opinions of the other ladies before you decide?" Lady Adams tested.

"I doubt these ladies know their own names right now, let alone anything else." Thea quipped pettily. Lady Adams nearly cackled, clearly quite inebriated herself.

"Lushes, the whole lot of them, I tell you." She eyed a fair-haired woman as she walked by. "And watch your jewelry around that one." She whispered.

"I will make a note of that." She slowly rose her hand to the necklace gifted to her by Kol, hoping to push the conversation toward him. "I am quite lucky indeed to have made your acquaintance. You must be absolutely full of helpful court knowledge, of which I am desperate for – being so new here. I admit I've been a little lost." She humbled herself; at least, she hoped it looked that way to Lady Adams. Her finger still traced the large gemstone at her neck.

"Consider me a friend then; we can't have the future High Queen lost in her own court." Her eyes darted toward Thea's strategically placed hand. "And we can't let that stone be snatched – it is gorgeous."

Thea played her role, though she did not have to try hard to act like a smitten fiancée. "They'll have to pry it off my cold, dead body. I scarcely take it off." Lady Adams' eyes grew wide at the dramatics. "It was a gift from Kol." She used his first name, knowing it would convey closeness.

"Well, I don't blame you. His Highness has exquisite taste." Jealousy was coming off her in waves. She subtly touched the small stone that hung around her own neck.

"Well, I'm sure you knew that; you've known him his whole life haven't you?" Thea took her shot. Dorothy listened beside her, anxious for her friend.

Jealousy was replaced by pride on Lady Adams' face. "I was invited to the High Queen's baby shower while she was pregnant with him. It was a very exclusive event."

"Amazing. Though, I'm sure you've been to many exclusive events." Thea continued the flattery.

"One or two." She feigned modesty.

Thea continued to play the role of a smitten fiancée. "I wish I could have been in the Palace to be with Kol as he grew up. We are getting quite close, but I feel as if a thousand lifetimes wouldn't allow me as much time as I want with him. And when we are together, we hardly want to spend all our time reminiscing on our childhoods."

Lady Adams took another drink of wine, "Scandalous!" She swatted playfully. "If my husband looked like the Prince, I wouldn't be able to keep my hands off him either." Thea's cheeks grew hot at her scandalous accusation, and she had to focus her mind on the task at hand as memories of his hands tracing lazy circles on her bare skin came into her mind. She shivered.

Thea cleared her throat. "I feel I know so little of him, and I crave to know more." This moment was crucial; either Lady Adams would grow suspicious or blindly see it as an opportunity to gain the future High Queen's favor. Thea and Dorothy exchanged a subtle but nervous glance.

"Darling." She paused as she took another long drink. "I know it all. What do you wish to know?"

Thea released a breath she didn't realize she had been holding. She dared another question. "And this conversation can stay between us girls? I wouldn't want Kol to feel like I'm prying."

"I won't tell a soul." Truth. A sense of relief washed over her – and at the same time, she felt lucky that she had yet to cross a royal loyalist in her time at court. While this had played to her favor, she noted that no one was to be truly trusted. If they gave up information on people they'd known their whole life to a stranger, they likely would feel they could do that same to her at some point. *Or maybe these rulers inspire no loyalty,* she worried in the back of her mind. "I've seen what happens to those that cross Mori men, and I have no interest in inciting that upon myself." Immediately her worries were confirmed. She swallowed against the lump that had formed in her throat.

"What do you mean?" Thea asked, trying and failing to keep her voice steady.

"You don't stay a High King without crushing a few thousand skulls, as my husband would say. And he would know. He is often one of the men administering punishments on the High King's behalf." Thea forced herself to relax, thinking that perhaps she was only referring to Kairo when speaking of the Mori's cruelty.

"The High King and Prince seem to be quite different from one another in their dealings then?" She hoped. She prayed.

"Oh yes." Thea's chest released its tension. "The Prince is much more charming and diplomatic than the High King, at least in public."

"What do you mean? At least in public?"

"Who's to say what any of us do behind closed doors." She remarked jokingly before her face grew grave, and she leaned in desperately close. Thea could practically taste the wine on her breath. "Though we all have heard rumors of the Prince's secret activities and dalliances." Thea grew faint, *dalliances*?

"Dalliances?" Thea repeated.

Clearly drunk, Lady Adams stumbled over her words. "He has pleased several ladies from the court in his time, not of late but in his youth – they were frequent." Thea's vision blurred, and she used all her willpower to stop tears from coming. She tuned the sound of Lady Adam's voice out. Her mind drifted, remembering a time when a boy had tried to kiss her as a young girl; she had wanted to but feared retribution so severely that she ran fast away and never spoke to him again. She had always held herself back – because of who she was to marry one day. She held back while Kol wasn't expected to. Sadness was replaced by anger and jealousy, though she reasoned that she knew he had a life before her, as she had – albeit hers was not so colorful – she couldn't help but grow uneasy considering who may have been in his life before her. *Or in his bed,* she cringed and tried to shake away those bad thoughts.

"The High King tries to hide it, though. In fact, my husband has helped relocate many girls the Prince fancied on behalf of the King. But he can't hide it, his Empire may be vast, but his court is rather small. And rather bored and prone to gossip." She giggled, unaware of the pain her words were causing Thea. Or, if she were aware, she didn't care. "We all know the Prince doesn't always stay in the castle perimeter at night. If you know what I mean."

Thea gulped, "I'm afraid I don't."

"Well, he turns up often enough covered in bruises. Whether that's from an underground fight club or kinky sex, I can't say." She hooted at her own joke.

Thea stood abruptly, chair scraping the floor loudly from the force. "Thank you, Lady Adams, but I must take my leave now." Choking back tears, she fled toward the door, earning chuckles from nearby ladies.

A birdlike woman chuckled and remarked, "I see poise isn't one of the gifts our future princess is *'Blessed'* with." The ladies around her cackled, but Thea was too distracted by her grief to care.

"Shame on you, harpies." Dorothy spat as she chased after Thea. "Thea, wait!" She hiked her skirt up and ran down the hallway; she rounded the corner and was knocked down after colliding with another. "What the hells!" Dorothy exclaimed. A hand appeared before her, tanned and smooth – not having seen a day of work in its life.

"Quite a mouth on such a pretty lady." A smooth, accented voice remarked. Dorothy looked up as she took the hand in her own. His hair was curly, golden ringlets spilling over his forehead, and on his nose perched glasses.

"You don't know the half of it." She remarked sarcastically. To her surprise, he laughed, deep and slow, as a smile pulled at his lips. He delicately pulled her to her feet and remained back a respectful distance as she straightened her skirts. "Thank you for your help, I know it doesn't appear dignified, but I was trying to follow my friend."

"Stalking isn't very dignified either." His satirical comment stopped her. She eyed him approvingly, a small smile playing on her lips.

A breathy laugh escaped her mouth as she replied, "I'm not stalking her, she was upset, and I need to find her. But I hope to cross paths with you again." She eyed him again, noting his flash-less attire but impeccable posture. "Are you...a lord?" She questioned aloud.

"Surely you can't think me something else, a court jester perhaps." He joked. Without warning, Dorothy snorted with laughter at the irony of his joke, earning her a bemused expression from the man in front of her.

"What is your name, sir?" She demanded easily.

"Martin, just Martin is fine. And what may I call you."

"Dorothy, just Dorothy will be fine." She mocked his previous, straightforward statement.

"Well, just Dorothy-" He bowed deeply in front of her. "It's been an honor." And he continued down the hallway. Despite herself, Dorothy dared a glance over her shoulder and was delighted – giddy in fact – to see he had done the same. It took her several minutes and a lot of willpower not to follow

118

him, but she was committed to help her friend. Still new to the Palace, she wasn't always aware of her body in space there, and she found herself running in the exact opposite direction of their rooms – where Thea had gone.

Thea callously sent the maids out of her room, slamming the door behind them. She regretted it as she did it, but at that moment, she could not hold back her emotions, and she wanted as few witnesses as possible. A million images ran through her head as she curled up on the couch and rage cried. A barbaric version of Kol, punching another man as he smiled wickedly, surrounded by degenerates at a fighting exposition. And yet she felt even worse when she imagined him entangled in the sheets with a faceless woman, tracing slow circles on her bare skin like he always does to Thea – she physically shivered in disgust. *A man – who had been taught he was better than everyone else, of course, he did whatever he wanted*, she thought sorrowfully. *Would I ever be enough?* She added, self-deflating thoughts abounding in her head. She felt foolish again – and then scolded herself for the constant flip-flopping she did regarding her feelings for Kol.

As if conjured by her thoughts, Kol's nightly rap came at the door. Panic seized her, knowing what a mess she must look and having no excuse for it. She didn't want him to know the truth of her investigative behaviors – or what thoughts she was grappling with. She hopped off the couch and ran toward her bedroom. "Just wait!" She yelled without thinking, but a moment too late, as he turned the door and caught a glimpse of her. His face flashed instantly to rage, which she feared was directed at her. "I'm so sorry." She began, worried her demand for him to wait had enraged him.

"Who hurt you?" He demanded, his tone quiet but firm.

"What?" She asked, shocked his anger wasn't directed at her.

"You're crying, and in the weeks I've known you, this is not a common state I come to find you in. I'm assuming someone did something, and I will rectify it. Immediately." He bit out as fire flickered in his eyes and his shapely jaw tensed. Despite her earlier findings, his protectiveness warmed her heart. Ruth's words ran through her head, remembering the truth that he would treat her well – and even more that he was going to love her. She relaxed, but not entirely, knowing she still had to answer for her current state. She needed to stall.

"Would you grab me a water, please?" Without question, he went toward a bar cart to grab her a glass. She racked her brain for a cover – and already regretted any lies she might tell, so she opted for a version of the truth. She watched his graceful movements – as he elegantly walked toward her and handed her a glass. He brushed a piece of wayward hair behind her ear, causing her to shiver under his delicate touch.

"Can you tell me what happened?" His voice, now gentle, calmed her. "I need you to be happy." Truth.

"I am feeling homesick." Truth. Not the whole truth, but a truth nonetheless.

"No one hurt you?" He asked to confirm.

"No one hurt me." *Only you, but not on purpose*, she thought.

"Just homesick?" She nodded. "Is there something you need? A better room? A bigger bed? Different foods prepared for you? More ladies to spend the days with? We can get you whatever you need." He sprang into problem-solving mode, though most solutions would be at the inconvenience of others, the gesture was genuine still. "Anything you want, you only have to ask." Truth. She suddenly wondered if his past mattered. That if he was kind to her, did his politics or where he went at night matter? At that moment, the answer was no; as long as his nights were not spent with other women, she would not care. And maybe there was a way to prevent that. She placed a hand to his cheek, and she felt as if lightning shot through her skin at this intimate touch initiated by her own hand. He froze and ceased his problem-solving prattling, eyes locking with hers. The worry lines faded from his face as he calmed down and waited for her to speak.

"You are too kind, but I have more than enough here. I can be happy for this change-" She paused, eyes turning sultry, "And thankful for you, and still grieve over what I'm losing at the same time. They are not mutually exclusive; they don't cancel each other out." She brushed a thumb gently over his cheek, plans formulating in her mind to erase all memories of other women from his head as she did so. He closed his eyes, leaned into her palm, and blew out a gentle, contented breath.

"I overreacted?" He asked. "I have been accused of that before, but the men who said so didn't live to tell the tale." At that moment, Thea was thankful for his closed eyes for she didn't have the willpower to hide the shock on her face as he casually mentioned killing a man – just for insulting him. She hoped it was merely a poor joke.

She cleared her throat, "Maybe I did as well." At least, she wanted to convince herself she did. "There are a great many things I love about being here." She added, knowing it didn't matter if it were true or not. She had no choice, and her life

121

would be long and miserable if she didn't find things to love about it. *And about him,* she thought, though that part was not proving to be difficult. He opened his eyes, intensity in their stare growing. Boldness and a desire to solidify her place in his life took over, and now it was her turn to close her eyes. She leaned toward him, lips puckering slightly as she did so. Any moment now, and she would know what those velvety lips felt like against her own. Time slowed down, seconds ticking by agonizingly slow. She felt his arms wrap around her and draw her near – *this is it.* But instead of flesh, her face was met with fabric smooshing against her lips as he wrapped her in a hug. She felt dejected, embarrassed even. Reading her mind, he spoke.

"I cannot take advantage of you in this emotional place, as much as I may want to know how every part of your body feels against mine..., especially your lips." He continued holding her – as if he could hold her together and squeeze the sadness out of her. The longer they stood there, embracing one another, the less embarrassed she felt. *He cares for me.* He smoothed her hair down with his hand and placed a gentle kiss on her head. "Why don't you get cleaned up, bathe, and dress yourself in some of those scandalously tight stretchy pants you love so much." Sincere tone gone, and typical flirting returned. "And I will bring you back a surprise."

She looked up at him from underneath her lashes, daring another sultry look. "Finding you in my room by the time I am finished is all the surprise I need." Shock and joy appeared instantaneously on his rascally face.

"Thea!" He placed a hand to his chest sarcastically. "If I weren't a smart man, I would say you're trying to seduce me."

"Maybe you're not as smart as you think then." She replied, again shocked at the boldness she felt she could speak with in his presence. She pushed away from him, walking toward her bedroom door, pushing it fully open. "Give me one hour."

He bowed, eyes glittering with mischief, "As you wish, Your Highness."

Thea sat in the large tub in her bathing room, thinking about what may occur with the rest of her night. The rest of her night with Kol. She sighed with contentment, sinking deeper into the tub as she did so. A knock sounded from the bathroom door, and excitement surged through her – followed quickly by shock. Shock at the boldness he had to come into a room she was nearly confirmed to be nude in. Her whole body blushed.

"Come in!" She replied with little hesitation. She closed her eyes and took a deep breath. The door opened and clicked closed behind her.

A female voice shocked her, causing her eyes to dart open. "Are you okay? Sorry, I didn't come sooner; I got lost." Dorothy sat down on a chair near the tub.

"Get out!" Thea yelled, covering her breasts with her hands.

"You told me to come in here!"

"I thought you were someone else!" Thea replied without thinking, nearly instantly regretting it as Dorothy's face went from confusion to devilish glee.

"Oo la la." She made kissing noises in Thea's direction.

"Shut up!" Thea splashed water toward her friend. "He'll be back soon; you need to leave. Throw me that robe." Dorothy did as her friend asked. Thea stood, wrapping herself in plush terrycloth before stepping out of the tub. "Seriously, whatever vibe we had going on tonight will be completely gone if he returns to find you here."

"There was a vibe, you say?" She shimmied seductively, raising her eyebrows in jest at Thea. "What exactly do you plan on doing tonight? Nothing I wouldn't do, I hope."

"That leaves nearly nothing out of the question." Thea quipped.

"As it shouldn't, you're an adult woman. You should have fun."

"Said no one to any woman ever, especially not to me." Freedom of choice was nearly non-existent, let alone freedom of sexual exploration.

"No time like the present." Dorothy grinned cheekily.

"I don't know about that. Where have you been anyway? You said you got lost?" Thea asked incredulously.

"Don't give me a tone; this place is huge, and I was a little frazzled."

"You? Frazzled? Since when does that happen? Did something cute walk by?" Silence followed her questions. "It did, didn't it? Who is it?" She shoved her friend playfully.

"He literally ran into me and knocked me to the ground; of course, like the gentleman he seemed to be, he helped me up. His name is Martin."

"Duke Martin?" Thea asked; Dorothy shrugged in response. "The only Martin I know of in the court is Duke Martin. Curly blond hair, very handsome?" Dorothy nodded enthusiastically.

"He's a duke?"

"You're here not even a month and you've snagged a duke! What will your mother say?" Thea joked.

"She'd be so excited it almost makes me not want to pursue it."

"But?"

"But he was so dashing I can't deny myself that. Plus, he seemed innocent, and I'd have fun with that as well." Dorothy remarked shamelessly.

Before their conversation could continue, the door to her bedroom opened and slammed shut. "I'm back!" Kol shouted toward the bathing room door. "No rush, though."

Dorothy's mouth dropped open as she playfully pushed her friend in excitement. "There's a boy in your room!" She exclaimed in hushed tones.

"Shhh!" Thea quietly, yet sternly, shushed her friend. "What are you going to do all night, sit in here?" She whispered.

"Like a creepy voyeur? I'm not into that, give me a break. Tiny little things like you always blow the doors off the barn in the sack. I'd be scarred for life."

"Shush, there's not going to be sex."

"No sex? Why no sex?" Dorothy pouted.

"I barely know the man."

"He's your fiancé," Dorothy added.

"While my heart may feel it knows him, he is basically still a stranger. Also, his nickname is the Prince of Death, which I still don't know why, not exactly panty-dropping tone to that name. Plus, not only a few hours ago, we learned he may sneak out of the Palace at night and get beaten up by prostitutes or whatever Lady Adams was insinuating." Thea whispered, perplexed.

"We should talk, my vanilla sweetie; that is not what she meant." Dorothy retorted.

125

"Are you saying something, Thea?" Kol yelled from the bedroom; she clamped her hand over Dorothy's mouth.

"No! I'll be out in a second!" Thea yelled, before squealing in surprise, Dorothy having licked the hand covering her mouth.

"Are you okay?" Kol asked, concern in his voice.

"Fine! Just…saw a spider." She responded lamely.

"A spider…really?" Dorothy whispered.

"Your fault! And I don't permit you to lick me ever again."

"Does Kol have the same rule? I doubt it." Dorothy teased.

Thea blushed. "Seriously, you need to go."

"I don't see a backdoor out of this bathroom, do you?"

"The sarcasm isn't helping." Thea sighed in irritation.

"Take him out on your balcony! Walk out there and ask him to point to the stables or something like that, and I will sneak out."

"This idea is stupid and sounds like something children would come up with." Thea rolled her eyes.

"Have any better ones?"

"No. Fine, we will do your plan." Thea walked to the door and cracked it open – before closing it quickly. "He's on my bed! Laying down!"

"Yeah, he is." Dorothy raised an eyebrow seductively.

Thea swatted at her friend – before taking a few deep breaths. "Okay, I can do this."

"Make me proud!" Dorothy whispered, swatting her on the butt as she exited the bathing room.

The door shut loudly behind her, making Kol turn his head in her direction. There he was, draped on her bed like a god from a painting, propped up on one elbow with one leg bent up casually. His face alone exuded seduction, from the fullness of his lips to the sharp bend of his jaw. Thea's breath caught in her chest, and she became acutely aware of how little clothing she was wearing. He seemed to be aware of the same thing. A slight blush tinted the apples of his cheeks and the bridge of his nose as he gently looked her up and down. His eyes lingered on her bare legs and chest, which were left partially revealed by the scant robe. Under his predatory gaze, she felt beautiful and desired in a way she never had before; it almost felt sinful. She pulled the fabric over her cleavage.

His voice, quiet and raspy, met her ears. "Do what you want, it's your body, but don't cover up on my account." She nodded and slowly removed her hand. "Good girl." His praise sent a shiver up her spine. She suddenly became aware again of the voyeur in her bathroom.

"Would you care to walk with me on the balcony? I've been here several weeks and not gone out on it once." She prattled nervously. "I'm sure the gardens are beautiful under the night sky."

"Now? Are you sure you don't want to sit up here with me and see your surprise?" He asked, sultry voice nearly undoing her.

Desperately, she thought. "After." She insisted, using all her willpower not to glance back at the bathing room and give herself away.

"In that scrap of fabric?"

"I thought you rather liked this scrap of fabric?" She flirted.

"I do." He smiled naughtily. "The reason I like it is the reason other men may like it, and I can't have a passing guard look up and be given a sight that belongs only to me." She shivered again, then crossed the room, grabbing his hands.

"Come on, you can kill them to defend my honor." She joked.

"Gladly." He replied; again, she was unsure if he was joking. He led her to the door, opening them before allowing her to pass through before him. A gust of wind gave her a visible chill. "I told you that measly wrap would do nothing; let me get you a blanket." He started to turn, and she spotted Dorothy out of the corner of her eye.

"No!"

He looked amused. "No?"

"You can keep me warm." She pulled him close to her, his amused face quickly becoming an aroused one, as she had accidentally pulled his hand to graze the curvy flesh of her breast. A gasp escaped her.

"Thea, I am so sorry." He pulled his hands back.

Unsure if she was giving in to the con or was just genuinely this daring now, she replied, "Don't be." She wrapped his arms around her, placing his hand back from where it had previously been, and stepped deeper into his embrace, allowing her back to press against his chiseled chest. Her heart pounded in her chest, relishing every place her body touched his. Heat radiated from the hand he had gently placed under her breast, knuckles grazing the sensitive flesh every time he moved. It felt like an eternity passed as they stood there, silently wrapped in this embrace. The door to her room closed, shaking them both from their daze.

"What was that?" Disappointedly, his grip on her loosened.

"I'm not sure." Lie.

128

"Let's go back inside; one of your surprises is getting cold anyway." He took her hand, fingers effortlessly intertwining with hers, and led her back toward the bed. The way he moved around her, the way he touched her, it was so effortless, as if he'd done it a thousand times. He sat her down and allowed her to get comfortable. "Close your eyes and open your mouth." She followed his instructions, hearing dirty retorts in Dorothy's voice in her mind. Her sense of smell kicked in, aromas buttery and acidic flowing in her nostrils. "Bite, gently." She did as he commanded again, immensely enjoying this game they were playing, whatever it was. Her teeth met with a flaky crust, and tangy citrus jam spread across her tongue.

Her eyes flew open. "It's a citrus tart!" She exclaimed in delight.

"Yes." A breathy laugh escaped his lips.

"I love these!"

"I know – that's why I made them." He replied, matter-of-factly.

"You made this?" She took another bite. "It's delicious."

"You sound surprised." He laughed.

"Princes don't bake, and if they did, I don't think it'd be so good." She took another bite, jam sticking to the corner of her mouth.

"I assure you-" He spoke slowly. "I am quite good at everything I do." He raised his thumb to her lip, wiping away the wayward jam before slowly drawing his thumb to his lips and sucking it off. And he did all this without breaking eye contact with her, his eyes gazing down at her in a seductive manner. Her mouth went dry, and she desperately wanted to respond in turn, but out of awkwardness, she continued the conversation.

"So, who taught you to bake?"

"My mother, she taught me many things my father despised. Baking, poetry, art history, dance." He paused, "But this I requested to master, once I knew they were your favorite." He looked her in the eyes, this time only sweetness in them instead of seduction or playfulness.

"Your whole life…." She paused.

"Yes?"

"Your whole life, you've been preparing for me?"

"Yes." Truth.

"You've been learning what I like just to… make me happy?"

"Yes." Truth. He answered as if it was so obvious.

"Why?" The question left her mouth before she thought. But no fear flashed through her this time; she knew him well enough now to no longer be afraid.

"Because you're it for me, Thea. You are my equal, and I want you to be happy here so that we can create a life together. A happy life." Truth. He spoke so simply – as if baring his soul to her was the easiest thing in the world.

A tear slipped from her eye. He caught it with his thumb, hand not leaving her face as concern grew on his. "Are you homesick again?" He asked.

"No." She paused. "Just the opposite, actually." He nodded knowingly – while giving her a small, satisfied smile. They sat there for several moments, enjoying the comfortable silence that had settled around them.

After many minutes Thea spoke. "This reminds me, actually, of the gifts I got for you." She hopped out of bed and headed toward the dressing room.

"You aren't going to change, are you?" Disappointment in his voice.

"No!" She giggled. "I'm getting your gifts that I brought with me."

"I already received them, the citrus fruits and lavender bundles. How do you think I made these tarts?" He asked, perplexed.

"I have other gifts! Ones that I picked out myself." She yelled from the dressing room. She rested the arrows in the bend of her elbow and carried the spice box in her hands. She walked out to find Kol, perched on the edge of the bed, eyes closed and mouth open. "What are you doing?" She giggled again.

"Waiting, as I had you do for your gift."

"It's not that kind of present." She retorted. "Open your eyes."

"You got me a wooden box?" He tried to act excited, likely to not hurt her feelings – but he looked utterly confused.

"Definitely starting to wonder if you are as smart as you think you are." He shot her a teasing look. "Open the box." He opened the lid, and his eyes went wide. "I knew you liked exotic spices; at first, I didn't know why and now I know it's because you like to bake. Nevertheless, I bought these for you. We often got spices like these, being so close to the seas and therefore shipments of goods from overseas." The arrows shifted in her arms. "I also brought these, I knew you liked archery, and I thought they were pretty so..." She handed them over to him.

"And the ribbon?"

"You like green." She said simply.

"Thank you, Thea, these are... so thoughtful. Truly, I love them." She thought back to all the gifts he had sent her over the years, feeling as if this was so small in comparison.

"It's no big deal." She dismissed it.

"It is." He looked up genuinely. "I haven't received a gift in some time, not since my mother's passing, actually. Father isn't big on gift-giving, or affection for that matter." He looked down at the box in his hands. "Perhaps we can bake something together with these new ingredients." He replied excitedly, changing the subject.

"I don't have the slightest clue how to do that." She laughed.

"Don't worry. I can teach you." Pause. "And I'll be gentle." He looked into her eyes again from under thick lashes.

"I trust you." Truth. She cleared her throat and changed the subject. "So, your father was not so warm and fuzzy then?" She asked.

He laughed cheerlessly. "The understatement of the century." He paused, considering his next words. "But he helped me become who I am. Strong, competent in the ways of ruling, a skilled fighter, and capable of getting what I want. He and my mother were a good balance in that way, I suppose."

"Just because she was kind, it doesn't make up for the fact that he wasn't."

"'Not kind' is the nicest way to describe him. He would beat me for small mistakes and make me do the same to others while he watched." Thea flinched, placing her hands on his in comfort. But he didn't seem to need it. "But, it was all necessary for me to become king. His father taught him the same way and so on." *Would he do the same to his children?* She wondered. But after spending time with him, she knew he was not like his father, and she felt that he'd never hurt their children, just like he would never hurt her. "And I get some level of payback on him, in my own way." He smirked.

"What do you mean?"

132

"Well, starting my fourteenth year, I started sneaking out of the castle most nights." *Here it comes,* she thought. "I would go anywhere I could: bars, brothels, dance establishments, plays, and fighting exhibitions." Her mind continued to hear the word brothel over and over again, and she had to force herself to listen to the rest of his story. "At first, I would just watch, and then I started to fight as well. Partly because it was fun and I was good at it, but mostly because it pissed my father off."

"Why did it? Shouldn't a prince be able to do whatever he wants?" She asked.

"Yes, but only if the King approves, and he didn't. Fighting is often looked down on. A sport for the poor. I hate that it has that reputation – because it helped me through the hardest years of my life." He recounted with sadness in his voice.

"I'm sorry that you felt like you had to do all those things because of what had been done to you." She replied in a quiet voice.

"I don't want pity."

"It isn't pity. It's empathy. I would not want to hurt as you have, and I'm sorry you had to." She replied genuinely, heart aching to know the man in front of her had gone so many years without love in his life.

His eyes shifted, confusion in them. "I'm sure your parents did the same."

"Well, they certainly weren't perfect, and I have my qualms, but I know they love me. Everything they did was because they loved me."

"What are your qualms?" She hesitated. "Go on." He encouraged her.

"Well, I was only raised to be a wife. Your wife. Nothing more."

133

"And this is a disappointment?" He asked, not offended, genuinely curious.

"No. And the more I get to know you, the more fervently I can say no. You're not a disappointment. I just wish I had belonged to me, even for a small amount of time." She explained, knowing a man of such power could not understand how that feels.

"What does that mean?" Confusion in his voice.

"I don't even know… be allowed to make my own choices on where I go and with who and what I wear and who is allowed to touch me." She stopped herself, hoping she hadn't crossed a line by wishing out loud she had been allowed more physical contact in her life. But he did not act concerned; he just waited, wanting her to finish. "It seems that I will always be someone else's property." She said sadly, looking down.

He placed a gentle finger under her chin and lifted it. "I do not see you that way. When I say you are my equal, I mean it. I will not tell you what to do or what to wear. I would request I only be the one to touch you, but I would not force that upon you either if you didn't wish it. I need you by my side, not behind me." She couldn't stop herself; she embraced him again, nearly climbing in his lap to do so. The box of spices clattered to the floor, followed by the arrows, as he pulled his arms tightly around her.

"Thank you." She whispered.

"Do not thank me for giving you something you should already have." He stroked her hair gently as they sat there. She pulled back, eye level with him, and wiped away the tears that had fallen from her eyes.

"Kol…can I ask you something?"

"Always." He brushed a lock of hair behind her shoulder.

"Can you tell me about the Dissenters?" He flinched when she said their name.

"How do you know about that?" Kol felt angry, but not at her, at whoever had told her. Telling her shouldn't have even been possible by anyone at court, as he used his Control to order it so. Not that Kol wanted to hide things from her, he just didn't want her to be unnecessarily scared in his home. *Her home,* he amended.

"They attacked us on our way here a few weeks ago. No one told you?" *No, they didn't,* he thought, *and they will pay for that.* "Kol?" He pulled his thoughts back to the present moment.

"No, I didn't know." He grabbed her hands. "I am so sorry. I'm assuming you weren't hurt?" Concern filled his blue eyes.

"No, we were fine. The head guard stopped it very quickly. These men in all black just gathered around the caravan and yelled 'Oppressors' at us." Thea tried to explain it away quickly, hoping to dissuade his anger and fear.

He sighed heavily. "They are a fringe group, a minority of people who oppose my family's reign, saying we are not fair to those without Control or Title."

"Is it true?" She asked.

"That living in the Empire is not kind to everyone? Yeah, it's true. It's hard to be a human sometimes, which is true of people with and without Control. But for whatever reason, God has allowed people with Control to also be the people in power, and the Dissenters hate us for it." Truth.

Thea paused before asking her next question. "Am I safe from them?"

"You are always safe with me." Truth. "As long as I live, I will do anything in my power to protect you." Truth. Thea's knees grew weak at Kol's unwavering devotion.

But next thing she knew, he was the one who sought to change the conversation. "Would you like your other surprise?" She nodded. Without moving her, he leaned back, shirt rising from his waistband as he did so, and grabbed a book from her nightstand. "I often see you reading novels, and I have occasionally picked them up, just out of curiosity, and found that you like the horror genre." She nodded again. "As do I." She smiled, thrilled to have another thing in common with him. "So I brought this, thinking you may want to read my favorite one. And you will be pleased to know it even has an element of romance in it, as many of those other ones you read do." She blushed, embarrassed at this particular attention to detail. "But it's not lascivious, so don't get too excited." Her mouth fell open, and he laughed in sheer delight at her reaction. "But I thought we could read some together tonight."

"I would really love that." She crawled off his lap and followed him to the other side of the bed. He propped himself against pillows and the headboard, sitting on top of the duvet, his legs straight out in front of him crossed at the ankle. A gesture she was convinced no other man could have done better. He patted the spot beside him, and she obeyed, nestling herself beside him and under his arm. Warmth engulfed her as he draped a blanket over her body and then wrapped his arm around her side, hand resting easily on her hip. The small leather-bound book he held fell open in his other hand, and then he began reading.

"Horace Walpole was the youngest son of Sir Robert Walpole, the great statesman, who died

Earl of Orford. He was born in the year in which
his father resigned office, remaining in opposition
for almost three years before his return to a long
tenure of power. Horace Walpole was educated at
Eton, where he formed a school friendship with
Thomas Gray, who was but a few months older-"

Thea interrupted. "You said this was a horror story. This is more like a biography."

"Woah, someone is impatient." He pulled her closer to him and started sliding his thumb up and down on the fabric that lay over her hip. "Does a story about murder, lust, and ghosts sound boring to you?"

She gulped. Not from the horror of the story but the constant movement on her hip and the proximity of his horizontal body next to hers. "No."

"Exactly, just be patient, my dear."

My dear. She missed many paragraphs of the story, repeating those words repeatedly in her head. The fiery trail his thumb left on her hip also remained a fervent distraction in her mind, and she had to actively work on breathing evenly.

As time wore on, her eyelids became heavier, and his body became more comfortable, and she found it hard to keep her eyes open. His melodic, deep voice became almost hypnotic as he read to her. Smell was the last sense to fall asleep; she inhaled his scent deeply – and then dreamed of him that night.

Thea awoke draped carelessly across Kol's hard chest. He had fallen asleep as well, sitting up, and the book lay close beside him. His chest rose and fell evenly, letting Thea know he was still asleep. Despite every lesson on decorum she had been taught her whole life, she snuggled closer to him rather than pulling away. Instinctually, his arm pulled around her tighter. At that moment, she didn't care that their legs were tangled together or that her robe was nearly scandalously pulled open – because she was happy. And even after forcing herself to think about it, she couldn't remember a time when she felt that doing as she pleased wouldn't result in her reprimand. Beside her lay the second most powerful man in the known world, and he declared her his equal. She smiled at this, remembering his tender words and comfort the night before. At this moment, she knew that she would be happy there with him.

He stirred, stretching his back as he turned over in the bed. This caused them to be face to face. His eyes opened, and surprise filled them, clearly forgetting where he had fallen asleep. But that surprise was quickly replaced by a look of bliss. "I don't ever wish to see anything else upon awakening ever again." He said in a sleepy, scratchy voice. A blissful smile to match his spread across her face. "But unfortunately, I must go." She puffed her lip out in pouty desperation. "Now that is cute, but time with you today will do me no good in negotiating with the foreign dignitaries that are no doubt waiting in my office as we speak." He kissed her forehead before getting up.

"Will I see you at the court luncheon today?" She asked.

"Do you wish me to be there?" She nodded fervently in reply, causing him to smile once again – an abnormal occurrence that he felt nearly unable to stop in her presence. "Then the answer is yes." He sat his book on her nightstand again and attempted to wipe the wrinkles out of his clothes, to no avail. "There will be no saving these clothes today, lest I wish to encourage rumors about me stirring in court. I'll have to leave the men waiting on me a little longer while I change into something less scandal-ridden." He joked. She loved listening to the easy tone he conversed with her in, but part of her ached when he said this as she remembered there were indeed many unpleasant rumors about him already in court. But after last night, she decided she didn't care. As long as she was his future, she didn't care about the past.

He turned to leave. "Kol." He turned back immediately. "Thank you for last night. You have no way of knowing but everything you said and did reassured me. I am so happy to be here, and I'm even happier that you are…that you are you and you are to be mine, and this is to be my life." She babbled, unsure how to articulate her feelings as well as he always seemed to be able to.

He strode back toward the bed, placing his hand over hers. "Of course. I hope I can always bring you comfort and reassurance." He waited for a beat. "Perhaps we can do this again tonight." She grinned in agreement. "I will see you midday." He looked at his gifts, still strewn across the floor. "Please have someone take those to my apartments." She nodded, and with that, he kissed her hand and left.

Once she was sure he was out of earshot, she covered her face and squealed in delight. She couldn't wait for thousands of more nights like that, and she couldn't want to tell Dorothy all about it. *Perhaps,* she thought, *I might even ask her for some pieces of advice.* This caused a blush to heat her cheeks, as she couldn't believe the lascivious acts she was considering. She sighed and looked around the room, which was suddenly less grand without Kol's presence. *He'll be back tonight,* she thought with another sigh of contentment.

Chapter 7

At some point, after Kol left that morning, Thea dozed off to sleep again. And unlike the easy and restful sleep of the night before, this nap was riddled with anxiety and unease. No concrete nightmare plagued her, just a stream of unhappy memories. She could hear many voices shouting at her and scolding her. The voices belonged to her parents, tutors, and other faceless adults who had disciplined her during her upbringing.

"Stop that. Ladies must not behave in such a way."

"Little girls do as they're told."

"You'll never make a man happy acting like this. You know he can refuse you, right?"

"You must remain pure of mind, heart, and body. No one will love a harlot."

"You belong to the Mori Empire."

"You belong to the Prince."

She twisted in her bedsheets, sweat beading on her brow. Memories flashed through her head of times she attempted acts of rebellion or independence – always to be thwarted by someone in her life. She was constantly reminded of her place, which was under the Prince and as property of the Mori Empire. When she wore pants for the first time: 'Crossdressing harlot!' When she held hands with a young boy at court: 'Slut! Ladies do *not behave so forwardly.'* When she asked if she could travel and learn more of the culture in her land: *'Not without the consent of the High King, and you do not have it.'* Manifested by her anxiety, an ominous voice boomed in her head: *'You will never belong to yourself!'*

She jolted up in bed, clutching her heart as if pressure and sheer force of will could calm her down. She tried to tell herself it was just a dream, but she knew all those words had been spoken to her at some point during her life. While some may call her desire for autonomy stupid, and others may even say that she was spoiled for wanting a different life as she had always been privileged – she knew that desire was born of the constant reprimands she had experienced her whole life.

Attempting to manage these negative feelings, she focused on the positives in her life. Kol cared for her. Kol was kind to her. She would never want for anything. Her family was well. Her friend was with her. *But you don't belong to yourself. The most significant decisions in your life have been made for you.* She physically shook her head, trying to shake the condescending voice from her head. Attempts to reason with these thoughts didn't help, she knew that most women don't get to choose, but it didn't make her feel much better. She felt lucky with the life she had, especially given recent developments and Kol's sweet demeanor. And if she were honest with herself, she didn't even know that she would choose something different; she just wished it were an option. And she knew the lack of choices would carry on in some form throughout her life.

"I will talk myself into a frenzy if I don't stop. I love my life." She whispered to herself with resolve, willing herself to believe it.

Thea found herself on autopilot that day, pushing through her morning routines and lessons with intentional effort. If she focused all her energy on tasks, she had no time to listen to the voice in her head that was plaguing her. She forced smiles as she walked through the halls and dutifully took notes as egotistical noblemen taught her more political nonsense. All day, she looked forward to seeing Kol, hoping his presence would calm her and reassure her as it had the night before.

Due to decorum, she knew Kol would be one of the last to arrive at the midday meal, leaving her with time to fill until he arrived. She walked in slowly, accepting nods from ladies around her as she passed them. The dining hall was dressed simply, nothing grand for a measly weekday meal. Several long tables were positioned in a u-shape in the center of the room, and a chair was left empty in the center of the center table for if the High King ever decided to grace them with his presence, which he hardly ever did. The chair beside the High King's, reserved for Kol, was often left empty as well. *But not today,* she smiled to herself. Kol would be joining them – at her request. She knew that was a big deal, given that most women couldn't get their husbands to stay out of brothels, let alone eat meals with them some days. *I love my life.* She reminded herself, and this time it felt truer.

She wondered how Kol spent his days. For that matter, she wondered how he spent his nights before her arrival. As tedious as they were, the meals broke up the day and gave Thea something to do, so she looked forward to them. Before living at the Palace, she would spend her nights alone, reading, or playing games with friends or family. She doubted the High King was a fan of playing games or dancing with his family at night. *So Kol must have friends*, she considered as she looked around the room.

He was elusive, she had never caught him speaking with anyone – other than for necessary and official courtly reasons.

Thea scanned the room again. She spotted Dorothy in a corner, who was flirtatiously twisting a piece of hair around her finger while giving undivided attention to whatever the Duke was saying. Thea smiled, happy her friend was finding her way in court. Her eyes flitted to the left, catching the gaze of a meek-looking man in the corner. He gave her an inviting smile. She took that as good a sign as any to ask questions from the male perspective on Kol. While she was willing to forget his past, she still wanted to know about his goings-on – especially the behaviors that would impact her. She walked her way toward the man, he looked young, perhaps a few years younger than herself, and he was dressed immaculately, making her think he was someone of importance or wealth. White-blond hair was slicked tight to his head, and his eyes were dark as night.

"I don't think we've been introduced yet." She said as she stepped in front of him confidently.

"We have not, although I was at your welcome ball. A hells of an entrance you made, quite the first impression." His gaze slowly moved up and down her body, giving her a shiver of discomfort. Unlike when Kol looked at her, she felt highly scrutinized and objectified under his icy stare. "Lord Heltman." He offered his name with confidence. "My father is on the council; I believe he is one of the men responsible for aiding you in learning and orienting yourself to our court." Indeed, he was. *An insufferable man,* Thea thought.

"I will be eternally grateful for the knowledge he has helped me obtain." Lie. "And I'm sure I need no introduction." She said haughtily, copying his air of condescension.

He laughed mirthlessly. "No, you definitely don't." He paused for a moment, shamelessly staring at her chest. She instantly regretted her corset today, as well as her decision to speak with this man at all. He had seemed so innocent from across the room. But now, she would rather never know another thing about Kol than have to talk to this insufferable man any longer. And deep down, she felt that Kol would tell her anything she wanted to know if she asked him herself. *Nothing good has come from my prying*, she realized with embarrassment.

"Well, I must find my seat before the meal begins." She offered a seamless goodbye.

"I'll enjoy watching that ass walk away as you do. Until we meet again, Althea." She felt lucky to have not been facing him as he said this. Her face heated in angry embarrassment, and her mouth dropped open. She had never been spoken to in such a manner, and while she knew didn't enjoy it, she also didn't know how to respond to it.

Befuddled and flustered, she accidentally walked straight into someone. She looked up, eyes meeting with Lady Lavina's, which were filled with fury. Red wine stained the front of her previously flawless dress, and if looks could kill, Thea would be dead.

"Lady Lavina, I am so sorry! I wasn't looking where I was going, forgive me. I can replace the dress, no problem."

"No problem?" She slurred, drunk in the middle of the day as always. "Other than my day being ruined when I was previously having such a good time."

"I am truly sorry, but there is nothing else I can do. Unless you know someone with the Control of Time I could bribe to come here and reverse the situation from ever happening." Thea attempted a joke, but Lady Lavina was not amused in the slightest.

She sucked her teeth, a calculated smile on her lips. "Well, who can blame you for being so distracted? I mean, with the state of your future marriage as it is." She looked around wickedly, gaining snickers from the ladies around her.

Thea's face heated in embarrassment. "I'm sorry? I don't think I know what you're referring to."

"You will be sorry – for making an enemy out of me."

"Enemy? It is just a little wine." Thea tried to reason.

"If the wine wasn't enough, your general existence is. And did you know that my husband is one of the most powerful men in this court? I can make your life here very difficult."

Thea stopped herself from laughing. "Though, he's less powerful than my fiancé. The Prince."

"The Prince is a spoiled rake with nothing between his ears, and everyone knows it." She swayed as she spoke, leaning on one of the women around her for support before she continued. She dropped her voice lower. "Though I know from experience that what he lacks between his ears he makes up for between his legs." She cackled wickedly, and even the demurest women in her circle couldn't hide their amused smiles.

Thea gritted her teeth. "You will remember who you are and with whom you are speaking." Tears sprung from her eyes, and her voice quaked, but she spoke with authority, nonetheless.

"I'm speaking with a girl who has yet to secure her place in this court. A little girl, not even strong enough to speak her mind without crying tears, like a pathetic child. If you even manage to make it down the aisle, you will be a powerless queen whom no one respects – and with whom her husband steps out on constantly. I mean, look at you." Thea's lip quivered.

"You will speak about Kol with respect. The Prince is a good man – who has been nothing but kind to me. And he will be your King, and if you had a brain between your ears, you would be more careful how you speak about him."

"Kol? Getting familiar, are you? Trust that you're not the first woman to call him that, and you won't be the last." She stared daggers. "You are not special."

"You will address him as His Royal Highness, as you will me."

"Not likely."

"Careful, what you're doing could be considered treason. And though I seem weak, I promise you I am not, nor am I feeling particularly forgiving today." Thea turned, walking briskly with her head held high out of the dining room – determined not to show even more vulnerability in front of the court.

From the shadows of the room, Kol watched this argument unfold. "Detain her until I otherwise instruct." He demanded through gritted teeth. *She will pay for hurting my Queen.* He ran after Thea, not ashamed to be seen in such haste when it came to her happiness.

Thea turned a corner and positioned herself in an alcove near the stairs to the servant's quarters, assuming no one would be there this time of day. She drew in cleansing breaths and allowed tears to stream down her cheeks as she attempted to understand why she was so upset. In part, it was an embarrassment that someone would speak to her that way – but it also spoke to her fears that no one in court was taking her seriously. And anger that others had the ability to wield Kol's past against her like a weapon. She knew some of Kol's history, and she felt close to him despite it – she just hated that no one knew the reality of their closeness. She hated that no one knew that they spent every night together and that he made her tarts and read books to her. And no one ever would because, truthfully, she wanted that to stay between them. *Maybe time will convince others of our affections for one another*, she hoped.

Despite her already growing affections for Kol, in the back of her mind, she wished she had the choice to love someone simpler. Someone without the baggage of the throne and jealous women at court who have known him his whole life. Someone discreet – that she could love in a quiet cottage in a town somewhere. Someone she didn't have to share with the Empire.

Her mind dashed back to Lady Lavina, her long silky hair and perfect porcelain skin. At one time, Kol had belonged to her in a way, and Thea hated that. Not out of jealousy, although she childishly wondered how she compared to her, but because it had the power to hurt Thea's reputation at court – and the opinions of her future marriage.

Lightning danced up her arm as long, gentle fingers wrapped around her wrist. "Thea." She was pulled in, the smell of cedar overwhelming her senses as her damp face met a silken shirt. She didn't need to look to know whose arms wrapped themselves around her body. He placed a hand to her head and shushed away her sobs. For a moment, she gave in to his comfort. Her body melded into his, and their breathing became one, as did the beating of their hearts.

"Everything will be okay." He tried to reassure her. She wasn't even focused enough to test it for truth or not.

She looked up at him, now calm, and responded, "You don't know that."

"I am the Prince. I can make anything happen. I will stop at nothing to make sure you are safe and happy." He wiped his thumbs across her cheeks, pushing away the wetness.

Part of her wanted to be comforted by this gesture, but his words incited irritation within her. "You cannot fix everything just because you're the Prince." Her tone turned accusatory. "You can't make the women at court like or respect me. You can't stop your father's council members from treating me like an imbecile. You can't make the women at court quit gossiping about you. And you can't turn back time and make it to where you didn't have sex with Lady Lavina." His shoulder slumped in defeat, face full of regret.

"I'm sorry. If I could go back and change ever being with those women, I would. I'm sorry it hurt you. But it meant nothing. I was young and far too powerful for my own good. Before I grew wiser, anyone looking to get ahead would use me one way or another. For women like Lavina, it was through sex. She likely thought it would better her life in some way. But it meant nothing to me, other than momentary release." Truth. "At one point in my life, I was trying to find connections with people, but it never worked. Probably because they weren't you, I was always just passing my time until I could be with the only one who deserved me. A woman who was kind, smart, and understanding – not to mention feisty, well-read, and gorgeous. Stunning inside and out. I could go on all day praising you." Truth. Tears formed in her eyes again, but for a different reason. "And you don't deserve me. You deserve better. I have hurt you, and my chest aches for that. Tell me how I can fix this." Thea softened into his arms again, resting her head on his chest. "I never said I was a perfect man, but I promise that I will never hurt you this way again. I won't be with other women or lie to you." Truth. A powerful truth. "Forgive me?"

She leaned up, looking into his eyes. "Kol, I'm not angry at you."

"You're not?" Confusion covered his masculine features.

"For having a life before me? No," Kol released the tension in his jaw at hearing that. "I can't lie and say it's my favorite thing in the world, knowing you've been with so many other women – mostly out of self-consciousness." She took a breath. "But I know you and your heart. You intend to take care of me – and to be a good partner to me."

"Then why are you upset?" He gently rubbed his hand up and down her back.

"Other than being humiliated in there today? Because others doubt us, and they have so many negative things to say about you." She admitted.

"I don't care." He replied confidently.

"But I do. They are using it to devalue our union and me. No one respects a queen that they think the king doesn't respect."

"I swear to you, it is my new mission to prove to everyone in this court just how devoted I am to you... if that is what you want." His features looked uncertain – as if scared to continue.

"What do you mean? Why wouldn't I want that?" She asked, almost annoyed.

"Thea, I have waited my whole life for you, you know this. But I want you to be here for the right reasons. I have enough sycophants in my life. I won't be married to one too. If we're going to do this, I want it to be real." Thea couldn't believe

149

what she was hearing. "I want you to choose whether or not you want to stay." Time froze; she had never heard those words before in her life. *I want you to choose.* Never. Fresh tears slipped down her previously drying cheeks, and she had to force herself to focus on the rest of what he was saying. "If you stay and marry me, I will always try to make you happy. I will learn your likes and dislikes and, hopefully, you'll do the same for me. We would be equals – in all ways. And I'd hope you could learn to love me despite what I've done." Her heart ached for the man in front of her, who despite his beautiful face, honey tongue, and generous spirit for her –felt unlovable. She saw a soul that was as much of a victim of circumstance as she was. "But if you want to leave, I will make that easy for you." His voice cracked. "I will take you wherever in this realm you wish to be and help you create a life there. And as much as it would hurt me, I would leave you alone." A tear rolled down his cheek. Thea watched it fall, frozen and in shock at everything he was saying. She felt as if her heart was filling, the corners of it bursting at the seams for the love that was growing in it for him. He saw her. He wanted her to choose. Her life, for once, belonged to her. But at that moment, all she wanted to do was give it right back to the man in front of her. "Of course, I want to marry you. It's all I've wanted since I was a boy. But I will not force my will upon you. I never will."

His eyes looked deep into hers; his mouth was still moving – but she could not hear him over the pounding of her own heart in her ears. She couldn't contain what she was feeling for him any longer. Her arms, previously on his chest, darted up. She placed one hand on the back of his neck and the other on his jaw. She used force to pull him closer to her, closed her eyes, and then crashed her lips to his. At that moment, years of desire and wanting took them both over. He picked her up, her legs instinctually wrapped around him, and he placed one hand under her as the other pulled her close to him. Though she had never done this before she moved her body with his like an expert. Temporarily, all decorum went out the door, she had to express how she felt. Futilely, he hoped never to be separated from her again. He didn't know what this kiss meant to her, if it was a hello or a goodbye, but he was enjoying every second of it regardless. He tried to memorize it all in his mind, like the way her body felt pressed against his and how soft her full lips were. She moved her lips with his, forgetting modesty and rules as they traded hot breath with one another. He traced the outline of her bottom lip with his tongue – before drawing it into his mouth and sucking. She gasped in surprise, which only fueled his efforts and desire for her more. She grabbed a handful of his hair and tugged gently, causing him to release a quiet moan from between his lips. He wished desperately that his hands could roam the terrain of her body, but to do so, he'd have to put her down, and at that moment, he wanted nothing but to hold her close. And when they finally pulled apart, he rested his forehead against hers.

"Thea." He breathed out quietly, closing his eyes, contentment on his face. He said her name like a promise. Never before had he wished to freeze time. In fact, as a boy, he had often wished the opposite – waiting for the day he could be with Thea. But as he stood with her in her arms in his face resting on hers, he wanted time to stop. Not only to cherish the moment – but also to put off what he assumed would be her telling him that the kiss had been a goodbye.

"Kol." She said, breaking the silence. *Here it comes,* he feared, *I will be alone again.* "I want to stay." She spoke, barely above a whisper.

"What?" His voice cracked, and he slowly dropped down to his knees, continuing to cradle her as he did so.

"I want to marry you. I want to stay." Truth. And all of it, her choice. "If we have time, I know we can figure everything else out."

His mouth hung open, and he looked as if he were searching for words. But when he found none, he simply just kissed her again. Softly this time, as slow and gentle as he could. They sat there on the floor together, his hands resting gently on her hips and his mouth on hers. Thea kept her hands resting on the back of his neck, sensing this kiss to be more emotional than physical. Only when his tongue grazed the bottom of her lips and then entered did the kiss turn passionate, and they both allowed their hands to roam. Though Kol wished to stay in that moment forever, the moment she chose him, he knew sooner or later someone would enter that hallway and part of protecting her was keeping scandalous rumors from being spread about her.

They never made it back to the meal, deciding instead to take a private lunch in Thea's room. They talked through all the rumors Thea had heard in court, and despite not asking for it, Kol apologized profusely for anything he had done that was causing her pain or embarrassment. Although she understood the Sway Kol's mother placed on him, she sometimes still couldn't believe the infatuation he had for her, but she was done questioning it. After that afternoon, she considered herself the luckiest woman in all the realms. All afternoon he peppered her with questions about herself, and in between conversations he would cover her in his hands and lips. She found it sinfully intoxicating, and felt as if her whole body would catch fire from the heat, but she couldn't get enough of his hands on her.

They eventually dragged themselves out of her quarters to attend dinner together, promising that they would go straight to bed together after, to read more of the book he had brought her the night before. They walked hand in hand, partly to work on Kol's plan to convince the court of his affections for her and partly because he couldn't bring himself to pry his hands away from her. Before they entered the room, he turned to her, "I don't want you to be caught off guard, but I will be punishing Lady Lavina tonight, during dinner."

"Punish? All she did was say words." Thea felt uneasy.

"She spoke careless, hurtful words to you. That is treason, and it will not go unpunished. Besides, if others know what she did, and know she got away with it, what will stop them from treating you the same way?" Thea shrugged. "This ends tonight." He drew his hand to her cheek and pulled her in for another kiss, and then sighed. "I will never grow tired of doing that."

She smiled. "I should hope not."

"If I do, feel free to plunge a dagger straight through my heart – because I clearly would have lost my mind and need put out of my misery." She giggled at his dramatics, following behind him as he strode into the dining hall.

She searched around the room, noting the surprised glances at their clasped hands. This made her stand taller. Kol noticed her swell in confidence and took it as an opportunity to show off. He pulled her close, kissing her in full view of all the court. Their lips met passionately, but briefly, earning awes and applause from around the room. When he pulled away, he noticed the blush that had grown on her defined cheekbones. "Kol!" She swatted his chest.

"Thea." He mocked her in a shrill voice.

"That isn't proper." She spoke quietly as she looked around, hand to her cheek.

"Everyone will know you're mine, and I'm yours. Modesty be damned." She blushed harder. "Now, let's take our seats."

Once seated, she noticed the empty seat beside Lavina's husband. "Lady Lavina isn't here."

"She will be." He raised a hand and waved toward his guards. Moments later, the doors opened, and Lady Lavina was dragged into the room. She wore the same wine-stained dress, though it was now also covered in dirt, and her usually gorgeous hair resembled a bird's nest. Her lip was busted, her eye bruised, and she could hardly hold herself upright.

Thea's eyes grew to the size of saucers. "What happened to her?" She whispered.

"Looks like she didn't fare so well in the dungeons, though I think she deserves worse."

Thea looked at him disbelievingly, "For hurting my feelings?"

"When it comes to protecting you, I'd do worse over less." Truth. A truth she didn't know how she felt about.

The guards pulled Lavina in front of their table, depositing her on the ground. Thea dared a glance at Lady Lavina's husband, who, despite the horrific state of his wife, looked unphased. Kol stood, the whole room falling silent to listen to him. "I'm sure rumors of Lady Lavina's behavior at the luncheon today have spread throughout court. She spoke maliciously toward my bride and spoke ill of me and our realm."

154

He paused for dramatic effect. "Which you all know…is treason." Hushed voices filtered throughout the room. "So now, I am announcing her punishment. No trial because, well, I don't feel like having one." He smirked callously and looked at her. "Anything you'd like to say?"

"I'm sorry." She choked out painfully.

Kol turned to Thea. "My love, would you join me?" Thea took his hand and stood, knees weak. Whether this was from his public displays of affection or the punishment happening before her eyes, she was unsure. "Now, is Lady Lavina telling the truth in her apology? Repeat it won't you?" He asked of her.

"I'm sorry." Truth.

"Yes, she is," Thea confirmed.

"As many of you know, Thea is as powerful as she is beautiful." She blushed again. "She can detect a lie, every time without fail. So it seems Lady Lavina is sorry… sorry for what, though?" He turned again toward Lavina. "Lady Lavina, what are you sorry for?"

"For hurting Lady Althea's feelings." Lie.

Kol looked toward Thea for confirmation. She shook her head no. He chuckled, "Lady Lavina, I knew you weren't bright, but only a fool would lie to a Veritas." He gestured to a guard, who on cue knocked Lady Lavina's legs out from under her. Her body made a sickening thump on the ground, all semblance of grace having left her. Thea gasped, and Kol pulled her closer, an act displaying a united front as well as an attempt to comfort her. "Try again."

"I'm sorry that all this has happened." Truth. Kol looked to Thea again, she nodded.

"Well, good enough, I suppose." He raised his arms and spoke loudly to the court, "You can't force sincerity." He

155

smirked and cocked his head to the side. "Now onto the fun part." He clapped his hands together, and a sadistic smile crept onto his face. "Everyone pay close attention – and know things will play out similarly for anyone else who disrespects my Thea." He walked around the table, crouching down in front of Lady Lavina. "Lavina, I am stripping you of your title, your land, your money, and the right to be in the Palace." She wailed in agony. "Cut the dramatics, and I will allow your husband to keep his, though…." Kol stood and faced her husband. "I also am graciously offering you the opportunity to annul your marriage from this wretched woman. Consider it and get back to me." He faced Lavina again, who was now a sobbing mass on the marble floor. "Be grateful. I could have had you beheaded." He turned on his heel and strode back toward his seat. Thea felt as if her brain was malfunctioning, having trouble negotiating the callous man before her and the angel who had washed her in praise and kisses only hours before. "Get her out of here." He sat beside Thea, gently kissed her cheek, and announced that dinner should be served. As if a woman had not just been stripped of her very life and dignity of his behest before them all.

They ate dinner as if nothing had happened, Thea conversing with Dorothy and Kol discussing the Strong realm with the noblemen beside him. At nearly all times, he had a hand on her. He felt that he had to be touching her always – to make sure this was all real. She used his touch as a grounding tool, keeping her mind from spiraling places she didn't want it to go. Kol was kind to her and protected her – that's all she was going to allow herself to remember right then.

When dinner was over, Kol and Thea stood, taking their time to exit as the rest of the court watched. As they walked, again hand in hand, she saw Lord Heltman leering to her left, sitting beside other noblemen. "I told you, look at the ass of our future queen. I'd bow down to that any day." She froze, because she knew if she could hear him, then so could Kol.

Kol released a breathy laughed, sounding both wicked and stunned. He released her hand and walked with purpose toward Lord Heltman. "What did I say about disrespecting my bride?" Quick as lightning, he picked up a dinner knife, still dripping in pig fat from carving their meal, and stabbed it through Lord Heltman's hand, pinning him to the table. His piercing screams echoed through the hall, and horror covered the faces of nearly everyone in the room. In shock, Hellman reached toward the knife. Kol spoke with authority, nearly motionless as he stood with his arms crossed over his chest, "Heltman, look at me." Lord Heltman's eyes glazed over as he stilled, looking at Kol as commanded. "I want you to grab that knife, twist it, and then slowly pull it out." *He's using his Control,* Thea thought as she watched in horrified fascination. She watched as Heltman did precisely as he was instructed – agony clear in his eyes as he did so. "Good. Now stab it in again." Thea jerked her head to Kol, shocked at his cruelty. A voice faded into her head, *Prince of Death.* She watched a calm, sadistic smile creep to her fiancé's lips. If he had ever done this before, it was no doubt his nickname was earned. Lord Heltman obeyed every command Kol gave him, screaming as he did so. "Shut your mouth." He clamped his lips closed, tears streaming down his face as muddled cries continued behind his sealed lips. "Again." She stood there, frozen in horror, as Kol instructed Lord Heltman to stab his own hand – over and over again. After many minutes Kol relented, "You can stop now." Lord Heltman threw the knife away from himself – as if that would stop Kol if he chose to use his Control again. "You will never speak about my bride that

157

way again. Are we understood?" Lord Heltman nodded, clutching his bloody hand to his chest. However, hand was a generous term, as it now resembled ground meat more than anything. "Get out of my sight." He stood and ran, a trail of blood following him as he did so. Kol picked up a wayward napkin, wiping off the blood that had splattered onto his hand. And again, as if nothing had happened, Kol walked to Thea, grabbed her hand, and bid the rest of the court goodnight. When they exited the dining hall, he ordered a servant to bring desserts to them in Thea's room; and she wondered how he could be thinking about cobbler after just stabbing and torturing another man. *Maybe it's so common that it doesn't even phase him,* she shivered at the thought. The walk to her room was silent, but as soon as the door closed, she pulled her hand from his. She paced back and forth, nervously rubbing her hands on her face.

Kol looked on in horror. "What's wrong?"

Now it was her turn to laugh humorlessly. "What's wrong? Are you serious?" She looked at his confused face, realizing she would have to spell it out for him. *Is he truly so desensitized to violence that he can't understand why she would be upset right now?* She exhaled and paused her pacing. "Kol, I just watched you strip a woman of all dignity and earthy possessions for making fun of me, and shortly after that, you stabbed someone and then made them torture themselves because they said something slightly inappropriate about my body."

"You're unhappy?" He said incredulously. "I am protecting you." He placed his hands in his head, something Thea interpreted as a position of shame. "This is the only way I know how." She sighed and joined him on the couch, placing her hand on his back and rubbing it in small circles. He leaned into her touch.

"I'm not angry at you, perse. I'm shocked and horrified at the violence. But I don't disagree that they needed to be punished; it's just that I don't feel the punishment fit the crime." She paused. "And honestly, it was a little scary to see you act in violence like that." She said quietly.

He snapped his head up, meeting her eyes with his. "I would never hurt you like that." Truth.

"I know, but I don't really like that you would hurt anyone like that." She admitted.

"I can agree that I acted out of protectiveness, and maybe it was over the top tonight. But being a king and a commander of armies requires acts of violence, especially in times of war. And it requires hard choices to be made at a moment's notice."

She nodded, "But our dining hall is not a war zone. And your court members, as rude as they may be, are not the enemy. You need them on your side, and if everyone is afraid of you, they won't be the happiest or the most helpful in their jobs here." She attempted to reason with him.

"This is one of the reasons I need you. You see the world differently than I do. You will help me be a better King." She looked into the eyes of a man who grew up with no friends and a harsh father. He was taught to solve all his problems with violence. But he was willing to change and admit when he messed up. She could work with that. "Forgive me." *I forgive him, he was protecting me. I forgive him, he was protecting me.* She repeated in her mind.

"Just no more rash punishments, okay?" He nodded. "No more stabbing people at the dinner table." Despite the horror of that sentence, she laughed.

"I will do my best." He matched her laughter and then leaned in and kissed her. "My sweet creature." He kissed the tip of her nose.

"My sadistic Prince." She teased, kissing the tip of his nose back.

"Now, that I like. Call me that again." He flirted, nipping at her lips as he did so. "Slap me a little this time as you say it, though."

"That's masochistic, you freak." She said with a laugh.

"Thea!" He faked shock and placed a hand to his chest. "Your mind must be dirty and corrupt. Who taught you such a thing?" He said in fake annoyance. "And know if you say a man's name, I will have to hunt him down and end him in a fit of jealous rage." She looked at him pointedly. "After a fair trial and much deliberation, as promised." He smiled sheepishly.

She rolled her eyes and suppressed a smile. "It's not what you're thinking. I've just read about it, in one of my lascivious books you so mercilessly mocked before."

He gave her an embellished sigh of relief, "So no real-life experience?"

"No, none to speak of." She confirmed.

"Maybe we could change that." The tone of his voice dropped, devoid of all jest. A lump formed in her throat, and she again felt as if her whole body was blushing. "Thea, earlier today, when you said thinking about me being with other women made you feel self-conscious, I want you to know that it's unnecessary. Those other women are erased from my mind. I don't even think about them, ever." Truth. "You are the most beautiful women I have ever seen, and I cannot wait to see more of you." He said all this with his voice as deep and sultry as ever. Before she could respond, a knock sounded at the door, saving

160

her. He sighed, dropping his head as he did so. Clearly, he was not thrilled with the interruption. "I'll get that." He whispered, voice still seductive, before he sauntered toward the door and greeted the servant. "Dessert is here."

She cleared her throat, which was now dry. "Great."

"Should we eat this in bed, or is that too risky?" He asked. She knew he meant because they could make a mess, but given their previous conversation, her mind was drifting toward other kinds of risks. The kind of risks that had kept her from being alone with men her whole life. The previous conversation notwithstanding, she was desperate for a replay of their previous night, so despite her better judgment she said, "The bed is fine."

They both were able to change into more comfortable clothing at some point during the night, Thea changed in her dressing room, and Kol had a servant bring him his clothes from his room. They lounged in the room all night, eating cobbler in bed, and playing cards on the floor by the fireplace – they even went outside to look for shooting stars at one point. The whole time they settled into the comfort of one another's presence, conversation shifting from flirtatious to serious and back again with ease. Thea started to think of it as their love bubble. Everything was perfect in the Palace, when it was just the two of them in her room. Toward the end of the night, they settled into her bed again, his arm around her and her head on his chest. He read to her, his deep, sultry voice lulling her into peace again. He would stop periodically, sometimes to kiss her and other times to discuss a point in the novel. And eventually, he placed the book down, blew out all the candles in the room, and pulled her close to him to fall asleep. As Thea lay there, waiting for sleep to take her, she thought through all the turns the day had taken. While she wasn't pleased with Kol's violent tendencies, he seemed genuinely open to hearing her perspective on things. But most importantly, he had given her a choice. And for that reason alone, he had earned the benefit of the doubt. She would give him slack, maybe more than he deserved, because even though she didn't acknowledge it yet – she was blinded by love.

Chapter 8

Thea awoke and attempted to stretch her limbs but found it difficult, as she was still tangled around Kol. She yawned and despite her best efforts not to, her stirring woke Kol.

"Good morning, darling." He murmured in his husky morning voice. He pulled her tight to him, her back against his front, and nuzzled his scruffy chin into her neck.

She giggled in reply, "That tickles!" She attempted to squirm away from his touch.

"Apologies, how about this?" He placed her earlobe gently between his teeth and pulled, causing a shiver to run down her spine. "Does that tickle too?" He whispered, hot breath coaxing shiver bumps down her neck.

"No." Was all she could muster out, her mouth dry.

He kissed her, right below the ear. "What about this touch? Do you like this touch?"

After a lifetime of being held at arm's length by everyone, she responded without even thinking. "I like all of your touches."

"All of them?" He asked coyly. She simply nodded in response. "Here?" He trailed a path of lazy circles on her hip. She nodded again. "And here?" He ran his hand slowly from her hip, over the top of her leg, and down the inner part of her thigh.

She swallowed the sudden knot in her throat. Again, she nodded. "Tell me you like it." He asked her gently.

"I like it." She replied confidently.

"Like what?" He demanded.

"I like it when you touch me." She said quietly, giving in to his command while blushing furiously.

"Good girl." She shivered under his praise. "What about here?" He gently ran a finger on the underside of her breast.

"Mhmm." She squeaked out, remembering the first time he had touched her there, by accident on her balcony. He had still been careful around her then, but quickly all pretense between them was being washed away.

"And this?" He flicked his pointer finger, which collided sharply with her nipple. She gasped at the sensation it sent down her body, and fire flooded her cheeks. "I'll take that as a yes." He chuckled gruffly, voice still raspy and seductive even in merriment, enjoying every moment of making her feel scandalized. *Look at how I effect her.*

The door to her bedroom burst open; Kol growled in irritation at the sudden interruption. He looked defiantly into the eyes of the intruder, his hands refusing to leave Thea's body.

Dorothy stood in the doorway shocked, but defiance also glistened in her eyes. "What do you want?" Kol spat out, and Thea sat in shock at his tactless greeting toward her friend.

"I am just here for our morning tea and meeting. Apologies, Your Highness." Dorothy responded with little respect in her voice.

"Dorothy, I'll be out in a few minutes. Just give us some privacy, please." Thea asked respectfully of her friend. Dorothy responded with a curt nod before closing the door and leaving.

"I'm sick of these incessant interruptions. After the wedding, I'm whisking you away, somewhere remote where we won't be bothered for days." He leaned in to kiss her neck, but Thea pulled away. "What? Do you not like that idea?" Surprise covered his features.

"No, the idea is fine. It's just…." She paused, unsure how to continue.

"What?" He asked, voice gentle as could be.

"I don't like how you talked to Dorothy."

"She barged into your room, unannounced, and she is below our station. That is not allowed. I could punish her worse than just giving her a stern talking to." He spoke so casually about this.

"She is my friend."

"I don't understand what that has to do with this." He remarked, and she understood that the concept of friendship was lost on him.

"Kol, she came here with me and left her whole life so I wouldn't have to come here alone. She is a kind person who has always treated me normal, even when no one else did." His eyes softened; she knew he could relate to that. "Not to mention she is with me all day when you're off doing who knows what."

"I am serving and working to better the Empire. For our future." He said defensively.

"I'm not criticizing you. I'm just saying that she is there for me, has been for years. She is my only friend, and I don't want you to disrespect her." In the back of her mind, Thea feared standing up to him. But she hoped that his constant preaching of being equals was true in practice, and here was his chance to prove it.

"As you wish." He stated matter-of-factly.

"Thank you." She released the breath she had been unknowingly holding.

He leaned in again to kiss her, pausing teasingly as if he expected her to pull away again. To his delight, she did the opposite, leaning into him as his smooth lips pushed against her. "I'll leave you ladies to your tea and planning then." The smile that followed devastated her, his features never failing to take her breath away.

He extracted himself from her bed with ease and padded his way toward the door. He pulled it open, wide enough that Thea could see Dorothy sitting across the room on a chaise. Thea watched as he walked toward Dorothy and began to speak. "I apologize for my terseness. I was surprised by your entrance, I am just very protective of my time with Thea." Dorothy snapped her head up in surprise the second he started his apology. "It won't happen again, I know how important you are to Thea, and I want you to feel at ease to make your home here. Forgive me?"

She stuttered in surprise, an uncommon occurrence for Dorothy. "Of course, Your Highness."

"Thank you for the grace. And please, call me Kol." He turned to Thea, still sitting in her bed with a surprised expression on her face, and then he bowed to her – that persistent mischievous glint clear in his eyes even from far away. And then, with that, he gracefully exited the room.

As soon as the door clicked closed Dorothy raced to Thea's room. "What the hells was that?" Dorothy exclaimed.

"What do you mean? He apologized because he was rude. That's a normal thing to do." Thea tried to play it off, but even she was surprised that he respected her enough to humble himself like that.

"Yes, it is normal, but not for a prince. Let alone one who has a malignant streak running through him." Dorothy added.

"Malignant streak?" Thea questioned defensively.

"Don't play that game with me. You know what I mean. We were both in that dining hall last night. I saw your face when he doled out his punishments. Remember? The fates of Lady Lavina and Lord Heltman, *the Prince of Death's* most recent victims." Dorothy put air quotes around his less than loving nickname.

"Don't call him that." Thea said quietly. "And he didn't kill anyone." Thea defended again, addressing her use of his nickname.

"If that's the best defense you have, I'll be the first to tell you that it isn't a good one." Dorothy crossed her arms defiantly.

"He was protecting me." Thea defended him.

"I don't believe you're fine with how everything played out last night."

"I'm not, but Kol and I had a talk about it, and he promised it wouldn't happen again. He assured me that we would talk about these things before just acting out of emotion." Thea stated with confidence.

"And you used your Control?" Dorothy asked wearily.

"Yes, and it rang true," Thea replied, annoyance clear in her voice. Not even Dorothy trusted her judgment. "Plus, he already listened to me today when I scolded him for being rude to you. I didn't even ask him to apologize. That was all him."

Dorothy stood for a moment considering everything Thea was saying, and she found herself lacking a response. She only hoped everything that was being said was true. She trusted her friend's Control, but she also knew that love can blind you.

She decided to change the subject. "So that happened," Dorothy remarked, gesturing toward the bed, disapproval in her voice.

"Don't act so surprised. You saw him in here just the other night." Thea blushed as she said this. Her sweet, innocent friend. *Is he going to corrupt her?* Dorothy wondered.

"That was before the events of last night. You let the hands that stabbed a man fondle your breasts, like twelve hours after the said stabbing occurred." She said disbelievingly. "Mind you, all Lord Heltman thought was that you have a hot arse, and if that's a crime to think, then we all are in trouble because you do," Dorothy added jokingly, trying to lighten the mood. It failed.

"We already discussed this," Thea said sternly, surprising Dorothy. "And Lord Heltman didn't just think it. He actively disrespected me, twice in one night, in front of my court. Don't pretend that what he said wouldn't have bothered you."

Dorothy exhaled loudly and ran her hands over her face. "I just want you to be smart about all this." Dorothy knew Thea, she knew how desperate for love and connection she was. And while Kol seemingly lived up to his devotion to her, he also lived up to his reported cruelty. "I don't want you to get hurt."

"Dorothy, I appreciate it. I do. But I'm not worried anymore. He has proven himself devoted and has treated me as his equal, as he said he would. He defended my honor twice last night, albeit not with the best tact, but we will work on it. The point is, his actions speak for themselves." Thea sighed as if she was remembering him lovingly in that very moment and trying not to swoon. "And if I'm not worried, then you don't need to be either."

As if on cue, a servant announced himself, interrupting their conversation. "Lady Althea, a gift from Prince Kol." Much to Dorothy's chagrin, Thea audibly squealed in excitement as a large box was carried into the room.

"See? Isn't he wonderful?" Thea asked with a childish twirl.

Dorothy didn't want to fight with her – because she knew she couldn't change her mind even if she wanted to. "All right, well…let us get on with the day then." She forced a smile and pushed her friend into the daily tasks, never forgetting the underlying hesitation toward Kol that lingered in the back of her mind. She could still see the horror on Lord Heltman's face as he stabbed himself over and over again; she could still hear the shrill scream of Lady Lavina when Kol took her whole life away from her; but what Dorothy remembered the most was the smirk of satisfaction on Kol's face as he did it all.

Dorothy paced in front of the fireplace in her bedroom, chewing her bottom lip as she did so. She was deep in thought, considering her earlier encounters with both Kol and Thea.

"You're going to burn a hole through the floor if you're not careful." Duke Martin teased from his seat across from her. She fixed him with a withering stare.

"I'm worried about my friend, and I don't know what to think of the Prince. He seems to be good to Thea, but I just don't know about him." She said as if it were so obvious.

"Oh, by all means then continue pacing, I've fixed many a problem by walking them out." He tried to use the sarcasm she was so fond of to calm her down, but it was not working.

"Well, what else am I to do?" She threw her hands up in frustration.

"You're going to put wrinkles all over that gorgeous face with that worried little pout. Come sit down, please." He patted the empty seat beside him. Dorothy blew a long breath out, dramatically puffing her cheeks in the process, but then joined him on the couch.

"Happy?" She asked, twisting her hands nervously in her lap.

"Ecstatic." Warm hands engulfed her own and helped to steady her nerves. "Tell me what's plaguing your mind." Earnest eyes found hers, holding her gaze with rapt attention.

"I don't know where to start." Her eyes rolled to the side and she shrugged one of her shoulders up. Dorothy had known Martin only a short time, but he was easily her favorite person in the Palace. He was trustworthy, respectful, and considerate. She knew he would happily listen to her talk about all of her problems or worries – but she was hesitant to burden him. She much preferred their joking banter or strolls through the garden to serious conversations.

"I truly want to hear this, perhaps I can help." He encouraged her to continue.

"I'm just worried for Thea." She admitted.

"Okay, what are you worried about?"

"The Prince is going around stabbing people and stealing people's titles from them and he yelled at me too!" Dorothy rambled quickly.

Martin straightened his posture, and a serious look covered his face. "He yelled at you?" Dorothy got a slight thrill out of the protectiveness in his voice.

"He apologized, said he was being overprotective of his time with Thea and that he wanted me to be happy at the Palace. He even told me to call him Kol." She didn't know why she was defending Kol, other than not wanting Martin to have to pay a high price if he were to try to defend her honor against the Prince.

"Well, good then." He said quietly. "So, you're afraid for Thea because of how impulsive Kol has acted?"

She laughed, "Impulsive? Me eating one too many pieces of cake is impulsive or kissing you up against a tree in the garden out in the wide open is impulsive," Martin's cheeks flushed thinking of that kiss. Dorothy continued, "What he does is more than impulsive, it's deranged."

"Have you talked to Thea about this?"

"Yes. We talked about it today."

"And?"

"And she feels everything is fine." Dorothy said, aggravation clear in her voice.

"She was fine with everything that happened?" Martin asked to clarify.

"Well, no. She said that he said that he would work on it and consult her in the future before he reacts out of anger or punishes people."

"That seems promising."

"I guess. She said that she used her Control and everything he says is true. That he will consult her and treat her like an equal and that he'll keep her safe. She trusts him." Dorothy considered her next words. "I guess I'm not afraid of him hurting her or anything, he does seem to care for her deeply. I don't know what I'm feeling I guess."

"Does she love him?" Martin asked.

"If she doesn't now, I think she will soon." Dorothy admitted.

"Has she been in love before?" He asked, Dorothy shook her head no. "She's likely all in with him then. It'd be hard to not fall under the spell of becoming a princess, especially when the Prince is showering her with praise and presents." Dorothy nodded in agreement. "Those do seem like good promises he's made her though. Maybe he'll change."

"Maybe, but its more than that. He is so handsy and sexual with her, it's so unlike her to be okay with that. She's changing too, I can see it." Dorothy saw in Thea what no one else was willing to admit. Everyone craves love, but Thea was a woman who was all consumed with the desire to be loved. And she might even be willing to do just about anything to get it.

"Change can be a good thing." Martin offered.

"He may be able to change his actions, but he can't change his heart. I saw his eyes when he did those things to Heltman and Lavina and, honestly, now I'm starting to not be so angry at what those Dissenters did to us. I've been here less than a month and I'm fed up with the tyranny I see."

Martin nodded thoughtfully, taking in everything she was saying. Dorothy hoped she hadn't overstepped by admitting she wasn't happy with the ruling in the Mori Empire. As a Duke, Martin was technically loyal to the throne – but if what she said offended him, he didn't show it. "Do you think she is safe then?"

"Yes, I guess so."

"Then you have to trust her judgement, she is an adult after all. She's allowed to make her own choices. We will just have to see what happens." Dorothy nodded. "Perhaps you can talk to Ruth more, she knows far more than people give her credit for. About Thea and the Dissenters. Maybe she can give you some comfort."

"Yes, that's a good idea." She nestled herself under his arm, scooting as close to him as possible. "Thank you, I'm happy to have met you." She admitted quietly, vulnerability not easy for her.

Warm lips pressed a gentle kiss to the top of her head. "Of course, and I'm happy to have met you too." He said with a smile.

Chapter 9

"We should just put this all on pause until after the winter. Let the soldiers go home and spend the holidays with their families, regain their strength, and then we can re-evaluate conquering the Strong realm in the Spring." General James, of the Mori military, said after much consideration. His men had not been home for months, many were injured and emaciated, and he felt he needed to speak for them. Powerful men sat around a map of the Continent, plotting its conquest. Kol, High King Kairo, several Generals, and the king's council all sat, brows furrowed, considering what this man said.

High King Kairo looked to Kol, urging him to answer. He had been allowing Kol's input more and more on matters regarding the Empire – knowing his time to rule would come to an end sooner than later. He was many things – a tyrant, a bully, a horrible husband, and an even worse father, but he wasn't stupid. Though that doesn't mean he was altogether supportive or kind during this learning curve.

"What will it say of our legacy if we allow the territory closest to us to time and time again defy our rule?" Kol asked.

"What will it say of *your* legacy if you make a foolish decision to continue a battle through the winter that results in the loss of your forces and continual defeat?" Kairo looked at him sternly, openly trying to embarrass him. "This isn't a time for flowery conversations about legacies. It's a time for realistic suggestions and strategy, Kol!" His tone was barking and belittling. "The Strongs have proven time and again that while their numbers are fewer than ours, their physical size and brute strength are nearly insurmountable. One of their men can easily take on a dozen of ours."

"And what will you do anyway, Kol, lead the men into battle yourself?" A nobleman asked mockingly.

Kol drew the dagger he carried on his hip and held it to the man's throat. "You know I'm well capable of that." He pushed the blade in softly, drawing a trail of blood from his throat and a gasp from his lips. "While you were sitting on your ass, manicuring your nails, I have been training every day since I was a boy, some of the time with the very Generals in this room." He pulled the knife back and then shoved the man to the ground. "And it's Your Royal Highness Kol. Or Prince Kol. Do not forget who I am or what I am capable of."

"Enough, Kol." His father said with no edge to his voice, as he entirely approved of violent behavior from his son, for he believed it would keep his Empire going long after he was gone.

A bell tolled in the distance, notifying the men that it was midday. "We will reconvene after the midday meal; I expect suggestions on how to move forward." He looked toward General James. "And not about giving up." He spat out.

"Your Highness, I wasn't suggesting we give up, only that we-"

Kol raised his hand, "Silence." He used his Control, and General James' mouth physically clamped shut against his will. "Kneel." His knees made a sickening thud against the marble floor, a sound all too common in the Palace – for more than one reason. Many I men were known for more than an appetite for

175

violence, and there was a reason lady's maids made themselves scarce when Kairo entered a room. "Do I make myself clear on the position this council has on giving up?"

"Yes." He replied between gritted teeth, old and war-torn knees aching from the harsh contact with the floor.

"Yes, what?" Kol smiled wickedly.

"Yes, Your Royal Highness." His voice cracked, his pain evident to all in the room.

Kol released him from his Control and turned to face the rest of the room. "Everyone understand?" He asked with an unhinged smile on his face. All the men in the room mumbled their agreements and nodded. "Good!" He clapped his hands together and turned back to General James, pulling an insincere look of sympathy onto his face. "James, my dear man, get up. No need to prostrate yourself in front of me." He helped the General to his feet and patted him on the back.

Kol walked toward the dining hall, having again agreed to join Thea for the meal this afternoon. He greeted her as always, a smile on his face, and even kissed her. He was pleased to be with her, he always was, but that day he found himself very distracted. He was concerned over the issues surrounding the Strong realm and the decades of effort that had not made much effort in denting their fortress or their power.

Thea was telling him about some wedding plan or another, but his mind was in strategy mode. He considered several attack options as he sipped soup absentmindedly. Catapult fires into their fortress, blast the doors to the hold open with a battering ram, or sneak men in through a yet to be discovered secret entrance – but all had flaws, and he knew it, and he couldn't risk looking like a fool in front of his father again. He had long ago learned the punishment for that, he had the scars to prove it, and he didn't feel like facing that ever again.

"Kol, are you listening to anything I am saying?" Thea asked, annoyance clear in her voice.

He had been caught not listening, and he felt terrible for making her feel sidelined. Gentle hands wrapped around hers, and she sensed genuine regret in Kol's eyes. "I am sorry, I am just so distracted."

"By?"

"I don't think you want to hear about politics or war efforts." He dismissed with a wave of his hand. "Please, just tell me more about the wedding plans. It is quickly approaching, and I want to be all filled in."

"If we are to be equals, I should bear the burdens of the Empire as much as you do. Plus-" she brushed a wayward curl off from his forehead and lovingly rested her hand on his cheek. "What upsets you, upsets me. Please tell me."

He sighed, so happy to finally have someone who cares enough about him to help shoulder his burdens. He told her everything, all the past attempts to infiltrate the Strong's realm in the last decade and some of the ideas he had been toying with over the last hour. "Their Control is just too strong."

She giggled, surprising him. He heard his father's voice in the back of his head, *This is no laughing matter,* but he would never speak to her that way. "Men are always so ready to go in with a battering ram, but they forget that the lack of subtly associated with it gives their opponent time to prepare, thus reducing their chances of success."

"What would you suggest then?" He asked – a smirk on his lips. He loved watching her confidently speak on matters of war and the kingdom like a natural – as if she had been doing it her whole life.

"Can I tell you something about myself? Something you likely don't know." She asked, already planning her next sentence in her head as he responded.

"I hope never to stop learning about you, my darling." He replied with a moony look in his eyes.

"I love herbology. I have studied it my whole life under various teachers, Healers, and cooks. I've learned about the healing properties of some and the flavors of others."

"As I said, I love learning about you, but I don't see the relevance." He wasn't often confused, but he was now.

"Patience Kol." She teased. "Have you ever heard of *Herba Hebeto*?" He shook his head no. "It is also called 'the plant of weakening.'" He nodded, encouraging her to continue. "Now we mostly use it to decorate, as it has a pleasant smell and beautiful blue hue. But some believe that ingesting it will temporarily weaken those Blessed with Control. Specifically, that it will make their powers simply not work until it has worked its way through their system."

He stared at her, in shock, mouth open. "You clever girl. How have I never heard of such a thing?" He asked, still in disbelief that a solution so simple could exist.

"They do say that poison is a woman's weapon. And you are a man." She shrugged, pleased with herself. She hoped that this was the first of many collaborative efforts she and Kol would work on the better the Empire. *Our Empire,* she thought with satisfaction.

"And if it does work, how would we get them all to ingest it at the same time?" Despite the thrill of this solution, he still didn't know how to execute that plan.

"I'm sure it would be easy to disguise someone as a cook in the enemy camp. Cook it into their soup." She mimed sprinkling and stirring, causing Kol to laugh.

"You're an adorable genius." He kissed her and stood up. "We have to find out if this works. Where do you think I could get some?"

"A gardener, probably." She shrugged. Kol caught her by surprise and kissed her once more before rushing off excitedly. He searched for a servant who could potentially locate these things for him: the herb itself, a cook to make soup to put it in, and a criminal being held in the dungeon with Control – all to be brought to an interrogation room.

"What was that all about?" Dorothy asked, noting a previously sullen Kol now nearly bouncy with glee.

"I helped him," Thea replied simply, a pleased smile on her face.

Several hours passed as Kol worked to test Thea's theory. He was able to get a groundskeeper to pick the flowers off one *Herba Hebeto* plant and take them to the kitchen, where a cook shredded it atop a stew. They then pulled a man into an interrogation room, a dingy stone room deep below the Palace.

He devoured the stew and then was left to sit – chained to the interrogation chair for several hours. Kol didn't know how long it would take the herb to kick in, or if it would work at all, but he assumed a few hours would be the minimum. The test subject was recently convicted of using animals to steal from local merchants. One such merchant had turned up dead after such an encounter. After a dog had helped this man steal, he released it from his Control, and the unfortunate merchant found the animal to be feral and ill-tempered. It ripped his throat out in minutes.

179

As fantastical as that story sounds, and though it was the dog who did the killing – the man was still partially at fault for the man's death. This prisoner had the Control of Fauna, which was the ability to bend the will of animals to whatever he wanted. He could make a dog walk on its back legs, a squirrel steal coins from a merchant's pocket, or even stop a bear from mauling someone mid-attack.

After several hours of impatient waiting, Kol barged into the interrogation room, startling the man in the chair.

"Why am I here?" He asked, not knowing what they could want with a thief after he had already been sentenced.

"You're here to help me with a little problem I am having," Kol answered.

"A little problem?" The man eyed Kol with a cheeky expression. "Takes a big man to acknowledge that, and an even bigger one to admit it. Not pleasing the misses, aye?"

Kol chuckled, darkness hidden under what is usually a happy action. "Choose your next words carefully."

"How can I help you with a problem?" The man asked, amusement clear in his voice.

Kol chuckled at the man's annoying arrogance. "You will see." He turned to the door. "Bring in the beast!" He yelled out. Moments later, a large black cougar was brought into the room. His long claws clicked on the floor and his lithe body slinked back and forth as far as the harness would allow him to go. He growled, low in his throat through a makeshift muzzle that was keeping his mouth clamped shut. The guards in the room jumped back each time the beast neared them, but the man in the chair sat, unamused and unafraid at the creature in front of him. Animals were the one thing he could always command in this world, so he felt he had nothing to fear.

"What do you want me to do? Prove I can Control it?" He snorted, thinking this was all a waste of his time.

Kol smirked, "The opposite, actually. I'm hoping you prove to me that you can't."

"That I can't?" The man scoffed.

"Mhmm." Kol nodded, a menacing smile still painted on his face.

"You do know why I'm locked up in here in the first place, right? I could turn this cougar on you now and kill you all if I wanted. Smirk at me one more time, and you'll find out too." He threatened. Kol liked this game, partly because his cocky opponent didn't even know the rules.

"Well, I've added an additional variable this time around." Kol strutted around the room confidently.

"What the hells does that mean? Because I'm tied up? I can still Control their minds from here." He stated obviously, his aggravation was getting more and more evident by the moment.

"Do you value your life?" Kol asked simply.

"Of course, I do?" The man retorted back.

"No desire to harm yourself or end it all?" Kol clarified.

"What the hells is wrong with you?"

"Watch it." Kol scolded back, temporarily putting him under his Control to straighten the man's back and seal his lips. "Answer my question."

The man sighed before answering. "No, I don't want to hurt myself. I'm getting out of here in a few months and I'll get to go home to my family. Why would I want to hurt myself?"

"Just making sure." Kol walked out of the room, gesturing for his guards to follow, leaving the man in the room alone with the beast. "Release the animal's restraints and exit the room." He told the guard who was holding the cougar's leash.

The man sat, a confused look on his face. Completely unaware of what was happening or why he was there. When the final guard exited the room, they shut and locked the door. The door was floor-to-ceiling bars, exactly like the doors on the jail cells several floors down. Kol stood directly in front of the man on the other side of the bars, no more than three feet from him.

"When was the beast last fed?" Kol asked the man beside him.

"Owner said last week, he has been low on funds and couldn't buy extra meat." The guard replied.

Kol grinned mischievously and tilted his head to the side. "Perfect." He turned his full attention back toward the cage and watched as the man sat unafraid, as the cougar prowled in a slow circle around him. Seconds ticked by painfully slow as the cougar did nothing but pace around. Kol clenched and released his fists repeatedly in irritation. "Come on." He whispered under his breath. As they all stood there in silence, breath bated, they started to hear a slow drip from somewhere in the cell. From hours of sitting with his wrists chained, the man had rubbed them raw and reopened a cut on his arm – which was now slowly dripping blood. The cougar was the first to notice, and he stalked slowly toward the puddle of red liquid on the floor, standing behind the man, and tentatively lapped at it with his tongue. This ignited his hunger, and he started licking the man's arm next.

"Stop!" The man demanded calmly, but when nothing happened, panic filled his eyes. "Stop!" He yelled this time.

Kol looked on in wonder. *Is it working?*

The cougar dug his teeth into the fleshy part of the man's arm and yanked, pulling a sizable chunk of flesh off. The man screamed, whether in terror or agony, no one knew.

"Get him off! Get me out! Please!" He begged.

"Should we stop it, Your Highness?" A guard asked, concern in his voice.

"No. I want to see what will happen." *I have to know this works,* he thought.

"May the Blessed burn you for this!" The man cursed as another piece of flesh was pulled from his arm. The sickening sound of dripping blood and snapping tendons could be heard by all the men watching. One guard turned pale-white, while another fought to swallow down the vomit that had crawled up his throat. The man continued to scream and beg for his life. Kol was unfazed, mind focused on one thing. *Will this herb be my deliverance?*

The cougar jumped up and placed his large paws on the man's shoulders, claws out. And as entirely predictable for his species, he opened his mouth, baring his long teeth to his audience, and then moved to clamped down around the man's throat.

"Stop!" The man yelled, a vein protruding from his forehead from sheer force and exertion. The beast froze. "Get away from me." The man ordered, tears streaming down his pale, sweaty face. The cougar obediently walked to the farthest corner of the room and sat down. "You-" He took a labored breath. "You will not hurt me again." The beast licked his lips but did not move to harm the man again. Tear-soaked eyes bore into Kol's, "What did you do to me?" He asked before passing out.

Kol had seen enough, and he felt almost giddy. He knew there were still kinks to work out and experiments to run, but that didn't stop his mind from racing as he thought of all the possibilities this herb had given him. *All thanks to my beautiful, brilliant bride,* he thought as he walked down the corridor toward the exit. *I must thank her.*

Kol walked briskly toward Thea's apartments, excited to tell her the good news. He had been told by staff that she was there having afternoon tea with Dorothy. He opened the door quietly, not wanting to interrupt, and found she was standing with her back to him, talking to Dorothy. Dorothy stared at him, eyes wide, as he snuck up behind Thea and quickly wrapped his arms around her waist. A gasp of surprise from her escaped her lips when he pulled her into him.

"You're a genius." He said in her ear before lovingly kissing her on the neck.

"Kol!" She swatted his arm. "You startled me!" She exclaimed with a giggle.

He spun her around to face him and placed his hands on either side of her face. "It worked!" He kissed her. "The herbs worked!"

"Kol, that's wonderful! What does this mean?" Thea asked.

"I don't know exactly and there is still much to figure out, but I think it means we can safely invade the Strong realm. Well, as safe as any invasion is, But they will be without their Blessed strength! We will win!" He kissed her again, high on excitement. She was also high, high on hope. Everything she had been hoping for was coming true. He cared for her, and he was letting her help in matters of the Empire.

"Not that I love the idea of war, but I'm so pleased I could help." She leaned back and placed a hand on his chest. *Damp,* she thought after placing a hand on him. She looked down to find both her hand and dress sprinkled in red. *Blood.* She looked at Kol and found that his whole front side was covered in the same red splatters. "Kol! You're bleeding!" She exclaimed. "Get towels and a physician!" She called to a lady's maid.

184

"Not necessary." He said, waving his hand to stop the maid.

Dorothy and Thea gave one another a concerned look. "Kol, if you're injured, you need to be looked at and helped." Thea insisted.

"Darling, don't worry. It's not my blood. I'm fine." Kol replied casually. Thea's face shifted quickly from concern to horror.

"Who's blood is it?" Thea asked, and that persistent voice in the back of her mind whispered, *Prince of Death.*

"Just a prisoner from the dungeons. It's not a big deal." Kol attempted to explain it away, but the look on her face told him that it might not be an easy conversation to just dismiss.

"What happened?" She asked sternly. Everyone else in the room exited, sensing a battle brewing, and left them there alone.

"The man we were testing out the herbs on ended up getting injured in the process, and a little blood must have sprayed on me," Kol answered. Again, his voice was utterly casual, inciting Thea's horror of the situation even more.

"Is he alive?" Thea asked, horrified. At her tone, Kol was immediately pulled back in time. His mind flashed vividly with memories of the first time someone asked him that.

"Is he alive?" Kol's mother asked, with terror in her voice.

Kol stood in front of her, dagger in hand, staring down at the crumpled mass of a man on the floor. Crimson blood dripped from the dagger and decorated his face and clothes in splatters.

"He stole from you, mama." His prepubescent voice replied.

"What?" She asked in shock. She knelt down and felt the man's punctured chest for a pulse.

185

Nothing. He was gone. She began to cry. He can't be a monster, not like his father, please! She begged silently to God.

"Don't cry, mama. I got your necklace back." He raised his arm and opened his hand, the one not clutching the bloody dagger, and a light blue gemstone on a long chain dangled down – swinging slowly back and forth.

"Darling boy, I'm not crying for my necklace. I'm crying for this man's life." She tried to reason with him, get him to see the error of his ways.

"But he did a bad thing. He stole from you, mama. I watched him do it. And father told me that we must punish people when they do wrong. That's what a king does." He explained it to her slowly, thinking she must be confused.

"Not every crime is punished with death. And that punishment is not to be doled out by a child."

"I'm not a child. I'm a prince!" He cried. Tears started to well in his eyes, and he didn't understand why his mother was so upset with him.

"Kol, come here." She opened her arms to him, and he leaned into her – finally dropping the bloody dagger, which clattered loudly when it encountered the marble floor. "It'll be okay. We just can't do this again." She started to use her Sway on him to help him understand the value of human life and the role of a ruler to be just – but his father stormed into the room.

"What is the meaning of this?" He yelled.

Kol rubbed his bloody knuckles under his eyes, pushing away the tears and streaking blood across his face, making him look nearly feral. "I killed him because he stole mama's necklace," Kol said, shame in his voice now.

His father considered the situation, before nodding in approval. "Good job. Prick doesn't deserve life if he would steal from the crown." He turned on his feet and left the room. "Clean this up!" He yelled to a servant.

Kol smiled – because he had made his father proud. Such moments were few and far between. But when he looked at his mother, he could see the fear and disappointment behind her forced smile.

"Kol?" Thea said, concern in her voice. "Kol? Are you okay?" She waved a hand in front of his face. He blinked a few times, settling back into the present moment after his reverie.

"Yes. Yes, I'm fine." He replied. He walked, still slightly dazed, toward a couch and sat down.

"So, a man is dead?" Thea asked diplomatically, trying a different approach.

"No." Truth. Thea blew a steadying breath out.

"What happened?"

"We were testing the theory out – to make sure the herbs would stop a Control." Thea nodded, encouraging him to continue. "And the only person in the dungeon with a Control was a man with the Control of Fauna. So, we gave him the herb, and waited, and then put him in a cell with an animal."

"And then?"

"And then it attacked him."

"You didn't try to stop it?" Thea asked, trying to keep the judgmental tone out of her voice.

"How am I to stop a cougar, Thea?" He asked dubiously.

"A cougar?"

"It had to be life or death because I had to be sure it worked! We have already lost too many men in the battles against the Strongs, and I can't lose more! I don't want that on my conscience. I'd rather the life of one convicted murderer and thief be forfeited than the lives of hundreds of innocent soldiers because I was too careless to test out this theory thoroughly." He spoke with conviction, and what Thea saw before her was a man who cared for his people and desperately wanted to make good choices for the whole Empire. She felt the means didn't justify the ends, but she also knew he was open to trying new ways of handling things. All she had to do was suggest it.

"It's just… human life is valuable," Thea said. *My mother would have loved you*, he thought. "I know with this situation there won't exactly be a next time, but next time a life-or-death decision comes up, will you discuss it with me? Please? Perhaps there would have been a better way to test this."

"Like what?" Kol asked, genuinely curious.

"Maybe…maybe you could have offered him his freedom if he could make a dog do a particular trick or something. Do you think he would have passed up the opportunity if given the chance? He would have tried and tried, desperate for freedom, and if it didn't work then you would have known."

"No, you're right. I'm sure he wouldn't have." Kol remembered the man saying how ready he was to leave. "I will consult with you next time. I promise." Truth. Thea wasn't pleased with his actions, impulsive and violent as they were, but she saw his willingness to respect her and change. *I won't give up on him. He is changing*, she told herself.

"Go get cleaned up. We will have dinner soon." She told him.

"I think I'll eat in my room tonight. I need time to plan my proposal of attack before the next council meeting," Kol said. And it was the truth, he knew better than to lie to a Veritas, but it was a half-truth. He was also struggling to be in her presence or look her in the eyes after seeing the horror in them only moments before. *For a moment, she was afraid of me*, he thought, and he hated it. "Have a good evening." He kissed her on the cheek and left without saying another word.

Thea couldn't help but feel something was off about Kol as he left. She assumed it was the pressure of carrying the weight of the Empire on his shoulders, and she decided to just wait patiently for the next time they could be alone together to discuss it. What she didn't know then is that their nightly visits would stop, and he would try to avoid her for fear of ruining everything and scaring her away. That night he would send a dessert to her room with a note saying his absence was due to working late with the council, but in reality, he would be avoiding her. He had thought she was afraid of him, and now he was afraid one wrong move would result in him losing her.

Chapter 10

Kol hadn't been around as much, and Thea convinced herself that it was because he was busy preparing for the upcoming attack on the Strong realm. In an attempt to spend more time with him, she had asked if she could help more with efforts to better the Empire. This offer led to her sitting on a cold metal chair in the corner of an interrogation room several floors below the Palace – as Kol interrogated a man from the Strong realm. *Not exactly the quality time I had in mind,* she thought.

Mori soldiers had ambushed this man on his travels, fed him a meal lace with *Herba Hebeto,* and brought him to the Palace. Kol was pleased to find out that the herbs worked on a Strong as well, as the man had yet been able to break free of his restraints. Unbeknownst to the Strong, each meal he ingested while there prolonged his weakness even longer. Kol had given instructions to all his soldiers on exactly how the herb worked – and then used his Control to order that they never tell another soul about the herb and that they never use it against a member of the Mori family.

"What is happening?" The man said anxiously as he looked at the simple rope that was holding him to the chair. Panic was etched into his face, and veins were popping out of his bald head as he strained against the ropes that held him down. He knew something was wrong, for he had been snapping ropes in half with his bare hands since he was a boy.

Kol turned his Control on the man. "Look at me." The man's head involuntarily snapped up, panicked eyes now looking into Kol's stoic ones. "Tell me what I want to know." Kol had been asking for hours for information that would allow them to sneak into a war camp or into the Strong castle itself, but the man would give up nothing. While Kol could Control nearly everything about a person, he could not Control their truth – only Thea could do that. Thea watched as the man was beaten and cut as they tried to get information from him. But he wouldn't give it up. She felt frustrated with herself, knowing she could help more, but Kol did not. Only a select few knew the full extent of her Control. After years of practice, her Control went past just detecting honesty, she could command it from someone. But she didn't use it often, as she didn't like taking someone's free will away. This was the very reason she cringed each time she saw Kol use his Control, as all it did was strip free will, but knowing his love for his Empire, she told herself it was for the best.

At one point, Kol turned around, and the look of him sent a shiver of terror through Thea's body as well as a gasp from her lips. It caused her to flee from the room, trying to erase the image of the man she cared for looking like that. He had just asked the Strong another question, and after getting no answer, he ripped the dagger from its position on his hip and swiftly stabbed the man in the thigh. The man had wailed, chilling Thea's already cold body to the core. And Kol had smirked. He smiled as he wiped the blood from the knife onto his shirt. Thea continued to reconcile in her mind how the man who was so tender to her was so ruthless to others.

Though not watching, Kol noticed a shift in the room when Thea left. He dropped the dagger, letting it clang to the floor as he ran out after her. *I knew this was a bad idea. She doesn't understand that this is necessary*, he thought as he followed her. He raced toward the staircase, climbing up after her.

"Thea!" He called when she reached the second floor. Hearing desperation in his voice, she paused and waited for him. Thea had wanted to spend time with him, but she didn't know how much more of this side of him she could see before it changed her. She didn't understand why the violence was necessary. "I'm sorry." He said, desperation also in his eyes.

"Sorry for what?" She asked.

"Sorry, you had to see that." He clarified, meaning every word.

"Not that you did it?" She asked, not hiding her judgmental tone.

"I had to." He pleaded with her.

"I don't believe that there isn't another way to do this!" She demanded. "And why are you always covered in blood?" She yelled, exasperated.

He looked down at his clothes; the Strong's blood was speckled across his chest and arms. "Does this bother you?" He gestured to his clothes.

"Obviously! People don't just walk around casually with blood on their clothes." She looked frustrated, almost frantic.

"Okay, I want you to understand. I don't want you to be afraid of me or think that I don't think these things through." He went to grab her hands – but decided not to when he remembered the blood that coated them. "Let me get cleaned up, and then I will explain my side to you. Okay?" He was desperate to get her

192

to understand. To stop her from fearing him. Thea wasn't sure how she felt, and she again scolded her fickle mind. She adored the man who met her alone in her room at night, but she was unsure of the brutal future ruler who seemed to choose violence nine out of ten times when confronted with an issue. She remembered a thought she had a few weeks ago. *As long as he's kind to me, I can tolerate a lot,* and she still felt that way.

"Okay."

"Okay." He smiled reassuringly at her. He walked her down the hall, toward the east side of the Palace. Toward his side of the second floor. Anticipation raced through Thea's veins at the thought of seeing Kol's room. She reasoned that he had seen her room, and this was no big deal, but seeing his seemed infinitely more intimate. *Is he trying to be more vulnerable with me?* She considered as she followed behind him. This moment felt monumental to both of them. For Thea, seeing his inner sanctum seemed relationship-altering; and to Kol, it was an easy choice, of which he had few of in his life. He had never let anyone, besides staff, into his rooms – but letting Thea in seemed indisputably right. She was the only one he felt was his equal, the only one he could be vulnerable with, the only one he truly trusted. Large golden doors sat at the end of the hallway, and without pretense or hesitation – Kol pushed them open, walked in, and turned toward the left.

"I'm going to get cleaned up. Please, make yourself comfortable." He said quickly before opening another door that led toward his bedroom. His room was set up exactly as hers was, a large sitting room with windows and bookshelves around the walls and then to one side a bedroom. While the layout was the same, the décor was completely different. It felt like an autumn night in the room, in the most comforting way. Dark green, black, and gray covered the room. Deep green, velvet floor-to-ceiling curtains were draped across the back wall, partially closed and covering the room in soft light. Black leather couches were positioned in a u-shape around a large, black fireplace, a fireplace so large she was sure she and four other people could comfortably stand in it. Thea turned around and her eyes scanned, in awe, the hundreds of leather-bound books that sat in meticulous rows. Shifting her gaze, her eyes found a grand piano in the corner, and she imagined Kol sitting at it playing soft music for her as she lay on the nearby couch reading.

Thea peered into his room, and with the positioning of a well-placed mirror, she had a perfect view to inconspicuously watch Kol change. She watched as he quickly discarded his stained shirt, to reveal rippling muscles – covered in long scars. From her position, she could count nearly a dozen scars on his pecs, abdomen, and back. *I wonder how he got those?* Sadness filled her heart for him. *The life he must have led to earn all those scars...must have been horrific.* Deep lines of V-shaped muscle led down toward his waistband and disappeared below. Her stomach clenched as she suddenly wished she could reach out and touch them, trace her fingers over and down them. *See where the lines lead,* she thought to herself.

Suddenly, Thea felt like a voyeur, but despite the shame she felt from watching him, she couldn't force herself to stop. Kol delicately cleaned and re-dressed his body, all the while with an audience. When he was pulling a fresh shirt over his head, he turned and caught her eye in the mirror. He smirked, but didn't say a word, granting her silent permission to watch him. For this she was grateful, and despite being caught – she still didn't look away.

Does she like what she sees? Kol wondered to himself as he finished getting cleaned up. For some reason catching her spying on him had made him feel even luckier to have her. He just hoped he could convince her not to fear him – that she may one day feel as grateful to have him as he was to have her. *Unlikely,* he heard his father's voice mock him in his mind. He physically shook his head, trying to shake the bad thoughts away. He needed to be sharp to explain the intricacies of his intentions to interrogate the Strong man to Thea. He took a deep breath, cleansing his mind, and then walked out to face her.

"What do you want to know?" Kol asked, unsure where to start.

"The beginning. Why do you have this man, and why is violence the only answer?" She asked plainly because she now knew that she could be direct with him if nothing else.

"Well, it's a very long story. But I guess…it starts with us wanting to add the Strong territory to our Empire. For so long we have engaged in battles with them. Recently, over this past summer, I decided to try to conquer them again – on my terms." He paused, causing Thea to wonder if it was because he was carefully considering his words or if he was regretting the truth. "We always have children in war camps, to help cook or clean or run messages, and it is usually safe. Because the fighting never takes place near the camps. But the Strongs decided to play dirty, and while most of our men were away on the battleground – they snuck some men in and took the children. All of them. And regretfully, we don't even know how many. A dozen families have reported a child missing, but some of the kids they took may not have families to report them missing, so it could be even more." He shook his head in defeat, his dark wavy hair shaking as he did so.

195

"So, you want to get information, in part to save these kids but also to defeat the Strongs?" She asked simply, making sure she understood. Kol simply shook his head in confirmation. "And why the torture, why is that how you handle everything?"

"That is all I know." Truth. She grieved for him, for she saw in him a small boy who had scarcely known kindness and therefore had embraced violence like a friend. "And this feels like life or death." Truth. "And if I can push this guy far enough, maybe I can save them. Maybe we can win." He looked desperate. He felt desperate. And he didn't want this failure to be his legacy.

"But you're open to other ways...besides violence?" Thea asked, and depending on his answer, she may be willing to offer him help.

"Maybe not every time, but I promised you I would hear you out on ideas. I stand by that." Truth.

"Okay." She considered what to say first. "I think I can help." He nodded, encouraging her to continue. "In two ways." She took another deep breath, not used to explaining her Control to people. "I can help you know if the kids are safe – and how many were taken." His face turned to shock.

"How?"

"It's part of my Control. I can detect if things are true, even if the person saying them doesn't know. So, you can say statements to me about the children, and I can tell you if they're true or not." She answered meekly, knowing her Control could not compare to his power.

"Thea...that is incredible! I had no idea you could do that." Pride burst throughout his chest.

"Many don't." She shrugged and tried to hide the blush on her face. No matter how she was feeling, she would always bend under the weight of his praise.

"Can I just ask you questions then? To know the answers?"

"Not questions, just statements. Being specific helps."

"Okay…" He considered before continuing, rubbing his pointer finger across his bottom lip and middle finger across his chin as he did so. "Twelve kids are missing."

"You have to be more specific than that – because it's true that in the world at large, there are at least twelve missing children. Make it specific to your situation." She instructed him.

"The Strong soldiers took twelve children from my war camp this summer."

"False."

"The Strong soldiers took fourteen children from my war camp this summer."

"True."

"All right, we knew it was roughly that many." He paused, got a pen and paper to write the information down, and then said his next statement. "The Mori children being held at in Strong realm are safe."

Thea's stomach turned as she revealed the truth to him. "No."

He clenched his pen tightly, knuckles turning white. "All of the Mori children held in the Strong realm are alive."

Again, anxiety churned in her stomach, and she shook her head. "No." He clenched so hard the pen in his hand snapped in half. Thea reached out, grabbing his hand to comfort him. "Say it again, but this time about a specific number of them!" She demanded.

"Thirteen of the Mori children being held in the Strong realm are alive."

197

"Yes!" Thea said with relief.

Kol considered the final question, thinking it may come across as gauche, and decided to ask anyway. "I will save the remaining children and add the Strong realm to my Empire before the end of this year."

"True."

Kol sat back in his chair, considering everything he had been told. Everything he had learned about his future wife. Everything he wished to say to her to find out the truth of. She was more powerful than he ever knew.

"There's more," Thea said as she studied Kol's face and after noting the admiration and affection in his eyes, decided that she wanted to trust him with her secret.

"Okay," Kol replied, still trying to wrap his mind around what they had just learned.

"I can make people tell the truth."

His eyes widened and drifted to the side as he processed what she said. "You can make people tell the truth?"

She nodded. "It's not easy, and requires much concentration, but I can."

"So, you can go to the interrogation room now and make that guy talk?" He asked, trying to confirm what she was saying.

"Yes."

"Why didn't you say this hours ago?" He asked, slightly frustrated with the effort that could have been saved.

"I don't like doing it, taking someone's privacy away from them."

"So why tell me now?"

"Because I see now that it's life or death…and that it's important to you." *She cares that it's important to me.* He thought as an unfamiliar feeling of warmth and comfort encompassed him. She continued, "And I want to help."

Chapter 11

"Remember, don't get closer to him than necessary. Know I could stop him from seriously hurting you, but I don't want to take any chances." Kol had spent the last hour preparing Thea for this interrogation. And she did feel prepared, at least logistically, emotionally was a different story. She cursed the person who refused to let her have political lessons growing up; perhaps if she had, then this whole thing wouldn't seem so foreign to her. She had figured out quickly that she was quite unknowing of what exactly it took to run a kingdom, and she was beginning to assume that she would have to become accustomed to the bloodshed and deception synonymous with ruling in the Mori Empire. And that epiphany would make her push herself, emotionally and physically, in order to help Kol rule. She tried to convince herself that by taking these steps in helping Kol, she was getting what she always wanted – a role to play in ruling and closeness with her future husband. Although what she didn't know until she arrived in Cativo, was what ruling actually looked like. Ruling wasn't only hosting parties and speaking with foreign dignitaries, it was getting your hands dirty, and she was about to do just that. *I'm going to get my hands dirty all right… or bloody*, she thought with a cringe. "Are you sure about this?" Kol asked, concerned brows furrowed.

"Yes. I want to be useful and prevent unnecessary bloodshed. If I use the Veritas to extract information from him, then we will have the information we need to save the children, and we won't need to hurt anyone else." Though becoming more aware of reality, Thea was naïve still. Many more would die on the road to growing the Empire. The guards at the door nodded, validating Thea's words, admiring her diplomatic approach. Thea took a deep breath to steady her nerves, a forever-increasing habit in her new home.

In addition to Kol giving her preparatory advice, she had also had an herbal tea brought to her from herbs in her personal collection. She had been taught that tea made from *Herba Augendae Vires* would increase one's Control, and today she felt like she could use all the help she could get. She told herself she could handle this, that she was strong enough to accomplish this for her Empire. *And for my Prince*, for some reason, that thought caused her to blush.

"Open the door." She spoke with authority, and without hesitation, the guard listened. They respected her, for now, simply because Kol respected her. Kol watched, burning with pride and seduction at the command she instantly took of the room. He followed her in and motioned the guard to follow as well.

"You protect her at all costs, no questions asked." Kol whispered to the guard, using his Control. The young guard nodded despite the fear in his eyes.

The Strong in the chair lolled his head up and blinked one eye slowly, the other was swollen shut. "A skirt. This should be interesting." He laughed, before a fit of wet coughing racked his body. When the coughing stopped, he continued, "Are they trying to seduce the answers out of me?" He looked her up and down, eyes trailing her in a predatory fashion. "Honestly, it may work." He laughed roguishly.

Kol's hands swiftly formed fists, and he switched his Control on. He had but a single, possessive word on his mind, *mine.* "Silence!" The Strong breathed out a ragged breath. "Watch how you speak in the presence of this woman." *He protects me with such passion,* she thought, *I like it.*

"I am here to ask you a few questions, which you will be answering." She spoke calmly.

"Listen, *bitch*, I don't know who you think you are, but they have been trying to get me to talk for hours. And I haven't. I don't know what you are going to do that will change that." Despite his chains, he leaned back in his seat, trying to use false confidence to cover up his anxiety.

Kol was becoming unhinged watching this man disrespect Thea. He drew his sword, ready to use it, but stopped when Thea lifted her head and met his eye line. It's as if she silently communicated, *I've got this.*

"Listen, *prick-*" Thea copied the cadence of the man's previous sentence to her. Kol's mouth opened slightly, and an amused smirk replaced the grimace on his face. *This woman,* he thought in awe, *she is incredible.* "I will tell you who I am. I am the future High Queen of the Mori Empire, including what will formally be known as the Strong Realm." Kol wished he could strip her bare and ravage her here, her confidence nearly his undoing in that very moment. "And I will get you to talk." She breathed in deeply and arranged her hands as if in prayer before her chest before looking into the man's eyes. Kol watched as the man's eyes suddenly glazed over, not unlike the eyes of the people he used his Control on. "You will say, specifically where all the children of the Mori Empire are being held captive in your keep."

Without hesitation, he began speaking. "Most are serving our king as slaves, and at night they all sleep in a locked room below the keep."

"Your false king is going to pay for these crimes." Thea held eye contact with the man. "How does one get to this room where the children are held?"

"There is a door, accessible from the back of the castle, and another door beside the dungeon. The stairs are between the servant quarters and the kitchen." He spoke as if in a trance.

"See, was that so hard?" Thea asked, and though he wasn't in physical pain, betraying his king had him in emotional agony. "Now, how can we infiltrate the Strong realm? Specifically, the walls around the city."

"You could wait until the change of guard at night – when the moon is highest in the sky."

"And why is that the best time?" Thea asked.

"The bell will toll, and for the next five minutes, there is often no one on the tower. They have grown lazy in recent years." A vein in his forehead pulsed as he tried to fight her compulsion over him. "Or you could take the secret tunnels."

"Where are the secret tunnels to the Strong Hold?" She asked, voice still calm.

He hesitated this time, a vein pulsing again, and his lips turned pale as he tried to force his mouth closed. To no avail. "The entrance is at the base of Mount Moraha."

"Where does this tunnel at Mount Moraha lead?"

"To the caverns and stores below the Strong Castle." He began to cry, the shame of his betrayal weighing on him.

"Is it guarded?" Thea asked.

"Those tunnels are never guarded."

"Thank you for your cooperation. We're done." She looked away from the man, and he physically slumped in his chair, the shame of his disloyalty crushing him.

He tried to fix it. "You better hope everything I said was true!" Not knowing Thea's Control.

"I know it is."

"How?" The man asked.

"Because she is powerful. She is Veritas." Kol answered and her heart fluttered under his praise.

While Kol and Thea stared lovingly into one another eyes, the Strong attempted an attack. He lunged, and though he was still weak and unable to break free, the guard in the room had no choice but to act on this aggression. The sound of slicing flesh and a heavy thud pulled Thea and Kol from their gaze, and Thea looked on in horror as the Strong's head rolled toward her – now detached from his body. The shaking guard dropped his bloody sword to the ground.

"What have I done?" He whispered.

"What happened?" Kol asked, as he placed a protective arm around Thea and pulled her head to his chest so that she could no longer see the severed head rolling on the ground.

"He lunged toward the lady and I just reacted. I killed him." He stared blankly at the headless body before him.

"You protected the future queen, and for that you will be rewarded." Kol reassured him. "Meet me in my office in one hour. I'm going to take care of her and you're going to take care of that." He gestured toward the body.

"Yes sir." The man choked out.

Quickly they exited the cell and rounded the corner, Kol led her out with his hand on her lower back. Once out of sight of the guards Thea slumped against the wall and pressed a hand to her head – which was pulsing with pain due to the exertion of pushing her Control.

"Are you okay?" Kol asked, and attempted to get her to make eye contact with him.

"I'm not sure." She was not accustomed to violence or death, but she didn't want to show it. She didn't want to seem weak or incapable of serving the Empire.

"I know seeing that must have been hard, but protecting you was our number one priority." Kol brushed a piece of hair behind her ear.

"I know." She replied without making eye contact. In her heart she knew his one desire was to protect her, and the means with which he did so was something she would have to get used to.

They stood in a comfortable silence for some time before he spoke again. "You were incredible." He praised. A desire to wrap his arms around her and kiss all over her beautiful face filled him, for she had done what he could not. Not only would they save the children and his legacy – but they could also now conquer the Strong realm, something decades of Mori leaders had tried, but only he would accomplish. And it was all because of Thea. His whole demeanor shifted, though, once he saw the state she was in. His heart nearly stopped as she sank against the wall with a look of agony contorting her features. "Are you okay?" Concern filled his voice, and his sharp features softened with worry.

"I have a headache. Pushing my Control that far usually results in this. Probably from lack of practice." Thea admitted.

"Then why did you do it?" He was upset, but not with her, with himself for allowing her to be placed in harm's way for his benefit. He wanted to protect her in all ways, even from herself if necessary.

"As I said, I want to help." She lowered her hand and stood up straight, but Kol could still see the pain hidden in her slightly squinted eyes.

"And help you did, this information is…it's invaluable. I don't know how to thank you." Thea's cheeks heated at this statement, she tried to smile, but the pressure in her head would not allow it. "Can I do anything to help you now?"

"I have some herbs I use for headaches, and resting will help as well."

"Then go do that, please. I will tell them to send Ruth up to check on you." Kol wished he could do more. She nodded and turned to leave, pacing herself as she traveled down the corridor and up the stairs. He watched until she was out of sight and then it was his turn to lean against the wall and sigh, but not in pain as she had – but in admiration. Kol remembered every second of the interrogation: her voice filled with authority, the movement of her supple lips as she demanded answers from him, and the draw of focus in her eyes as she called on her abilities. *She's perfect.* Kol was utterly captivated by her, and his most primal side was starved for her. *Beauty, intelligence, seduction, and bravery –all qualities she has. Will she ever stop surprising me?* He stood staring at the doorway she had departed through, desperate to see her again, desperate to wrap his arms around her. A hungry desire hid behind that, a desire to place his hands on and in all the places he knew he shouldn't. *Not yet.*

Reality pulled him from his seductive thoughts. *Would she even want me to do that?* Doubt replaced these thoughts, fear that seeing this violent side of him would burst the love bubble they had been living in together. Doubt led him to decide that he would again not spend the night with her, and this choice filled him with anger. Anger that was to be unleashed on the next person who crossed him.

On his way back to his rooms, he found Ruth and ordered her to get Thea a whole night of pampering to help her relax and recover. This did help to dissuade his anger some, caring for Thea always did, but it also made him jealous that the maids would see more of his bride that night than he would allow himself to. So, he busied himself with tending to the corpse and rewarding the guard, but Thea danced in the back of his mind all night.

The walk back to the room was long for Thea, as she had to stop several times to catch her breath and steady her vision. But despite the pain, she was filled with such an overwhelming sense of pride. She knew she had made Kol proud, and she hoped the more helpful she was, the more he would include her in the business of court. Mixed feelings about the now dead prisoner flitted through her mind, but she just repeated Kol's words over and over again. *They were protecting me. He is always protecting me.* Regret danced around her mind, for how harshly she had judged his actions, she now doubted she would have acted any different in his position – with the lives of so many children at stake.

While she would be lying to say she didn't want part of him to change, she continued to tell herself that in the little time she had asked for change from him – he had tried. He seemed willing to hear her perspective and handle things without rash violence. *Because he cares for me.* As she crawled into bed, she couldn't wait to see him again. Thea longed to have a private moment to discuss everything that had transpired with him, and to get on the same page before their wedding next week. They definitely had much to discuss, but she felt confident they would sort things out and continue to grow together. But Thea was naïve in this way too, for Kol would continue to avoid her, out of fear, and this would leave room for doubt to continue to seep into both of their minds.

Chapter 12

Thea felt a gentle shake pulling her from her sleep. *Kol?* Was her first thought. But it wouldn't be Kol, he hadn't stayed with her since the night he tortured the Fauna man – when he began to fear his bride would reject him if she knew anything more about his dark side. The side his father had cultivated to make him a more effective ruler. Thea didn't know why he had stopped their late-night visits, the thing she loved the most about living at the Palace – and she hoped it was because he was only busy but her mind feared the worst. That he was bored of her already, Lady Adams's words of his torrid love affairs racing through her mind. Or worse, she worried that she had done something to elicit second thoughts on his end.

Thea opened her eyes to see Dorothy standing beside her bed. "Ready?" She asked. *Ready? Only one word, but such a loaded question.* It was Thea's wedding day, and despite twenty-three years' worth of time to prepare herself for this day and previous excitement she had felt – she was unsure how she felt that morning. In reality, she was feeling so many things at once. Fear of tripping as she walked down the aisle or embarrassing herself in some other way. Excitement for everything she had ever known to be coming to fruition. Confusion as to why in the week leading up to their wedding Kol had been less and less present in her life.

He had continued to be sweet and attentive when he was around, but the kisses and caresses were few and far between, making her worry about his desire for her. All the lessons she had on sexual pleasure swirled in her mind, causing heat to rush to her cheeks and tension to pull at her stomach. Tonight, once their marriage was ordained before God, was the night they would be permitted to join as one – but his distance of late made Thea wonder if that was even something he wanted. She thought back to all the sultry moments of tension they had experienced together, even from the first night they met when his identity was still hidden from her. Since then, she had craved his touches and even tried to push him further, but he had declined her advances. Thea assumed it was out of respect and decorum, but now she was not so sure. Part of her worried he was moments away from changing his mind, that the life she had been dreaming for herself these past few weeks would be ripped out from under her. A life as Queen, helping further the Empire, and evenings wrapped in Kol's arms. She thought of his obsession for her, that he couldn't possibly go from being infatuated to nothing all of the sudden. But an anxious voice in her mind feared that he may just be very hot and cold in all ways, including his feelings for her. She held onto faith in her Control, that despite the worries or words of the court, she knew with certainty that Kol cared for her and that he would one day love her.

If she closed her eyes, she could image Kol's calloused hands rubbing the sensitive parts of her body, that he had only teased so far, and his breaths coming out in heavy pants as Thea returned the favor. But that nagging voice in her head caused her chest to clench at the thought that this may never happen, that her whirlwind romance was over even before it really even started.

All they had were stolen glances and fleeting embraces, and she was desperate for more. *I will have more.*

"Thea?" Dorothy asked, pulling Thea from her thoughts.

"Yeah." She sighed, releasing an audible breath. "I'm ready."

Moments were all she had, the rest of the day passed by either in slow motion or fleeting wisps – nothing in between. Time swirled by quickly as several lady's maids fluttered around her, twisting her hair, and painting her face. And then moments ticked by slowly as she watched her mother and father come to greet her. They were dressed in black and deep purple, coordinating with one another. She watched them come toward her, smiles plastered on their faces. *If they only knew,* she thought, *that Kol had slept in my bed, that I had tried to seduce a man who was not yet my husband, that I had watched a man get beheaded, that I helped torment a man for information with my Control – they wouldn't be smiling at me.* She wondered if they knew what they had thrown her into – if they truly knew Kol's reputation and the expectations a woman at his side would have thrust upon her. As her parents wrapped their arms around her, she remembered the last time this had happened and who she had been then. Only just a month ago, she felt small, powerless, and resigned to a life of servitude beneath a powerful man. But now, she stood before them, feeling stronger and knowing her place was not beneath anyone – but beside. *My equal,* she heard Kol's voice echo in her mind – it slowed her racing heart and banished her worried thoughts.

After her parents left, she continued pondering her relationship with Kol. She knew she had to put all doubt to rest and trust him fully – in every way. She had to trust her Control. *Perhaps this week has been a fluke,* she hoped, *and tonight will change everything.* She knew she had his heart and his respect, and with the final addition of his body, she doubted his loyalty would ever waver again. *He won't go another night without warming my bed, that I can be sure of.* Confidence rushed through her as swiftly as the blush flew onto her face. Though seduction would be a move to cement their relationship and her place in his world, it was also her deepest desire. A desire that intimidated her.

Before she knew it, it was time to get her gown on and leave. This reminded Thea of the first time she got ready for a grand occasion at the Palace, her arrival ball. She had been so nervous then – unsure of what to expect from Kol or her new life. *So much has changed.* Everyone but the lady's maids left her bedroom, allowing her privacy to be laced into her wedding gown. Beneath it, she was wearing a sleeveless silk slip held up by an under-bust corset. The dress itself was a work of art, hand-sewn and meticulously designed for the last year by several seamstresses. It hung on Thea's body perfectly; the bodice hugged her chest and abdomen before effortlessly fluttering away from her body at the hips and then flowing down. It was sleeveless, but delicate flutter sleeves hung pointlessly off her shoulders, and the skirt boasted dozens of handcrafted three-dimensional flowers. Once she was all cinched in, she couldn't help herself from twirling around and watching the skirts flow around her.

"You look beautiful, my lady." One of her lady's maids, Elaine, said.

"Thank you, Elaine. Thank you all for helping me get ready today." Thea looked at them all genuinely, making a point to make eye contact with each lady in the room, lingering on Ruth a little longer than most. She was pleased that Ruth, unlike the rest of the Palace staff, would be allowed to attend the wedding today – Thea felt as though Ruth was a surrogate grandmother to her now and would be saddened if she hadn't been able to attend.

"You look lovely," Ruth said as she wrapped her in a hug. "Ready to show everyone else?" She gestured to the next room, where Thea's parents and Dorothy waited for her.

"Definitely," Thea answered with a smile, but more than anything, she was ready to get all the pomp and circumstance out of the way so that she could be alone with Kol.

They opened the door to reveal Thea to the room; her mother gasped, Dorothy covered her mouth in delight, and her father stoically nodded in approval.

"You look amazing!" Dorothy shrieked as she wrapped Thea in a bone-crushing hug.

"You do too!" Thea responded. And it was true. Dorothy's dress was silken and hanging off her body as a sheath dress hung off of a Greek Muse, and the color was a deep mauve that complimented her dark skin. She had left her hair down, natural curls bouncing with every move she made.

Thea's parents stepped up next. "I have no words." Her mother began, tears immediately coming to her eyes.

"We are so proud of you, and we know you will do great things as our queen." Her father finished as he pulled his wife to the side to console her. *Our queen.* Thea found the statement so odd, realizing that after her wedding, she would be a princess, officially outranking her parents in power. Crazy to think of that shift in their power dynamic when they had spent her whole life controlling her. *Never again.*

"The carriages are ready, my lady." A servant announced before bowing and dismissing himself. Thea pulled herself from her thoughts and charged the door.

Excitement coursed through her veins, and she had to restrain herself from shouting. "Make haste! I'm ready to get married!" She said with glee, and Dorothy pranced along, matching her infectious energy, despite the pause she may have for the groom in question.

They would be taking a carriage ride through the city to the cathedral church on the other side of the Capital. The people would be given a chance to see their future princess in her gown and throw flowers at the feet of her carriage as they had the day she first arrived. And after all of that stimulation and excitement, she would be led to a room to be alone a few moments before the ceremony.

Once outside, Thea saw the gargantuan white carriage sitting at the bottom of the Palace stairs with two comparably sized white horses standing before it, waiting to pull them through the city. The doors were painted with delicate gold detailing and crystals, much like most of the Palace.

"Do you ever think one could ever get used to the glamour here?" Dorothy asked in awe as she walked toward their carriage. Thea didn't answer, choosing instead to be inside her mind for a little longer as they traveled.

Once they were all settled in, the carriage took off, and they didn't even have to get through the Palace's outer walls before they heard the crowd. Thea had been shocked at the number of people who had come to see her arrival that first day in Cativo – but the amount this day was more than double. People lined the edges of the streets, body to body, hoping to experience just a moment of the royal wedding. Flowers of all kinds were thrown at her horses' feet, and children threw woven crowns toward her in the carriage. Thea reached her hand out, catching one, and the children cheered when she placed it on her head, and she threw her head back in carefree laughter as she watched the joy on their faces. While she was enjoying the merriment, another moment seemed to come into her vision in slow motion – only this time it was a soul-crushing one. She watched as a child was shoved to the ground by a man in all black, and their hand was crushed under the weight of the carriage. The child's screams of pain were masked by shouting. Several Dissenters stood before the crowd. A group of people, faces covered and mourning colors donned, pushed the celebrating people out of the way and chanted toward the carriage.

"No new queen, end this regime! No new queen, end this regime!"

One pivoted his body directly at her, pointed, and screamed. "Princess of Death!" She flinched as he used an altered version of Kol's fear-mongering moniker at her. *Why would they call me that?* The Dissenters all raised their arms, half in the signature fist of Dissent and the other half held chunks of black rock that they swiftly threw at the carriage. Someone screamed, and Thea ducked as the black objects pelted them. She opened her eyes to see one lying at her feet. *Coal?*

"Burn it down!" They began chanting.

"Guards!" Thea's father yelled. "Do something!"

"Clear the streets!" Someone outside the carriage yelled and the people in the streets scattered. The driver whipped his lead, causing the horses to break into a full run – jostling the carriage back and forth as they flew down the road.

"Are you okay?" Thea's father asked.

"I'm fine! Are those people okay? Are the guards helping them? Did someone help the child?" Thea could still see the fear on the child's face as the faceless Dissenter shoved them to the ground. Thea visibly winced, remembering the child's wail of pain as her bones crunched under a wheel of the carriage.

"They are fine. They are being helped as we speak." He said reassuringly. Thea was scared, so much in fact she was unable to use her Control to detect truth in her father's statement. She was speechless and unsure how to process an attack like that, especially on her wedding day. She wished she could talk to Kol, tell him what happened, and let him reassure her that he would do anything to protect her. *I wouldn't even care to watch him torture that man who hurt the child,* her vengeful thoughts surprised her. "Don't worry, my dear. We are almost there." Her father gave her a comforting pat on the hand.

She allowed herself to become re-immersed in the positives of the day, knowing there would be time to deal with the Dissenters later, there had to be. They pulled up to the church, and Thea noted that its pointed steeples and black windows felt very gothic in comparison to the ethereal white and gold of the Palace. She had been inside this building only once, when she toured it with Ruth and Dorothy weeks ago, and she knew the inside was much like the out. Tall ceilings draped in black chandeliers with tall candles to light the room, with help from the large windows that overlooked the river and mountains beyond the city. She also knew the inside was decorated with deep greens, lanterns, and flowers, pulling natural elements into the otherwise gray aesthetic. She felt it poetic, almost as if it represented she and Kol. Him, austere, and she, whimsical.

Guards flanked the fronts and sides of the building, letting guests filter in unbothered by the throngs of people on the streets. Once her carriage pulled to a stop around the back entrance of the building, Thea was ushered in by several guards. Her parents and Dorothy kissed her good luck, before leaving her to her moment of solitude.

Traditionally, a bride was to use this time to pray and find peace before her ceremony, but Thea had been doing that all day, so instead she used this time to worry about the Dissenters. Part of her was hurt they would use her wedding as an opportunity to push their agenda, but a larger part of her knew that it didn't have anything to do with her. They were unhappy, and she could potentially understand why. If Kol's father had led his whole reign with an iron fist and ruthless tyranny, they had a right to be upset. *Perhaps I can help. Kol and I can be different in our reign.* Thea paced back and forth, trying to think of ways to help the people and heal the broken parts of this land she was to help rule. The door opened and Thea, assuming it was her father coming to get her for the ceremony, spoke out. "Just a few more moments, please."

"Thea, it's me." Deep, baritone tendrils danced into her ears.

"Kol?" She whirled around quickly to face him, her dress fanning out around her. "You aren't supposed to be here. It's bad luck." Thea wasn't usually superstitious, but weddings seemed to pull superstition out of even the most atheistic people.

"You look-" He paused, a look of devastation on his face. "Stunning."

She blushed and twirled her skirt a little. "You do too." And he did. He had for once taken great care in taming his wavy mane and his black tuxedo was sinfully fitted to him. His black and gray pique vest clung to his abdomen in a way that made Thea desperate to see him without it, to see more of the scarred

217

and muscled torso that clothes hung on as if they too couldn't get enough of touching him. "But why do you look sad to say so?" She asked with jest in her tone, but when her joke didn't reveal his dimple or cause his lip to twist up even slightly, she grew somber too. "Why do you look sad?"

He sighed and exhaled; it sounded as if he had been holding his breath since the moment he got there. "Because I'm trying to be a good man, for once in my life – because that's what you deserve." He swallowed the knot that had formed in his throat. "But seeing you now, looking even more beautiful than I thought Blessed possible, is making it... incredibly hard." Thea's stomach dropped, not only at the heart-wrenching tone to his voice – but because of her perceived implications of his words. *He's calling off the marriage.* She went rigid and felt as if ice-cold water had replaced all the blood in her body.

"What do you mean?" She wasn't sure how she managed to get those words out.

He strode toward her, with all the elegance of a skilled dancer but all the intensity of a trained warrior, and took both her hands in his. "I heard about the attack on your carriage, and I want you to know how sorry I am."

"Kol, you don't have to be sorry. You didn't do it." Thea tried to reach up and touch his face, but he grabbed her hand again and looked into her eye.

"Please, let me finish." He sounded broken. "I am sorry that marrying me would mean marrying my family's enemies – which are numerous. I want you to know that I believe you deserve the best life – love, safety, and adventure. Not fear and darkness and undeserved hatred." His lip quivered and she wanted so badly to reach out to him, to kiss away the sadness and let him know she was fine, but she also wanted to respect his

218

wishes and allow him to finish. "I came to you today because I had to see for myself that you were actually here. That despite all you've learned of me and my Empire and what you've endured even today that you would still want to marry me. I gave you a choice weeks ago," He released a heavy sigh. "A choice to leave and not marry me, and this would be your last chance to do so. I had to see if you were still choosing me, because I would understand if you didn't want to." His eyes glistened. "You are powerful and smart and shouldn't be saddled with a life your father bargained for you over twenty years ago. A life you never asked for. One where you're always looking over your shoulder for my enemies. A life with a man who doesn't deserve you." He cursed, "But Blesses burn me for not wanting to let you go." Thea watched as a single tear rolled from Kol's left eye and felt it when hot liquid splashed onto her hand. She could see the doubt in his eyes, and suddenly she understood his absence for the last week– she had feared he didn't want her, and he had been fearing the same. When Kol was alone, he didn't regret any of his actions but looking into her eyes when she found out he had allowed the Fauna man to be harmed for his personal gain had made him wish he had the Control of time – so he could reverse time and take back everything he had ever done that made him unworthy of her. *Could she grow to love a man who is so feared and ruthless?* He had asked himself that question hundreds of times in the last week. But when Thea looked at him, all she saw was a man who made her feel more alive than she ever had before, a man who was willing to compromise and hear her opinions, and most importantly, a man who let her choose her own destiny.

"I will only be leaving this church one of two ways. Married to you or dead." Thea stately confidently. Kol's brows furrowed in confusion, but his eyes glimmered with hope.

"You don't want to leave? Not even after today or all the brutality you've seen?"

"I don't want to leave." She said with confidence.

"You don't want to marry me." False. Her Control detected the deception in his statement.

"That's not true." He looked surprised.

"Have you considered the fear or regrets-" Kol began, but she interrupted him.

"The only thing I regret about this last month is not making sure you were completely clear on how I feel about you." She racked her brain for words, unsure how to speak as eloquently as he was always able to do. "Kol, when I look at you, I feel many things – pride, intrigue, adoration, lust – but never regret or darkness or fear you would hurt me." His lip quivered again, but this time she caught it with the edge of her thumb and rubbed it as she cupped his cheek in comfort. "I won't lie to you, some of your world is surprising and scary to me." He looked disappointed. "But at every turn, I have been faced with a man who treats me like an equal and is willing to not only hear my voice but also to consider it and allow it to change him. And I know your world isn't without its dangers, but I also know you will protect me."

"Even with my own life." He vowed to her.

She nodded, her tears threatening to brim over. "So, I say it again, either I am marrying you here today or those sycophants will have to haul my corpse out the door."

He smiled at her morbid joke. "I've missed this."

"Me too." She agreed. He leaned down and kissed her, a week's worth of want and passion all coming undone in a single moment. He held her close as he let the light of her words fill the dark places in his soul. "Can we get married now?" She asked with a laugh.

"Let them try and stop us." He nipped friskily at the tip of her nose, suddenly his confident self again – as if her words had mended him instantly.

"You need to leave!" She swatted him playfully. "And forget you saw me, like I said, it's bad luck."

He wrapped his arms around her once more. "Thea, I won't forget. I will remember the way you look and the words you've said until the day I die. We will just have to combat the bad luck together." He kissed her on the forehead once more and then turned to leave. "See you down the aisle, Princess of Cativo." He winked, and as quiet as he arrived – he left.

Before Thea had a chance to collect her thoughts and wrap her head around what had just happened, her father knocked and entered the room, and instantly time moved quickly again. Her father ushered her out of the room and gently guided her in front of the massive doors that led into the chapel – the room where she would become a wife. The building pulsated with excited energy; everyone was eager to see the Prince of Death wed. Thea only hoped everyone there had good intentions; she thought briefly of the Dissenters but refused to allow them to taint that moment. She shifted her thoughts back to Kol as the doors to the chapel opened.

The attendants gasped at her angelic appearance. She didn't care, she focused all her thoughts on him. *The sharp curve of his jaw. His deep dimple when he smiles. That little laugh he does when I amuse him.* Kol turned to watch her descend the aisle, and despite having seen her only minutes ago – he looked as if a feather could have knocked him over. That dimple appeared and his smile grew larger with each step she took closer to him. He couldn't hold his normal cold, indifferent façade – not in her presence. *How I feel when he touches me. The sound of his voice when he reads to me.* Positive memories filled Thea's mind, causing her smile to match his.

Her father kissed her cheek and handed her off to Kol, but all she saw was Kol. The priest started the ceremony, filled with symbolism and heart – but Thea and Kol didn't hear a minute of it. They were lost in one another's eyes. *Eyes so warm and loving I never want to leave their embrace*, he thought. They were so distracted that the priest had to repeat the instruction to say their vows twice – which elicited a gentle laugh from the audience.

"I, Kol Arius, take thee, Althea Torianna, to be my wife. I vow to protect you like I protect this realm. I vow to provide for and safely keep you and our future generations. There for you, I will be, in good times and in bad, until the end of time." As he repeated the pre-approved vows from the priest, Thea considered their beauty, *they're almost perfect,* she thought, *the only thing missing is the word love.* She knew she was idealistic, she had hoped to be in love before she married but arranged marriages hardly allowed for that. And despite the slight disappointment in that, she wasn't worried – she knew their love would grow in time, as her Control had confirmed.

"I, Althea Torianna, take thee, Kol Arius, to be my husband. I vow to nurture you as I nurture this realm. I vow to stand by your side as you reign and raise future generations to do the same. There for you, I will be, in good times and in bad, until the end of time." Thea repeated as the priest instructed.

"And with the power given to me by God and High King Kairo – I now pronounce you Prince and Princess Kol Arius of Cativo. You may kiss your bride." Thea fought the urge to roll her eyes at the subtle misogyny of the King's approved vows, but it was hard to remain unhappy with Kol approaching her – lips puckered. She leaned in as his lips crashed into hers and he placed his hands on her, one on her jaw and the other on her lower back. The priest cleared his throat – disapproving of their prolonged display of affection. Kol pulled back and nipped at her lips playfully – before shooting the priest a withering glare. "Ladies and Lords of Cativo and visiting realms – I present to you the Prince and Princess of Cativo." Kol swept her into his arms, causing Thea to gasp in surprise, and carried her down the aisle, covering her face in kisses as he did so. Much to the chagrin of his father, who stood glaring at the front of the chapel.

Kol placed her back on the ground once they were out of eyesight of everyone, back in the room they had spoken in before the ceremony, and in less than an hour, so much had changed. They stood before a large mirror and he pulled her close to him, his front to her back, and stared into her eyes through the mirror as he whispered into her ear.

His deep, sensual voice raised bumps on her arms. "You're mine." He traced a finger lightly down her bare arm, causing her to shiver. "And I am yours." He took her arm and pulled it back, placing it on his upper thigh and moving her thumb to caress his leg. She broke eye contact with him and looked to her hand as she drew in a sharp breath, surprised at the intimacy of the touch. He pulled his fingers away from her arm and placed his hand on her abdomen, slowly trailing it up until it cupped her breast. She bit her lip as heat flooded her cheeks. "I

223

love watching how I effect you." He kissed her neck. "My expressive Princess."

Boldness filled her as she twisted her body to face him. His hands quickly found their way to her bottom, as if he'd already memorized every curve of her body. She moved her hand, inching it up his thigh, dancing into uncharted waters. A combination of shock and approval covered his face, and Thea found herself reveling in it.

"I just wanted to see how I could effect you." She removed her hand, causing him to growl in disapproval.

"Careful, Princess." He teased with a wicked smile on his face.

"No, thank you." She teased back, attempting to find her stride and engage him in playful banter.

"Curse them for planning a reception directly after this."

"Why?" She asked in genuine confusion.

"Because it means we have to wait several more hours to finish this."

"What's wrong with this room?" She asked as she slipped a few fingers into his waistband.

"There's not enough privacy or surface area for what I have planned for you." He placed her chin between his fingers and drew her mouth to his. "But I appreciate the eagerness." Smile, wicked as ever. "First the innocent fun, we will eat and mingle and dance-" On cue, he pushed her out from him and twirled her in a circle, causing her to giggle, "And then the real fun will begin." He pulled her back to him, held her close, and looked deeply into her eyes. "If that's okay with you?" He asked coyly.

"I suppose it has to be." She matched his demure yet sensual energy.

"Then let's get this over with." He grabbed her hand in his, intertwining their fingers, and guided her to an awaiting carriage, which would take them back to the Palace. Unlike her ride there, the ride back would be more discreet. The windows of his black carriage were cloaked in dark shading – allowing them to see out but no one to see in. They would greet the public as a married couple by waving from a balcony of the Palace later in the week, but until then, they were being permitted more freedom and privacy for the remainder of the day.

Once settled in the carriage, Thea turned to Kol, "So I understand from my meeting with the council yesterday that this reception is more business than pleasure?"

"You're already becoming more savvy to the ways of my court, I see." He drew his lips in a tight line and briefly looked out the window. "Unfortunately, my father sees everything as an opportunity to show off his wealth and power. Including our wedding."

"I see," Thea said, not trying very hard to hide her disappointment.

"I'm sorry, you don't deserve this." He looked down and loosened his grip on her hand. "This day should be about us, not the Empire. We have the rest of our lives to deal with the Empire." He ran his other hand through his hair, un-coifing it.

She pulled their hands into her lap and squeezed tighter. "It's part of the package. And the perks outweigh the deficits." She pushed away a rebellious wave of his hair, the one that often defied all attempts at taming, and then rested her hand on the back of his neck, pulling him firmly toward her. She bit playfully toward him, as he often did to her, trying to elicit a laugh from him.

The right side of his mouth tugged upward. "You never stop surprising me." A little laugh escaped him, and he put an arm around her and tucked her under his arm. He planted a tender kiss on the top of her head.

"So, what do we need to do?" Thea asked.

He sighed. "Well, members of the Strong realm will be in attendance – including their king. We are to appear diplomatic and not reveal any of our cards, regarding the future raid of their castle and attack on their camps."

"Obviously." She said in a mockingly grim tone.

Kol nudged her playfully before continuing, "And to everyone else, we must just appear powerful, put together, and in love." Thea froze when he said the last part. The word love had never come up in their conversations. *What will he say next?* "Which won't be difficult at all, at least on my part." *He basically just said he loved me, without saying it.* Thea was both aflutter with this turn of events and also annoyed that he wouldn't just say it outright. But she wouldn't let his reticence make her hold her feelings back.

"It won't be hard for me either." She looked up into his eyes – and was met with an adoration and softness that he had never looked at another in all his days – and never would again. *Is it possible that she could love me?* Joy and panic seized Kol's chest, both unfamiliar emotions to him. He panicked, for if he loved her and she him, then he had something to lose and something for his enemies to use against him. *Father didn't even love mother, and they still used her against him until her death.* He knew he had two choices, his mother had told him as much, either he could build walls around himself and be alone, or he could let one person in – Thea. And he was sick of being alone.

At that moment, he wanted to tell her just that, so he decided, *I will tell her I love her – tonight.*

The carriage pulled to a stop and a servant opened the door for them. Kol jumped out first and held his hand to her. "Allow me, my wife." He said with a wide smile.

Thea blushed after hearing her new title from his lips for the first time. *Wife.* "Thank you, *husband.*"

"Please never stop calling me that." He pretended to swoon, and Thea laughed and thought about how unbelievable her life was. She was walking into her wedding reception with her husband, the Prince, who made her laugh and was sinfully handsome. *I must be dreaming.* She sighed happily, and for once, she was not plagued by the demons of her husband's past when she thought of him.

"As you wish, *husband.*" She curtsied before him. "Anything you wish, *husband.*" She tried not to laugh.

"So now you're mocking me? That's what we're doing?" He asked with an amused expression on his face. Thea nodded in response, laughing as she backed away from him. "No, no, get back here." He chased after her and quickly captured her around the waist. He spun her around as she continued to giggle. When he placed her feet back on the ground, he didn't let go of her. "Anything I wish, you say? Be careful what you promise." He whispered into her ear, causing a shiver to shoot down her spine. "For right now, I wish to forgo this party, take you upstairs, and-"

"Are you two quite finished fooling around?" A condescending voice boomed from the top of the stairs. They both snapped their heads to look at Kairo. "Foolish children." He scoffed as he turned to walk back into the Palace. Once he was gone, they noticed Dove still standing there. She waved demurely at them.

"You look beautiful today, Althea," Dove said.

"Dove!" Kairo yelled, she flinched and quickly walked away to follow him. Thea hated Kairo, and she was beginning to notice that his wife was not a huge fan either.

"Are we quite done fooling around them?" Thea asked Kol, mocking his father's tone.

He snickered. "Not at all, though it seems as if we have to push our merriment for later." He kissed her temple and grabbed her hand. "As I said before, let's get this over with."

They walked through the hallways and then through the grand door of the ballroom. Kol, back straight and smug smirk on his face, and Thea beside him with an effortless closed-lip smile. The picture of poise and power. Invisible masks covering who they truly are.

Kol walked into every room as if he owned it, and Thea was quickly learning how to match such energy with her powerful husband. He walked them toward the center of the room, the dance floor, and made a show of sweeping her in a large circle before pulling her into an embrace.

"I have a little surprise for you," Kol said, and before Thea could question him, the music swelled. The melody of her favorite waltz began to play, the same one they shared on her birthday. Her eyes snapped to Kol's, finding them in an instant, as he had already been looking to her for a reaction. Delight and surprise covered her delicate features.

"How did you do this? They told me we weren't allowed to do this dance because it was 'too *provincial for a royal wedding.*'" She quoted the council member who had shot down her request.

"Darling, I am the Prince. I can do nearly anything I want. Including adding a dance to a party to make my wife happy." He lovingly bopped her nose with his finger. "Plus, it means a lot to me as well." Thea thought of their first dance together at her birthday party, which felt like a lifetime ago. She had insulted him and kicked him out of her home, and she was still unsure how that was endearing to him.

"Yes, that fateful night when I mocked you in a room full of people and kicked you out of my party." A laugh came from deep inside of him, and he threw his head back as it came out. He couldn't remember the last time he had laughed so hard.

"Yes, that night. The first time I saw you." He pulled her tighter to him. "The first time I touched you." He trailed a hand down her spine. "The first time I saw how fiery and passionate my future wife was." He again locked eyes with her, and his blue eyes glistened with adoration and passion. "The only regret I have in life is that I temporarily have to let you go." He effortlessly released her and joined the line of men who had got into formation behind them. Thea turned and joined the women behind her in line, waiting for the musical cue to begin dancing.

They moved through the dance effortlessly and though dozens of people surrounded them, they felt as if they were alone – floating in their own world, dancing to their song. Thea remembered how Kol had brazenly touched her finger with his own during one touchless turn of the dance at her party, and feeling touch starved without his hands on her; she decided to copy this notion. As they turned, she sequentially tapped her four fingers against his, provoking a wicked grin from her husband. But he was not to be outdone. As soon as the third touchless turn ended, he threw propriety out of the window. While the other couples danced inches apart, only touching where their hands laid, Kol pulled her so close a breath couldn't squeeze between them. Thea grew hot under the disapproving stares of those around her, but instead of the judgmental eyes pressuring her to pull away from him, they fueled her rebellion. *I am the Princess now, and I can do almost anything,* she thought, copying what Kol had said earlier about himself. She leaned her hips into his, relishing every curve of his body and reveling in the sharp intake of breath it extracted from Kol.

"Blessed, burn me." He cursed under his breath. "This is delicious torture." Thea delighted in the power she was discovering held over him. She swirled her hips against him. "You wicked creature." He said this as a compliment. And all too soon, the dance was over, and they were forced to extract themselves from one another to mingle with their guests. As they walked on the dance floor, he whispered to her. "You will pay for that."

"Do you promise?" She asked as she discreetly swiped her hand across the front of his trousers. He gulped and nodded in response. "Good. That's what I'm counting on." Thea felt daring and acted unflinching in her efforts to let Kol know it. He was, after all, the one that freed her from the invisible chains society had kept around her for her entire life.

"As I said, you are a wicked little thing." He praised her. She shrugged in response – as if it were blasé and not a new bold feature of her character.

"That was," A man cleared his throat. "Quite the show." Thea and Kol extracted themselves from their private love bubble to engage the man who had approached them.

"Malcolm." Kol greeted tersely. The man before them, Malcolm, was extraordinarily tall and broad. He stood more than a head taller than every man in the room and was twice as wide.

"King Malcolm." A tall woman beside him corrected, presumably his wife, if one could assume by their physical proximity and handholding.

Kol stared, refusing to acknowledge the authority of the man in front of him. Thea deduced from his sheer size and title that the leader of the Strong realm was in front of her. "Can I help you?" He asked.

"We came to offer our congratulations-" He paused before continuing, attempting to give Kol a withering stare, but he should have known that Kol doesn't scare easily. "And to inquire about the location of one of my men, he never returned from his patrol of the border of our two lands." *So, he came to wish us false congratulations and make veiled threats,* Thea thought.

"I'm sure he will turn up soon," Kol replied indifferently.

"I should hope so." Malcolm stared at Kol – like he was trying to burn a hole through him.

"Is that all? This is a party, after all, and we have many guests to see." Thea interjected.

"The men are speaking." Malcolm dismissed her, igniting a white-hot rage through both she and Kol. She feared Kol's response and placed her hand on him, hoping he remembered his promise not to react impulsively or out of rage anymore.

Through gritted teeth, Kol responded. "You will not speak to my wife in that way ever again if you value your life." A vein throbbed in his neck, tension pulling in every muscle in his body, as he used great force to not overreact. "Lucky for you, I promised her I would not act rashly, but I do think you and your wife would better enjoy the rest of the night in your rooms." A shift in his eyes was all that clued Thea in that he was using his Control. "Leave now." Immediately Malcolm and his wife turned and left the room without another word. Kol turned to Thea instantly, "I am so sorry they disrespected you." All venom that was previously in his voice was replaced with sincerity. But Thea didn't care about them; all she cared about was that he had kept his promise to her.

"Thank you." She hugged him. "For keeping your promise and not responding to him, even though I know you wanted to."

"Of course. I will always keep my promises to you." Truth. Thea's heart swelled with love, and she couldn't contain the joy on her face. "Let's finish our duties for the night so we can be alone." He kissed her forehead softly.

Thea and Kol then followed around his father for much of the night, speaking to several Lords and Ladies from various lands important to the Empire. Toward the end of the night, her parents approached them, but Kairo was the first to greet them.

"Grayson! Josephine!" He patted her father on the back as if they were old friends.

"Your Majesty." They said in near unison. "We came to wish our daughter congratulations and to let her know that thanks to your generosity, we will be joining the royal family for Christmas this year. For two whole weeks!" Her mother beamed with excitement as she said this. Thea turned in shock toward her father, wondering how he had gotten Kairo to agree to this.

As if on cue, her question was answered. "Now that you mention that, we should discuss how your men will travel here for their militia training. We need all the men we can get and we need them trained soon." Thea watched as her father's face paled. He had given up much (in the way of other people's lives) to be granted more time to see his daughter. Without thinking, Thea pulled her father into a hug.

"Thank you." She whispered, and he squeezed his arms around her tight. She turned and hugged her mother. "I am so happy you will get to be here to celebrate. Truly." She looked them both in the eyes, feeling the finality of her time as their child coming to an end. She looked to Kol. She was his wife now, no longer a daughter of Veritas but a wife of Mori.

Thea's parents looked at her lovingly and then continued their conversation of logistics with the High King. Thea turned, and saw Kol finishing a whispered conversation with a guard. "Now's our chance," Kol came up behind her and pulled her into the shadows. With hardly anyone noticing, he walked them out a servant's exit and then bolted for the stairs. Kol couldn't stand to be apart from her any longer, and every inane conversation he was having at the party pushed him closer to madness.

"Where are we going?" She asked with a giggle.

"My bedroom." He stated obviously. Thea felt tendrils of excitement flush throughout her body, and she instantly thought back to the first time she had an education on sexual pleasure. A new tutor showed up at her house with anatomical models and sage wisdom. Thea had nearly fainted from embarrassment, she never dreamed of the day where the idea of sex wouldn't frighten her. But here she was now, eager, sick of waiting to the point of near hysteria. *I may go mad if I'm not touched by him soon,* she thought with grave certainty. She didn't even care anymore about Kol's *experiences.* As Dorothy had told her in previous conversations, it may play to Thea's favor.

They burst through the door of his room, and no sooner than the door clicked closed behind them did his feverish hands grasp onto her waiting body. He couldn't contain himself as his hands searched roguishly up and down her figure. Hot lips found their way to her neck, and he whispered between each wild kiss.

"Mine." He breathed on her neck before crashing a wanting kiss to her skin. "Mine." Teeth nipped and then were replaced by his tongue. "Mine." His lips refused to leave her skin even as his words vibrated off her skin as he spoke. She had resented feeling like property her whole life, but under Kol's cerulean gaze and expert hands, she didn't mind belonging to him. *He also belongs to me.* With that thought, she took off, hands matching his pace as she explored his body. Teeth nipped harder at her neck, causing a gasp to escape her parted lips. Kol leaned up, capturing her gasp with his mouth as he kissed her lips fervently. The back of her legs bumped up against something; she opened her eyes to see his bedroom. She hadn't even realized they had slowly been stepping their way toward the bed since entering the room. He took her bottom lip into his mouth and sucked.

"Mmm." She moaned and sighed simultaneously, leaning further into his body. Suddenly and without her consent, a rumble reverberated from her abdomen. Not desire this time, but hunger. Thea blushed, again not in desire but embarrassment. A deep, rueful laugh escaped Kol's lips, and he placed his forehead against hers.

"Hungry?" He asked. She shrugged and nodded in reply. "Have you eaten at all today?" She shook her head no. Dove had made it abundantly clear to the staff that Thea was not to be fed today. Under the order of the High King, she wasn't to look 'fat or puffy' for the ceremony. All she had managed to eat was a piece of fruit Ruth had snuck out of the kitchen. "Darling, why didn't you eat anything?" His tone had gone from seductive to gentle in no time at all.

"Your father said I wasn't allowed to be fat today and food would do that. I suppose he isn't pleased with how I look."

She shrugged, not that she cared about the opinions of a tyrannical jackass.

"I hate that man." Kol practically growled. He grabbed the fat of her bottom in his hand and squeezed. "This body is perfect." Another knee-weakening kiss was placed on her lips. "Let me go get you something to eat." He released her and she instantly felt the absence of his hands.

"Kol, it can wait. We were kind of in the middle of something." She says bashfully.

"Believe me, I know." He said as he adjusted himself, a look of pain on his face. "But I want to take care of my girl." Her heart warmed at his tenderness. "Besides, you're going to need your strength for what I have planned for tonight." Other parts of her warmed at that comment. He kissed her again, long and slow, with one hand on her cheek. "I will be back soon."

"Maybe I'll have a surprise waiting for you when you return." She tried to match his sultry tone as she walked to the bathroom and held up the lacy scrap of fabric she had stowed away in there.

He groans in agony. "You're making leaving right now really hard."

"Hopefully, that's not the only thing I'm making hard." She teased.

"Blessed, burn me." He groans again. "I will be right back!" He yelled as he raced out the door.

Thea, thoroughly proud of herself, strode into the bathroom and managed to get herself out of the dress that had taken two women to get her into. She pulled on her new lacy outfit, a strappy, see-through mini corset and scant matching bottoms, and then pulled on a silk robe and belted it closed. Once released from the pins, her hair fell in thick waves over her shoulders and down her back. Shortly after getting dressed, she heard the door click open.

"That was very fast. Maybe I should give you an award for speed." She said as she slinked around the corner.

"A reward? I'm intrigued." A male voice replied, but not Kol's voice. A body emerged from behind the doorway and stepped into the bedroom, dressed in all black and facial features shielded. *A Dissenter.* Panic clutched Thea's chest as she backed away slowly, trying to gather her thoughts enough to formulate a plan, but time was not on her side. The dressing room door burst open from behind her, revealing another man who had been in the closet the whole time. She spun to the side, trying to keep her eyes on both of them at the same time.

"Help!" She screamed. "Someone's in here with me, help!"

One of the Dissenters laughed. "Gorgeous," Her skin crawled. "No one will hear you. They are all downstairs at your pretty party."

This wouldn't stop her from trying. "Help!" She screamed again.

"Shut her up, please." One of the men said to the other.

"Gladly. Grab her." She tried to jump to the bed, but one of the men grabbed her by the arm and pulled her toward him. Her arms were then pinned behind her, and the other man pulled something out of his pocket – a small vial of clear liquid.

"What is that?" She yelled and attempted to wiggle out of the man's grasp. *Kol, where is Kol?* She screamed internally. The man dumped the vile out onto a cloth and stepped closer to Thea. She pushed away from him, but the man behind her was stronger than she.

"Night, night. *Princess.*" He said mockingly – before he covered her mouth and nose with the soaked fabric.

She tried to yell from behind the fabric, but it was muffled. She kept attempting to fight them – but all at once, her limbs felt as if boulders weighed them down, and her heart rate slowed to a dangerous pace. Thea's vision blurred and despite her willpower, her eyes sagged. And finally, she went limp, rendered unconscious by the poison she had breathed in.

"Stuff her mouth and tie this around it." The man put a piece of fabric in her mouth and tied another around her head to secure it, while the other man placed a piece of paper on the bed. "Let's go." The larger of the two men threw her over his shoulder and walked toward the balcony door, the same way he had gotten in all those hours ago. Several more Dissenters waited below the balcony and about halfway down the ladder the man dropped Thea's limp body down to his comrades below.

"Blessed, she barely weighs anything." One of the men who caught her commented.

"Hardly wearing anything either." Another commented, earning sniggers from the rest of the men.

"Quit fooling around." The man who had drugged her said with authority. He was overseeing this operation. "You have your orders." The men covertly carried her outside the Palace gates to a small, black carriage. They threw her in, tied up her hands and feet, and ordered the driver to take off.

As Thea was being bumped around and whisked to an unknown location, Kol was re-entering his room, pushing a tray covered in food with him. He laughed to himself, remembering the first night Thea had been at the Palace and he had pushed a similar tray of food into her apartments and pretended to be a servant just to see her. *So much has changed.* He thought as he rounded the corner into his bedroom.

"I'm back, and sorry I wasn't as fast as I said I would be, but I brought back literally one of everything in the kitchen, so hopefully you won't be too upset with me." He said with a light-hearted tone as he started taking the lids off the various plates he had brought back with him. "Thea?" He asked playfully. "Are you hiding from me?" He laughed. "As adorable as that is, I would love to feed you so we can get back to what we were doing." He walked toward the bathroom. "Oh! And so I can see you in that scrap of fabric you taunted me with earlier." He peeked his head into the bathroom and saw her heap of a wedding dress crumpled on the floor. "Darling, this dress is too gorgeous to leave lying around. I honestly may ask you to put it back on just so I can stare at you in it." He opened the dressing room door, no Thea. His heart started to race a little. *Have I upset her by being gone so long? Did she go back to her own apartments?* Distraught, he threw her wedding gown on the bed and planned on running across the second floor to her rooms to find her. But as her dress hit the bed, the breeze it created disrupted the piece of paper left by her captures, causing it to fall off the bed and float to the ground. The fluttering paper caught Kol's eyes and he leaned over to snatch it up.

Red hot fury boiled in his veins. *They took her.* Devastation and fear threatened to steal the show in his mind, but he remained steadfast. Devastation and fear would leave him a sobbing heap on the floor, but fury would help him find her. Fury would help him kill the ones who took her.

Chapter 13

Thea awoke, disoriented, but almost instantly, the reality of her situation came back to her, and fear threatened to consume her. *I've been taken,* she remembered with absolute certainty. She waited as her senses slowly turned on, allowing her to make better sense of her surroundings. The smell and sound of burning wood was the first thing she noticed, and when she opened her eyes, she could see several men sitting around a fire. They were speaking in hushed whispers that no amount of strained listening could distinguish. Looking around she could only tell two things; it was night and she was in the forest. But she didn't know how long she was out, what these men wanted, or where they were taking her. Checking in with her body, she noticed how cold she was. The brisk autumn air was freezing her bare legs, but her legs were only slightly colder than the rest of her – her whole body shivered beneath the silk nothing she had draped around her body. Next, she noticed that her body ached, she felt exactly as sore as she had the time she had fallen off her horse as a girl, and she discerned without looking that her body was covered in bruising; the hard dirt beneath her was doing nothing to ease her discomfort.

Thea had been made almost completely immobile and mute. Moving her tongue, she found a cloth gag had been secured around her mouth and after attempting to sit up she found that ties adorned her wrists and ankles. Her ankles were tied together, the restraints left only a foot of space between them – making running away nearly impossible. *What am I going to do? Is anyone going to find me?* Silent tears fell from Thea's eyes as she assessed her situation. Her eyes darted back and forth, pointlessly searching for an ally or escape.

Laughter boomed from the firepit, and all the men raised pints into the air.

"To a successful mission." One shouted.

"Aye!" They all shouted in unison.

He continued. "And to the eventual downfall of the Mori Empire!" At this, the men hooted in unison again.

What if thoughts darted disturbingly around Thea's mind. *What if I had refused food from Kol tonight? What if I fought back harder? What if no one finds me? What if I die? What if I had said no to marrying Kol today?* She hated herself for wondering that last one. She knew that somewhere in the Palace Kol was panicking and using every resource at his disposal to find her. *I hope he finds me.*

Thea closed her eyes and imagined she was sitting with Kol in one of the Palace's gardens. In her mind, they're having the picnic he promised her they could have once winter turned to spring and the air warmed. *He's telling her of an adventure he had on one of his various travels, she laughs, and he smiles as he watches her. His blue eyes are swimming with love as he delicately reaches out and brushes windblown hairs behind her ear. "I love you." He would say.*

Tears began freely falling down her face again. *I will never hear him say those words,* she thought. Dread and grief washed over her as she began to mourn the life she would never get to have with him.

A branch snapped in the distance, pulling Thea from her wallowing, and the sound of whinnying horses followed. *Someone is near! I must remove this cloth.* Determination filled her as she aggressively pushed her face to the earth and tried to use the ground as leverage to push the gag away from her mouth. Pebbles and twigs scratched her face as she frantically brushed at the ground. She felt it pulling down and hope filled her chest, but as soon as she raised her head to start again, it slipped right back into place.

Thea could now see lanterns of the approaching caravan in the distance. *I need something stationary to pull it off!* Now acclimated to the darkness, her eyes spotted a raised tree root near her. She looked to the firepit, the men were too drunk on ale to have noticed that she had woken up, let alone to see that her salvation was pulling up the dirt road beside them. Twigs snapped as she rolled toward the root. Pain pulsed through her right eye, she had smacked it right into the tree root. "Burn it!" She tried to curse at the tree, blaming it for her pain instead of her jerky, hurried movements. A low hiss escaped her mouth as she processed the pain. Deciding to ignore the throbbing ache that was now pulsing from her eye, she reached her neck out and snagged the corner of her gag on the tree root. Luckily, it was with ease that she pulled her head down and rolled away – leaving the cloth stuck to the tree root behind her. "Thank you, God." She whispered after she spit the remaining fabric from her mouth.

Her eyes darted back to the dirt road, but she was no longer the only one to have noticed the approaching carriages. All the men around the fire were now standing and looking toward her. Lucky for her, they were too drunk and frazzled to notice her lack of gag. All she had to do was bide her time.

"Cover her up!" One shouted as he threw a blanket at his companion. She was again cloaked in darkness, but this time not without hope. The carriage pulled to a halt, and she listened as a door opened and shut.

"I'm not interrupting the merriment, am I?" A male voice asked.

"No, my lord, just resting on our travels." The man who seemed to be in charge answered.

"Your name?" The mystery man asked.

"Marcus, my lord."

"Marcus, did you know you were trespassing in the Strong Realm?" He asked. The *Strong Realm?* Thea thought. *We've traveled that far?*

"We are just passing through, my lord," Marcus replied in a diplomatic tone. "We will be gone by morning."

"Very well." The man turned to leave.

Now is my chance! "Help me! I've been taken hostage!" She yelled as loudly as she could.

"What was that?" The man asked. "Answer me!" He demanded after a moment of silence.

"I'm on the ground! Under the blanket! Help!" She yelled again. The large Dissenter beside her kicked, landing his boot directly in her stomach. She cried out in pain, alerting the lord instantly to her location.

"Guards!" The lord yelled out, and within moments he was flanked by half a dozen men. "Uncover her!" The breeze from the blanket being torn off her was as much of a surprise as a kick to the gut, but this one she welcomed.

"Thank you!" She almost started to cry, and then the large Dissenter to her left shoved her to the ground.

"Shut up!" He yelled.

242

"Arrest these men." He instructed and placed his hand before her face. Thea grabbed it and looked up, finally looking upon the face of her savior. Before her stood Malcolm, king of the Strong Realm.

"Malcolm, thank God you came by. I feared for my life." Thea started to cry. A look of confusion crossed his face, he didn't recognize her.

"Malcolm, what is going on?" His wife asked as she stepped from the carriage. Immediate recognition covered her face. "Princess Althea?" His facial features turned from confusion to rage.

Malcolm's expression mirrored his wife's. "Althea? The Prince's wife?" Thea nodded, confused herself at the hostility. *I know our realms are not allies, and Kol had been terse with them earlier, but why do they look like they hate me?* "Men, change of plans." They released the Dissenter men. "Arrest her. And place her in the carriage." *Arrest me? For what?*

"What is the meaning of this?" She asked as she was roughly seized by Malcolm's soldiers.

"Vengeance." He answered. "God fated vengeance." He laughed grimly. "Knock her out." A sharp blow to the head stunned Thea, a moment of pain and then darkness greeted her once again.

For the second time in her life, Thea awoke unsure of where she was, but with absolute certainty, she knew it wasn't home. *Home, at the Palace, with Kol.* Her heart longed for comforts that felt like home: Kol's embrace, Dorothy's laugh, or the tangy-sweet taste of citrus tarts. But all she had was a cold, rock floor beneath her feet, the taste of blood in her mouth, a lingering headache, and the stench of mildew filling her nose.

She blinked slowly, her eyelids feeling heavy and sluggish – not to mention the right one smarted with pain each time she moved it. The room she was in much resembled the dungeon rooms below the Palace. The stone floor, caked in layers of dust and debris, steadied her as she pushed her top half off the floor with her shoulder. Shackles clinked as she moved, inhibiting her movements as the ties had in the forest, only allowing her the ability to sit up with her feet together. Her head swam as she sat up, and she had to close her eyes and wait for the room to stop spinning. Questions filled her mind, mainly she wondered how long she had been knocked out this time, but she also was confused as to why Malcolm had saved her – only to imprison her again.

"Why is this happening to me?" She whimpered, tears brimming in her eyes and threatening to spill over.

"I asked myself the same question just yesterday." Malcolm's voice boomed from the shadowed corner of her cell, startling Thea and urging her to scoot as far away from him as possible. He laughed at her pathetic attempts at protecting herself. "Good luck trying to get away from me with no use of your hands or feet, *Princess.*" He mocked her title, just as coldly as Kol had refused to acknowledge his.

"Why are you doing this to me?" She shouted, anger temporarily winning the war of emotions swirling inside of her.

"Silence! You Mori whore." She gasped as if that insult had been a physical slap to her face. He rose from his chair in the corner and stepped into the shred of light a lantern was providing her cell. "As I was saying." He cleared his throat. "I asked myself the same questions yesterday, 'Why me?'" He mocked the sorrowful voice she had first asked that question in. "When I went to my guest room at your Palace, well more like was 'Mori'

Controlled and forced to go to my room by your husband. And there I found a large golden box sitting on my bed." He walked a slow circle around her, eyeing her like prey the whole time. "Do you know what was in the box, Althea?" She shook her head no. He laughed again, a laugh drenched in darkness. "I was gifted the head of my brother." His voice cracked. "My only brother, my younger brother, who had been sent to patrol the borders of our lands and had the displeasure of crossing paths with the *Prince*." He spat Kol's title out like it was rancid food. Thea didn't know if it was her newfound hate for Malcolm, her desensitization to Kol's violence, or being left emotionally barren after her two kidnappings – but she didn't care at all about the fate of Malcolm's brother. She stared at Malcolm, no emotion crossing her face. This angered him more. "You have nothing to say?" He shouted. "No words for my fallen brother or apologies on behalf of your husband?" She tried not to flinch as his spittle rained down on her face.

"If he was anything like you, there seems to be no loss in my eyes." She muttered, and knew it wasn't the right thing to say even as the words left her mouth. But she couldn't bring herself to care. White, hot pain stung her cheek as Malcolm open hand slapped her. Strong strength coursed through his veins, but even in his fury, he restrained himself, knowing the full force of his slap could easily snap her neck. And he wanted her alive a bit longer, to suffer.

"I'm going to enjoy every ounce of torturing you – as you did my brother." He said sadistically. "And when I'm done, I'll send that pretty little head of yours back to your husband. See how he likes the taste of his own medicine." This stirred the fear inside her. *I don't want to die,* her soul whimpered. She said a silent prayer as she watched Malcolm remove his formal jacket

245

and take a knife and leather strap from a guard outside the cell. She prayed that by some miracle Kol would find her, and soon.

"I didn't hurt your brother." Thea cried out.

"You might as well have." Blood trickled down her arms as Malcolm daintily scratched a path from her wrist to her elbow. Not deep, but just enough to sting and draw blood. "While you're here, you might as well be useful. Tell me, *Princess*, what are your husband's plans for attacking my realm?"

"My loyalty lies with the Empire and the Prince. Even if I did know, I wouldn't tell you." She spat each word at him as if they were venom. He laughed again, a bone-chilling and spine-tinglingly evil sound.

"I hoped you wouldn't give in too easily." In one swift motion, he grabbed the material of her silk robe and ripped it from her body and cracked the leather whip hard across her bare back.

"Ahh!" She cried out in agony. Thea had never known such pain. The welted skin on her back pulsed with a significant ache, taking on a heartbeat of its own.

"Such a pretty girl you are." Bile rose in her throat as he trailed his grubby hands on her neck and chest. He crouched in front of her, getting as close to eye level with her as his large frame would allow, and grabbed her left breast in his hand. She tried to pull away from him, but he squeezed harder. "I am so tempted to carve my name right here." He poked the tip of his knife into the swell of her upper breast. "But to maim such a supple breast seems a crime." A small drop of blood rolled down her chest, staining her white corset. Her breath caught in her throat, and the various pains of her body and traumas in her mind threatened to knock her out – but they didn't get the chance.

"May the Blessed burn you and this whole realm to the ground. May you and your children be ashes in the wind, you vile, perverse creature." Thea said with eerily calm conviction – before she spat in his face. A few seconds passed as shock froze him, but he quickly recovered and slapped her again – harder this time. Thea was knocked unconscious before she hit the floor.

Light kissed the sky, causing beautiful hues of orange and purple to dance on the horizon, in stark contrast to Kol, who rode against the rising sun in all black with determination and purpose. His destination was a Dissenter camp. The letter he had found on his bed, in place of his wife, had directed him north, just east of the Strong realm. He was to bring gold, food, and a decree to change several Mori policies – only then would they release his wife. Instead, he brought his trusty dagger, various other weapons, and enough supplies for his journey there and back. They were going to release her or they were going to die and then he would take her. Either way, he was leaving with Thea – at the expense of their lives.

He had ridden into battle countless times, even looked death in the face, but the feelings of fear he had resting in his gut this day were worse than when he had looked across a battlefield filled with hundreds of enemy soldiers. Thea had grounded him his whole life. As a child and he felt restless, she was a story to get him through the day, and as a lonely adolescent, she was a light shining at the end of a very dark tunnel. But now that he had met her, she meant more to him than she ever had. She was his joy, his purpose, his only friend, his only confidant, and the only one who helped him grow. *I only just got her.* He fought back tears, and his resolve strengthened. *I can cry tears of joy when she is back in my arms again.*

Riding half a day's journey behind him were Mori soldiers. He had left the Palace as soon as he could get dressed and inform the council of his needs. He demanded a unit of soldiers be sent fully equipped to take on a small army to follow him. Despite his father's dislike of his son's frivolous love, he wouldn't pass up an opportunity to launch an attack on the Dissenters, an anarchist group who he felt had long overstayed their welcome in his Empire. Kol found himself counting the steps the horse was taking or forcing his eyes to follow along with the birds in the sky, all in an effort to not think about what could be being done to his Thea. He thought back to the cesspools of war camps he had seen in the past, a place where the depraved men were left unsupervised and able to act out their darkest fantasies. He had heard horror stories of rapes or beatings that men had doled out – these thoughts made him ride harder.

By the time daylight had broken out across the sky, his horse was galloping full force into the Dissenter camp. He had no time for scouting out the situation, and he was coming in with swords drawn. The first men he encountered at the entrance to the gate simply stepped aside, gawking at him in fear as he rode confidently into their camp. Wise *men,* he thought. He knew his way around a war camp, so he rode with determination toward the middle of the camp, where he knew the leader's tent would be. He barged in without an announcement and demanded sternly to the man sitting behind a desk:

"Give me back my wife." Unwavering authority laced every word he said, and if looks could kill every man in that tent would be dead. Kol kept a steady eye on them all, tracking his gaze back and forth between the few men in the tent, watching to make sure none of them made a move on him. He noted that none of them wore the signature Dissenter mask, and despite the havoc they were wreaking in his heart and Empire – they just looked like ordinary men. Ordinary, non-Blessed men.

"Prince Kol, I assume?" The man asked with a smirk. "Marcus." He placed a hand on his chest in introduction.

"Where is my wife?" Kol asked, teeth bared. "Release her, or I will start killing." Kol never minced words, especially not when the most important thing in his world was at risk.

"Come now, we are all civil gentlemen, and we can settle this as such. Did you come with the demands we had?" Marcus asked diplomatically.

"I will not negotiate with the likes of you," Kol stated plainly. "Bring me to her." His mind was one tracked.

Marcus clicked his tongue in disapproval. "I'm afraid without the demands I put forth in the letter, or at least a negotiation, my answer will have to be no." He smiled maliciously.

In one fluid motion, so fast that had one blinked they would have missed it, Kol plucked a knife off his belt and hurled it toward the Dissenter closest to him. The man gasped and gurgled as he pawed at the knife lodged in his throat.

"He'll be dead in less than five minutes; I severed his carotid. My negotiation is this – if you give me Thea, I will not do that to every single one of you." Kol stared at Marcus, challenging him to deny him what he wanted.

"No," Marcus stated with authority, though his voice slightly wavered.

"Okay, you don't care about your men. Noted." Kol looked around the room, considering his next move. "But I'll bet you care about someone." A bead of sweat formed over Marcus' lip, Kol had hit a nerve. "A family, perhaps? A wife? Children?" Marcus didn't speak, but the subtle twitch of his eyebrows let him know it was true. Kol pointed to a man close to him and beckoned him over. "You there, come here." The man hesitated, fear on his face. "If I wanted you dead, you'd already be dead, just come here. I just need to tell you something." The man walked over slowly, eyes darting back and forth between Marcus and Kol, and once he was close enough, Kol clamped a hand on his back. The man nearly jumped out of his skin. "Now, I cannot force you to tell me the truth, but I can make you do other things." He looked the man in the eyes, turning on his Control. "Touch your nose." The man did. "Dance around." He did. "Pretend you're a little girl." He twirled an imaginary skirt. "Pretend you're a goat." He plopped down on all fours and began to chew on the corner on the rug. Kol laughed and even Marcus had a tentative look of amusement on his face. "Stand back up now." Once he was standing up Kol stood before him and placed both hands on his shoulders. "When you get home from this long journey – you're going to go to Marcus' house and slaughter his whole family."

Marcus gasped. "Darius wouldn't do that!"

Kol smirked, he knew he had him now. "Don't you get it, you daft fool – he has to." Kol walked toward Marcus defiantly. "I am more powerful than you could even imagine, and I will ruin your life, and make it a lonely, tortured life at that if you don't give me back my wife," Kol said sternly.

Marcus looked back and forth between Kol and Darius, trying to decide if what Kol commanded would be done – if he was willing to risk the gamble. Marcus groaned in agony, "We don't have her!" Kol's smirk fell, and devastation filled his heart.

"Where is she?" He tried to sound authoritative, but it was so hard when he felt so devastated.

"The Strong king took her. He happened upon us and discovered her and took her for his own vengeance, he said," Marcus answered.

"What vengeance?" Kol asked.

"He said you killed his brother, sent him the head or something. Said he wanted to show you what it felt like."

Kol screamed in frustration and agony. He hadn't known that was the king's brother, not even Kol was brazen enough to offend an enemy to that level while they were staying in his own home. Kol's heart pounded in his chest, and he began to mentally calculate how quickly he could ride to the Strong realm. *I can get there by nightfall, and she will be alive. She must be.* He stormed out of the tent, only to be followed.

"I gave you what you wanted! Call off the death hit on my family." Marcus yelled. Kol turned back to look at him. "Please." He begged.

Kol looked back to Darius and used his Control on him one final time. "Kill only the wife. Leave his children be." Kol continued his walk toward his horse and jumped on its back.

"Please! No! Take it back. I will give you whatever you want." Marcus dropped to his knees and begged.

"An eye for an eye, you took my wife – I will take yours," Kol said callously and then rode away. He shouted over his shoulder, "You could always kill Darius or write your wife and tell her to leave and never see you again or you could disband your little group here and run away with her. Either way, you're losing something, therefore I win." But it was a lie. He wouldn't feel like a winner until he knew his Thea was okay. He snapped the reins and kicked the horse into a run, leaving the misery he had created in his wake. Marcus sank lower to the ground and tearfully considered his options, regretting ever having crossed the Prince of Death. Kol returned to counting each step his horse took, pushing away the thought of Thea's beautiful head sitting in a golden box. *Perhaps she was right – that not everything should be addressed with violence. And now she will pay for my sins.*

Chapter 14

Thea had never felt so much pain. A pampered life of dancing and tart eating had not prepared her for hours of torture or interrogation. Her cheek was raw and swollen from all the hits it had taken. Her delicate arm was hanging at a sickening angle, dislocated. The once beautiful lingerie she wore was now covered in mud and blood. Its once ornate neckline was ripped, and the matching hem lay against her bruised ribs, now wholly tattered. Thea winced when she licked her dry lips, discovering yet another bleeding wound. But, to her horror, she was so dehydrated that she welcomed the blood, for at least it was something wetting her dry tongue.

Time was incalculable without sunlight to mark the days, but Thea figured her captors had detained her for no more than two days. However, she had passed out from pain so frequently that any amount of time could have passed. They were currently holding her in what looked like a grand, yet small, dining hall. Two men had chained her to the leg of a table. Not that it was necessary. With the combination of injuries and general weakness, she doubted she had the strength to stand, let alone escape or fight back against them. She cursed her family for never exposing her to any kind of combat training. Maybe if she had that, she wouldn't feel so helpless or hopeless. Perhaps if she had training, she could at least pretend she stood a shot of surviving this. At that moment, she didn't even know if she would survive the night, not if the gusto with which they had tortured her most of the day continued much longer. In stark comparison to the hell she was experiencing, revelry took place all around her as her tormentors took a break from tormenting her. The king had gone to bed – and left his men to their own devices. After taking turns spitting and pissing on her, the tormentors had taken to drinking ale and dancing around the room. About a dozen men and women drank and laughed around her, acting as if there wasn't the crumpled mass of Thea's body lying on the floor beneath their feasting table. They callously sang victory songs as she lay broken, covered in her own blood and their bodily fluids.

Thea's fevered and exhausted mind drifted to Kol, of his smile and how he would often brush his soft lips against her knuckles. If she closed her eyes, she could almost feel his fingers rubbing lazy circles on her bare legs. In stark comparison, she also remembered how he had looked when he had stabbed a knife into the hand of a man who had disrespected her. Fierce and unforgiving. He had promised to always protect her, and he had meant it, of that she was certain. She knew that the promises he made her came from a place of unwavering devotion, maybe even love.

In her heart, Thea knew Kol would be willing and capable of saving her – if he knew where she was and if he realized she was missing in time. But panic and sorrow gripped her again, as the fear in her mind told her that neither of those things were possible. She had to force herself to hold on to hope, for without hope, she knew she would surely die.

For what reason she had initially been taken was a mystery to Thea, but with sudden clarity, she realized what Kol had been saying the morning of their wedding. She had gained more than a lover or noble title with her marriage; she had also gained a slew of enemies. A lifetime of charity and benevolence on her part was now mute, as she had married the Prince of Death, and he had acted in no shortage of violence or malevolence during his lifetime. And now she would pay for that.

After hours of revelry, someone had remembered her presence there. The sound of heavy boots ambling toward her pulled her from her thoughts of Kol. Her swollen eyes peeled open and her head lulled painfully toward the direction of the shuffling feet. A large ruddy hand placed a cup on the floor near her.

"Thirsty?" He offered, gesturing toward the cup. Despite herself, she lunged toward it, primal thirst taking the reins from her resentment for the people around her. The chains around her ankles pulled, clinking loudly as she fell flat on the ground. She groaned in pain – but continued crawling forward and braced her weight on her good shoulder as she stretched toward the cup. It was just inches out of her reach.

"Please." She begged, voice raspy and barely above a whisper. Her sandpaper tongue rubbed roughly on the roof of her mouth.

"Let me help you." The man offered, before he callously kicked the cup over and spilled its contents all over the floor. He cackled maliciously as she wailed in disappointment.

Thea used all the will left in her, actively fighting the urge to give up and collapse to the ground, to look up at him with death in her eyes. "You will regret that." She swore defiantly

The man laughed again, looking around at his comrades as he did so. "Little lady, no one is coming to save you, so you can keep your threats to yourself." Lie. Hope filled her chest as she detected his lie, and then the door to the room was kicked open. Splinters shot out as the wooden mass burst open and then hung to the side, tittering off its hinges.

"Where. Is. My. Wife." Thea shivered, even knowing his anger would never be directed at her; at that moment, his very voice incited fear. She looked up at him from under the table, he had yet to see her, but she could see him. Blood dripped from both swords he held, and his dark, curly hair was dripping with sweat. Rage-filled eyes scoured the room, and his chest heaved with substantial breaths as he searched desperately for her. "I will not ask again!" He shouted.

The women screamed and fled the room knocking over chairs and dropping their glass cups as they ran. Metal chinked as the five remaining men in the room pulled their swords and began to walk toward Kol. He ignored them – as if driven by a single desire that turned off even his self-preservation skills. Kol had to know she was alive.

His eyes finally found her, and then he allowed himself to draw in the first steady breath he had inhaled since he discovered her missing. A strange combination of relief and horror flashed through him. He was relieved to find her – but also horrified and filled with shame that any of his past actions had led his enemies to do this to her. Horror reigned supreme in his mind to see the state she was in. Though he never raised his own hand against her, he felt as if every bruise on her body was directly his fault. It took all his willpower not to run to her immediately. He vowed to take care of her, but first, he had a job to finish.

"They did this to you?" He asked her calmly, strangely calm given the circumstances. She nodded – slowly. "All of them?" She confirmed with a weak head nod. He nodded grimly, before raising his gaze back to the men around him. He smiled sharply, showing nearly all his teeth in a wicked smile. "I want you all to know – I'm going to enjoy this immensely."

And then the killing began.

Kol's body moved with the precision of a trained killer, but his eyes darted wildly about like a feral animal. No one could touch him. He was driven by primal rage and armed with years of practice, and he sliced through each man who attacked him with ease. Superficial wounds were all they could land on him, a cut on his arm here or a punch landed there. He took down three men in a matter of moments. The remaining men screamed, calling for backup when they saw Kol easily topple their comrades. A dozen more men entered the room, some armed and others not. One of them, who had been a very active participant in her torture, smirked when he saw Kol standing in the middle of the room – thinking Kol's odds were not very good.

"He came to save you, just like you said." He spoke as he towered over Thea's crumbled body. "Too bad you're about to watch lover boy die." He crackled maniacally. "And you're going to watch." He crouched down and grabbed her by her hair, pulling her head up. She cried out in pain, and Kol froze. He froze long enough for one of the guards to push a dagger straight into his shoulder, but he didn't flinch – his focus was on her. Using all the power inside of him, he turned on his Control and pushed it out into the entire room.

"Halt!" He yelled, and instantly every man in the room froze in place. They moved their eyes in terror, back and forth to one another they looked as they shouted for help. "Silence!" Kol added. The room instantly became quiet; all Thea could hear was the sound of the crackling fireplace in the background and Kol's steps coming toward her. He jumped over fallen guards and ran to Thea's side. "Release her!" He yelled desperately at the man, whose grubby hands still held Thea's hair within their clutches, and he instantly released her. Kol placed his hands beneath her head, catching it as it fell from the man's grasp.

"Thank you." She choked out, and it nearly shattered Kol's heart hearing how weak she was. He finally took inventory of her condition, and on a single glance he could see several bruised ribs, black eyes, swollen lips, dehydration, and a dislocated shoulder. She also smelled of waste. This only fueled his desire to kill them even more. They had treated her worse than a prisoner, but he would do worse yet to them.

"Feck." He cursed under his breath. *I will spend the rest of my life trying to make this up to you, Thea.* Kol noted her restraints – locked shackles. *I need a key,* he thought. He observed the man crouched beside them and noticed the keys dangling from his hip.

"Unlock her restraints," Kol ordered, and the man did. Thea rubbed her wrists and looked around the room. Awestruck, she looked around at all the men Kol held under his Control. The vein popping in his forehead was the only evidence of how taxing Controlling that many men at once was for him. "Now stand," Kol instructed him. "Take this." He pulled the short sword from his hip and handed it to the man. "And slowly push it into your heart." He turned to Thea, "Look away, darling." He said as he wrapped her under his arm.

"No, I don't need to." She swallowed. "He deserves this." The arm hanging out of the socket at her side served as validation for her feelings on this man's life. She watched as he looked around in horror as he moved the sword up to his chest and positioned it over his heart. He opened his mouth as if to scream as the blade pushed into his flesh inch-by-inch, but not a sound came out – because Kol had silenced them all. Once his body hit the floor, Kol turned to Thea once more.

"Let's get you out of here." Kol picked her up, carefully placing his hands on her body, trying to find places to hold her where she wasn't injured.

"What about them?" She asked and tried to gesture toward the men, but her arm wouldn't cooperate with moving.

"Getting you to safety is more important than vengeance. I will come back for them later." Kol said, even shocking himself. The pre-Thea Kol wouldn't have forsaken vengeance for anything. He watched as a look of uncertainty crossed her face. "What's wrong? What can I do?"

"Kill them." She whispered.

"What?" He said out of shock more than confusion.

Using all the strength she had left, she moved her head and looked up at him. "Kill them all." Darkness filled her eyes as she requested this from him.

A small, wicked smile pulled at his lips. "With pleasure." He continued walking out of the room – and with all confidence simply said, "Drop dead." Thea watched in awe as every man in the room dropped to the floor, blood spilling from every orifice. *How powerful is he?* She wondered in reverence. He carried her through the halls, and she noted the several bloodied, dead bodies lining the walls of every room they walked past. Despite her previous distaste for violence, she couldn't find it in herself to be upset at the slaughter before her. She was just glad he had found her. In her darkest hour, she hadn't needed a well-mannered courtesan – she needed the Prince of Death. Her savior may come with darkness and trauma, but now so did she. *A perfect pair – fated to end up together and destined to rule the Empire with unwavering dominance. He sees me as his equal,*

259

and now I must act like it. Thea thought, thoughts of power and revenge controlling her mind.

Kol found a couch in an alcove of the front room and delicately sat her on it. His eyes trailed up and down her body, assessing her injuries. He noted the unnatural angle her arm dangled at and counted her visible bruises and scars. This was relatively easy as most of her body was visible, as she had long ago been stripped of her robe and had spent the entirety of the last day in nothing but lingerie.

"Most of your wounds look superficial, but the arm we need to fix. And you'll need clothes before we travel. It gets cold this far north when the sun goes down." Kol said, avoiding eye contact with her. He was filled with shame, knowing his actions led to this. Thea watched as he dug through his satchel. "Drink this." He pushed water toward her and she realized that he had yet to make eye contact with her since leaving the dining hall massacre. She watched quietly as he pulled the blood-soaked jacket off his body and draped it around her. "I'm sorry it's bloody. I know you hate that, but you're freezing. I promise I will find you something more suitable as soon as I can." He rambled nervously. She caught his hand with hers and he froze, ceasing his anxious babbling.

"Thank you," Thea said, and she tried to catch his gaze, but he continued to avoid it. "Please look at me." He swallowed, she watched as his Adam's Apple visibly bobbed, and he reluctantly turned his head to face her. His lip quivered as he stared into her eyes, vulnerable and tired, and he began to weep. It instantly made Thea feel uneasy, to see someone so powerful and stoic weep and fall to the ground under her gaze.

"I am so sorry, Thea." He choked out between cries.

"You saved me!" She took a deep breath, exhaustion from what she had endured threatening to pull her into a deep slumber. "Why are you sorry?" Thea asked.

"Thea, it's my fault they wanted to hurt you. Because I did the opposite of what you keep telling me to do. I acted out of violence, and you paid the price." He rubbed his hands over his face and began pacing in front of her. "This is exactly what I tried to tell you the morning of our wedding – you will always be a target now. Because of me."

"So, what do you want me to do? Leave?" She asked, growing frustrated.

"If that means you'll be safe, yes!"

"I'm not going anywhere, not without you." She said stubbornly. He ran his hand down his face again. She closed her eyes and slumped against him, getting too tired to even hold her own head up. "I love you." She said quietly.

"I don't want you to leave. I just don't know how to protect you all the time. I could always train you to be able to defend yourself." He was rambling again, not having heard her confession. "And we can assign guards to you." She leaned away from him and wobbled as she worked to hold herself upright.

"Kol." He snapped his eyes down to her. "I love you." He knit his brows together in confusion, before falling before her again. He crouched in front of her, a mystified look on his face.

"What?" He uttered, barely above a whisper.

"I love you." She took a deep breath. "I knew I liked you for a while. I liked the way you made me feel about myself and how much you believed in me." She drew in a labored breath. "But once they took me, and I thought I may never see you again – that's when I knew I loved you." He searched her face, still in disbelief. "And when you burst through those doors and saved

261

me, there was no question. So no, I'm not leaving. You can give me guards or train me to fight or whatever else will make you feel better, but I'm not going anywhere." Kol reached his hands out to her slowly, so delicately, as if she may shatter into a million pieces under his touch. He placed a deliberate and unhurried kiss on the unbruised corner of her mouth.

He was at a loss for words. "I never thought it possible." His voice cracked. "Especially after all you've seen and been through because of me." He looked away from her again, ashamed. She used the hand on her good arm to pull his gaze back toward her, and with his hand he gently grazed the corner of her busted lip. "Who did this? Is he dead now?"

"No, I don't believe so. The king did this one when he was interrogating me." Rage filled Kol's chest yet again.

"Then he must die too." He stood up, and watched as Thea followed him, wincing as she did so. "You can't travel like this." He looked her over again. "Thea, can I use my Control on you?"

Without hesitation. "Yes." He smiled, still surprised she loved and trusted him. "Why though?"

"I can take your pain away in your mind. Truthfully, it probably isn't a wise thing to do, because you can hurt yourself even further if you can't feel pain, but I need to push your arm back into the socket, and we have at least an hour on horseback to the closest town – and I don't want you to feel that." She nodded, understanding his rationale. "Once we get settled I can track down a Healer, but until then, this is the best I can do." He looked her in the eyes and called on his Control. "Thea, my love." She shivered. "You will feel no pain the rest of the night." She nodded, and instantly her body was washed in warmth – pushing away all the pain with it.

"Kol! It worked! I can't feel any of this." She gestured to her body.

"Good." He kissed her brow. "Now, let me fix this arm, kill the king, and get you out of here." He rattled off that list as if each were so casual – instead of the reality that he was rescuing his kidnapped wife and killing a king. Thea closed her eyes as he grabbed her arm and swiftly rotated it, but as he commanded, she felt no pain as he did so.

"Did you know you could use your Control in this way?" She asked.

"Not really, but of all the things I have Controlled, I didn't see why your pain couldn't be one of them." He put his hand on the small of her back and directed her down the hallway. "Did they hurt your legs? Can you walk?"

"They're just bruised." She answered.

"Then let's kill Malcolm and leave." He grabbed the hand of her uninjured arm and held it, clutching her fingers so tight she wondered if it would have hurt had he not taken her pain away. He led her to a staircase. "If this is anything like our Palace, Malcolm's room will be on the top floor." They started up the stairs but halfway up encountered a crouched and cowering maid. "Stand." Kol used his Control. "Take us to the king's room and do not make a sound or alert anyone else to our location." She silently climbed the stairs and led them directly to Malcolm's room. Thea would never get over the power of a Mori, the ability with just words to take ones free will away. The maid stopped in front of a large set of doors and pointed, before running away down the hall. Without hesitation, Kol pushed the doors open, letting them bang the walls loudly. Malcolm and his wife both sat up in bed, a hazy alarm on their face.

263

"What is the meaning of this?" Malcolm asked as he rubbed his eyes. "Prince Kol?" He laughed. "I wondered when you would get here." His demeanor shifted when he saw the blood covering both Thea and Kol's clothes. "What have you done?"

"You hurt my wife, and the punishment for that is death."

"You don't get to come into my realm and demand things of me," Malcolm said, irritation evident in his voice.

"I'm not demanding anything, I'm telling you." He looked at them both defiantly. "I only wish I had time to drag this out, make it painful for you as you did to my Thea." He spread his arms out. "But sometimes one doesn't get what they want."

"If you think you can beat me in hand-to-hand combat, you are mistaken. I have twenty more years of training and my Control on my side." Malcolm said as he stood from the bed and rolled his shoulders out.

"Of course not, but you forget I also have my Control." He looked to Malcolm's wife. "Die." And she immediately slumped over in bed, eyes dripping blood and her body unmoving. Malcolm screamed and dove toward her, pawing at her chest as he felt for a pulse.

"What have you done?" Malcolm screamed.

"The same thing I'm going to do to you. But first, I want to assure you that I will take good care of your realm." Malcolm stood and posed as if he were going to lunge at Kol. "Die." But he never got the chance. His body crumpled to the ground beside his bed, his lifeblood leaving his body. "Let's go." Kol grabbed Thea's hand again and led her toward the stairs, passed the dead bodies, and outside to his horse.

"Why couldn't you have done that all along? Kill him, I mean. Like, years ago to save all the wars." She asked, genuinely confused.

"Well, it's not exactly diplomatic. People usually respect the results of wars, maybe because both parties knowingly engage in it, but they don't always respond well to their ruler being killed without warning in his own bed in the night. Also, until today I didn't know I could do that." He admitted. Thea thought back to all the men in the banquet hall he had killed with only two words. *He is more powerful than even he knows*. Thea allowed him to place her atop his horse, and when he hopped on behind her, she couldn't help herself from leaning into him. He put both arms around her, his massive body completely encompassing hers. She didn't know if it was her exhaustion or the rhythmic jostling of the horse beneath her, but soon she was asleep against him.

Chapter 15

Kol took comfort in feeling the rhythmic rise and fall of Thea's breaths against him as he rode them into a nearby town. *She is alive. I saved her. She is alive. I saved her.* He repeated this over and over again in his mind – because he almost couldn't believe it. More than that, what he really couldn't believe and what he refused to let sink in – is how he had almost not succeeded. He wondered how much longer the king would have allowed her live had Kol not arrived that night. By the look of her and the lack of life-sustaining care they had given her, he doubted she would have been kept alive even a single day longer. He shuddered thinking about it. *She is alive. I saved her.* But he doubted this mantra would fully keep the demons that currently haunted his mind at bay. He attempted to busy his mind with listing the tasks he would need to accomplish once they arrived in a town: find a Healer, find housing, find food. But aside from the horrors that plagued his mind, he also caught himself being distracted by a much more pleasant thought. *She loves me.* Her utterance of those words had nearly erased decades of his father telling him he was undeserving of such affections.

He played back every second of their conversation. "I didn't say it back." He whispered. This realization hit him like a punch to the gut. He thought of the horrors she had faced, the terror she must have felt because of his actions – and he couldn't even say he loved her back. His desire for vengeance had distracted him, but at that moment he vowed that she wouldn't go another day without wondering where his affections lie.

Though the ride to the nearest town wasn't terribly far, the journey felt excruciatingly long to Kol. He was dreadfully aware of every injury on Thea's body, and he knew hours on horseback wouldn't help matters at all. But once they rode up upon town, his comfort in seeing civilization wasn't long-lived. He noticed it first at the entrance of town, where his family's flag had been torn and a large X had been placed on it. Then he saw that nearly every door they rode past bore the mark of the Dissenters, his family crest marked over with a large X. They had stumbled across an anti-empire town. He wondered what the odds were, that the one time he needed help he would find himself in the midst of enemies, but the odds were more likely than not the farther north one went. Pockets of anti-empire civilizations had started to crop up all over the Continent – particularly near areas yet to be conquered. The Strongs had been sympathetic to the cause and had allowed the anti-imperialists to congregate, so long as they didn't cause strife for their realm. *Fecking Malcolm.* He cursed the king again, still causing trouble for Kol even in death. Kol considered his options: find another town or lie about who he was. He considered the former greatly, considering he also didn't know the likelihood of finding a Healer in an anti-empire town – for those that were anti-empire were often also anti-Control. But he dismissed this plan when he considered Thea's injuries and the likelihood of finding another place to stay any time soon. Night and the chill that came with it had already settled into the air – and below his bloody riding coat, she wore no actual clothing. At least for the night, they would stay to sleep and gather supplies.

Kol pulled his horse to an abandoned corner of the town. He needed to wake Thea and inform her of their situation, neither of them being in the position to fight off a whole town if their identities were found out. Once he pulled his horse to a stop, he released the reins and carefully wrapped his arms tighter around Thea. He kissed her temple and watched in rapped awe as her eyelids fluttered open.

"Kol?" She asked in a sleepy voice, making his heart beat out of turn for a moment. He'd never tire of hearing her say his name.

"We've made it to town, love." He kissed her temple again.

"Home?" She asked; his heart clenched again, just knowing she considered his home hers did something to him.

"Not yet, but we will rest here, and I will take you home as soon as I can." She nodded, and then started to take in her surroundings. An audible gasp escaped her lips when she saw the Mori crest marked out with a large X, knowing the punishment for such disrespect was usually death. He shushed her. "I know, it will be okay."

"Where are we?" She whispered, fear gathering in her stomach as she noted all the anti-empire propaganda littering the alley.

"We are in a town just outside of the Strong realm. And it is, as you can see, anti-empire and pro-Dissenter." The fear was etched on her face now. "It will be okay. I will keep you safe. No harm will come to you here." Truth. She allowed herself to calm down after this realization. "We just have to lie about who we are and not let them know of the Mori family. Okay?" She nodded slowly.

"Who are we then?" She asked, getting on board immediately.

He smiled at her courage of spirit and ability to persevere. "We will keep it simple, middle names. I am Ari, and you are Tori. We are fleeing the Strong realm after they brutalized you for stealing. Okay?" She nodded again. "It's a simple enough story, one they will believe." He pointed up the road. "I believe that is an inn, we will go there and request a room. I will figure out our next steps from there."

"Thank you." She said quietly.

"For what?" Kol asked.

"Taking care of me."

"I will never stop taking care of you." He turned and started walking toward the inn, but he stopped abruptly, remembering the vow he had made. He turned around so quickly that it startled Thea and caused her to bump into him.

"Are you okay?" She asked with a small smile. And he loved that after the last two days, she still had the ability to smile within her.

"I love you. I need you to hear that and know that, and I realize I didn't say it before...." Thea watched, amused, as he rambled nervously again – clearly unaccustomed to this level of emotional vulnerability.

She pressed a chaste kiss to his lips, capturing his words mid-babble. "I know. And I love you too." She grabbed his hand with hers and started toward the inn again. "But let's talk about this somewhere warm, preferably with food in front of us." She gave another small smile, but this time Kol saw through it. Behind her attempts to calm him, he could see that she was still shaken – and incredibly tired.

"Yes, let's do that."

The inn looked fairly new, built three modest stories tall with red bricks. The wooden door opened to a room filled with jovial action: men playing cards, couples dancing, and food being served. Kol walked toward the bar with authority. Thea thought, *if anyone in this room had any sense, they would see a Prince walking amongst them.*

"Who do I talk to about getting a room for the night?" Kol asked. The bartender pointed to an older woman standing behind a wooden counter at the other end of the room.

"That would be my wife, right over there," Kol grunted a thanks and walked slowly with Thea over to the counter.

"We need a room for the night." He said again.

"I think we can arrange that." She said cheerfully before looking up at them, the second she did though, her face fell. "What the hells happened to the two a'you?" She covered her mouth in shock as she took in each new horror in front of her. Thea's lack of clothes, the amount of blood, the scars up and down Kol's bare arms.

"It has been a long night, and we just need a place to lay our heads." Kol tried to deflect, but the women didn't budge. He sighed, "My wife was beaten by the Strong king and his men for days. She worked in their castle and did something they didn't like and they didn't spare her any brutality. Please, just let her rest."

The woman spit on the ground. "Burn 'em all." She spit again. "I'll take of ya, sweetheart, don't ya worry." She pulled the sleeve of her shirt up to reveal a decades-old burn mark. "I've been on the receivin' end of a Controlled fury a time or two." She shook her head. "They're all the same, I tell ya." She came around the counter, key in hand. "I'll take yous up to room three, just one floor up, so ya don't have to walk up too many stairs, and then send up some food."

"Thank you, we appreciate it." Kol thanked her.

"I should thank you, from the looks of ya, you didn't leave without a fight – I've had an ax to grind with the Strongs for some time. Last Strong king killed my brother." She said sadly. And suddenly, Thea felt guilty for lying to her. Not only because truth was a vital part of Thea's nature, but also because this woman was being so genuinely kind to them.

"I'm so sorry for your loss," Thea said, speaking for the first time since entering the inn.

"Thank you, dear." She stopped before a door marked with a three and looked to Kol. "At least tell me the king will suffer the loss of a few men in his guard?" She asked.

"The king won't suffer anything anymore," Kol replied. When the innkeeper's face contorted in confusion, he continued. "Because I killed him."

"No shit?" She asked, an amused expression on her face.

"No shit," Kol confirmed. A smile spread across her face.

"I like ya." She laughed and slapped him on the back. "Dinners on the house tonight. I'll let you two get settled in." She walked back down the stairs and yelled. "King Malcolm is dead!" Elated shouts echoed up the stairs.

"Seems you've done the whole realm a favor," Thea said.

"Yes, but we'll see how happy they are when the Mori's take over the realm in place of Malcolm," Thea noted a sense of sadness in his tone. Kol didn't always love how feared and hated his legacy was.

They entered the small rustic room together. A small bed with a handmade quilt sat on the far side of the room, and scant

271

furnishings covered the rest of the walls – a desk, a washing bowl, and a small, three-drawer dresser.

"Bed is small. I'm not even certain it can hold both of us." Thea joked.

"I can sleep on the floor if you want, but…." Kol trained off mid-sentence.

"But what?" Thea asked.

"I'm trying to decide if I should impose my desires on you, given what you've been through."

"Why don't you say it and allow me the ability to choose what I want for myself."

Kol smiled, forever impressed by her spirit. "Fair enough, my love, fair enough." Her heart fluttered, as it always did when he called her a term of endearment. "I thought I had lost you, my hope and light just, poof-" He flicked his fingers in the air to simulate a vapor fading away. "Gone." He drew in a shaky breath as he sat on the edge of the bed. "And I'm afraid if I don't wake up with you in my arms – I will forget you're okay." He hung his head in sorrow.

She sat beside him on the bed and took his large hand in her. "Kol, you must stop mourning me – I am right here." She placed her other hand on his back and rubbed it in small circles.

A single laugh escaped his lips. "I don't know if I'll ever forget how you've been victimized." That word shot a hot arrow through her heart.

"I am not a victim. I am not 'a' anything anymore. You taught me that." She said with conviction. "I am not just a daughter or a wife or a woman. I am Thea. And you will treat me as such, because I'll tell you this, with your help I'll be able to get over what happened to me, but I will never be able to get over you looking at me like I'm broken or treating me like I'm made of glass."

Kol paused for a moment, considering her words. "You are so…" He looked at her with awe. "I don't have words to describe how incredible you are." He pulled her hand to his lips and kissed her knuckles. "But I can't forget what happened. How would that make us better or safer?"

"Then don't forget, guard me and train me – but you will not continue to mope as if I am dead or look at me as if I am damaged. Treat me as you always have. That is what I want." She said definitively.

"Then that is what I shall give you." He kissed her hand again before releasing it. A knock sounded at their door. "Enter." The innkeeper pushed the door open with her hip and came in carrying a tray.

"I've got food, water, ale – and a little something extra." After she said this, a middle-aged man entered the room behind her.

Kol became instantly suspicious, fearing his identity had already been found out, so he stood protectively in front of Thea. "Who is he?" Kol asked.

"Guard down, boy." She instructed Kol, and the flash of annoyance from being told what to do did not go unnoticed by Thea. "And you, close that door." She instructed the man, before clapping her hands together. "I realized that we got right into it without proper introductions." She placed a hand to her chest. "I'm Hannah, this is Enzo."

When Kol didn't answer, Thea did it for him. "I am Tori, and this is my husband, Ari." She spoke slowly, making sure to get their cover story correct.

"Why is he here?" Kol was relentless, but Hannah liked him. She laughed before answering.

"I want the twos of ya to have an open mind for a moment. After what you've been through, I realized that you'd be right to fear all Blest. But Enzo is good people. I say that on my grave." She crossed her heart over in a cross and kissed her fingers. Thea looked him over, a question on her face, playing the role of a scared and skeptical peasant.

He nodded. "I have the Control of Sana." Thea noticed an unplaceable accent coming from his lips.

"Sana?" Thea asked.

"I am a Healer, but Sana is what my people are called." Thea had known several Healers in her life, and none of them had requested to be called Sana. Her face must have looked confused, for he continued. "My healing is a special kind."

"I didn't know there were different kinds of Healers." Thea looked to Kol for clarification, but he shrugged his shoulders in response – he didn't know either.

"Sana are Healers of body and mind. We are rare now, scattered across these great Continents." That is all the explanation he was willing to give. "If you allow me, I will tend to your wounds and ease your mind of suffering and be on my way." Thea looked to Kol, wondering if there should be any reason she should object.

"And what do you want in return?" Kol asked skeptically.

"You slew the king of Strong?" Enzo asked.

"Yes," Kol replied.

"Then it shall be my gift to you." Enzo bowed respectfully, and Thea noted the long strand of prayer beads that stuck out from under his shirt.

"You are a man of religion?" Thea asked Enzo.

274

"We all are, my lady." He replied.

"And how is that?" Kol retorted.

"We are all created of the same, equal in God's eyes. We are all His people." Enzo responded, his accent growing more noticeable by the syllable.

"Where are you from, sir?" Thea asked.

"I believe you call it the Lesser Continent."

Thea's mouth dropped open. "I've never met someone from the Lesser Continent!" She exclaimed. "I have so many questions. No wonder I couldn't place your accent."

"I'm afraid I have no answers for you tonight. I am to heal you and be on my way." Enzo countered. Thea didn't even try to hide her disappointment, but she sat back on the bed and allowed him to begin healing her; she wasn't about to argue with a man who was helping her. "The physical healing will not hurt," Enzo explained. Little did he know Kol's Control had stopped her from feeling any pain no matter what he did to Thea. "But the mind healing may feel strange, just don't fight it. It may lead you to sleep. That is all right." Thea nodded and allowed herself to be laid flat on the small bed. "I don't want to be invasive child, but the mind healing is in its way…invasive."

"What do you mean?" Kol asked defensively.

"Whatever injury I heal, I must see – in order to know how to heal it. The mind is no different. When I go to give her peace, I will become privy to the sight of what injured her mind in the first place."

"You'll see my thoughts?" Thea grew concerned, fearing she and Kol's identities may be revealed.

"Not at all. I will be given glimpses of what is plaguing you, what caused your fear or anxiety. For example, it is likely I may see the face of the person who made this cut on your

275

mouth." Thea looked to Kol again for silent input on the matter of letting a stranger, the anti-Mori man, into her head. But he was concerned with her safety and well-being first that night – the days after he could worry about other things.

"Love, it is your choice." Kol encouraged her to choose as he crouched beside the bed and held her small hand in his. She looked at him and noticed all the cuts and bruises covering his skin.

"Enzo, if it's not too much trouble – would you mind healing my husband's injuries as well?"

"I am fine, my love." Kol tried to convince her, but she had seen him wince when he crouched down beside the bed, and she could still see the labored effort it was taking for him to stay squatting upright.

"Just let him heal you, for me." She batted her eyelashes up at him innocently, earning her a smirk from Kol.

"Fine." He bopped her on the nose with a single finger.

"Enzo, can you?" Thea asked again.

"For the Kingslayer, I can," Enzo confirmed. Kol suppressed a laugh. Kingslayer, *better than Prince of Death, I suppose,* he thought.

"Okay," Thea said. "Go ahead." With that, she leaned her head back and closed her eyes, fully surrendering herself to the healing process.

Kol watched over her possessively and protectively. He watched, with a hand on the hidden dagger beneath his tunic, as Enzo moved his sun-aged hands over her body, never touching her. Enzo would hover over injuries, humming deeply in his throat, and Kol watched in fascination as dark purple bruises went through the entire healing cycle in seconds. Thea felt no pain, as both Enzo and Kol had promised, but what she did feel was sensations of warmth in the places Enzo worked on – as if she had a fever in the areas of injury. The heat nearly tipped over into a burning sensation in her shoulder, the sight of the most damage, but it never tipped over the scale into being a painful sensation. She wasn't sure how long she lay there, eyes closed, but after a while, Enzo spoke again.

"I've done what I can with your body. All the bruises and cuts I could sense are mending now, as well as your shoulder and rib injuries. Now I will move onto your mind." He placed one hand over her head and the other over her heart, both still suspended over her utterly still body. "Quiet your mind, just take deep breaths." Enzo encouraged her. Flashes of the last two days sparked through her memory, not so much in visions but emotions. Joy, surprise, fear, anguish, loneliness, hope, disappointment, pain, relief. Her emotions flowed through in the order she had felt them, from Kol leaving her alone the night of the wedding all the way to his rescuing her. She felt her lip sting as she remembered Malcolm hitting her, hitting her just because she wouldn't do what he wanted. She lingered the longest on the emotions of anguish and loneliness, the former because it was one she had never felt before yesterday and the latter because it was all too familiar to her. But slowly, those emotions began to drift away from her mind and be replaced with peace – just as Enzo had explained. She allowed the peace to flow through her body and settle into her heart. And for the second time this night, she found herself falling asleep.

Kol watched Thea's torment expression fade and her breathing turn slow and steady, which he knew to be a sign of her having fallen asleep. Enzo sensed the same and shortly after she fell asleep, he moved his hands back to his side and stood to leave. Kol followed them out the door and paused before closing it.

"Thank you." He looked them both in the eyes.

"I almost forgot." Enzo used his hands like a wand, tracing the hard angles of Kol's body up and down. Kol watched again in captivated interest as the wounds on his body faded before him. "And thank you. Remember, this is what it is to be human – to help one another and strive for the best world. You did that by killing the king and I did it by helping you." Enzo bowed before Kol. "Blessings." He said before turning down the hall and beginning his journey down the stairs.

"Not particularly chatty, that one." Hannah joked. "Get some rest. We'll be here in the mornin' to feed ya and get the two of yous on your way." She patted Kol's shoulder and then followed Enzo's path downstairs. He tried to close the door silently, but the creak in the old hinges and the latching of the lock stirred Thea from her sleep.

"Sorry for waking you." Kol apologized. "We'll have to leave in the morning – I can't trust what exactly that Healer saw in your mind," Kol said briskly after he closed the door.

"Okay.," Thea responded sleepily.

"I'll go in the morning to get supplies and we will head out to another town." He continued.

"Sounds like a plan." Thea yawned.

"I wonder if I should get another horse. We would travel faster, but I doubt I have enough coin on me to buy a horse here." He paced the room as he babbled.

"Kol," Thea said, stern but loving. "I'm sure you will do a great job protecting us and creating a plan. But I'd love for you to just come be with me now." She patted the bed beside her. Kol exhaled, allowing himself the luxury of taking in the sight of his wife, healed and safe. He sat softly on the bed, careful not to jostle her too much, and then placed his arm gently around her. "I wish we had that novel of yours. I love passing the night close to you, just listening to your voice." Kol's heart warmed. He sunk deeper into her and placed a tender kiss on her forehead.

"I'm sure they have a book around this place somewhere," Kol said, and he moved to get up.

"That's okay. Just hold me." She snuggled herself under his arms and closed her eyes. "I love you." She whispered as she threatened to fall asleep.

"I love you too." He held her tight against him, for he was afraid if he didn't he would wake up and she would be gone again.

Chapter 16

The sun shining through the window woke Kol up, and then his stirring woke up Thea. "The sun is just now rising. Why are you getting dressed?" Thea asked in a sleep-hazed voice.

"I need to get a few things before we leave, clothes for you and some food mainly. You can go back to sleep." He reached down, placed his hand on the back of her neck and leaned in to kiss her. He paused an inch from her face, both allowing themselves the luxury of basking in her presence, something they both only a day ago feared they would never be able to do again. Thea leaned in the last inch and placed a soft kiss on his lips. They pulled apart and stared into each other's eyes before meeting their mouths again in a feverish and wanting display of affection. His hands searched her body endlessly, with every touch making sure she was actually there with him. He had woken several times in the night in a panic, his nightmares having weaved stories of her demise and his failure. But she was real, and every caress made him believe it even more. Her hands roamed his body, and for the first time she felt free to explore the peaks and valleys of his physic without society telling her it was wrong. Her hand grazed over the spot where she had watched him get stabbed the day before. Instead of a festering wound, she was met with a healed scar, and she had Enzo to thank for that. Kol found himself horizontal again, his lust taking the reins in his mind. His fingers found their way instinctively to Thea's chest, and she gasped when his fingers expertly pinched the sensitive flesh. He smirked, satisfied in getting a visceral reaction out of her. But trying to match his energy, she pressed her hips against his. He groaned softly in her ear – a deep sound from the back of his throat.

"Can you remove this barrier between us, please?" She asked, desperately tugging on his trousers. Kol leaned up to do just that, but when he opened his eyes, he began to feel panic's sharp fingers squeeze his heart. Thea's blood-stained undergarments peaked out from under the blankets, and Kol's mind flashed back to seeing her chained to that table in the Strong banquet room. His breath started coming in short, uneven pants. "Kol?" Thea asked, concern in her voice. She watched him, a dazed and pained expression on his face. All he could see was her blood. "Kol!" She placed her hands on his shoulders and shook him.

"I'm sorry, I-" He slowly started to come back to the present moment. "I don't know what came over me. I must still be tired from yesterday." Truth, but not all of it. "I really must go get our supplies, and you need to get cleaned up. I will tell the innkeeper we need warm bath water up here." Kol hopped up from the bed quickly and walked to the door. "I will be back quickly, don't open the door for anyone besides Hannah. Okay?"

Thea pulled the blankets over her chest and nodded. "Okay." She said quietly. When he left, she couldn't help but place her hands over her face and grieve the loss of that moment together. *He feels distant from me,* she thought. She glanced down at her body, slightly bruised and cloaked in tattered, blood-soaked lingerie, *unsightly*. Her hair hung lifeless against her face, and when she reached back, she felt a large matted tangled, caked in dirt. *Not exactly the most alluring I have ever been.* She hoped his only issue was seeing her like this, for that she could change. She paced the room anxiously, waiting for Hannah to knock at her door so she could bathe away the dirt and blood from her body.

The knock finally came. "May I come in?" Hannah's voice boomed from the other side of the door. Thea wrapped herself in the bed's quilt and unlocked the door. Hannah pushed her way inside. "Yer husband said ya needed clothes. I have a daughter about yer age, so I told him I would take care of that, an' I have water coming up so you can bathe."

"Thank you so much. Your kindness and generosity mean the world to us right now." Thea thanked her with all sincerity.

"Well, we all should be thankin' you. Yer husband killed a tyrant. He wasn't as bad as the Mori King but still, words already spreadin' about his death. His lords are fightin' for power as we speak." She laughed to herself. Thea was desperate to change the subject.

"Well, we appreciate it nonetheless," Hannah grunted in acknowledgment and took a large pitcher of water from a girl at the door. "So, what can you tell me of Enzo and the Lesser Continent?"

"Well, as ya likely noticed, he ain't much of a talker. But from what I gathered, the kingdom is divided there just as it is here. It seems that everyone has Control there though, noble and commoner alike. From what I can gather, half the continent is fairly safe an' normal, but the other half is extremely dangerous and run by thieves an' assassins. Their king, reportedly, is a coward who's locked himself and his family inside the castle." She laughed. "Imagine that, a king afraid of his people instead of the other way around."

"I can't imagine." Thea tried hard, but she was unable to imagine what that would look like.

"Not at all, around these parts if ya aren't Blest, yer pretty much in fear all the time," Hannah said dismissively.

"All the time?" Thea asked.

"Well, look at what happened to you, a perfect example of the power a Blest has over those who aren't." As Hannah explained this, Thea felt herself shrinking smaller in her chair.

"But what could we even do about it?" Thea asked out of curiosity.

"Well, if ya ever find yourself around these parts on the night of the full moon, there's a meetin' that could answer those questions. And I'm sure they'd welcome the Kingslayer into their ranks." While she wasn't saying it, Thea knew Hannah was talking about a Dissenter meeting.

"I'll keep that in mind," Thea replied, Hannah winked in response.

"Okay, baths all ready for ya, and clothes are on the chair in there. Just holler if you need anything else." Hannah said as she closed the door.

Thea was surprised at the lack of pain she felt as she moved, most remnants of the last few days gone from her body already. When her body was slipping into the warm water, she became aware of how much privilege she had always had in her life. Never, before this week, had she wondered where her next meal would come from or if she would have water or if she could clean herself. So, as she sat there, scrubbing her skin of the foreign gunk and blood, she started to cry; and when she started, she felt as if she may never stop crying again. The night before she had been too grateful to be rescued to be sad over what she had experienced, but now it was all coming back to her. When she washed her face, she remembered the pain she had felt in it only a few hours ago. As she looked at her healing body, she sat in silent gratitude for God blessing people with the Control of healing. She didn't even want to consider the pain she would be in today had her body not been healed by the Sana. All that aside, the horrors in her head still danced around her mind, threatening to take hold of it, the menacing looks of her captures, the fear of impending death, all of it. She tried to focus on the good in her life, on Kol and her newfound freedoms, but it was challenging to do so in certain moments.

Thea stepped out of the tub and began to dry her body with the towels left by Hannah. The clothes Hannah had left for her were very plain, provincial in every sense of the word. A white wool sweater, a floor-length brown linen skirt, and a thick scarf. Thea gentle fingered the hand stitching on the scarf, knowing that while this fabric wasn't expensive or fine – it was made with love. Warmth engulfed her as she wrapped her arms around herself, relishing the feeling of being clean and fully dressed for the first time in days. She didn't have the slightest clue when Kol would return, so she made herself busy as best she could while waiting. She took inventory of their supplies, repacked Kol's travel bag, and then busied herself with cleaning the weapons he had left in the room. She assumed swords were not unlike the silver jewelry she had been taught to care for, delicate in their own way and needing special care, so she simply used a damp cloth to clean the blood and mud off the blades. Kol returned to find her doing this. A mix of feelings entered his heart at seeing her handle a weapon, the first and main one being fear, but he restrained himself from reacting out of this emotion.

"I see you're familiarizing yourself with the blade." He commented coolly, and his heart skipped a beat when she turned

284

and smiled – looking so pleased that he had returned. She carefully placed the sword she was cleaning down and hopped up to wrap him in an embrace. Thea buried her head in his chest and inhaled; he smelled of soap and that underlying masculine smell that was all his own.

"I missed you." She said, and Kol realized no one had ever said that to him before.

"I missed you too." He pulled her in tighter. "And this is quite the ensemble." He pulled her away from him and twirled his finger, encouraging her to spin around. Thea obliged with a giggle on her lips, and turned slowly before dropping into a low curtsy.

"This old thing?" She asked playfully.

"I assume you'll require all your gowns to be brown and made of wool from now on?" Kol teased.

"You know me so well." Their laughter slowly died, and smiles shrunk as they looked meaningfully into one another's eyes. He looked her up and down slowly, not in jest or a predatory manner, but as if he were checking to make sure every piece of her was still intact.

"I heard you last night, so I'll only ask once and hope you let me know if anything changes. Are you feeling okay?" He asked. Thea considered his question before answering.

"Physically, yes."

A pained expression flashed across his beautiful face. "And not physically?"

She paused for a moment, not sure how she would answer until it left her lips. "I will be."

Kol nodded, appreciative of her honestly but worried for his wife. "Are you ready to begin our travels? I asked around, and there seems to be one more small town on the road between our home and here."

"We can't make it home tonight?" Thea asked with disappointment in her voice.

"Alone, I could, but I was unable to get us another horse, and with both of us on mine, he will be slightly slower than normal." He sensed her disappointment. "But we will be home tomorrow, and I will personally help you burn that skirt." He wrinkled his nose playfully at it.

Thea laughed. "I won't stop you, but I rather like the sweater and scarf." She made a show of dramatically tossing the scarf end over her shoulder.

"Then you shall keep it, and I'll have one of every color made for you just like it." He bopped her on the nose with one finger and then pulled her close. "Shall we leave?"

Thea nodded. "We shall." She reached forward and placed a quick kiss to his lips. "Let's get this over with." She stated dramatically.

Kol released her and added the rest of his supplies to his pack. "Not looking forward to our travels?"

"Definitely not. Honestly, I think I'd much prefer doing this leg of the trip passed out from exhaustion again. I didn't notice the discomfort of riding two people in a one-person saddle, and time went by quite quickly."

"Now I know you're feeling better. Someone is particularly sassy today." Kol commented.

"You love it." She teased.

"As I love you." He agreed. "But I cannot help you with the boringness of the trip. You will simply have to suffer in my company." He threw his pack over his shoulder and grabbed the blanket from the bed.

"What's that for?" She gestured to the blanket.

"I thought we could put it under you, between your legs and the saddle, so it doesn't rub. I tried to find you pants, but no one in this town makes women's trousers. I can try again in the next town." Thea's lip began to quiver, and then she threw her arms around him. "It's okay." He rubbed her hair. "What's all this about?"

"You're so considerate of my needs. Thank you." She replied, holding back tears of gratitude.

"Considering your needs is part of protecting you, which I promised to do." He said as if it were the simplest thing in the world. "Now, let's go." He kissed her head and ushered her out the door and down the stairs. Kol kept his head down, but Thea waved to Hannah as they walked through the main floor toward the door.

"Leavin' so soon?" She asked.

"Yes, afraid so," Thea replied simply, not wanting to give too much away.

"Not headin' home, I take it?" Hannah asked.

When Thea paused too long, Kol stepped in. "We're out to make our way in the world."

"Nothin' wrong with that," Hannah said. She walked the short distance between the counter and them, slapped Kol on the shoulder affectionately, and then hugged Thea. She leaned in and whispered in Thea's ear. "Remember what I said about the full moon."

"I-I will." Thea stammered. Kol looked at her confused, but she simply waved her hand dismissively.

"Blessings upon ya both and safe travels," Hannah shouted as they walked out the door. The air was crisp, so much so that they both could see their breath with each exhale.

"Please tell me it will get warmer the closer we get to home," Thea whined.

"It will, but not by much," Kol said grimly. "Come, our horse is saddled around back." Once they reached the horse, Kol took great care to lay the blanket on the horse's saddle and gently help Thea up. "Up you go." Thea watched as he threw his leg over the horse with ease. "Comfortable?"

"As much as I can be," Thea confirmed.

"We're off then." He clicked at the horse and pulled him to a steady trot out of the town gates.

"How long until we reach the next town?" Thea asked no more than an hour into the trip.

"We'll be there before dinner." He assured her. But by her estimation, that was hours from now, as the sun was only just past its highest point in the sky. Her stomach growled loudly. "Hungry?" Kol asked with a laugh.

"Yes." She replied sadly.

Kol leaned over slightly, reaching his hand into the saddlebag behind him. "Here." He handed Thea a small canvas bag. "I had the barmaid at the inn wrap up some food for our trip."

"If I didn't love you before, I would now." Thea grabbed at the bag ravenously. Inside was a baguette, a hunk of cheese, an apple, and dried meat. "Is this all the food?" Thea asked.

"It's not a lot, but I'm sure it will hold you over before we get to the next town, my love." Kol quipped.

She playfully smacked one of the arms he had draped around her thighs. "I know that." She said dryly. "I'm trying to be considerate, as in is this all the food for me and there is more for you, or do I need to save you some of this bag?"

Kol's face grew somber, still unaccustomed to being cared for or considered. "There's another bag of food for me."

"Okay, good," Thea replied quickly before tearing into the baguette.

"I'm sure whatever is happening up there is very becoming and ladylike. I'd akin the sound to a horse chewing straw." Kol teased.

"I think God birthed you into the wrong role in life," Thea responded.

"That right?"

"Yes, clearly, you think yourself a jester. Perhaps I'll stage a coup d'état and become High Queen but allow you the honor of entertaining my court with your hilarious japes." Thea jested sarcastically.

"You're generous even during a hostile takeover, be still my heart. I am truly fortunate." Kol replied.

When Thea couldn't think of a witty reply, she said, "This conversation is making me tired."

"Giving in so easily?" He clicked his tongue at her. "I expected more."

"Well, if you forgot I was recently kidnapped, forgive me for not being at the top of my game." She said innocently, trying to gain his sympathy.

"You're forgiven," Kol replied, causing Thea to snort in amusement. "Let me know when you're done eating, I have a surprise for you."

"I can be done now for a surprise." She mumbled, mouth full of cheese.

"Your full mouth and rumbling stomach say otherwise." He replied in jest. Thea quickly swallowed her mouthful and tied the bag closed, having already eaten half of its contents.

"Ready for my surprise now." Though Thea could not see, Kol made a playful show of himself by dramatically rolling his eyes as he reached into his saddlebag again. His fingers wrapped around the small leather-bound book he had sought out for her earlier that day. "Here." He placed it in her hands. "I thought you could read for us while we ride, and I'll read for us tonight after dinner, just like we do at home." He leaned forward and kissed the back of her head. "I asked the man I bought it from for either a romance or horror story because either we would enjoy, but he gave me this."

"You would enjoy a romance?" Thea asked, shock in her voice.

"Hearing you read aloud the seduction scenes to me? Yes, I would enjoy that very much." He leaned forward and whispered in her ear, "I'd just request you read them nice and slow." And then he nipped at her ear playfully.

"You're too much." She giggled as she leaned away from him.

"To quote a beautiful woman, 'You love it.'" He mocked in a shrill tone.

"I don't sound like that." She insisted.

"No, but it's the best I can do. My talents lie more in comedy than mockery." He joked. Thea rolled her eyes and began to investigate the cover of her new book. "Apparently, it came over on a ship from the Lesser Continent. It has it all: romance, murder, and ghosts."

"Ghosts?" Thea asked.

"So, the man said," Kol confirmed.

"Well, all right. I'd be interested to see how stories are written from the Lesser Continent." Thea turned to the first page. "Why is everything so spaced apart?" She asked curiously.

"Yes, he said it was a play."

"A play?" Thea asked. "I've never seen a play written down."

"Well, you aren't a performer. Maybe they're the only ones who normally see these things." Kol suggested. "But it's all I could find." He replied, fearing he had disappointed her.

"I'm eager to read it. Just different is all." Thea reassured him as she leaned back into him. "Thank you."

"Of course." He kissed her head again. "Now go on, read us a few pages.

Thea read until the sun started its descent, and she could no longer make out the words on the page. She was enthralled by the story, never really having read anything like it before. Now she was desperate to make it into town not only to stretch out her aching legs – but also to continue reading.

"Do you think he is mad, or truly seeing the ghost of his father?" Thea asked.

"I think him mad. Ghosts aren't real." Kol said definitively.

"You think these the actions of a mad man, though?" She asked.

"Yes, he's being driven mad by his own emotions."

"Well, in the confines of this story, perhaps ghosts are real." Thea pondered.

"I suppose so." He agreed. "And who's to say the lore of the Lesser Continent. Maybe they all believe in ghosts there."

"Maybe." Thea considered. "Do you think we could ever travel to the Lesser Continent?"

"You want to?" He asked.

"I don't know, maybe." She replied. "I'd just like to see as many different places as possible." She paused, "We could visit your sister that lives there!" She offered.

"I suppose, though I haven't spoke to her in years." Thea couldn't imagine having a sibling and not being close to them, but Kol's siblings were likely strangers to him. All his sisters had been sent when they were very young to live in foreign lands and marry to strengthen relationships with other realms and increase Mori power.

"Have you ever seen the Southern Sea?" Kol asked, changing the subject.

"No, only the Eastern Sea near my home realm."

"We have a small manor by the Southern Sea. We could go there once things have settled down, perhaps in the Spring." Kol offered.

"Can we?" Thea replied delightfully.

"Anything for my Princess." He kissed her head. "I've kissed the back of your Blessed head so many times this trip. I can't wait to get off this horse and kiss you properly." He said in frustration, causing Thea to giggle.

"Tell me of the Southern Sea." She demanded as she closed her eyes.

"It's the most beautiful part of the Continent." He replied. "It's a few days journey to get there, but it is worth it. The Sea is so clear that you can see your whole body while underwater. In fact, you can see the sea life as well. There are beaches stretching up and down the water, and they're so beautiful. The sand is pure white and it's contrasted by the black mountains in the distance."

"What makes the mountains black?" Thea asked.

"Legend says the god of the mountain got angry one day, long ago, and spewed fire from his head and it rained black down for weeks, leaving the mountains black to this day," Kol said in an eerie voice.

"And you believe this?" She giggled.

"I did as a boy. Whenever we would visit the Southern Sea, I would be on my best behavior, for fear I may anger the mountains."

"That's funny." She said in a sleepy voice.

After a few moments of silence, Kol spoke again. "Want some good news?" Kol asked.

"Always."

"We are here." He said. Thea's eyes snapped open, and she strained her eyes to see the dimly lit torches flanking the entrance to the town ahead. "So, if anyone asks, we are living in Midtown, that is where we just left, and we are headed to visit your parents in Mountain Place. Mountain Place is a fishing and lumber town outside of Cativo. Rural, in the mountains by a large river, with lots of hardworking people in it. I am Ari, you are Tori, and we are newly married. Since we both are basically healed, our appearance shouldn't arouse suspicion, so we don't need to talk about what happened in the Strong realm." He ran through their back story in a rushed voice, should listening ears be closer than they think. "Got it?"

"Got it." She replied. "So, where are we?"

"They call this place Trinity," Kol answered. "Though, I don't know why. Midtown was named for its distance between the Capital and Strong Castle, Mountain Place is named for the large mountains that surround it, but Trinity...I am unsure."

"Maybe we'll find out." She replied.

"Best not to ask; all locals probably know why it's called that. Asking too many questions may stir up suspicion." Kol responded.

"That makes sense. You're concerningly brilliant with espionage." Though she was teasing, he still shivered under her praise.

"You're handling this all wonderfully, too; I'm just more used to having to read these situations. I've dealt with politics enough times to learn its best to hold your cards close to your chest and just observe what goes on around you." Thea nodded in understanding.

"Maybe I will observe why this town is called Trinity." She retorted.

Kol chuckled. "Perhaps." They rode upon the town, which was much like the one they had left that morning, just older and dustier. Dirt roads led to muddy alleys, and log cabins and stores lined the streets. Candle-lit streetlights dotted the path and led them to the town square, which had prominent showings of anti-empire literature posted on them. "Remember, we are not amongst friends here." Thea nodded slowly. "Oy, which way to the inn?" Kol shouted at a passerby, who in turn aggressively pointed up the road. Kol pulled the reigns and directed their horse in the direction they had pointed.

"I cannot wait to get off this horse and walk around. My whole ass fell asleep hours ago." Thea complained, causing Kol to sharply exhale in amusement. The inn was a small two-story building, constructed of light, knotty wood. Unlike the previous inn, this one seemed quiet. Kol led their horse to the small stable beside the inn and paid the stable hand for a night of care for it.

"Come on then," Kol said as he grabbed Thea around the waist and pulled her down from atop the horse. Her legs wobbled beneath her, sore and tingly from half a day without use, but they held up despite it. "Let's go inside." He grabbed her chapped and frozen hand in his and pulled her toward the inn.

"Do you think they have soup?" Thea asked.

"What?" Kol replied in an incredulous tone.

"Soup. I'm freezing and hungry." She replied.

"I'm sure they do, my love." He said as he tucked her into him and rubbed her arm for warmth. "But just being inside will help, plus they have smoke coming from their chimney, which means there is a fire somewhere in this building." On hearing this, Thea quickened her pace and beat Kol to the door; she threw it open and immediately rushed in.

"Thank God!" She exclaimed as she ran toward a roaring fire and stood as close as possible to the warm flame.

"Cold travels, I take it?" The man behind a desk said in amusement.

"You have no idea," Kol replied. "We need a room for the night, if you have one available."

"There's always a room available. Trinity isn't exactly a popular destination, mostly just weary travels and visiting families stay here." The man said. "Your name?"

"Ari." He said briefly.

"Henry." The man extended his hand, Kol shook it briefly before sticking his hands back into his pockets. "What brings you through Trinity, Ari?" Henry asked.

"Just on our travels, headed to Mountain Place." He tried to be brief.

"What's in Mountain Place?" He asked. *Why is everyone so fecking nosy?* Kol thought in irritation.

"Family."

"Well, all right," Henry said, sensing Kol's lack of friendliness. "Suppose you're tired after a day of traveling. I'll show you to your room." He walked from behind his desk and headed toward the narrow staircase.

"Come Th-Tori." Kol nearly slipped and said her name. "Our room is ready." She begrudgingly pulled herself away from the fire and walked to meet them by the stairs.

"Are there fireplaces in the rooms?" Thea asked Henry hopefully.

"No, but I can bring you a bed warmer."

"I would appreciate it. And is there food here?" She asked.

"We have bread and stew today," Henry answered. "I can bring up two bowls of that as well." Thea nodded enthusiastically. "I'll be back shortly. Here is the room." He handed Kol a key and gestured to the door at the end of the hallway. Inside was a double bed, adorned with a quilt and fur blanket, and a dresser with a water basin on it. They silently started unpacking their scant belongings and removing their sodden clothing. Kol unpacked a pair of cotton trousers and a heavy, floor length nightgown from his bag.

Thea held the gown up with a disgusted look on her face. The thick fabric went nearly down to her knees. "What is this?" She asked, amused.

"It was the only thing I could find. I assumed you wouldn't want to sleep in the clothes we rode in with or nude, much to my dismay, due to the cold temperature." He explained.

"Just don't let this change the image you have of me." She half-joked, though secretly she was horrified that the first night they truly spent together married, other than the night before when she passed out from exhaustion, she would be wearing a grandmotherly dressing gown to bed.

"You're gorgeous in anything you wear." He kissed her temple. Henry knocked on the door and entered the room without invitation. Lucky for him Thea had only removed her boots, socks, and scarf – else Kol may have killed him. Henry placed the food on the dresser and returned a moment later with the hot pan for the bed, placing it under the last layer of the blanket layers.

"You can sleep with it in there, but don't touch it while it's hot or the metal will burn you," Henry instructed. "Have a restful night." He said as his farewell. Both being exhausted, Kol and Thea ate in near silence, side by side on the bed, only occasionally talking about the length of their ride or the quality of the food. When they were done, Thea asked Kol a question.

"What are you most looking forward to about being home tomorrow?"

"Having you there with me, safe." He responded instantly. She leaned in to kiss him.

"Thank you, Kol." She leaned back. "But I mean the food or amenities that we have missed out on while away."

He considered her question. "I look forward to bathing in the large obsidian tub in my room, fully to the brim with hot water. And then laying in my own bed with an excessive number of pillows around me." He closed his eyes as if he could imagine it at that very moment. He opened his eyes slowly; they were dark and hooded in seduction. "All those activities would be made even more pleasurable by your presence in them, though."

"I'm sure we can arrange something," Thea replied, drawing her body closer to his.

"Promise?" He nearly growled, a feral look in his eye.

"Promise." She purred. And in the next moment, he was on her, without warning, but she would never complain. As much as he wanted her, is how much she needed that to feel their relationship was completely secure. He hovered over her body, a silent question hanging in the air, did she consent to his desires.

"If you don't touch me now, I may cease to exist entirely." That sent him. His lips were everywhere, her neck, her mouth, her chest. She relished his touch. Her fingers scratched a pattern up and down his back, sending a shiver down his spine. Teeth crashed against teeth as he aggressively captured her mouth with his, actively being driven mad by her touch. He groped wildly at her clothing, hating himself for purchasing the gown that had led to her current state of overdress.

"I've never hated a single piece of fabric so much." He groaned.

"Then get rid of it." She demanded. He didn't have time to be shocked at how forward she was, for his desire only allowed a single thought to command his mind. *Worship her.*

"As you wish, Your Highness." Her oversized nightgown hit the floor in seconds, and he was left staring at her bare flesh. In that moment, he wished he had the ability to paint, so that he could render every freckle and stretch mark into a permanent existence; one in which he could spend hours staring at her beauty whenever he wished. He stared, trying to sear every curve and dimple into his mind, as Thea laid there watching Kol trail his eyes up and down her body. To her it felt like an out-of-body experience. She always thought she would be shy and insecure, under the naked scrutiny of a man, but with Kol it felt so right.

"Your turn." She begged as she pulled on his trousers. He didn't put up a fight as he slid the material off his muscular legs and discarded them by throwing them across the room. She didn't jump or shy away from his touch as he trailed his expert hands up and down her body. He took the lead, and she followed his moves like a dancer follows their partner around the dance floor.

Gasps and moans filled the small room, as they both gave themselves over to their desires. Despite his primal hunger, Kol took special care in preparing her body for his. But these touches were not enough for him, and she knew what she wanted – the final step in sealing their marriage.

"Kol." She begged. "Please."

He knew what she wanted, but he hesitated. "Darling-" He kissed her collarbone. "I don't want to hurt you."

"I'm not afraid of a little pain." She met his gaze with a look of confident defiance. A sultry, wicked grin spread across his face. Though a lie, she wanted to play this game with him. The truth, which she usually valued but in that moment was ignoring, was that she was afraid. Afraid of pain and afraid of this new step in her relationship. She had thought about it for weeks with fondness, but now that the time had come – she was overwhelmed with feelings. But she was sick of being scared, and her heart was already hardening against fear and any other emotion she considered weak.

"I'll remember that." His wicked grin remained as he leaned down and bit the sensitive flesh of her breast, bruising it instantly. Thea worked to hide her shock as he pulled her close to kiss her lips again, gently and slowly, before giving himself almost completely over to his most primal wants. He remained partially restrained, not wanting to inflict Thea with his sadistic and depraved desires. Not yet.

After, Thea rested motionless against Kol, relishing the warmth of his body and trying to time her breaths to his. He had one hand resting on her waist and the other rubbed circles on the bare leg she had carelessly tossed across his thigh. Her chest

299

rested on his, and he twisted his finger on the skin of her hip as if he were drawing small circles on her skin.

"How do you feel?" Kol asked.

Thea thought, considering her answer before speaking. "Alive." She sighed. "Tender in some places." They both let out a whispered laugh. "But utterly alive." She turned her head, resting her chin on his chest so she could look him in the eyes. "And you?"

"There are too many adjectives, my darling."

"Choose a few." She pressed with a smile.

I adore her, he thought. "Amazed, sated, humbled, grateful, and alive as well. I feel more alive than I ever have before." Thea kissed his bare chest before returning her head to its rightful place there, she was satisfied with his answer.

"I always thought I'd feel different after sex, but I lay here and realize that I'm still just me." She paused before continuing. "Everyone made me feel that I would be somehow damaged or besmirched if I did it at the wrong time. They made such a big deal about it – that I did too."

"And now?"

"It feels the most natural thing in the world...to be with you." She decided.

He shivered, a feeling of acceptance and belonging pulsing through his veins. "I would have waited a thousand lifetimes for you, Thea."

"Good thing you didn't have to." She nestled closer into him. "Kol?"

"Yes?"

"Do you feel like finding out what happened next to the Prince of Denmark?" She pointed to the leather-bound book lying on the small bedside table. Kol laughed, something he only found easy to do in her presence and nodded.

"Yes, yes I do." He picked the book up, leaving one arm around her and using the other hand to hold the book up to the light of the candle. She closed her eyes, listening to his gravelly voice turn words into pictures in her mind before eventually drifting off to sleep.

Chapter 17

Thea closed her eyes and listened as a soft wind rustled the grove of lavender bushes on the left of the road. The horse she sat upon, no doubt tired after days of travel, walked sluggishly, bumping she and Kol around with each step. Her legs ached and her butt felt numb, but she knew each step the horse took was one step closer to being home. They had left the inn early, with little fanfare, and after gathering a few supplies were on the road. Feeling bored and peckish, Thea had already eaten all the food Kol had packed for them and tried to pass the time as best she could. Gentle wafts of lavender blew into her nose as she inhaled deeply. And then she had a thought.

"Kol?"

"Yes, love?"

She didn't think she'd ever get over the little jolt of excitement she got from hearing him use a term of endearment toward her. "You know how I've helped with a few things, in regards to the territory battle against the Strongs?"

"Of course. Your interrogation using your Control and your knowledge of *Herba Hebeto* were invaluable." He said matter-of-factly. "But I doubt you think I have forgotten these things. What is it you want?" He asked, a flirtatious tone to his voice.

"How is it you know me so well?" She asked.

"Darling, you are the only thing in this world I care to know anything about at all." She shivered.

"Well..." She hesitated. "I want to help more," Thea stated firmly.

"Okay."

"Okay?" She said, in shock. "Just like that?" Thea was used to decades of people telling her no, shielding her from things like danger and her own desire.

"If that's what you want, then, okay." He said again. "Obviously, we will train you up, find a proper place for you in the command. But, of course, you can do what you want. This is your Empire too." She often forgot just how devoted to equality Kol was.

"Thank you." She wrapped her arms tighter around him and squeezed.

He patted her hand. "Anything for you." Truth. "Thea, look." She peered over his shoulder, and through the foggy haze she could make out the Palace, resting in all its gilded glory in the cleared basin of the forest.

"Home." She signed with contentment, causing Kol's heart to clench in his chest. He didn't have the words to express how much he loved that she felt at home there, with him.

The final moments riding up to the Palace felt surreal. They entered the gates from behind the Palace, avoiding the bustling city streets and eyes of the people. The gardens were eerily calm as they rode through them and around to the front of the Palace. Since no one knew they were coming, no elaborate welcome had been planned. In fact, inside the Palace, many people were acting grieved, waiting with bated breath for word on the Prince and Princess. A weepy Dorothy sat in bed, unable to get out of it that day, in despair over her missing friend. She prayed all day and night, silently to herself, for the safe rescue of her friend. Duke Martin had been extremely attentive to Dorothy during this time, he sent gifts and read with her and sat with her during meals, but he knew his presence only nominally helped ease her mind from the worry of what could have become of Thea. Ruth was similarly plagued with worry, but she was not afforded the luxury of isolated depression; she had work to complete. So, Ruth bustled around the castle, ordering maids and servants around, and in moments when she was reminded of Thea, she would excuse herself for a brief moment – before getting back to work. Thea's parents had stayed at the Palace as well, but stoic as they are, they simply tried to look indifferent and busy. Grayson sat in meetings with the High King, easily distracted by strategy and battle debate; he often did not come to bed until the wee hours of the night and was up again at dawn. Josephine worked on needlepoint and knitting so much that one of her fingers had started to bleed, at which point she pivoted and began to complete correspondence letters to all the high-ranking members of her realm, announcing her daughter's marriage and pretending nothing was wrong at all.

On Kol's side of the family, High King Kairo worried for the future of his kingdom more than his actual son. He sat, lips pursed in displeasure as he complained to his young wife. "My ignorant son is going to get himself killed, over what? A wife of one day who could easily be replaced. What will become of my Empire?" He shouted and slammed his fist down on a table. Dove flinched whenever he did that. She worried about Thea and Kol, though not in a maternal way but in the way anyone empathizes when they hear sad news about a fellow human. She also had grown quite fond of Thea, and prayed often she would be returned safely, but she hoped for Kol's return primarily out of selfishness. Dove would look at Kairo when he would complain about Kol's potential death, and she knew what his solution would be. Though Dove could not be Queen, her children could be royalty. She shivered in disgust as she looked at the mean, fat, and balding man before her and imagined him, forcing himself on her in hopes of producing an heir. She felt her morning breakfast coming up. He had done it a few times before, forced himself on her. She did all she could to go to a different place in her mind when it happened, eyes closed, wishing for it to be over. She felt lucky that women more beautiful than she would willingly throw themselves at the High King in hopes of finding favor, she knew their ambition saved her from much trauma – for he was often too spent from his romps with her lady's maids to turn his sexual lusting onto her.

Bells began to ring throughout the Palace, signaling to everyone inside of urgent news. Whether it was good or bad, no one knew. Dove and Kairo gracefully paced themselves down the stairs to the foyer, while Thea's friends and family raced toward it in all manner of dress. Dorothy had one shoe on and was wearing a night robe over her sleeping gown; Josephine was sporting bed head from her recent nap; Grayson left a meeting so briskly he took the document he had been reading with him, only to discard it in the hallway as he ran; and finally, Ruth walked as fast as possible toward the front of the Palace covered in the suds of the laundry wash she had been supervising.

The emotions upon seeing Thea and Kol were as vast. Upon seeing them, Thea's father, stoic as ever, allowed a single tear to roll his cheek before clearing his throat and wrapping a supportive arm around his sobbing wife. Dorothy, throwing all decorum out the window, crashed into Thea with her whole body and wrapped her arms around her.

"Thank God!" Dorothy cried. "I missed you so."

"I missed you too." Thea hugged her back, using all her strength to stay upright as her emotions threatened to blow her over.

And finally, "What the hells were you thinking?" Kairo shouted as he walked toward Kol and smacked him across the face, hard enough to draw blood. Thea gasped and protectively pulled Kol toward her without thinking. This incited even more rage into Kairo's heart. He saw it as an act of defiance. He gritted his teeth and squinted his eyes at Thea – before raising his hand to strike her as well. She closed her eyes, waiting for his slap to come, and behind her eyes, she saw flashbacks of being tormented by the Strongs. Flesh slapped against flesh, but Thea felt no pain. Kol had wrapped his hand around his father's wrist to stop him.

"Touch her and die." Kol snarled.

"You will burn for disrespecting me. I am your father! I am the God-ordained High King!" Spittle spewed from Kairo's mouth as he yelled. "Let go of me, boy. I'll forgive you this one transgression, but any more, and you will regret it." He spoke with confidence, but the strength of Kol's grip was inciting a minute amount of fear into him. Thea could see this fear in his eyes.

"What will you do?" Kol twisted his father's arm behind his back. Kairo winced in pain, and the whole room watched in frozen silence.

Kairo's eyes narrowed in concentration. *He's going to use his Control on Kol,* Thea thought in horror. "Release me and bow before me." He commanded. Kol instantly released him, but did not bow. A vein in his forehead throbbed as he concentrated, fighting his father's Control. "I said bow!" Kairo screamed.

"No, you bow," Kol spoke, voice low and menacing. Kairo shook as he fought Kol's command and the whole room held their breath, seeing who would win. Kol cocked his head to the side, a small smile playing on his lips. He knew he was winning. He stood under his father's Control unwavering, while his father shook under Kol's commands like a terrified child. Kol thought about the injustices he had faced, mostly under his father's hand, and used that anger to power his next command. "Bow." The crack of Kairo's knees hitting the ground echoed throughout the foyer. "And one more thing-" Kairo's eyes were now fully glazed over, under Kol's Control. "You will do nothing about this. Nor will you punish anyone in this room for seeing your weakness. Understood?" Kairo reluctantly nodded. Then Kol simply smirked and walked away, leading a stunned Thea upstairs toward his room.

Once out of earshot, Thea asked, "Has that ever happened before?"

"No." He responded, his voice a combination of shock and pride.

"What does this mean?" Thea asked. Kol considered her question, and slowly began to remember the first time his father had won a Control battle with his grandfather. That moment marked the turn of the tide in regards to power, and within a year, his grandfather had died.

"He's growing weak. Old age is taking a toll on him." Kol responded.

"Are you okay?" Thea asked, knowing how she would feel if she had to confront her parents' mortality.

"Of course, we're home. You're safe. Why wouldn't I be?"

"Yeah, of course." She responded, silently wondering if she would feel the same as Kol did, had her parents been as cruel to her as his father was him. Sure, she had been placed in a box and forced to repress aspects of her nature by her parents. But Kol had been brutalized and given little to no love. She thought his path worse.

"So, what would you like to do now that we're home?" Kol asked.

"Get into bed." She said definitively.

"Thea, I'm hurt."

"What? Why?" Thea asked.

"You only want me for my body." He placed a hand to his chest, looking every bit like a victim.

A blush crept up Thea's face. "No! I mean to go to sleep." She defended with a stutter.

"No, no. I get it." He placed his hand on the doorknob and turned. "Listen, I'm going to do it for you, but I know that I feel used." He said sarcastically before winking at her. She let out a small giggle and followed him into the room. He closed the door behind them and instantly placed his hands on her body. Sweltering kisses trailed down her neck as he walked them toward the bedroom. His mouth found hers in a frenzy of passion, and desperation coated each bite and suckle of her lips. It was as if he needed to breathe the same air as her to stay alive. Thea's hands scratched gently up and down his back, causing shiver bumps to break out all over his arms. Kol stepped into his bedroom, and instantly the memory of coming there to find her missing filled his mind. This fueled his desperation; he had to replace the bad memories with good ones.

Thea opened her eyes and found herself standing in the exact location she had been attacked. Before her eyes, Kol's face began to morph and darken, and all of a sudden, she was looking into the featureless black mask worn by the Dissenters. The room flashed with every blink of her eyes. One minute she saw the present, and the next, she saw the past. In her mind, she was flickering between standing in the bedroom kissing Kol and fighting for her life. Panic rose in her throat as she began to question which was reality.

Kol watched as her eyes, once hooded with lust, shot wide open in terror. She shook her head, as if trying to physically shake the traumatic memories from her head. Kol released her and called out to her, "Thea?" But she did not answer. Instead, she clamped her hands down over her eyes, sunk to the ground, and began rocking back and forth. She mumbled something to herself. Kol crouched down beside her and wrapped an arm around her. "Thea, what did you say?"

"Let me go!" She screamed, her voice unrecognizable to him; it was cloaked in pure animalistic fear. He removed his hands from her and watched as her eyes darted wildly around the room. She was desperate to find a way out, away from the men who sought to take her. Her breaths came in labored puffs, and her clothes felt as if they were threatening to suffocate her. She aggressively tugged the sweater she wore over her head and threw it across the room.

"Tell me how to help." Kol tried to remain calm, but a tinge of panic coated his words.

"Get me out of here!" She cried, tears now freely falling from her eyes. Her vision was becoming spotty, and her breathing even more erratic. She was on the verge of fainting. Thea did not protest as Kol scooped her into his arms and carried her out of his room. She allowed him to carry her through the door, down the hallway, past the peering eyes of Palace staff, and to her own apartments. Every step they got away from his room she felt the burden of fear lifting from her shoulders. By the time Kol closed the door of her apartments, she could stand on her own again and her breathing had steadied.

"Are you okay?" Kol asked as he led her to a couch.

"I-I think so," Thea replied, voice shaky.

"What happened?" He asked, with so much gentleness in his voice it nearly broke her heart to hear. She wanted to tell him, but every time she opened her mouth, the horrors threatened to consume her mind.

"I'm...not sure." Not a lie. But not the whole truth. She knew the horrors of days past were haunting her, she just didn't want to say it allowed. Not to him. Not to anyone.

"Okay." He nodded understandingly. "Come here." She crashed into him, and melted into his embrace as he rubbed gentle circles on her back. "I'm going to take care of you, always." Truth.

Kol waited until she had calmed down enough, then gave her a book to read and then set about caring for her. He ordered food and tea to be brought to the room and then went himself to draw her a bath. Once the warm water was ready, he went to the sitting room to get her. There he found her sitting, entirely still, knees hugged to her chest and staring blankly out the window.

"Thea?" He spoke gently, barely above a whisper, but it still managed to startle her. "I'm sorry, love." He apologized for spooking her. "Your bath is ready." He gestured to the bathing room and then sat on the couch, fully intending to give her privacy to soak.

Thea walked slowly to the room, partly in a daze, and closed the door to the bathroom behind her. The smell of the room was intoxicating, bouquets of lavender wafted into her nose, and the bubbles that she saw dancing on the top of the water looked more than inviting. She disrobed and sank her body into the hot water. But despite all Kol's effort, she couldn't find it in her to relax. The room felt too big, and at the same time, the closed door made it feel like a tiny jail cell.

"Kol!" She yelled, and the sound of running footsteps shortly followed.

"Yes?" He asked from the other side of the door.

"Will you-" She took a deep breath. "Will you sit in here with me?"

The door opened slowly. "Of course, I can." He turned to close the door.

"Will you leave it open?" She asked quietly. Kol simply nodded and left the door standing ajar. Thea watched as he pulled the chair from the corner of the room closer toward the tub's edge. She tried not to flinch as the chair's legs scratching on the floor hit her ears and caused her heart rate to quicken.

Instead of being enrapt in the beauty of her naked form, he was worried for her. Kol replayed what happened that evening repeatedly in his mind. *Fear filled her eyes. She hit the ground. She demanded I let her go.* He knew not to take it personally. He had watched many soldiers go a little mad from witnessing violence and knew it wasn't him she feared. The fear she had experienced those days in the Strong realm and before that with the Dissenters – are fears he couldn't fathom.

"I'm sorry," Thea said quietly.

"Whatever for?" Kol asked.

"That you have to watch me like a child. That I allowed myself to be taken. That even though I should be happy to be home, I feel less okay than I did yesterday or even the night before that."

"You never have to be sorry for that. Being taken was not your fault. If there is to be blame placed on anyone in this room, it should be placed on me. I promised to protect you, and I failed on my first night as your husband." He pushed a piece of wet hair behind her ear. "And you are not a child, anyone would be fearful after enduring-" His voice caught in his throat, and he took a moment to steady his emotions before continuing. "Enduring unspeakable torment. Adjusting to life back home may take time, and I am here to help however I can." She nodded, grateful for his continual kindness toward her. "Plus, I have had worse jobs than getting to sit and watch my naked wife bathe for an hour." He teased, attempting to lighten the mood. Thea giggled and splashed water at him. "Watch it." He said, pointing a finger at her. The laughter subsided, and Thea became thoughtful.

"Train me. I have to know how to fight."

"Okay," Kol said.

"That's it?" She asked, wondering how her father would respond to a similar request.

"Thea, I have no intention of ever keeping you from things you want." Truth.

"Can we start tomorrow?" She asked sheepishly.

"We can start tomorrow." He replied with a nod.

Chapter 18

Thea sat on the floor of the padded training room and attempted to stretch as she had before dance lessons as a girl. Out of the corner of her eye, she watched Kol, dressed head to toe in skin-tight training clothes, perform intricate warm-ups. She stood and attempted to copy him and grimaced at him when he laughed at her inability to do so.

"It looks so simple. Why can't I do that? It makes me want to forget this whole thing." She said in frustration.

"You need to get over that attitude right now, Princess, because almost everything we do in here today – you will be bad at." Thea scoffed. "That's not to say you aren't agile or athletic in your own right, but training and moving your body in these ways-" He dipped into another low stretch. "Takes practice. You will get there, don't let ego get in the way." Thea wasn't sure why, but his little speech was very impressive. It was as if he were a born motivator and teacher. *Perhaps all the things that will make him a good king,* she mused. Kol clapping his hands together pulled her from her thoughts, "Let's get started." Thea walked toward a wall covered in weapons, and as impressed as she was by the size of many of the swords, she opted to reach for a small one to start with. "What do you think you're doing?" Kol asked, amusement in his voice.

"Getting a weapon?" She said obviously.

"You're not ready for a weapon, my love. Do you think they gave me a sword when I began my training at five years old?"

"No, but I'm not a child. I can hold a sword." She answered.

"I know you can hold one. But you are not there yet. All the things before the weapons training are crucial: agility, balance, hand-eye coordination, endurance. These are all things we will work on before you ever get a weapon in your hand." Kol replied. "We are starting with these today." He picked up a handful of fabric and dangled it in front of her.

"Scarves?" Thea snarked skeptically.

"Yes, scarves." He mocked her tone with a smile. "This is how I started, and it is how you will start too. Here." He tossed her a small wooden dagger.

"What is this for?"

"I am going to swing these scarves at you, and all you have to do is use that wooden dagger to block them from hitting your body. This is learning defense in slow motion. If all else fails, you need to be able to protect yourself. Attacking is secondary." Kol dipped into a fighting stance, feet spread apart, and knees bent at a slight angle. "You want to stand like this. If your feet are too close together, you are easier to topple, too far, and you won't be quick enough on them. Arms are always up. You want to be able to protect your most important parts fast. Head and abdomen." He gestured to his core as he said this. Thea mirrored his stance, and even bounced on her toes a little for good measure. Kol smiled at her spunk, "Good girl." He winked. "Ready?"

Thea nodded. "Yes, I think I can handle scarf attacks." Kol tilted his head to the side – before quickly snapping the scarf in his left hand toward Thea's neck. She brought her dagger up a second too late, and she felt the soft fabric brush against her skin.

"Fatal wound, dead within minutes," Kol commented.

"You didn't say go. I wasn't ready yet," Thea grumbled.

"Not that your enemies will say go. But okay…go." Kol said before he began to move around her, flicking the scarves at her every few seconds. To her credit, she was able to block some, and eventually, she got into a rhythm of movement, dancing around Kol with her arms never dropping to her side. After an hour, Kol brought their training to a close. "Good job. I'm proud of you." He said as he took the wooden dagger from her and placed it with the rest of the training equipment.

"I was inflicted with about a hundred 'fatal wounds' today." She placed air quotations around the words fatal and wounds. "I 'died' dozens of times today, so I don't know what there is to be proud of." She replied sullenly.

Kol walked over and leaned down to Thea's eye level. "I am proud you showed up. I'm proud you tried. I'm proud of the many times you blocked me." He kissed her slowly on the mouth, inhaling her scent as he did so. He nearly became intoxicated by her. "You will improve. It will only take time."

"Okay." She muttered.

"Okay." He mocked her and pulled a fake pouty face, causing a small smile to break through Thea's melancholy. "Let's get cleaned up and eat. We have a strategy meeting soon." Thea followed behind Kol as he walked his way toward her apartments. He made no attempt to take her back to his room, leave her side, or exclude her from his daily duties. As promised, Kol was eagerly adding Thea into all the conversations around the Strong conquest. And it did not go unnoticed by Thea. They ate lunch quickly and then bathed one another slowly. Then,

315

filled with power, adrenaline, and impulsivity, they took time to ravish one another's bodies on the edge of the bathing tub.

Thea eyed herself in the mirror as Kol got re-dressed. Both hips bore dark marks from his fingers and her neck was dappled in bite marks and bruises. What once would have horrified her, now brought her a sense of pride. She was proud at her ability to satisfy Kol and at his desire to mark her as his. With a smile, she dressed herself in a new gown – not bothering to hid her purple neck, and then walked with all confidence and authority toward the next council meeting. Surprisingly enough, even to herself, Thea felt confident as she engaged in political discourse at these meetings. In addition to feeling confident, she also felt at peace. She had been free from her horrid flashbacks all day and hoped that her ambition and desires were strong enough to push the memories back forever.

Thea sat at Kol's side, on the edge of her seat, and listened to the strategy and discord happening before her. Everything in this room moved quickly: ideas, words, hand gestures, and more. One man would shout out an idea, to be immediately shut down by another, and harsh words and insults were tossed around carelessly. Kol explained to the men again the success of the *Herba Hebeto* and Thea's idea of discreetly feeding it to the Strong soldiers before battle.

"Your bride's ideas are of little value here, Kol. Just buy her diamonds and pleasure her in bed to shut her up. You don't need to make her think you value her mind or ideas in regards to political affairs." Lord Geoffrey spoke callously. Thea's face reddened and she instantly felt stupid for even trying to insert herself into this world. She looked around the room, not another woman to be found.

Kol slammed his hands on the table, silencing the men in the room. Kol narrowed his eyes at the lord who had spoken out of turn. "Silence." His mouth continued to move, but no words came out. "She is your Princess and will be respected. This is our Empire." He gestured between Thea and himself.

"High King, how do you feel about this little girl coming in here and trying to tell us what to do?" Geoffrey asked once released from Kohl's Control. Kairo sat sunken into a chair toward the middle of the table, silently observing everything unfolding before him. Kairo wanted to tell the girl to bugger off, but he feared his son's growing power. He worried that if he angered Kol, then he would show everyone in the room just how powerful he was becoming. Powerful enough to put Kairo on his knees, and maybe worse.

"My son is correct. All members of the royal family are more important than you and will be respected." That was the best Kairo could do in the way of support.

"And you forget her ideas and powers have already given us valuable insights into the weaknesses of the Strong's realm and castle," Kol said.

"Oh, her little powers of truth and persuasion." Geoffrey mocked. "The men of my family can throw fire from our hands. That is power." He said smugly. Thea stood suddenly, her chair scraping against the floor as she did so. Her heart pounded wildly in her chest, and anger raged in her mind.

"Kol, silence him. He only speaks when I ask him a question." She demanded.

"Silence," Kol said with a smirk, and again Geoffrey was muted. "You will answer Princess Althea's questions."

"What is something you don't want the men in this room to know about you?" Thea asked. Kol watched her, nearly spellbound watching her command the room. Lustful thoughts and desire for her filled his mind. He imagined taking her, right there on the table. *I will do that after this very meeting,* Kol promised himself. He was seeing a whole new side of her, and he liked it. His whole life he had been around women who were quiet, demure, and did whatever he said in an attempt to win his favor – they bored him. Thea was coming into her power, and he couldn't wait to see more.

"I cheat on my wife." He blurted out before slapping both hands over his mouth.

"Kol, make him move his hands," Thea demanded.

"Hands at your side Geoffrey," Kol said, an amused smile on his lips, and so it was done.

"Anything else you don't want us to know?" Thea asked.

"I pissed myself the first time I visited a brothel, right in front of a woman." He said, shame on his face.

"Why?" She asked.

"I was drunk on two ales and intimidated by her beauty." The men in the room laughed.

"Lord Geoffrey, what is your greatest fear?" Thea asked. Her temples pulsed as she used her Control to extract answers from him.

"Small spaces." He announced quickly. "And rats." A look of embarrassment crossed his face, causing the other men in the room to laugh again.

Thea looked to a guard. "Lock him in a dressing trunk for an hour and see if you can find a rat to put in there with him." She commanded. The room fell silent. All the men wondered if this woman, who could extract their deepest fears from them, had the authority to punish them. The guards didn't move, instead, they looked to Kol for approval.

318

"You heard her." He said to them. They grabbed Geoffrey, who fought them kicking and jerking as they pulled him from the room, though thankfully, he was still silent.

"Anyone else want to question my authority?" Thea asked, looking around the room. All the men shook their heads no, emphatically so. From the corner of his eye, Kairo watched an approving smile on his lips. "Good." She sat back down and gestured to Kol to continue. With a smile on his face, pride in his heart, and blood pulsing in his loins, he did just that.

"Without their king, they will be weak. Even his second in command is dead. There are likely few people ready or prepared to take the throne. They are likely even weak because of that now, fighting from within for power. We need to seize this opportunity and declare our intent to attack as soon as possible."

"With all due respect, why would we announce our attack?" An advisor asked, voice even and respectful.

"We will write, saying we want a fair fight and announce the battle location and date, then they will set up a camp, and that will allow us the opportunity to poison them with *Herba Hebeto* the night before the battle. It will weaken and confuse them. It will allow us to win." Kol explained as simply as he could.

Kairo cleared his throat. "While not the most traditional method of attack, planning a battle is not unheard of. Tell us the details." Kol didn't know if that was approval, or simply continued submission after being bested, but he would take an affable father to the tyrant he was used to any day. He began to lay out his plans and allowed the advisors and lords around him to give input on logistics. When the meeting ended, everything was all but planned. They would send the letter that night and wait for word back.

When everyone had left the room, Kol and Thea stood leaning against the table. Kol took the smile on her face as an invitation. He placed his legs on either side of her and pressed his body against hers.

"I think that went well," Thea commented.

"Do you?" Kol asked, an amused expression on his face.

"Yes. We have a plan, and more likely than not, the Strong realm will be under Mori rule before the end of the month." She answered with a shrug. "What's with your face? You look very smug." She asked.

"I'm just thinking about how you commanded this room and made a boy out of one the most wealthy and respected lords in our Empire." Kol said, leaning into her even more. "It fills me with lust just thinking about it." Truth. She pushed him playfully, but his body stayed glued to hers. If her Control hadn't verified his last statement to be true, then the pressure on her hip would have.

"Stop it." She swatted at him playfully.

He leaned down and nipped at her ear before whispering, "Also, who's the rash punisher now?"

Thea considered his words and thought back to all the times she had criticized Kol for doing exactly what she had done today. "He's alive, isn't he?" Was all she said.

Kol laughed and leaned further into Thea until she lay flat against the table, scattering the maps and battle figurines that had been carefully placed during their meeting. "Fair enough, my love." He kissed her exposed collar bone as he climbed up on the table, hovering over her. "Now, can I show you what I've been thinking about all meeting?" Thea nodded knowingly and Kol fulfilled his earlier promise to himself and took his wife on the table – uncaring of her moans, the open office doors, or the voyeuristic glances of curious passersby. In fact, those things fueled his lust even more. She was his, and he wanted that to be clear to everyone.

~

"No," Thea whimpers quietly in her sleep, not loud enough to wake Kol, who lay mere inches from her. In her nightmare, she saw flashes of the past. Men emerge from hiding spots in Kol's room to grab her. "No." She awakes in the wood, cold and bruised. "No." The Strong king backhands her face. "No." Guards take turns hurting her, one kicks her in the ribs then another punches her in the jaw. "No." Most disturbing of all, Thea sat in frozen horror as a guard slid a hand up and down her body. Even in her slumber, the memory of those touches felt real, as if it were happening to her again in that moment. She felt herself shudder under his calloused touch and felt the bile rise in her throat as his rancid breath wafted into her nose. He kissed her, roughly shoving his tongue into her mouth. "No!" She screamed, waking both herself and Kol.

Kol placed a hand on her thigh. "Thea? What's wrong?"

"Stop! Get off of me!" She screamed, thrashing in bed to get herself untangled from the covers. She fell from the bed and began looking around frantically, searching for an escape. The room was disorienting her, remnants of reality and traumatic memory mixing – plush chair sat beside a tree, a cell door where her windows used to be. Kol rose to his knees and crawled to the edge of the bed, arms stretched toward her. "Stay back!" Thea cried. Before her she saw flashes of the men who had hurt her.

Kol lowered his voice to barely above a whisper, tone soothing and even. "Thea, you are safe."

Safe. The word broke through her terror-filled haze like a torch slashing its way through fog. "Safe?" She asked, blinking rapidly. The room around her shifted back to normal, and before her was only her beautiful Kol.

"I am here. I will protect you. You are safe." Kol's mantra slowly helped lower her heart rate and steady her breathing. She ran her tear-stained cheek on the sleeve of her robe and then crawled into Kol's lap. He held her close and rubbed small circles on her back. "Want to talk about it?"

She released a shaky breath before answering. "I just can't get it out of my head. The fear, the pain." She shook her head softly. "I don't want to talk about it."

"Then we won't." He assured her.

"Kol?" She whispered.

"Yes, love?"

"Can you-" She paused.

"Can I what?" He asked gently.

"Can you tell me a story?" She asked. "A happy story."

"Of course, I can." He leaned back in the bed and propped them both comfortably against pillows, all without releasing his hold on her. Thea pulled a blanket over her legs and then nestled herself into the space between Kol and the pillows. "When I was a boy, I thought I'd catch a fairy." Kol started, all seriousness in his voice.

Thea snickered. "A fairy? What would you want with a fairy?"

"The mothers at court had always told all of us children about the fairies that lived in the gardens. Little spritely things, no bigger than a pinecone. Legend said that if caught, a fairy would grant you one wish to earn its release."

"What did you want to wish for?" Thea asked, voice already drenched in sleep. Kol couldn't bring himself to admit the sad truth of his wish. At five years old, all he wished for was a friend. The children at court were either jealous or afraid of him, which meant most of his days were spent playing in the gardens alone.

He hoped she was too sleepy to use her Control. "I don't remember." He said, and when she didn't remark on his lie of omission, he continued. "One day, I found a perfect circle of mushrooms near a large tree. So, I took a piece of mother's jewelry, laid it under a small rabbit trap, and waited."

"Then what happened?" She asked, eyes closed.

"I fell asleep waiting, and when I awoke, the trap was set off – but empty. And the ring was gone."

"The fairy was smarter than you." She whispered.

Kol smiled. "I suppose so." He kissed her forehead. "Goodnight, Thea."

"Mmm." She said in reply, snuggling deeper into his side before falling asleep.

Kol laid awake the rest of the night, unable to sleep with a head full of worry for his wife and unwilling to try lest she wake again and need him. Kol thought of the Sana man they had met in Midtown, who used his Control to settle Thea's mind after the attack. He wondered if there was anything else the Sana could do for her.

Once Thea had been asleep for several hours, and the sun was peeking over the horizon, Kol extracted himself from bed and padded quickly out of the room. He threw a robe over his topless form and walked briskly toward the General James' chamber. He knocked, hoping the General was still in the habit of waking with the sun.

"Enter." A voice boomed from the other side of the door. Kol opened the door and shut it quietly after entering. "What is it?" General James groaned. He was sitting at a desk. The candles that surrounded him were already burned down halfway, alerting Kol to the fact that the General had also endured a night with little sleep. Papers and maps covered the desk, and an ink-drenched quill lay beside a ledger. "I said, what is it?" General James snapped and looked over his shoulder. His eyes widened when he saw Kol, and he immediately jumped up from his chair and dipped into a low bow. "Apologies, my Prince. I didn't expect it to be you." Kol ignored him.

"I need you to send men to Midtown and bring me a Healer called Enzo. Tell him I will pay any price for his services." Kol turned to leave.

"We have plenty of Healers in our very court, Your Highness," James added.

"I didn't ask for your input, do what I say, or I will make you. I expect a report by sundown." Kol said, darkness in his tone.

"Right away," James replied quickly as Kol walked away. *I must protect her, even from her own mind,* Kol thought.

"Excellent, Thea." Kol praised as he watched her block his scarf with her wooden dagger. He looked down at her feet, noticing how close together they were, likely causing her stance to be unstable.

"Ha ha!" She yelled as she used his distracted observations as an opportunity to slash her dagger across his side.

"Good slice, my love." He pushed on her shoulder, toppling her over. She landed flat on her back. "Watch your footwork, though." He hopped up and gave her a hand, with great finesse transitioning this aid into an opportunity to pull her into a kiss. He held her tight against him with one arm and used his other hand to caress her face. When he pulled away, he looked deeply into her eyes, unable to ignore the faint dark circles nights of sleeplessness had bestowed upon her. *That Sana cannot get here soon enough.* "Great session today. You're learning quite fast." Kol complimented.

"I suppose those years of dance were not useless after all, at the very least, they've given me the stamina to continue through these hours of training." She suggested.

Kol nodded, a smirk on his face. "I suppose so." He said sarcastically.

"Do you not agree?" She asked, slightly self-conscious but also somewhat annoyed.

"No, I agree you're doing well. I just enjoy teasing you." Kol replied.

Thea rolled her eyes. "Race you to the bath!" She took off running, getting a head start. Kol jogged lazily behind her, enjoying the view. She often came to their training sessions in fitted trousers and a tank top – both clung to her body now, drenched in sweat. When she rounded the corner to her apartments, she dismissed the maid that had just finished making the bed.

"Shame she put so much work into that bed when we're about to mess it all up." Kol grabbed Thea around the waist and spun her, attacking her with kisses as he did so. She pushed him away, giggling and quite amused with his constant flirting. Out of nowhere, she pulled a pout onto her face. "That is quite the face," Kol commented.

"You let me win. You didn't even try to race." She replied.

"Why race for a prize I'm going to share." He put her feet back on the ground and released her. "Besides, the view was better from behind." He walked past her and roughly smacked her round glute, the sound satisfying to his ears. "Water hot or cold today, love?" He asked as he walked into the bathing room, eyeing the massive tub.

"Very presumptuous of you to assume I'll be sharing my bath with you today." She teased.

"I'll make it worth your while." He said with a twinkle in his eye as he ran a finger up her inner thigh.

"Fine." She said with a shiver.

Once the water in the tub was filled, both settled into the tub. Thea closed her eyes as Kol massaged soap into her hair. The warm water, steamed around them, and bubbles danced along the water. Cedarwood and lime, a smell she had come to associate with Kol, wafted into her nose. She loved bathing with him, not only for the obvious reasons but also because she loved smelling like him for the rest of the day. He rinsed the soap from her hair, taking care to block her eyes with his free hand as he did so, and twisted her hair into a lazy braid.

"What do you have on your agenda today, my love?" Thea shivered when he placed a wet kiss on her naked shoulder.

"Nothing at all." She leaned back into his chest, allowing his legs to fall beside hers. He groaned quietly, a sound deep from within his throat. She pushed back into his lap further.

"Beautiful, wicked creature." He said with a strained voice as one hand trailed over her thigh and another inched up toward her chest. "Be careful, my love." He roguishly clamped two fingers around the sensitive flesh of her breast, eliciting a gasp from her. "Two can play this game." He whispered roguishly into her ear.

"Maybe it's a game I want to play." She gasped out, trying to ignore the pain.

326

"Are you sure?" He asked. In an act of uncharacteristic boldness, Thea nodded and initiated her actions with a daring touch. "Blessed, burn me." He cursed under his breath in pleasure.

"Is that proof enough?" Thea asked. She was no longer surprised when she did something that used to be out of character for her, she thrived on it now. Every daring or wicked thing she did made her feel that much more powerful, and that much more connected to Kol. *Kol, my redeemer.*

∾

Kol and Thea lay in her bed, wrapped in each other's arms after leaving their romp in the frigid tub water.

"Can I finish my earlier question?" Kol asked.

Thea giggled. "Yes, sorry for my rude interruption." She replied sarcastically.

"My, my, someone's feeling feisty today." Kol teased.

"I thought my actions in the tub made that obvious." She replied, a glint in her eye.

He cleared his throat, which was suddenly dry. "True." He held her intense gaze a moment longer before continuing. "I asked if you were busy because there are some goings-on in the town I think you'd be interested in."

"Oh?" She asked with interest.

"A festival to celebrate a good autumn harvest and to honor God in hopes of an easy winter," Kol spoke with reverence.

"What is there to do?" Thea asked.

"There is dancing, performers, food, drinks, wares to be bought, and other things like that."

"You go to this?" She asked, surprised.

327

"Not since I was a boy." He answered. "But I thought you would enjoy it. You've told me many stories of your attending similar events in the town near your childhood home. Plus, with your parents still being here, I thought you may enjoy their company there as well."

"So, are you telling me about it or asking me to go with you?" She asked skeptically.

"I will go anywhere with you, my love." He answered, staring at the strand of her hair he had absent-mindedly twirled around his finger.

"I'd like to go with you." She looked up into his eyes. "Thank you." Her genuine gratitude pierced his heart.

"Of course." He leaned down and kissed her.

"When do we leave?" She asked.

"Celebrations are from sunrise to well past sunset, so we can go whenever." He said casually.

"Okay, you must leave then." She hopped up and shooed him off the bed and toward the door.

"Why am I leaving?" He asked with a laugh.

"Because I want to look presentable tonight and need to get ready!" She insisted.

"You realized I've seen you nude? But you don't want me to watch you get dressed?" He asked, emphasizing 'get' with much irony.

"Yes. Bye-bye!" She waved dramatically. When the door to her apartments opened, Thea was surprised to find Dorothy and Duke Martin standing quite close together outside her bedroom door.

"Your Highnesses." The Duke bowed. Dorothy dipped into a demure curtsy before Kol, a formality she wouldn't bother with for just Thea.

"Lady Dorothy, Duke Martin." Kol addressed them. "Good day." He said before excusing himself. "I await your call, Princess," Kol called to Thea with a wink.

"I must bid my farewell as well," Martin said sheepishly, looking awkwardly between Thea and Dorothy.

"Duke, before you leave," Thea started and then turned to Dorothy. "There is a festival of sorts in the city proper today. Would you like to come?" She leaned in and whispered teasingly, "Would you like the *Duke* to come?" Dorothy pinched Thea's arm.

"Stop," Dorothy whispered back. "Martin, would you like to attend the festivities today with myself, Thea, and Kol?"

The Duke blinked in surprise, both at her forward ask and her use of the Prince and Princesses first name. "Of course. Shall I wait in the library for you to be ready?" He offered.

"That will be fine, Martin. Thank you." She put her arm through Thea's. "Just allow us to get ready, and I will send someone to fetch you before we leave." The two women stepped back into Thea's room and closed the door.

"*Martin?*" Thea said. "Since when are you on a first-name basis with the Duke?" Thea asked, excitement for her friend clear in her voice.

Dorothy blushed, uncharacteristic for her, and answered quietly. "A lot happened while you were away." Thea froze a little, uncomfortable with the mention of her 'time away' sounding so casual – as if she were on vacation and not being tortured and assaulted.

"Yes. It did." Thea said grimly. She was desperate to change the subject. "What shall we wear?" They both busied themselves with getting ready. Thea twisted her hair into a crown of braids and dressed herself in a warm dress made up of maroon and orange hues. "Ready?" Thea asked after Elaine finished tying her into the corseted top of her dress.

"Yes." Dorothy nodded and then turned to face Elaine. "Please go to the library and ask Duke Martin to meet us in the foyer."

"My parents as well!" Thea added.

"Right away, ma'am," Elaine said before bowing and excusing herself.

Dorothy and Thea linked arms and started down the hallway. "So, you and Kol are...?" Dorothy asked.

"Wonderful." Thea sighed blissfully.

"That good?" Dorothy said with a laugh. Thea nodded empathically.

"He is so tender and attentive and funny." Thea bragged on her husband.

"Really? Rumors at court and my own eyes wouldn't peg him as such." Dorothy said tentatively.

"Perhaps not, but he is so with me and mine, and that is all that matters," Thea said definitively as she began her descent down the stairs. If Thea had bothered to look at her friend's face after she said this, she would have seen her disagreement, but Dorothy would not say as much aloud at this time. Dorothy watched, half in romanticized awe and half in court-rumor-filled confusion as Thea jumped off the stairs into Kol's arms. He smiled as he spun her around and pecked a gentle kiss onto her cheek, and once she was on the ground, he laced her fingers with his own. Dorothy was happy for her friend, but wouldn't lie to herself and say she wasn't surprised the two opposites made such a match. The Duke appeared beside her as she stepped off the last stair and offered her his arm.

"Ready?" He asked with his smooth accent. Dorothy nodded and wrapped her arm around his, allowing him to escort her to the awaiting carriage. Kol and Thea sat on one side, ogling one another and giggling. Dorothy tried to hide her shock, that a man she had seen casually stab another at dinner could giggle like a child. *Must be love,* Dorothy thought to herself.

"What shall we do first?" Kol asked the group.

"We've never attended this festival before," Thea replied, gesturing between herself and Dorothy.

"Neither have I, Your Highness," Martin added.

"Then you are to be our guide today, my love." Thea decided. "What did you like most the last time you attended?"

"Well, I was a small child, so I enjoyed the puppet show." Everyone in the carriage laughed, though Dorothy couldn't help but notice how stiff and uncomfortable Martin was acting. "But also, the food. Perhaps we can start there." Their short carriage ride ended abruptly, and they all piled out, finding themselves amid a bustling crowd of celebrating peoples, Lords and peasants alike. It was so busy that they almost went unnoticed in the chaos...almost. Children dropped flowers at their feet, and everyone bowed as Thea and Kol moved through the crowd. They navigated the streets, addressing the people appropriately while also simply enjoying their day.

One couldn't help but notice all the effort that had gone into creating the festivities before them. Every shop along the river was decorated in autumnal colors, and vendors of all kinds lined every street for at least a mile. They turned down one street, and Thea's mouth immediately watered as a multitude of smells accosted her.

"Something smells amazing!" Thea grabbed Kol's arm dramatically.

"You don't say." He replied, clearly amused with her, gesturing around to the many food vendors around them.

"Yes, I do." She ignored him. "It smells like cinnamon and apples."

"Let me find it for you." He said, as if he were a soldier on a mission.

"My hero." She teased. Kol scanned up and down the street, trying to find who could be making the thing Thea desired. His eyes fell upon an elderly woman, who had a bowl of apples on the table in front of her serving stall. She bowed when he approached her.

"Highness." She said quickly.

"What are you selling?" He asked tersely.

"Apples, baked with dough, spices, and syrup." She answered as gruffly as he had asked.

"I'll take one." He placed a gold coin on her table, a value much higher than the food she was peddling was worth. Her mood instantly shifted.

"Right away, Prince Kol." She smiled, showing a mouth missing many teeth. Kol grabbed the wooden bowl and spoon from her hand and turned back to Thea.

"Is this what you desire?" He asked as he presented it with a flourish.

She inspected it with a sniff. "Yes!" She snatched it from him. "Thank you." As they rounded the corner, they spotted a troupe of performers acting out skits on a stage near the river. When Thea saw this, she pointed excitedly. "Can we watch them?" She asked Kol.

"Of course." He led them to a bench near the back. "You all wait here. I'm going to get you a surprise." Thea's faces contorted into amused confusion.

"Okay, we'll wait here," Thea replied. Once he was gone, she turned to Dorothy. "Would you like to try this? It's amazing. We'll have to tell our cooks about it at The Palace and ask them to recreate it." She looked at the food in Dorothy's bowl. "What do you have?"

"It is hog, covered in some sort of sweet and savory sauce over a bun," Dorothy answered.

"What is that?" Thea pointed at a shriveled green vegetable.

"Vinegar cured cucumbers," Dorothy answered. "They look weird, but I promise they are quite good."

"Taste swap?" Thea offered her bowl up.

"Taste swap." Dorothy nodded in agreement. They switched bowls temporarily and, after tasting, switched back.

"Those are good!" Thea exclaimed. "I wonder if our cooks know how to make them." Dorothy shrugged before turning her attention back to the performers. Not long into watching the performance, Thea felt a tug on the back of her dress. She turned to find a small girl, no older than six years old, staring up at her. The first thing Thea noticed was that the girl was thin, far too thin to be healthy, with sallow skin and sunken cheeks. Then Thea noticed that she was quite dirty, with soot covering her face and caked under her fingernails, and her clothing was tattered. "Are you all right?" Thea asked the girl. The girl didn't speak, she simply just pointed at the bowl of food in Thea's lap. "Would you like this?" Thea offered, a little sad to be giving away such a delicious treat but knowing the girl needed it more. The little girl nodded in reply. "Okay, here you go." Thea handed her bowl over, and smiled at the girl, she gave her a small, closed mouth smile of her own before running away with the food. Thea made eye contact with a peasant woman sitting behind her. "Do you know who that girl is?" The woman nodded her head yes.

"Orphan, she runs around town often begging. Never stealing though, not after what she's been through." The woman replied.

"What do you mean?" Thea asked.

"Her parents were killed after her father stole bread from a cart that was headed to The Palace." She said simply, as if that were such a normal thing to die over. *Perhaps here it was,* Thea considered. But before she had much more time to consider this, Kol re-appeared, two mugs in hand.

"Get ready for the best hot chocolate drink you've ever had." He said with a smile.

"Bold statement." She replied before taking a drink. "But not untrue. This is amazing." She took another sip. "All the food here is incredible. I wonder if we could serve things like this in The Palace sometime. Maybe even invite these vendors to come and serve it." She suggested.

"Anything you want." He kissed her. "Where's your food?" He asked.

"I was done with it." Not a lie, but not the truth. She wondered why she didn't tell him where the rest of her food had gone, but didn't allow herself to ponder on it long. "What shall we do next?" Kol smiled at her, but before he would answer, they heard someone shouting for him.

"Prince Kol! Prince Kol!" General James ran through the crowd, a piece of parchment in hand. "The Strong's...they have responded!" He said, breaths coming in harsh pants. Kol snatched the letter from his hands.

"And what of the other assignment I gave you?" Kol asked about Enzo.

"No luck in locating him yet, Highness," James responded quietly.

Kol read the paper swiftly, then looked up at Thea and spoke with a most serious tone. "They've agreed to battle. We must leave and prepare at once." He looked to General James. "Begin readying our soldiers and gather the *Herba Hebeto* as soon as possible. We ride out at dawn." He paused, eyes meeting with Thea's. "In two days' time."

Chapter 19

Thea looked at the small travel trunk that sat on the foot of her bed. *What does one even pack for battle?* She wondered. So far, she had settled on several pairs of her training outfits, a thick coat, riding boots, and a small dagger that she had stolen from the training room. *Meager and embarrassing.* She sighed and sat on the edge of her bed. The bedroom door burst open, drawing her attention toward them.

"I'm bored. Can we please go for a walk in the city or something?" Dorothy begged dramatically. "What's that for?" She pointed to the trunk.

"I'm trying to pack up the things I'll need at the battle camp," Thea replied drearily. "But I don't really have much that feels appropriate for the occasion."

Dorothy snorted. "The *occasion*? This is a war, not a party. And of course, you don't have the things you need to wear, you shouldn't be going!" She looked distraught. "You only just got back from being kidnapped. Kol expects you to go to the battlefield?" She said incredulously.

"No, I expect me to go. This is my Empire now too, and I was kidnapped by the Strongs. The very men we will be fighting. This is my battle as much as anyone else."

"You don't know the first thing about war! You will only be in danger." Dorothy tried to reason with her, but her words were only angering Thea.

"Kol has been training me," Thea said defensively. "And I am not powerless."

"Kol has been training you for a week! You told me yourself he's only allowed you to hold wooden swords. You cannot go." Something inside Thea snapped.

"Don't tell me what I can and can't do!" She screamed. "I am not going to sit idly by and allow others to make my choices for me. Not again." Dorothy's eyes widened. She had scarcely heard Thea raise her voice like this, and definitely not directed toward her.

"Who are you?" Dorothy asked quietly.

"I don't know what you mean." Thea responded, eyes refusing to meet Dorothy's.

"Yelling at lady's maids, screaming at your friends, demanding things of people." Dorothy ticked off Thea's offenses on her fingers. She paused to emphasize her last point, placing her right pointer finger of her left pinky. "Having sex on the table of the council room with the door wide open. For all to see and hear." She chuffed. "That is not the Thea I know and love."

"The Thea you knew was weak and easily manipulated. I am powerful now."

"Power without grace is tyranny." And with that final statement, Dorothy turned on her heel and left.

Thea wasn't proud of how she had just spoken to Dorothy, and she wasn't even sure where all the rage came from. She heard the door to her room open and close again. Expecting it to be Dorothy, she turned, ready to apologize, but before her was Kol, all hard angles and brooding charm but he, just like

Dorothy, had a perplexed look on his face. He gestured toward her trunk.

"Going somewhere?"

"Obviously." She huffed, her irritation still high after her tiff with Dorothy. "With you. Tomorrow."

"Oh…Thea, I don't know-" He began, but she cut him off.

"Don't you dare tell me I can't go." She ordered through gritted teeth.

"My love," He began slowly, trying to use a docile tone to soothe her. "Battles and camps are not always the safest place one can be." She refused to look at him. "Understand that your safety is what matters most to me in this world." He tried to step in front of her, to catch her gaze, but she simply turned her head away from him. "I don't know that it's wise for you to come with us."

"You said I was your equal. That I was to rule with you." She said, tears threatening to fall from her eyes.

"I meant that." He agreed. "And you have been. We are using a plan you developed as our main offensive in this battle."

"Then why don't you agree I should go with you? I can help more." She asked, lip quivering. "I am powerful." She said again, and though upset she still whole-heartedly believed it.

"Thea, I want you to be safe. Nowhere is safer than the Palace."

"The Palace? The one I was kidnapped from right under your nose?" She bit out. Her words stung, and Kol felt a pain in his chest after the words left her mouth.

Kol sighed and drug his hand down his face slowly. "You really want to go?"

"Yes." She said, finally making eye contact with him.

338

"All right, I won't stop you." He riffled through the trunk, eyeing the meager and unhelpful belongings within. He picked up the small dagger and dangled it between two fingers. "What were you going to defend yourself from with this? A squirrel?" He suppressed a laugh.

She snatched it from his hand. "It's all I could get my hands on."

"You mean it's all you could smuggle out of the training room behind my back." He replied. She looked down, ashamed of herself. "Come with me."

"Where?" She asked as she trailed behind him.

"We're going to get you proper gear and weapons. I won't have my wife showing up to a near winter battle in training tights and a peacoat."

Frigid air blew against Thea's wind-burned cheeks as she and Kol rode on horseback, regime behind them, finishing the final leg of their travels to camp. She tried not to think of the cold, it was only midday, and she knew it would only get colder. Though freezing to the bone, she held her head high. Thea radiated confidence as she rode. Her hair was braided back, and she was outfitted like every soldier around her; black leather head to toe, and at her hip was her stolen dagger and a small sword. Kol had a seamstress work all night to get the smallest pair of fighting leathers he could find to fit Thea's measurements. And around her shoulders hung a thick fur to help fight off the chill of the autumnal air. Thea inhaled deeply, chilled air tickling her nose as it went in. She knew they were close to camp from smell alone, a combination of burning wood and feces hung heavy in the air. She tried her best to hide her disgust, but Kol could see it all over her face.

"You never get used to that putrid scent." He commented. "I instructed a servant to close the flap to our tent and burn incense. Hopefully that will help." Thea nodded; though she didn't want special treatment out here, she wouldn't shoot this particular favor down. "Almost there." He clicked and nudged his horse, urging him to speed up, Thea's followed suit. "General!" Kol yelled, and General James' horse quickly caught up to Kol's.

"Aye?" He replied.

"You know what to do." James nodded and rode ahead of them, shouting orders as he went.

"What is he doing?" Thea asked after making sure no one was around to hear her. She didn't want her lack of knowledge to be broadcasted, as she knew the men already thought little of her.

"Make sure all the men have what they need and that all the weapons are in order for our attack tomorrow. We want this to be over before it even begins." She nodded, pretending that alone was enough information. "We will discuss it in further detail once we are settled into camp."

Thea followed behind Kol, doing her best to use her senses to orient herself to the environment as she did so. The ground beneath her, mostly comprised of mud and horse excrement, squished audibly with every step her horse took. Smoke from multiple fires wafted through the air, causing her eyes to water. She couldn't make sense of the sound around her; too many were occurring at once for her to process: men yelling, swords clanging, horses whining.

"Here we are." Kol stopped before a large, circular, canvas tent. He helped Thea off her horse, and she immediately sunk a few inches into the mud. "I feel compelled to remind you that you wanted to be here." Kol joked. She looked down at her fortified leather boots, and silently thanked God she wasn't in those riding boots she had tried to pack.

"I'm not going to let a little mud stop me." She remarked as she mucked her way toward the entrance to their tent. Kol pulled back the flap and gestured for her to go in. Instantly the smell of war dissipated, replaced with the Cativo signature scent of lavender. The tent was sparse, though more furnished than the inns she and Kol had found themselves in on their recent travels. The floor was canvas and covered in many animal skin rugs, a large table covered by a map and several little figurines sat in the middle of the room, and nestled in a far corner was a plush nest of blankets and pillows.

"Glamorous, no?" Kol joked.

"I never want to leave this luxury." She meandered her way around the tent, picking up a piece of fruit from a buffet of food on her way to view the map. "What is all of this?" The apple crunched as she bit into it.

"That is a map of the battlefield, and each figurine represents a piece of our attack plan. Catapults, soldiers, men on foot, men on horseback, barricades, and this one represents the Strong Castle." He named each piece as he picked it up.

She nodded thoughtfully. "Where will I be tomorrow?"

He pursed his lips in consideration. "That we still need to discuss."

"Your first thought is?" She asked.

He pointed to the map. "Here, on a hill, guarded by a handful of soldiers, and away from the action but still aware of what's going on."

"Okay." She replied.

"Okay?" He huffed out a breath, face suspicious. "I figured you'd fight me a little more."

"Were you willing to make concessions on this?" She asked genuinely.

"I'm willing to do anything for you." He replied, but in the back of his mind, he knew the reality was he was prepared to protect her from anything, even herself.

"Look-" She placed both her hands up, as if she were holding back an invisible wall. Kol raised his brows and smirked in amusement. "I'm not delusional. I have no misconception about myself to think that I belong in the mix of all of that." She pointed to the map. "I cannot fight well yet and would only be a liability." She took his hand in her own. "I just didn't want to be left behind, and there is plenty I can contribute before the fighting begins. Such as, supporting you and boosting the morale of the men."

"I agree." He leaned down and kissed her slowly. "Are you ready to go to the General's tent? We must finalize all strategic moves."

"Yes," Thea replied, and when Kol turned to walk out, she grabbed his hand and pulled him in for a kiss. "Thank you."

"For what?" He asked.

"Including me." She said quietly before walking her way out of their tent and into the chilly, putrefying afternoon air.

"All of our plans, the future of our realm, are riding on a bunch of herbs we have once tested on a singular man on the word of a girl." Commander Reese remarked sarcastically, and with that comment, the tent was divided – half the men nodding in silent agreement and half waiting in horror for Kol's response.

"Careful Commander," Kol warned. "On the word of the Princess of Cativo, who is to be respected."

Reese, a sensible man, nodded and placed his hands up in concession. "I mean no disrespect. I only worry for our men who are to face the enemy soldiers tomorrow. And also, for the man who is to sneak into enemy camp tonight and successfully poison every person in their encampment."

General James cleared his throat, "At that point, we have another complication to discuss."

"Go on then," Kol said with irritation.

"The man we had briefed and prepared to complete the poisoning mission is missing," James said, voice filled with tired exasperation.

"Missing?" Thea asked.

"Likely fled." James clarified.

"Because why?" Thea asked.

"The last man we sent into a Strong encampment to gather intel was found outside our camp the next morning, flayed and disemboweled...and still alive," James replied grimly. "It is likely this mission will be a hard one to convince many to take. Not to mention our best men will be sneaking into the Strong's castle to free the enslaved children tonight."

"Just pick a man, and I will not give him an option," Kol said, a twinkle of Control in his eyes.

General James continued speaking, temporarily disregarding Kol's suggestion. "It is a dangerous mission. Their numbers aren't minuscule – but small enough to notice an unfamiliar man snooping around in their kitchen tent. Not to mention all the men, even cooks, wear the same uniforms."

Thea sat in quiet contemplation as the men around her argued. Kol was trying to get traction with his 'force of a man to complete the mission' idea, and both the General and

Commander warned him of the danger associated with any man going into the Strong's camp.

"You are sending any man in there on a suicide mission, and the success of this part of the plan is our main strategy tomorrow," General James continued with his speech.

"What would you have us do then?" Kol remarked sarcastically.

"What about women?" Thea said quietly. All the men continued to speak over her, except for Kol.

"What did you say, Thea?" He asked respectfully.

"What about women? Are there women in the Strong camp?" She asked again, loud enough to silence the other men in the tent.

"Whores and scullery maids." Reese snorted indignantly.

"And do they wear uniforms?" Thea asked.

"You think whores have uniforms?" Reese said with a laugh, which was cut short by Kol's withering stare.

"I can do it," Thea said.

"Do what?" James asked.

"I can sneak into the camp; they won't notice an unknown woman in the camp. They'll never suspect a woman. I will be like a ghost. In to poison their food and out before they notice." Thea said, with excitement tinging her voice. She was eager to help, so much so it blinded any fear she had in facing the Strongs again. Revenge was commanding her brain. James and Reese sat in silent contemplation.

"No," Kol said. "It's too dangerous."

"Consider it, Your Highness. It's not a bad idea." James reasoned.

"Let's send your wife into the enemy's camp then," Kol snapped back at him. James glared.

Thea stepped in front of Kol. "Look at me." He did as she said. "I can do this." A thousand thoughts raced through his head. The pragmatic side of his brain, which his father had trained, told him that letting her do this was a logical idea – but the emotional side that loved Thea could only remember how he felt when he thought he might lose her. These two sides warred in his head. "Let me do this." She begged quietly so that the other men couldn't hear.

"Fine." Kol conceded. "But I'm coming with you." He said with authority.

"That is the opposite of the point. We are trying to be discreet. You are not discreet." Thea insisted.

"I can be," Kol responded. "This is nonnegotiable." He replied with finality in his voice.

"Fine." Thea agreed. "Let's get ready. There are only so many hours left in this day."

Hours later, after the sun had gone down, Kol and Thea rode silently toward the Strong's encampment. Thea's teeth chattered loudly. She had never before had cold seep so deeply into her that her bones themselves felt cold.

"I can hear your teeth from here," Kol commented.

"Well, it's colder than a witch's titty out here. What do you expect?" Thea retorted.

Despite himself, Kol released a small laugh, "A witch's titty?" He asked.

"I don't know, it's something my Nan used to say." She replied dismissively. The moment of levity passed quickly, and Kol looked at her with concern etched into his face. He called their horses to a halt. "What are you doing?" Thea asked.

He hopped down off his horse. "Come here." He helped her down and moved her bags onto his horse.

"Care to tell me what's going on?" Thea asked, annoyance clear in her voice.

"We're going to share a horse and share body heat. Plus, one horse riding in will be less noticeable than two." He slapped her horse and it quickly responded, whinnying, and riding off in the direction they had come. Kol made quick work of settling them both on his horse and continuing their journey. "Had you decided to be a scullery maid rather than a sex worker, you could have worn more clothes."

"Anyone can be a sex worker. The scullery maids and cooks probably know one another." She reasoned. Kol grunted in disgruntled agreement.

"Tell me the plan again," Kol ordered.

"Someone's bossy." Thea jested, but Kol was not in the mood, anxiety making him disgruntled.

"I want us in and out of there as fast as possible. I want no mix-ups." Kol explained. "I will take no chances with your life."

"Okay." She leaned into him and he placed his chin atop her head as she talked. "Walk into the camp through the back, locate the tent in the middle of the encampment with the largest fire (because that is likely where the food is being prepared), and, finally, put the herbal extract into the ale barrels, water supply, and dinner stew." She repeated succinctly.

"Good girl." Thea shivered, whether from the cold or his praise, she wasn't sure. "Thankfully, we had herbalists working on this for us. They were able to concentrate the herb into a syrup. It will be more discreet and make this whole thing much easier for you." Thea nodded in agreement.

The familiar smell of camp assaulted her nose. "We're close, I take it?" Thea commented.

Kol snorted. "What tipped you off?" He leaned in close to her. "I will tie our horse to a nearby tree. We will meet there when you are finished." He pointed to a darkened part of the woods.

"Meet? Where are you going?" Thea asked.

"I will be your shadow, watching from the darkness as your protector."

"And if you're caught?" Thea asked.

"I will make them forget or tell them to drop dead," Kol said casually.

"Oh yeah.," Thea said. "I sometimes forget you can do that." Slowly, the camp became visible, and then Thea felt as if she blinked and then it was time to fulfill her mission. With eight vials of poison in a satchel around her waist, she stood with shaking knees in the shadows of a tree, staring at the camp in front of her. All previous confidence was gone.

"You don't have to do this if you don't want to." Kol offered. This fueled her resolve once more.

"Yes. I do." She decided. "Kiss me before I lose the nerve." He obeyed.

"Use your Control on me." He said. "We will be leaving the Strong's camp in less than an hour, with our mission having been a success." Truth. "Is it true?" He asked hopefully. Thea nodded. "Then we have nothing to worry about." He kissed her again. "Go burn it down, my love."

Thea gave free rein of her mind to her revenge. She imagined the very men who facilitated her torture would be the ones drinking the poison. The shock that would be on their face when they found themselves powerless on the battlefield fueled her. She stuck to the shadows as much as possible, head on a swivel for the tent with the largest billow of smoke coming out of it. As she searched, Thea couldn't help but note the goings-on of the men in the camp. Many sat around fires drinking, while others snogged women in the shadows. Moans, giggles, and boisterous laughs filled the air. *I think anyone could have walked into this camp. Their merriment and debauchery are distraction enough,* Thea thought.

She eventually spotted a large tent with a cloud of smoke above it. This tent was directly across from her, a short distance but one in the direct path of many soldiers. Thea closed her eyes, took several deep breaths, and tensed her shaky hands.

The Icy wind blew hard against her nearly completely exposed breasts, and she cursed her lack of clothing. She thought warm thoughts. First, she envisioned her bathing tub back at The Palace, filled to the brim with steaming water, and then she imagined how a warmed chocolate drink would feel sliding down her throat. "I can have all those things soon. But first, I have to do this." Thea whispered this pep talk to herself. She considered running to the tent but thought that would draw more attention than slinking down the pathway would. Casually, she made her way to the entrance of the tent and stuck her head inside. The smell of broth and spices filled her nose. Inside she could see a single cook, mixing spices into the giant vat of what would be dinner. She made note of the layout of the tent and then stepped back, fading into the shadows, and waited on the diversion they had planned.

"Supplies are here!" Men shouted as the decoy carriage rode into camp.

A soldier ran into the tent beside her and yelled to the cook. "Bread came in. The men are fighting over it."

"Burn 'em all, daft scoundrels." The cook cursed before following the soldier to the supply carriage.

Thea slipped inside and quickly ran toward the barrels of ale that lined the far wall of the tent. The glass vials in her satchel clinked together loudly as she reached to grab one. She expertly tipped a vial into the small, uncorked hole of the three barrels of fermented drink.

The stew was next, but she tripped on her way to the pot. She closed her eyes on impact, but the sound of glass breaking was undeniable. "Fecking hell." She cursed. Inside, her bag was coated in sticky liquid and glass shards. Two vials had broken on impact. Carefully she picked two vials out of the mess and quickly dumped the syrup into the vat of broth.

Only left to contaminate was the water. She stepped confidently toward the large barrel of water and reached her hand down into her satchel. The flap to the tent ripped open. Thea turned her back to the barrel, successfully snatching the vial out of the bag, but cutting her hand in the process.

"When's the grub gonna be ready, Cooke?" A drunk soldier slurred. Thea's heart slammed erratically in her chest, and bile threatened to crawl up her throat. He looked around before his eyes landed on her. "You're not Cooke." He said with an arched brow. "Can't say I'm disappointed, though." He tried to flirt.

"Just getting a drink of water," Thea said slowly, trying very hard to keep her voice steady. She turned around and quickly dumped the vial into the water, using the ladle to stir it around.

"You are a drink of water." He slunk both hands around her waist and blew hot, rancid breath on the back of her neck. She forced away the horrid memories threatening to take her

349

over, the memories of the last time she was amongst the Strongs. "How about you show me a good time around back? I'll make it worth your while." Two small bronze coins materialized nearly out of thin air, and he rubbed them together miserly. Thea wanted to vomit, but she forced herself to nod, knowing an escape would present itself. Her Control had said as much. She focused on the positives as the old drunk beside her pawed at her chest and led her from the tent. Once out of the tent, the man's advances became more forward. He tugged on her corset and then began to loosen the strings on his own pants.

"Take me to the woods?" Thea asked suddenly. Her brain was working in the simplest assumptions in that moment. She last saw Kol in the woods. Kol must be in the woods. Kol is safe; therefore, the woods are safe.

"Someone shy? What away from the prying eyes?" He teased. "Whatever you want, milady." He grabbed her hand. Thea watched as his sagging pants slipped lower and lower as they crossed camp and were engulfed by the shadows of the forest. He pushed himself up against a tree. "Kneel." He ordered her.

"Kol!" She yelled as quietly as possible.

"Not Kol, kneel." The man corrected.

"Kol!" She repeated.

"What the feck is a Kol?" The man shouted, irritation clear in his voice.

"I am," Kol said from behind him, and before the man could say another word, he added. "You will not speak or move a muscle." Kol walked briskly to Thea and quickly inspected her for apparent signs of harm. "Are you okay?" She nodded. He kissed her quickly before turning his attention back to the silent soldier. "Did he touch you?" Kol asked.

"Yes." She answered grimly.

"How do you want me to handle this?" He asked, murder on his mind.

She eyed the man hesitantly, shivering as she remembered the feeling of his hands on her. her heart quickened as she considered how Kol would like to handle the situation, and then finally, she whispered, "End him."

Without pause, Kol ordered the man. "Arm out." Kol brought his sword high above his head and swiftly brought it down, slicing the man's right hand clean off. Horror covered his face, but he could not scream. "Did he speak to you?" Kol asked.

"Yes."

Kol tossed a small knife at the man's feet. "Cut out your tongue." The man's body responded without consent from his own mind. He gripped the knife in one hand and sawed painstakingly low through the flesh of his tongue. This task made all the more difficult without the use of his other hand. Tears streamed from his eyes as he sliced through the light pink organ that protruded from his mouth. Mere moments later, his tongue lay beside his hand on the forest floor.

"Did he look at you?" Kol asked, with every intention of forcing the man to gouge out his own eyes.

"Kol, just end it," Thea asked of him. "I want this to be over."

Lucky for the silent soldier, Kol's love for his wife outweighed his desire for revenge. "Die." And instantly, the man was a bleeding heap on the ground. "Let's go." Kol draped his black cloak around her shoulders and helped situate her on his horse.

"Were you successful?" He asked.

"Of course, I was." She replied haughtily.

351

"That's my girl." He kissed her head and allowed Thea to settle back into him for the whole ride back to their camp.

General James met them at the camp's entrance upon arrival. "Were you successful?" James asked desperately, mirroring Kol's question from earlier.

"Yes," Thea reported with forced nonchalance, but inside she was ecstatic.

"Praise be," James replied.

"And the children?" Thea asked.

"Report came shortly before you arrived. Twelve children were rescued and are being taken back to the Mori realm to be reunited with their families."

"Twelve?" Thea asked, a lump in her throat. James only nodded in reply.

"And several of the Strong's men were injured or killed in the sneak attack; all of our soldiers survived," James reported proudly.

"This calls for celebration!" Kol shouted. Soldiers stood around, and though typically cautious around Kol, they hooted in response to his excitement. "Two ales each and bed thereafter. We still have a battle to win tomorrow." Kol commanded sensibly.

Sometime later, Thea found herself sitting by a large fire in the middle of the camp. A warm mug of tea was in her hand, and she fought the cold air off with a thick fur shrug. Kol had long ago retired to finalize some things, stating, "The men will celebrate better without me around anyway." That made Thea sad for him, to be an outsider in his own world.

"Heard you're to thank for giving us a leg up tomorrow." A burly, bearded man said as he plopped down on the bench to Thea's left.

"A poison that takes away Control. How was this not heard of sooner?" The man on her right said. He held out his hand to her. "Jon."

"Thea." She shook it.

"We know." Jon laughed. "Everyone knows." He pointed to the man on her left. "That's my brother Rodrick," Rodrick grunted.

"Bet *Herba Hebeto* becomes outlawed now. Can't have the powerless getting any ideas. Not that they care, but it has other benefits to the un-Blessed. My family has been using it to treat things for generations, and now we won't be able to have it." A man nearby replied.

"Shut the feck up, Vincent. You and your conspiracies. We're going to win now. We get to go home to our families after we win. Put all this behind us." Jon said.

"You're stupid if you think they just won't find another war for us to fight, while they sit in their ivory towers." Vincent snorted.

"Kol is not sitting in an ivory tower. He is going to lead your ungrateful arses into battle tomorrow." Thea said, glaring at Vincent.

Jon slapped his leg and cackled. "I like the Princess. She's got bite!"

A quiet man sitting across the fire spoke; up until then, he had sat quietly and listened while he played a tune on his guitar. "I'm just ready to go home." His voice cracked. "One of the kids they rescued today was my little girl."

Jon leaned in and whispered. "Roger hasn't slept well since his daughter went missing', never seen a man cry so hard as when he found out she was rescued today. He picked up that

353

guitar and hasn't stopped playing. Think he's trying to keep his hands busy."

"It's taking every bit of his honor to not go AWOL and run home to his family as we speak. He even volunteered to cook breakfast with the cook tomorrow, figured cracking several hundred eggs would keep his mind busy." Rodrick added.

"Can't cook for shite, though. Hope you don't mind eating eggshells." Jon jested, causing both brothers to laugh.

"Tonight, we celebrate, but tomorrow we celebrate even harder," Rodrick shouted before he downed the rest of his drink. "Memento Mori!" He yelled.

"Memento Mori!" All men within earshot shouted back. They all tossed the remainder of their drinks into the fire, causing it to temporarily poof from the accelerant. Roger began to pick a fast, jaunty tune on his guitar; all the men responded in turn, moving their bodies in time with his song.

"What does that mean?" Thea asked.

"It means more than I could explain, but essentially it means this: 'Remember you will die.'" Jon answered her.

"Why would you want to remember that? It's so depressing." Thea said, a crinkle in her nose.

"So you don't forget to live before that happens." Jon winked and offered her a hand. "Join us in our revelry?" He asked with a smirk. Thea considered his offer, and how would it look for the Princess to be dancing around a fire in the mud with soldiers and peasants – but she soon decided she didn't care. She grabbed Jon's hand and allowed him to haul her up, immediately stepping in tune with the other men. Thea twirled, kicking up mud around her as her body and hair swirled around her.

"This one's more fun than she looks." Rodrick teased.

"This one's not a stuffy royal. She's a Princess of the people! Just look at her." Jon praised, a slight slur to his voice.

Thea ignored them both and let the music take her. She twisted and turned until her legs felt as if they might fold beneath her at any second. The fire turned to ashes, and one by one, the men left to go to bed. Roger was the last to leave, having played until his fingers hurt and he could hardly keep his eyes open, but even when he was gone – Thea stayed. She sat, staring and the crumbling embers of the once roaring fire. Many thoughts filled her head: the battle the next day, her life, Kol, the people of her realm, and her future.

"I began to wonder if you'd run off." Kol's voice said from behind her.

"No, just sat here, considering my mortality is all," Thea replied.

"Ah, Memento Mori?" Kol asked.

"You've heard of this?"

"All soldiers in the Mori Empire have." He paused. "You know you have nothing to fear for tomorrow, right?" Thea shrugged. "You and I will make it out of here alive tomorrow." Thea strained her Control, unable to sense the truth.

"Say that again." She demanded.

"You and I will make it out of here alive tomorrow," Kol said, confused. She pushed her Control to the limit, harder than she had to in order to force answers from people, and only barely could she detect the truth in his statement. *Weird.*

"You only keep me around to be a makeshift fortune-teller." Thea teased as she leaned into his invitation for embrace.

"You've figured it out. It's not at all because I adore you," Kol replied. "What was that all about?"

"I must be more exhausted than I thought. I could hardly detect the truth in the statement you made about our safety tomorrow."

"Let's get some rest, my love. Morning will be here before we know it." Thea nodded and allowed him to pull her into their tent. He helped strip her of her 'sex worker' costume and pull on something warmer. "I can't believe you wore this all night?" He clucked in disapproval.

"Honestly, I kind of forgot about it." She shrugged. "Especially once I had those furs wrapped around me and was by the fire."

He held up the small corset stop she had worn all night, which scarcely covered her breasts and flaunted most of her midriff. "I rather liked this piece, though." He raised a brow at her seductively.

"I'll wear it for you someday." She said dismissively as she nestled herself down into their makeshift bed.

"Promise?" Kol got down on his knees and crawled toward her.

"Swear."

"Can I have a timeline? It's cruel to not." He whined.

She considered the unpleasant garment, how it sucked the breath from her lungs and made her chest ache. "I will wear it for you when you become High King."

Kol pouted. "Not until them?"

"Nope."

"I must add killing the current High King to my to-do list then." Kol joked.

"Shut it," Thea said sleepily and then cracked a small smile. She closed her eyes and felt sleep nearing.

"As you wish." He kissed her gently on the temple. "Goodnight, my queen."

"I'm not the queen." She mumbled.

He leaned in and whispered, "You will be once I kill the King."

"Okay." She replied, half awake.

"Okay? That's it. No telling me that killing is wrong?" Kol said in jest.

"I'm too tired to argue with you, and I don't like your father anyway. Do as you will."

Kol laughed, startling Thea from her sleep. "I love you." He said with a smile.

"And I you. Now goodnight." She allowed him to pull her close to his chest, and there they fell asleep together, momentarily forgetting the horrors the next day may bring.

Chapter 20

Thea considered watching a battle to being much like watching a tragic play one had never seen before. She had been introduced to the players, the world, and the stakes – but she didn't yet know what the outcome would be and who may be lost along the way. She felt it almost unreal as she watched both sets of soldiers line up on opposing sides of the battlefield, all equipped with weapons and dressed in armor. Before the fighting started, Kol rode toward the Strong's line, meeting one of their men toward the center of that battlefield. They were discussing terms, Kol urging them once more to consider surrender. Thea figured the Strong man would laugh, knowing that on his side he had Controllers of Strong and Fire to fight, as well as Faunas to Control the Mori horses into disobedience from beneath their own masters. What he didn't know was that many of them had been rendered useless, and the shock of discovering their loss of Control would mute their reaction momentarily as well.

As expected, Kol and the Strong rode away from one another, and Kol commanded the catapults to fire. Massive balls of destruction were lit aflame and sent flying toward the Strong's men. Several men, those with Control of Fire and Strong, stepped forward, planning to use their Controls to extinguish the flaming masses and catch them midair to avoid destruction. Thea waited with bated breath. Of the twelve flaming masses, only two were extinguished. One confused Strong caught a flaming mass, and did succeed in stopping it from causing destruction, but he quickly became engulfed in flame and crumpled beneath the ball of fire. All the other masses did their job; with the flames still lit and the Strong's not strong enough to catch them – they bulldozed through the men and destroyed several of their catapults. Mori soldiers quickly reloaded the catapults and sent a dozen more blazing orbs toward the enemy. Chaos had broken out on the Strong's side of the battlefield, men screaming and Generals and Commanders riding frantically around, trying to reassess their situation. In this chaos, Mori soldiers successfully took out dozens of men and all the Strong's trajectory artillery. Strong soldiers lay dead and dying, when not a single Mori man had yet been taken down. Hope filled Thea's chest for their chance of victory, and the only regret she had was not having Kol test the question of their victory with her Control.

Not knowing how, but realizing they had been sabotaged, the Strong Commander ordered his men to run, to engage the Mori's in hand-to-hand combat. Though without Control, the army, made largely of Strong Controls, still had size to their advantage. Behemoths of men ran toward the Mori Army, swinging absurdly large maces and swords wildly, the anger of being stripped of their powers fueling them more than honor for the realm ever would have. Throughout the field one could hear the clash of metal and the sickening crunch of bones as Strongs ripped their mace into the bodies of Mori soldiers. Though the Mori's had a head start on the death tally, the Strongs were quickly catching up. Catapults were forgotten and traded for crossbows as the Mori men above worked to pick off the approaching Strong soldiers.

Thea wanted to ask the soldiers that flanked her, the men Kol had ordered to protect her at all costs to even their own lives or safety, how the battle seemed to be going. She wondered if they had some military prowess or life experience that allowed them to know the potential outcome of the scene before them. But one look at their faces told her they didn't know any more than she did, and they were actively grieving their fallen brothers below, feeling helpless as they watched. Thea thanked God for her Control, and that at the very least, she knew that both she and Kol were making it out of there alive that day.

Kol maneuvered the battlefield as a fish swam through water – effortlessly. His sword moved as if an extension of his arm and his horse followed his silent orders as if he were a Fauna. Kol ducked when approached by enemies and expertly sliced his sword into fatal locations every time he passed them by. Thea tried to keep track of how many men he felled, but she quickly lost count. At that moment, she saw him – a machine of war, the Prince of Death. And she was unafraid. Instead, she was mystified.

Kol was moving his way toward the Strong General, hoping death to their leaders would leave the men confused and directionless, ending the battle even faster. He bobbed and weaved and sliced his way across the field. Eventually, he found himself positioned right in front of their General. Immediately, sword crashed against sword – neither man open for conversation or concession. Kol landed several superficial wounds to the General, and he returned them slice for slice.

"Fauna!" The General screamed, and the single Fauna with Control left on the Strong side came running.

Thea watched as Kol was thrown from his horse, and time moved slowly as she watched the General jump from his horse, landing with practiced provision, and stab Kol clear through the chest. His scream could be heard from her perch on the hill far above the battle. *He's going to be okay! My Control said we would make it out of here alive today!* Thea screamed internally, but then it clicked. Her oh-so literal Control. They had been in camp when he had said it, and they both had made it out of the camp alive that morning. The General kicked Kol in the face, causing his head to snap back violently and his lip to bust open. *He may not survive,* Thea thought with anxious devastation filling her heart.

"Die," Kol called on his Control, and he found that even speaking required much energy from him. But despite his injury, his raw emotion and the added power from taking *Herba Augendae Vires* that morning sent his Control out and all the men within a twenty-foot radius instantly dropped to the ground.

"Holy hell." The soldier beside Thea whispered as he watched twenty men fall at Kol's Control.

Kol stood, laboriously, and stumbled toward the men who had stood just outside his previous fell radius. He coughed, blood spewing from his mouth, and at this, he raged even harder. He knew Thea's Control and had strategically asked the question he knew would give her comfort today. He had never been under any illusion it meant he would survive. But being confronted with his own mortality when he just felt as though he had begun to live enraged him to his core.

"Die!" Kol screamed, dropping six more men instantly. The few leaders left began to panic, scrambling away from the beast that prowled toward them, the true Prince of Death. The next in command, a small, young Captain, stood before Kol – visibly trembling. Kol could see weakness in this man. "Save your life, call the fecking surrender." The man hesitated. "Or die."

"Blow the horn!" The Captain conceded, and a loud horn blew, pausing nearly every soldier on the battlefield. A few men continued, giving the final blow to their current opponent, but after that, they stopped. A white flag rose above the Strong battlefield, and Mori soldiers shouted, celebrating their victory, without care that their Prince had just collapsed.

Thea screamed and pulled her horse's reins, urging him forward as fast as possible. "Healer!" She screamed repeatedly, begging someone to bring a Healer back from camp to help Kol. James and Reese quickly rode up to flank her, racing their way to the heap of unmoving, bleeding flesh on the ground. Thea did her best to ignore the stench of death and masses of dead bodies as her horse navigated through the battlefield. Once close enough, Thea jumped from her horse, running the last bit to him herself. Pain shot through her knees as she dove down to the ground beside him, but she didn't care. All she could feel was panic. "Kol?" He didn't respond. "Kol!" She rolled him to his back, at this, his eyes fluttered, and he released a small grunt. Thea gently rubbed his face. "Open your eyes, my love." But he did not. Thea, filled with adrenaline and fear, reacted on impulse. "Kol!" He slapped him across the face, hoping to elicit a response from him.

Kol groaned and cracked his eyes. "Holy hells, Thea." He coughed, blood trickling from his mouth again. "You are nothing but gentle grace, flipping an injured man about." He winced as he tried to sit up. "Slapping him in the face." He lolled his head to the side to look at her. "I've never been more turned on." Hearing him flirt, Thea released the tension she had been holding in her chest ever since he fell from his horse.

"It worked, didn't it?" She grabbed his hand with one of hers and used the other to swipe falling tears off her face.

"I suppose it did." He said weakly, closing his eyes again.

"Kol!" Stay with me, don't make me slap you again." She teased, but his eyes continued to close anyway. "Can we get a Healer here, please!" She looked to the Strong Captain who stood nearby, watching them. "Do you have a Healer close?" She yelled at him. His response was to nod. "Get them!" She ordered. The Captain hesitated, likely wondering what benefit saving Kol would give him. "Get the Healer, or I will kill you myself, and it will be painful, and I will enjoy it." She growled, and then the Captain went running.

"Uh- oh." Kol coughed. "You've been around me too long. I've corrupted you." Kol whispered, a weak but teasing smile on his lips.

"No, no, you didn't." She leaned down and kissed his bleeding cheek. "You freed me." She leaned back up. "Follow him! If he isn't getting a Healer, run him through with a blade and then find someone who will do as I'm demanding!" She commanded James.

"You're a natural," Kol said.

"What was that, my love?" Thea asked, desperate to keep him conscious and talking.

"A natural, you're a natural leader." He took a labored breath and forced his eyes open. "Even in times of panic, you default to command and order those around you. You are going to be an amazing queen."

"And you, an amazing king." She said in turn.

"Maybe." He whispered, eyes fluttering closed again.

"I refuse to be queen without you there to be king, Kol Arius. If you die here I will be very displeased with you." She scolded.

Kol laughed, and then winced in pain. "If I'm dead, I doubt your displeasure will upset me much."

"I will find a way to ruin your afterlife if you don't make it off this field alive today. I swear it." She said, tears falling from her face again. A few drops landed on Kol's hand.

"Don't cry." He gave her hand a weak squeeze.

Thea sniffed loudly. "Don't tell me what to do."

"Wouldn't dream of it." The corner of his lip pulled up into a small, sad smile. "I love you."

Thea's lip quivered, and her tears were unstoppable now. "I love you." She kissed him on the lips, but when he didn't return, she leaned up and screamed. "Healers! Now!" Reese looked around helplessly, uncomfortable with the grief before him.

James rounded the corner, the Captain and a small woman running behind them. "She's the Healer," James announced.

"Help him! Please!" Thea cried. The woman hesitated, clearly contemplating in her head the value of the man's life before her. "I will give you whatever you want – money, power, anything." Thea looked her in the eyes. "Please." The Healer looked to the Captain, who urged her to help out of his own self-preservation, remembering Thea's previous threat.

The Healer hiked up her skirts and moved forward. "Everyone stand back." She kneeled in the mud beside Kol and placed her hands over his body. Despite the woman's order, Thea stayed right where she was, knelt on the ground with Kol's hand in her own. Energy pulsed from the woman's hands as she moved them over Kol's chest. "His heart is still beating." Thea breathed a sigh of relief. "He is still breathing, though it is labored. Puncture in his left lung and several cracked ribs." She moved her hands over his face. "Only superficial wounds here." She went back to working on his chest.

"He'll live?" Thea asked, hope threatening to shatter her heart.

"He'll live. Though maybe not had I not been here to save him." The woman opened her eyes and looked to Thea. "I will be calling on my reward."

Thea fought the urge to scream at the woman, bringing up favors and money when Kol's life hung in the balance. "Of course!" Thea said with irritation, "Just heal him." Thea kissed his hand and stood, making her way toward James. "Is there a plan in place? Everyone knows what to do?" She asked.

"In the immediate time, yes," James answered. "We will need Prince Kol and the High King to make decisions on what comes of this land and the transition of power, but that can wait." Thea nodded.

"Get the men and camp situated then and send a carriage here to pick up Kol and the Healer. We will outfit her with her reward once Kol makes it safely back to the Palace." James nodded.

Thea watched as the woman healed Kol, sitting on the floor of the carriage as they rode slowly back to the Palace. She sat, stroking his hair or kissing his face, all the while asking the Healer many questions about Kol's state.

"He is fine? Why isn't he waking up?" Thea asked.

The Healer rolled her eyes and sighed. "He is resting, his body exhausted from the injury. Give him time, ma'am."

Thea didn't like this woman's attitude. "It's Your Highness." Thea corrected.

The woman nodded, fear in her eyes. "Apologies, Your Highness."

"Thought you didn't care for the titles?" Kol asked.

"Kol!" Thea squealed in delight. "You're all right!"

"You didn't really give me any other options than to be all right." He said, slowly picking his arm up and placing Thea's chin in his hand.

"Don't forget that either. That rule extends out until further notice." She replied.

"Duly noted, *Your Highness*." Had he not been on death's door hours ago, Thea would have slapped at him for that remark. "Come here and kiss me."

She stole a line from him. "As you wish."

Weeks went by, Kol healed, and slowly order began to restore itself in the realm. Several councilmen had been sent to the previous Strong realm to handle the transition of power. To Thea's knowledge, many resistant lords of the Strong realm were killed, while others fled. And much to Dorothy's dismay, Duke Martin had been amongst those to volunteer to maintain order there until further notice.

Under General James' recommendation, all future battle plans had been put on hold until winter was over – allowing the men to heal, rest, and spend the holidays with their families. Another occasion they all had to look forward to was the ball Thea was hosting to honor the bravery of the soldiers and the many lives lost in the Battle of Stronghill.

One morning, weeks after the battle, Thea lay exhausted in bed with Kol, his long sinewy arm draped across her taut abdomen. She relished his touch as he traced lazy circles around her left hip bone.

"I've never noticed this before." He commented, finger pausing around a discolored patch of skin.

"My birthmark? Yes, well, we've not been this…close very often." She giggled. "You've never stopped to inspect every inch of my body. And I don't want to alarm you, but I have another birthmark on my right foot." She teased.

"I suppose you're right, and that is something I plan to change. A pro of halting manifest destiny until the Spring, I have months where my only job is to do this." He placed a searing kiss on her hip bone. "I look forward to many more years of discovering new things about this body." Truth. Thea shock herself as she pulled on her Control for that, as she realized she had stopped using her Control on Kol long ago, except for those rare moment when he asked her to. When they first met she felt as if she used it on every sentence that left his mouth, but not anymore. This realization gave her peace, she trusted him so explicitly that it turned off her second nature to detect truth in his words. He continued, "It reminds me of the cosmos. A group of stars." He looked up at her. "My star." He stared at her birthmark, deep in thought, before sitting up and stretching his arms over his head, back muscles bulging with the movement. The sheets hung dangerously low on his hips, accentuating his vee of muscle there, reminding her of their activities from the night before. Her face reddened at the thought, he turned to see her staring and noted her blush. "I'd ask if you liked what you see, but I already know the answer." *Cocky, but not untrue,* she thought. "There are some council matters I must attend to, but with Her Majesty's permission, I'd love to meet later, to lavish you in fine wine and cheese and ravage your body again."

Speechless to his latter comment, she ignored his innuendo, "I am not 'Her Majesty' yet."

"You have been the Queen of my life since I met you." He kissed her hand, bowed, and left with a wink. "Speaking of which," Kol yelled over his shoulder. "I have something for you." She watched him open the door to the dressing room, naked as the day he was born, and confidently strut out of view. In recent weeks he had requested that many of his belongings be moved into her room, as she still found it hard to be in his apartments. Thea laid back, feeling drunk, and laid a hand to her forehead. Kol returned quickly, a wooden box in her hand and a smile on his lips.

"What is this?" Thea asked with a grin.

"Why don't you open it to find out?" Thea sat up, allowing her hand to trace the smooth surface of the box before she opened it. "Just do it already! The anticipation is killing me." Kol urged.

"Yes, sir." She replied – before quickly opening the lid. A gasp escaped her lips, and without thought, her hands covered her lips. Inside sat a beautiful crown – with obsidian jewels and ornate carvings.

"Do you like it?" Kol asked, a smirk on his face.

"It's beautiful! But what do I need such a thing for?"

"Princesses need crowns." He stated obviously.

"Yes, but I have a crown. The one in your family jewel vault."

"Well, now you have two. And this one I designed myself." Kol said with pride as he placed it upon her head. "Beautiful." He kissed her, slowly, before exiting the room again. Thea sighed, for, in that moment, she was utterly content. But moments only last a short while.

"Your Highness!" Lord Geoffrey burst into the bedroom; Thea screeched in surprise and scrambled for a blanket to cover herself with.

"Kol!" She yelled.

He exited the dressing room, still shirtless but now dressed from the waist down, and quickly assessed the situation. He moved to the bed and threw an extra blanket toward Thea for her to cover up with. "What is the meaning of this intrusion, Geoffrey? I have killed men for less disrespect." Kol growled.

"Apologies, Your Majesty. But I have urgent news." Geoffrey said, diverting his eyes away from Thea. *Majesty?* Thea thought in confusion.

"What is it?" Kol asked, still irritated.

"Your father is dead," Thea said.

"What?" Kol asked, looking between Thea and Geoffrey. "Why would you say that, Thea?" He looked to Geoffrey. "Is that true?"

"He called you Majesty, not Highness." She said simply, shock rippling through her brain.

"He died in his sleep last night, cause to be determined," Geoffrey confirmed. "We will discuss the transition of power and further details in the meeting." He bowed. "Good day, Majesties."

Thea watched Kol from the corner of her eye, as he slowly came to terms with the news he had just received. Thea did not care at all, Kairo was awful, and she felt the world was better off without him, but she was worried for Kol. Even though she knew he hated his father, his lack of grief shocked her. He didn't cry or even frown.

"Kol? Are you okay?" Thea asked, crawling toward the edge of the bed to be closer to him.

"I'm okay, just a lot to take in." He took a deep breath and looked at her. "My time to rule has come. But I am ready-" He grabbed her hands in his own. "We are ready." She nodded in agreement, and couldn't help but smile as she watched a devilish grin spread onto Kol's face.

"What?" She asked, but Kol didn't answer. Instead, he raced to their dressing room and began rifling through drawers. "What are you doing?" He exited the dressing room and tossed a bag at her. Inside was the corset she had worn the night before the Battle of Stronghill – and with it an extremely short, matching skirt which she had never seen before. "Did you have this made?" She asked with a laugh. Kol nodded enthusiastically and propped himself up on the bed, legs stretched out and crossed at the ankle and arms folded behind his head. Waiting for a show.

"You made a promise." He winked.

"Already mad with power?" She teased.

"If I were mad, there's no one to stop me now." He replied in jest, though it was true. He was the High King now, the most powerful man in their known world.

"I can't believe I'm a queen," Thea replied.

"You are ready." Kol kissed her. "You are capable." Another kiss. "My Queen." And Thea didn't even test the truth of these statements, for she completely believed them.

I am power, I am Mori.

Acknowledgements

All glory be to God, for all things in general but specifically for blessing me with a desire and ability to create stories. It has brought me comfort my whole life and hopefully it can bring joy to others now as well.

Tyler, so many thank yous. For believing in this project and encouraging me when writing a book was still only a dream, for not complaining when I sat for hours staring at my computer screen and ignoring you, for going to bookstores with me while I endlessly debated things like cover art and price points, for listening to me sort plots points and characters when it all was yet to be a fully formed idea, and ultimately for being my safe space and always believing in me.

My family. To my mom and dad, thank you for always believing in me and encouraging my creative pursuits. My whole life I have never felt that the things I wanted were out of reach, you helped foster in me the confidence to aspire and did everything you could to help give me the tools to succeed. I feel so blessed to have you guys in my corner. My brothers, thank you for allowing me to engage you in conversations of plots you didn't know and characters you had never met, and for watching endless movies with me growing up that helped fuel my love of characters and fantasy. I wouldn't be who I am today without our shared love of cinematography and characters.

My friends. Hannah, A.K.A. my ultimate hype woman, forever first reader, and creative partner. Thank you for the conversations and helping bring this book to what it is today, I credit much of the success of this literary process to our friendship and you always believing in me. Also, a huge thank you for creating my cover, you're a talented artist and I can't thank you enough for bringing my vision to life. (Maybe someday I will share the hilarious and un-artistic idea I sketched out for her that she somehow turned into this gorgeous and haunting cover). Danae, the first true reader of DOT. Thank you believing in this project and encouraging me along the way. Without your insight, ideas, and feedback this book would have likely stayed on my computer unread for all of time. Finally, thank you to all my other friends and book club who helped encourage me and hype me up throughout this whole process, you know who you are and I love you all.

And a finally, thanks to all those I've met along my life's journey who inspired me, as well as other creators who drove me to want to create myself.

Follow me

Instagram and Tiktok @frasherwritesandreads

Sign up for my newsletter for exclusive content, bonus chapters, and information on my upcoming projects!
https://frasherwritesandre.wixsite.com/sfrasher

Made in the USA
Columbia, SC
01 July 2022

62584061R00224